EDIBLE

A TRAVELER'S GUIDE

FRANCE

GLYNN CHRISTIAN

EDITED BY JENNI MUIR

INTERLINK BOOKS

An imprint of Interlink Publishing Group, Inc.

NEW YORK

First American edition published in 1997 by

INTERLINK BOOKS
An imprint of Interlink Publishing Group, Inc.
99 Seventh Avenue • Brooklyn, New York 11215

Copyright © Grub Street 1997
Text copyright © Jenni Muir and Glynn Christian 1997

Originally published in Great Britain by Grub Street

Library of Congress Cataloging-in-Publication Data

Christian, Glynn.
    Edible France : a traveler's guide / Glynn Christian : edited by
Jenni Muir. — 1st American ed.
        p.   cm.
    Includes index.
    ISBN 1-56656-221-X (paper)
    1. Cookery, French—Guidebooks.   2. Grocery shopping—France-
-Guidebooks.   3. France—Guidebooks.   I. Muir, Jenni.   II. Title.
TX719.C4545   1997
381'.4564'02544—dc20   96-44282
                                                                    CIP

Printed and bound in Canada
10   9   8   7   6   5   4   3   2   1

CONTENTS

INTRODUCTION

I have written this book of journeys both old and new that I have made in France, and collected the opinions, advice and experiences of French men and women, young and old. Sometimes the opinions may not coincide with what others have written, but no matter, for they are not presented as seminal but anecdotal. From knowing the circumstances in which I was told these things, and comparing your own experiences, you will develop your own understanding of France.

Even so, it will come as some surprise to most enthusiasts to learn that France's reputation for fine food is not based on long-held traditions but on constant change, and that a general expectation of good eating is a relatively new experience for the French.

When the Bastille was stormed in 1789 at least 80 percent of France's population were self-sufficient or subsistence farmers. Bread and cereals were the basis of the diet, as they had been since the ancient Gauls; cabbage, broad beans, haricot beans, chestnuts and dried pulses were the main supplements. Until the end of the 19th century you were five times more likely to be nourished from vegetable proteins than from those of meat, cheese included. What meat you might find on your plate was likely to be pork, air-dried or preserved with salt. Where you were too poor to feed pigs you raised geese, for they fattened faster and on less feed. In most places, game might augment diet, or salt cod or herring if you lived close to a trader's route. Olives helped those in the south, fresh fish those on the coast. Most milk and cheese was from goats and sheep rather than the greedier cows of the north,

and such wild things as snails and thrushes and songbirds made welcome seasonal contributions.

From 1820, new farming techniques resulted in more productive agriculture, but it was only in 1885 that a French government could first announce that the country need no longer fear famine. Even so, not much had changed on the table. In 1885 a mere 15 percent of the population were able to spend freely on food. The advantages were still with the minority of that privileged percentage.

Food as a conspicuous symbol of social position had swiftly been adopted by the new ruling class of bourgeoisie. Having axed the aristocracy, they then sub-limated all ideas of equality and recreated the sumptuous meals they had so criticized before. But they were a minority; the Prefect of the Seine, reporting in 1849, said that of 900,000 Parisians, 600,000 were either starving or ill fed. Yet when the restored Bourbons gave way to Napoléon III in 1851, the great kitchens of Paris responded by reaching their highest pinnacles - up to their toques in foie gras and cock's combs, truffles, lobster coral, oysters and sole. This was the golden age of haute cuisine. There was more money (untaxed) and more social competition at the top than ever. The beast of inequality gathered speed and fat as it lumbered through the naughtiness of the nineties and into the 20th century. It took a greater beast, that of a world war, finally to halt the gross parading of unequal wealth at the table and to bring a more even distribution of the nation's produce.

The French listened gratefully after World War I when a man who had adopted the pseudo-Russian pen name Curnonsky began writing seriously about the importance of simple local and regional foods. They had been all but erased from the national consciousness for over a century and were always beyond the means of most. Now there was not only interest but the need and, slowly, the affluence. The chickens that Henry IV had wished to see in every peasant's pot on a Sunday were available at last.

Improved transportation, especially by train, brought culinary revolution to the regions - it is still easy to find men and women in Provence who remember the arrival of the first cows in the 1920s. Trains also brought tourists; well, not at first - first came travelers, who traveled to appreciate everything that was different. Tourists largely like to look without touching or being touched by those differences. Tourism fanned into flame the crackling embers of slow change in France's commercial kitchens. Those who traveled to experience for themselves France's newly discovered enjoyment of old foods hastened its end. It stands to reason. A chef in an international hotel in Lyon, say, must make new fish dishes: a Japanese person eating ordinary French food would have fat intoxication in only three or four days. How do you remain hospitable and profitable when Middle Eastern visitors won't eat pork and order Coke instead of wine, or when the British want to keep red wine for the cheese they insist on eating *after* dessert? And, perhaps even more important, how do you retain the interest of the French men and women who have traveled and who have read and wish for new experiences? To believe the French are shackled to tradition in food, or should be, is patronizing humbug.

Those changes have been fastest this last century. In some cases the reasons are palpable. When the silk industry declined in the 1880s, Monsieur Faugier kept Privas and its surroundings afloat by setting up organized centers for making and distributing *marrons glacés*. When the *Phylloxera* pest from America wiped out most of France's vines at the turn of the century, Burgundy expanded her plantations of black currants and began making a sort of liqueur from them; and the Charentes planted grass, imported Normandy cattle, and started making butter.

Fast food and the industrial canteen have been welcomed in France too. They answer the needs of new ways of life. The long lunch eaten at home and family dinners are no longer the touchstones of French domesticity or a spur to the cook. Fast food solves one problem, but it has caused others. At the 1984 Dijon Food Fair, research commissioned by disoriented modern chefs revealed a major influence of fast food centers to be the removal of that most honored and reliable aperitif, the smell of food cooking. Modern restaurants of all kinds go to lengths to prevent customers sharing the odors, educating them to expect neither restaurants nor kitchens at home, nor food, to smell of food. This was especially true of nouvelle cuisine restaurants, many of which so far lost their direction as not to put flavors on the plate either.

Fast food centers seem deliberately to serve a confusion of flavors, particularly in hamburgers, menacing any attempt by the palate to learn to like subtle, clear or simple tastes. This serving of sensation rather than flavor was considered responsible for inexperienced, panic-stricken or incapable chefs adopting the mantle of nouvelle cuisine, encouraging them to use fancy and expensive ingredients in bizarre combinations, not in competition or emulation of the fine food of the initiated chef, but to capture the attention of palates which had been mislead or poorly educated.

The term nouvelle cuisine was invented by the French writers Christian Millau and Henri Gault in the 1970s to describe something that was not new but a continuation of what Escoffier had preached earlier this century: to serve food simply and tasting of itself. But the palette of ingredients available had become so magnified that the possibilities were limitless. The novelty of something apparently different was welcomed with relief and hyperbole by food writers, with open check books by tourists and the rich, and with freshly scrubbed fingernails by thousands of aspiring young chefs (well, you can't arrange three peas and a puddle of pear purée with a spoon and fork). Silver service became sliver service, as everything was sliced thinly and fanned on the plate. It should have been cheaper, since there was less on the plate and the chef hadn't had to buy half a beef to make a pint of stock. But it didn't work out that way.

The tide has turned, not just against small portions but because the essential commitment to presenting food tasting of itself was forgotten in search of sensation. It became possible to sit through several courses in some of France's culinary temples and not recognize what you had eaten, for each course would be little more than a series of warm textures, especially if it was pounded and puréed and whisked into egg white and cream and steamed and called a mousseline. It became a culinary gaffe to put committed flavor in front of a client. Technique, not taste, ruled.

Now that nouvelle cuisine has largely fallen from favor, the French have begun to rediscover their traditional foods and actively campaign against their near demise. They have not, however, attempted to turn back the clock, nor should they. As tourists or travelers, we would be arrogant to expect to benefit from the innovations of the modern world while the French live in a vacuum. Changing work patterns, feminism, health concerns, immigration and the world economic crisis have naturally had their effects on French society, although perhaps the way France has coped with these trends has been typically French. Among the *egalité*, *liberté* and *fraternité* of eating that has evolved, there is also increased polarization: a tendency to distinguish between daily and special occasion meals, a growth of fast food outlets and frozen ready-prepared foods and yet a noticeable cooking renaissance and increased patronage of fine restaurants.

In the (hopeful) aftermath of recession, the French are more concerned with value for money, as opposed to cheapness, yet the percentage of the household budget spent on food has fallen regularly over the last 30 years, and since 1990 there has been a particular growth in discount stores and supermarket chain store-brand products. Luxury foods such as smoked salmon, champagne, foie gras and caviar are still in demand, it is just that they are discounted as well, forcing established brands also to lower their margins.

The role of women in society has been one of the most important influences on French eating habits; indeed, it has always been the case, but as women's expectations of employment have grown throughout this century, so the time they have spent in the kitchen has decreased - good news for food manufacturers and restaurateurs. Households with women who work spend twice as much on eating out as the rest. Frenchwomen have always used the *traiteur* for convenience, although they may now purchase the prepared foods from the hypermarket, but 85 percent say they try to cook in the traditional way as much as possible. After the Second World War, many middle class women ceased to pass culinary skills on to their daughters; these daughters and with them the sons are now having to educate themselves, and hence, sales of cookbooks have soared, the classic *La Vrai Cuisine de Tante Marie* alone having sold well over 10 million copies.

EC directives have prompted French food manufacturers and consumers to recognize the need to preserve the quality, identity and integrity of their traditional foods. But even though France has hundreds of societies devoted to its food and wine, you are more likely to fall into a scholarly discussion of "the good old days" with tourists. The average French men and women know they are eating better and with more variety than at any time in their history, albeit bemoaning the changes in the customs and traditions they remember from *grandmère*. As visitors we must not impose our ill-founded and cookbook-romanticized views of French cooking on those we visit for such a short time, nor should we encourage too many wistful looks backward. How far do you look back? To Provence before the tomato arrived? Languedoc before the haricot came from the New World? Brittany before wheat could be successfully grown there, or further back, before buckwheat arrived with the Crusaders? Only a fool would think things were better then.

A hamburger in Reims or a pizza sprinkled with chili oil by the Opéra is just as much a part of the French eating experience as tucking into a *cassoulet* (you'll be lucky) in the Languedoc. What is not representative of France, and never was, is whisking from starred restaurant to starred restaurant. It's a wonderful thing to do, but it isn't France. What is then? And how do you share it?

To enjoy a visit to France and to enjoy eating there you need to think like the locals, to know what they do. The France promised by most cookbooks and culinary guides simply does not exist. No local willingly drives to a destination recommended by a guidebook, and most of us don't want to either.

To search only for local or traditional dishes is to court disappointment, for where they do exist they are mainly in private kitchens. To eat only in restaurants recommended by guides cuts you off from the experience of France and its food as it is today. Everywhere there are enthusiastic, talented cooks and chefs who will never be famous but who are cooking honest, exciting and creative food, and are recognized as such by the locals. The key to sharing the excitement of discovery is summed up by what André Daguin said to me in Auch: to enjoy a meal you must know the fields behind the restaurant. Exactly. It is local ingredients you need to know about, for then you will be able to pick the restaurants, the markets and the shops that most accurately reflect them, and whether they produce traditional or new dishes, they are likely to be the most interesting.

Edible France is a guide to the reality of being in France, of what to eat rather than where. Once you start to use it, you will find your own snippets of information, your own windows into France. Only through food and wine and through eating and drinking do the landscapes and the buildings, the markets and vineyards, the beaches, mountains and lakes become stitched together into a country and a people.

I hope *Edible France* will help you to eat and drink better in France, and thus help you to discover the France the French know, the France the French eat.

Le Shopping

Shopping hours in France are leisurely. Most small food shops open early in the morning, usually 8 or 8:30 AM. They close for a fairly long lunch, generally 12 noon to 2:30 PM, sometimes 3:30 PM, but they are open for business again right up to 7 or 8 PM. Almost all food shops and markets are closed all day Monday, but they open on Sunday mornings to brisk trade. Here's a brief guide to the names of specialty shops and what you are likely to find in them:

• Boucherie: The classic butcher's shop sells beef, veal and lamb, leaving the charcuterie to specialize in pork and the volailler to sell poultry. But times have changed, and while many butchers still do not stock pork, they frequently sell poultry and game. Many also have a rôtisserie roasting chickens outside the premises. In France, meat is cut with the grain, not across it.

• Boucherie Chevaline: The horse butcher, recognizable by the horse-head sign over the door. Horse meat is darker than beef and has a sweeter taste.

• Boulangerie: The baker's shop, where bread is baked on the premises at least twice daily, sometimes more, sometimes less. This is the shop to come to for croissants, brioches, petits pains au chocolat and the long loaf, the baguette. Wholegrain bread (pain complet/intégral) is increasingly available in France, as are other loaves of alternative grains. Breads that keep longer are the pain de seigle (rye bread) and the round loaf pain de campagne. When touring, you may have to buy bread instead from the general shop (epicerie) displaying a depôt de pain sign. Under a 19th-century law, every village must have at least one store either making or selling bread.

• Charcuterie: Traditionally a butcher's shop selling only pork and pork products, but they are now expanding to become what was once a separate shop, the traiteur. Always ask to taste the pâtés and terrines; it's a fallacy that they are uniformly marvelous. As the French do not often hang their game, pâtés of pheasant (faisan) and partridge (perdreau) can be very bland. When faced with air-dried sausages, all you need to know is that the coarser the grain, the sweeter and milder the flavor - and that garlic is rarely used in them, as it would become rancid. Salaisons are small pieces of salted pork. A small picnic ham is a jambonneau or petit-salé.

• Confiserie: The confectioner's, which is either a shop in itself or part of a pâtisserie. The specialty is hand-made chocolates and sweets, made on the premises.

• Epicerie: Grocery shop, usually self-service, except for cheese, fruit and vegetables.

• Fromagerie: Devoted entirely to cheese. The fromagerie may still refuse to use refrigeration to maintain its cheese properly - go elsewhere if you find the shop hot and smelly, especially in summer, or if you are a cheese novice.

• Marchés: Markets are the best places to buy fruit and vegetables. The vast majority will be produce of France. Markets include good charcuterie and cheese stalls too, and even fish markets. The variety and the place of origin of the fruit or vegetable is usually displayed. The most interesting artisanale stalls are usually found at the edges of the market. Flowers, cheap china and kitchen tools are also for sale. This is where I buy my bouchons-champagne, handy gadgets for resealing open bottles of fizz.

• Pâtisserie: Cakes, pastries, sorbets and ice cream are made on these premises. The standard of presentation is high, as the French housewife depends on her local pâtisserie for her dessert course. The Frenchwoman has never been ashamed of buying prepared food to take home.

• Poissonnerie: The fish market. The range of fish available in France is enormous, particularly shellfish. Fish merchants frequently have stalls in street markets, and often the displays of oysters and other fish outside restaurants can be bought.

• Traiteur: The original takeout, where prepared dishes such as casseroles and salads can be bought. Often such shops no longer call themselves traiteurs but some smarter name, or they use the proprietor's name. Beware in outlets such as Fauchon (in Paris) or Hediard (throughout France) of paying more for the label than the contents.

• Triperie: Shop specializing in tripe, sold on its own or prepared in different sauces.

• Volailler: Poultry shop also selling game birds.

BEST BUYS

When you have found your supermarket, specialty shop or market, what should you bring back home? Frankly it depends on what you are already able to buy at home, when you plan to leave France and the exchange rate (see also, U.S. Regulations). Fine food importers tend to select the products they feel have

HYPER HYPER

Having haughtily ignored the idea for years longer than anyone else, the French now build the biggest hypermarkets in Europe. Names like Auchan, Leclerc and Carrefour have become as commonplace in France as *boulangerie* or *boucherie*. Certainly the small specialty shop still holds charm, but the French enthuse about *les grandes surfaces* as well, for nothing can beat their practicality . . . if you have a car.

France's first supermarket opened in 1957; now there are over 6,000, accounting for some 70 percent of sales of packaged foods. Meanwhile, the total of small tradespeople has fallen from 943,000 in 1954 to 700,000 in 1986 and the figure is still falling.

Hypermarkets are supermarket cities where the quality of food can be as high as that of the specialty shops but the prices lower. There is ample space (typically 250,000 square feet) for a staggering variety of food

and wine; china and kitchen equipment are recommended non-food items. Look for the extensive counters (around 150 feet each) of fresh meat, fish; rows and rows of regional cheese; ingredients for international cooking and prepared meals (the French have gone mad for precooked meals but they typically come family sized, not for one or two).

You are never far from one of the big names and there is little fear of missing the signpost, for they are well indicated in towns, on beltways and on the highways.

Today there is very little difference between the various hypermarkets except perhaps a few centimes or slightly different opening hours and you are best advised to go to whichever one is the most conveniently located. Hypermarkets tend to be closed on Sunday but open from 9 AM until 10 PM Monday through Saturday. Visa is generally the only credit card they accept.

• Green peppercorns: buy them packed in brine or dry, but never in vinegar.

• Jams and spreads: unusual flavors like *reine-claude* (greengage) and *mûres* (mulberry - *mûres sauvages* or *mûres de vonce* are blackberries.)

• *Lentilles du Puy*: are there any others worth having? Their quality and delicious savor are protected by an AOC (see p. 11 for explanation of AOC).

• Oils: much better value in France. Stock up on very cheap but good-quality oils, or enjoy the opportunity to buy best-quality oils more cheaply.

• Olives: rinse away the brine and repack in jars with olive oil. Flavor each container with an herb of your choice, lemon peel or crushed garlic, coriander seeds - anything. By the time you get home they will be ready.

• *Rouille*: a rich sauce

U.S. REGULATIONS

U.S. Department of Agriculture regulations on bringing food into the U.S. are very strictly enforced. Any forbidden items will be incinerated at the port of entry.

• Fresh meats and animal products are forbidden as well as fresh fruits and live plants.

• Meat, animal products and fruits and vegetables are allowed if they have been canned or bottled (where the usual canning process is used - that is, the food is heated in the can or bottle to form a sterile vacuum).

• Dried beans and legumes are allowed as long as they are not infested with insects. Any questions can be directed to the USDA in Chicago:

• Animal Products (meat, cheese, etc.): (301) 734-7633

• Fruits and vegetables: (301) 734-8393

the widest appeal in the country to which they are trying to sell. In France you will certainly find familiar and unfamiliar quality food brands. You will also find them more widely available, possibly cheaper, and be able to select many seemingly unusual varieties traditionally popular in France. Here are a few items you might consider bringing home:

• Chestnut purée: once

tried, you'll find both the plain and the sweet vanilla-flavored varieties of *purée de marrons* indispensible.

• Coffee: beans and freshly ground coffee.

• Fish pâté: small jars are excellent for picnics and for use in canapés.

• Flageolet beans: very cheap. By them dry by the kilo or canned.

• Glacé fruit: this is always expensive, but far less so in France than elsewhere.

flavored with saffron and hot peppers. Dollop into fish soup.

• Smoked garlic: a specialty of Boulogne markets.

• Tableware: plain white or embossed white dinner plates can cost next to nothing, with extra savings on prepacks. Decorative plates or the scalloped green and yellow styles from the south are sensationally cheap; so is the amusing pink glass tableware made by Arcopal. Also look out for crystal glasses and Biot glasses (in Provence).

• Vinegar: herb-flavored vinegars and oils, a relatively new invention, can be made by your own hand much more cheaply. Buy your herbs at the market or pick them from the hills, and steep them in oil or vinegar from the supermarket.

• Wines and spirits: I tend to forgo the wines and buy alcohol that can be both drunk and used in cooking - *eaux-de-vie* such as pear and raspberry (*framboise*), *kirsch*, *cassis*, and black rums. Unflavored 40 percent alcohol (*eau-de-vie pour conservation des fruits*) is sold universally and is best used for drinking after soft summer fruits have macerated in it for a few months rather than as a preservative for the fruits. Add sugar to make a liqueur. Serve ice-cold in iced glasses or as a mixer for wine, sparkling wine and champagne.

SELF PRESERVATION

Pack your clean, dry jars with alcohol-soaked fruit during the summer months and they will be ready by Christmas. Try these combinations: greengages or white peaches in cognac, strawberries or raspberries in vodka or cognac, black figs in black rum, pears in gin. Peel or prick thick-skinned fruit and add just a little sugar.

Eating Out

Don't be a bore and eat only in restaurants recommended in someone else's listings, or to which you have to detour for miles. Be brave and eat where and when you like. There's just one rule to follow: the only good restaurants are busy restaurants, with the possible exception of those considered fashionable, which can be dreadful.

THINGS TO KNOW

To be treated seriously when you walk in without a reservation, always ask for a number of *couverts* (covers) rather than places: "*Vous avez deux couverts?*"

• Menu: A fixed-price meal, usually of four courses, which every French restaurant must offer. There will be a choice of dishes at each course and the menus may include wine, but not coffee. Unless there is something you particularly want to try, ordering from the special menu or menus is better than à la carte. The quality is invariably good and the tax and service are included. Many restaurants offer several set menus at different prices, the more expensive ones including extra courses or pricier ingredients or wine. There may be a *menu du jour*, a set menu of the day, which will generally be freshest and best, but always look around to see what others are eating.

• *Menu dégustation/ menu surprise*: The tasting menu. You'll be presented with a procession of small servings (chosen by the chef if it is the surprise menu) with the simple restriction

that everyone at the table must have the same menu.

• *La carte*: Everything offered which is not on the special menu. À la carte dishes that are not on the inclusive menus will be more expensive. Main courses will arrive with a garnish of vegetables. Usually there will be a *plat du jour* (dish of the day) and if you are not very hungry, go for this and a salad.

• *Table d'hôte*: Traditionally a chance to try real home cooking. The words posted outside a farmhouse once meant 'the host's table' and invited anyone to eat with the family at a single sitting and at a fixed price. The idea caught on in many a country restaurant and simply indicated that you would be offered little or no choice.

• *Menu touristique*: Generally you should look elsewhere, as this is not often French food but dull Eurofare aimed at the tourist. Yet some simple places do try, and sometimes an honest tomato salad, steak and pommes frites followed by ice cream will be just what you want and the best possible value. The French do eat such things too.

NB. Although the French still eat relatively little frozen food, 70 percent of French households have a freezer, and since 1954, there has been an increase of 45 percent in the ownership of freezers and microwave ovens. Throughout France, 84 percent of households now buy some sort of frozen food, typically frozen vegetables, complicated dishes such as *cassoulet* and *bouillabaise* and prepared ethnic meals. A third of freezer owners say they only use it for unexpected guests - hardly a warm welcome, then.

PLACES TO EAT

- *Auberge*: Restaurant, usually attached to a country hotel or in rural areas.
- *Auberge de Campagne*: Not commonly seen but an *auberge du terroir* with guest rooms.
- *Auberge du Terroir*: A restaurant that offers traditional, regional dishes and is approved as one using only local produce.
- *Bar*: Rarely serve food or coffee - when they do it will be simple dishes or sandwiches.
- *Bistro*: In the provinces, a cross between a café and a restaurant. City bistros often rely on the romance of the name to excuse cramped space, noise and rudeness, but there's often good food to compensate.
- *Brasserie*: Meals, drink and coffee any time of the day. It was usually Alsatians, dispossessed or disillusioned by war and border disputes, who went to cities to open such businesses and so *choucroute* and sausage are served in most. Modern Parisian versions can be a combination of American drug store and old-fashioned brasserie.
- *Buffet*: Usually found at stations and airports. Food and drink are available at all times, often much better than customers of British Rail or Amtrak would dream possible.
- *Buvette*: A kiosk selling drinks, sandwiches and ice creams.
- *Café*: Drinks and coffee at the bar, where prices are lower, or from a waiter. Sometimes offering simple meals, but snacks (*casse-croûte*) are always available. Croissants and brioches in the early morning give way to baguette sandwiches, usually with thin slices of ham or cheese, and *croque-monsieur*, a toasted ham and cheese sandwich. They all serve tea gladly or will make a fresh lemon or orange drink (*citron/orange pressé*). Don't

be embarrassed to sit a while with only a cheap drink. Everyone else does it.
- *Cafétéria*: For quick, basic meals and drinks. The ones at hypermarkets are often very good.
- *Crêperie*: *Crêpes* with sweet or savory fillings, usually associated with Brittany. Crêperies can usually be found in tourist haunts. (The savory crêpes are often made of buckwheat, sweet ones of wheat flour.)
- *Drugstore*: The hot dog and other American fast foods with simple French dishes.
- *Estaminet*: Small bar, often seedy.
- *Ferme-Auberge*: A working farm that also offers meals of traditional regional dishes. To be recognized as such, the ingredients used must be predominantly from the farm itself and any that are not must be from the immediate locality.
- *Hostellerie*: A restaurant, usually attached to a country hotel.
- *Libre-service*: A self-service cafeteria, often part of a hypermarket.
- *Relais routiers*: Motorway or main road truck stops - the truck drivers *qui roulent pour nous*. Popular with English Francophiles. Good plain regional food, and lots of it.
- *Restaurant*: For meals only.
- *Restoroute*: Restaurant set near a motorway.
- *Rôtisserie*: A restaurant, sometimes called a grill, which once specialized in grills or roasts. Now, most serve everything.
- *Salon de Thé*: Tea room and coffee shop, often part of a *pâtisserie*. Besides cakes and pastries, light meals are often served. Havens for lone women, who may feel more comfortable here than in cafés or restaurants.
- *Snack-bar*: Basic food served quickly.
- *Taverne*: Usually a rural restaurant.

THE AOC SYSTEM

As far as the French are concerned, when it comes to matters gastronomique, *imitation is most definitely not the sincerest form of flattery. The protectionist instinct is deeply rooted in the French psyche and the recent introduction of parallel European legislation to safeguard quality standards is patently based on the French* Appellation d'Origine Contrôlée *(AOC) system.*

This label recognizes the unique qualities and characteristics of certain food products, the result of a special conjunction of traditional skills, specific methods, local geography, climate and conditions. Regulations are detailed and carefully monitored and apply, most famously, to a long littany of wines, spirits and cheeses, as well as to assorted items such as Le Puy lentils, Bresse poultry, Grenoble walnuts, Charentes-Poitou butter, Belon oysters and olives from Nyons.

Larousse dates the origin of the AOC back to pre-French revolutionary laws, but the present system was really developed after the

LE LABEL ROUGE

At its simplest, the Label Rouge means you are justified in paying a little extra for the product and can feel a little more secure. All the labels are crammed with information, but some of the advantages you are promised will be:

• *Boeuf/veau de lait*: Beef and veal. Only from the *départements* of Cher, Allier and Puy-de-Dôme. Beef will come from an animal which has been suckled by its mother for 8 or 9 months and have spent summers at grass and winters fed on grass and cereals. Not slaughtered until at least 18 months, usually over 2 years. *Charollais* beef must have both mother and father of the same breed. Milk-veal must be born at special veal-raising farms or raised by them up to no later than 15 days old. They must be fathered only by *Limousin* bulls, but their mothers may be *Limousin*, *Charollais*, *Salers* or crosses of these breeds. They will be no more than 120 days old.

• *Emmental Grand Cru/ Central Est*: Made in every eastern *département* from the Vosges to Savoie. The Label Rouge guarantees it to be made only from milk produced from grass and hay (no silage, etc.) aged at least 10 weeks, and ensures standards of shape, crust, body, flavor and aroma.

• *Jambon cuit*: Cooked ham. Only hindquarter meat, salted without phosphates, full muscles and meat only from one animal (not tumbled or reconstituted).

• *Jambon sec*: Dry or raw ham. Dry-salting of the meat and controlled times of salting and curing.

• *Pâtés*: Guaranteed percentages of the major product - 30 percent liver and lean meat in a *pâté de campagne*, 25 percent pork liver in a *pâté de foie*, and so on.

• *Saucisson sec/saucisse sèche, jésus, rosette*: A guarantee that only the noble pieces are used and only hard fat, with a maximum proportion of 25 percent. No color or polyphosphates, coarse texture so that the quality of meat and fat can be appreciated, and controlled curing.

• *Volaille*: Poultry. 90 percent of Red Label poultry is chicken. Guinea fowl (*pintade*), duck (*canard*) and turkey (*dinde*) make up the remainder. If chickens are raised outdoors with at least 2 square metres of space each, they may also carry the fermier label. Otherwise they will have been confined but under rigorously controlled conditions of limited numbers. Diet must have been at least 70 percent cereal rising to 75 percent for the last two weeks, and some brands are fed only wheat or corn during the last week. Red Label chickens must be at least 81 days old, guinea fowl 94 days, Christmas turkeys 140 days and barbary ducks 84 days. The labels for poultry are more complicated than others and are worth checking. In order from the top they tell you:

* How long they were raised (*durée d'élevage*)
* What they were fed (*alimentation*)
* Last day of sale (*date limite de vente*), 7 days after slaughter for chickens
* Method of raising (*type d'élevage*), such as fermier
* Producer and area (*provenance*)
* Production number (*No de l'étiquette*).

Among over 100 products that have the right to sport a red label are the following: *La Belle de Fontenay* potatoes, *La Bintje de Merville* potatoes, Lautrec pink garlic, Créance carrots, Auxonne onions, Nice olives, Picholine and La Lucques green olives, Nyons black olives, Golden Delicious apples from the Haut-Diois, and *Passe-crassane* pears from the Haut-Diois.

HEALTHY EATING

"The French paradox" - that they are inclined to eat a great deal of fat and yet not die of heart disease - has been attributed variously to walnuts, goose fat, long lunches and red wine. Yet the French do die and while they are generally busy not having heart attacks like the Americans and the British, their mortality rates for cirrhosis of the liver and "sudden death" are remarkably high. Something in the red wine perhaps?

The 1980s saw a significant growth in France in sales of low-fat spreads, low-fat charcuterie, low-calorie drinks, yogurts and so on. But sales have dropped in recent years as the French acquire a healthy scepticism about the claims and benefits of these products; only low-calorie drinks and creams seem to have kept their market share. Nevertheless, the French are having smaller meals, more simply prepared and with fewer rich sauces. According to Francoscopie, a surprising 50.7 percent of French people now never drink wine, as against 38.7 percent in 1980. The number of daily drinkers has also fallen.

Michel Montignac is France's most popular dieting guru; his book *Dine Out And Lose Weight* has been in the country's top 10 best seller list for over three years. Now like his fans (including fashion designer Christian Lacroix who claims to have lost 30 pounds with the Montignac method) you can visit Montignac stores and restaurants to buy his approved foods. There are whole-grain croissants and brioche, sugarless confitures and Saumur sparkling wine, plus high-cocoa solid chocolate and unpasteurized cheeses.

organic produce and in 1988, the Certification de Conformité was launched for products of distinctive traditional character.

The AOC system plays a major part in the French economy. France tops the league of agro-food exporters and AOC and other quality labels are worth an annual 100 billion francs, although the bulk of this comes from wine and spirits. In a major speech in 1995, the French Agricultural Minister, Philippe Vasseur, stressed the value of developing these quality brands and stated that the government's long-term objective was to see 10 to 15 percent of all French produce carry such endorsements.

In July 1993, the EEC introduced equivalent legislation under which registered food and drink products are given protection against imitators throughout Europe. PDO or Protected Designation of Origin (AOP - Appellation d'Origine Protegée) is meant for producers whose craft and product is unique to their area; PGI or Protection of Geographical Indication (IGP - Indications Géographiques Protegées) is the somewhat lesser recognition for those who can claim their process is unique even if the materials are brought in from outside the region; the CSC (AS - Attestations de Specificité) is a certificate of specific character. These EC designations, however, are not so much labels as regulatory instruments of judicial protection. In other words, just keep looking for the AOC or Label Rouge logos.

devastation wrought in French vineyards by phylloxera in the 19th century. Regulations for AOC wine, for example, are complex and can extend to the exact area in which the vines are grown, the varieties of vines, the way they are grown and pruned, the permitted yield and the alcoholic strength. By the end of the 1970s the system had been extended to over 30 varieties of cheese - although there have been criticisms in more recent years that in some cases the rules have become elastic as a result of commercial pressures.

In 1960, the red and white seal of the Label Rouge was approved by the French Ministry of Agriculture to be awarded to certain food products, a guarantee of superior quality and taste. Although mostly associated with poultry (20 percent of French poultry production is now at this standard), the label can also be found on other meats, charcuterie and dairy produce. In 1980 the green and white Agriculture Biologique (AB) logo was introduced to authenticate

☙ NORMANDY

A Heart of Butter & Cream

Normandy rather creeps up on you. There you are driving expectantly south through what you think is sugar beet (so few people actually know) and remarking on the grayness of the northern villages, and the next minute you are in England's Kent. At least that is the way it seems, for all of a sudden there is green ruralness and a thatched, half-timbered farm or cottage.

Lots of rosy brick is used too, for inward-facing, seemingly fortified conglomerations of farmhouses, islands in an ocean of agriculture. Timber construction here was not chosen for cosy aesthetics but because Normandy has plenty of chalk (Pays de Caux) and little or no stone suitable for building. In any case, the black and white architecture may be neither British nor French, but one of the many relics of settlement by men from the north, Vikings, who invaded in the 10th century. Once their leader, Rollo, had extracted from the king of the Franks a dukedom for himself and grants of land for his marauders in return for some sense of peace, the new men of North Man's Land (Normandy) sailed their big-boned cattle from their old Scandinavian homes and started breeding. By perspicacious choice of cow and bull they produced the brown and white, spectacled Normandy breed, prodigious producers of fragrant milk and cream.

The renowned Norman table, set with brimming bowls of cream and slabs of thick, creamy butter is rooted in the same Dark Ages. The Vikings had relied on bland cheeses and sweet butter as relief from the relentless rations of salted and smoked produce. As new French men, they gratefully switched to fresh fish and meats, but kept their creams, butters and cheeses. The 15th-century Butter Tower in Rouen is said to have been financed by the selling of dispensations to eat butter and cream in Lent.

It's worth repeating the still surprising cliché that an area that does not make wine should have such a reputation for its food. Few of Normandy's traditional dishes are complicated. Those that are have been invented recently for demanding travelers or Parisians too bored to eat simple food. Normandy's real food and its culinary reputation relies on that rarest of modern things, intrinsic quality, plus a climate encouraging to produce that does not require excessive flavor or bite to compensate for coarseness or blandness. Normandy is neither too hot to grow frost-sweetened root crops, nor too cold to grow delicate cherries or raspberries. Its plains and meadows are suitable not just for dairy grazing but also for raising sheep, especially spring lambs of the salt meadows (prés-salés) of the coast. Windfall apples and pears, buttermilk and skimmed milk make perfect fodder for pigs and there was plenty of salt from the sea to preserve their flesh before refrigeration helped develop a year-round taste for roasted fresh pork.

It's not a broad or mountainous region, so the smallest hamlet might regularly find the fish from its rivers supplemented by mussels and oysters and fish from the sea. Honfleur's merchants once even took locally salted cod to China. Wheat and other grains grow well, both for use in baking and for feeding poultry. Britain was importing 7,000 dozen eggs a week from Honfleur 150 years ago. Thus the choice of produce has always been exceptionally wide, even if not always eaten. Those root vegetables so readily puréed for modern plates were rarely used for anything other than soups and stocks until after World War II, except in times of extra hardship. But there was simply no need to make complicated dishes, even if you had the time and facilities, when boiled cream or butter could make simple food luxurious.

Hard cider and eau-de-vie de cidre, called calvados only when it is of top quality and from the right départements, have also had their distinct influence on Norman tastes. Hard cider is more subtle than wine in cooked dishes and, like the rest of Norman ingredients, does not need a large palette of added flavors to balance its contribution. A little onion or shallot will do, perhaps some chives.

The person I know best in Normandy is a princess, Marie-Blanche de Broglie, granddaughter of Princess Henri de Polignac of the astonishing Pommery champagne family and latest in a formidable line of influential women. Marie-Blanche used to teach cooking in the gardener's cottage of her château, La Coquetterie, outside Rouen, and taught me much about the realities of modern French food. For although her family life is based on traditions and customs reflecting ancient aristocratic, social and climatic seasons, her food reflects change. Soups and stews there are, of course, but the soup may be iced red peppers from Provence, the breasts of chicken stuffed with green beans from her own garden, and garlic cloves may be used whole, as they are in Gascony - ingredients and methods which are eclectic but never eccentric.

I suppose that most people come to Normandy expecting to eat good fish, which they will; to try Rouen duckling, which they should; to order pré-salé lamb, which they must; and to drink sparkling cider (cidre bouché) and calvados. Well and good, and they are the basis of some excellent times. A less considered but equally edifying pursuit is

A FAR, FAR BUTTER THING

Essentially there are - or were - just two styles of butter, sweet and salted. Sweet butter can be made only from unpasteurized sweet cream, called sweet because it has not been allowed to age and develop acidity before being churned. But today's creams are pasteurized, which kills the bacteria that would have developed the character. Modern technique replaces the heat-slaughtered goodies with a carefully controlled mixture of lactic bacteria to reflavor the cream.

The industry's name for what is sold as "unsalted" butter is actually "lactic" butter. Differing mixes of bacteria and differing aging periods after inoculation explain the broad variety of un-creamlike flavors found in continental "unsalted" or "lactic" butter. It is the discovery of these differences that so repays experiment. To my mind, Norman butter makers add the least intrusive flavors of all and most of their unsalted butter honestly reflects the full, natural voluptuousness of rich, whipped cream. It is a revelation to use these butters in baking, but they are not, properly, 'sweet' butters.

Salted butter is made savory (after inoculation with a different mixture of bacteria) with salt, which also enhances its keeping qualities. You may or may not find unpasteurized butter (*beurre nonpasteurisé* or *beurre cru*), or sweet butter (*beurre doux*) in markets in Normandy. I keep some in my deep-freeze for cake and pastry making or for smearing onto hot scones with strawberry jam when I cannot get clotted cream.

The bonus of a butter search for the cook is the discovery that these butters perform differently from others. Their waxier texture is smoother in the mouth and their slow resistance to melting and oiling makes them matchless for adding satin thickness to butter-mounted sauces, made by whisking clumps of butter into fiercely reduced stocks.

a study of Normandy's butters. Butter flavors vary not just from area to area but also through the treatment of the cream. A fascinating and complete background to butter and cheese making can be found in the *Musée de Normandie* in Caen.

Before the motor car and train began shunting us inexorably towards uniformity, there was a difference between the table of Normans who lived east, and those who lived west of the River Toques. Rouen, capital of upper Normandy, and Caen, capital of lower, still offer their specialties of duck and tripe respectively. You will enjoy comparing the different merits of butter from Neufchâtel-en-Bray and Gournay and Isigny, where they credit the salty air and spray from the Atlantic for the special flavor of their butter and cheese. And there are wonderful local sights to be seen - in autumn in the Valleé d'Auge when its peculiar varieties of hard cider apples are tumbled into courtyards before pressing, and in the Pays de Bray, where farmhouse cheeses are made in small tin shacks thick with humidity in the company of ancient infestations of benevolent bacteria and molds.

Yet essentially Normandy is one of the most homogeneous of regions. Although the bowls of cream have disappeared from the Norman tables you are likely to encounter, they are nonetheless the unifying touchstone, used to make acceptable anything that has come from outside.

The dairy is still the very heart of Normandy and of Norman cuisine, perhaps the only heart in France that beats more robustly because of butter and cream . . .

Charcuterie

As well as enjoying a rich choice of fresh meats, the Normans make a limited range of charcuterie from their fine pigs, fattened and sweetened on the windfalls of cider and eating apples and pears - at least those lucky enough to live on free-range farms. Normandy is rather too damp for the successful manufacture of air-dried sausages, so most of the prime cuts are eaten fresh (frozen probably) with a little included in pâtés and terrines. Les restes are treated with such respect as to make them nationally famous and none more so than blood turned into blood pudding. Yet, perversely, it is boudins from other regions and countries to which Normans often give the most adulation.

The epicenter of the blood pudding world is Mortagne-au-Perche, also the home of those dignified giants of war and the furrow, the Percheron horses. Usually over the last weekend in March, the Confrérie des Chevaliers du Goute-Boudin, the Brotherhood of Pudding Tasters, organize an international Concours du Meilleur Boudin. Over three days, puddings and their makers come from every district of France and most countries of western Europe. It is a serious business, with secret recipes guarded, new

fantasy shapes and new ideas paraded. The French win prizes, of course, but so do the Germans and the blood-pudding makers from Britain, Lancashire particularly. Over six ton of blood pudding are eaten during the three days and there are blood pudding eating competitions - one person ate 1.25m of pudding in 17 minutes in 1969. Since then they keep forgetting to measure.

Where you find blood puddings, you invariably find my least favorite things, large and small tripe sausages, andouilles and andouillettes respectively. If you are uncertain and want to make your mind up once and for all, then seriously confront those of Vire; they are supposed to be among the very best in France. There, andouilles often also contain veal chitterlings and the andouillettes (also said to be good from Caen, where they are more robust) are usually smoked before they are grilled. Apples are a common accompaniment, sometimes puréed or sliced, sometimes in the form of hard cider, which may turn out to be the better idea. If you are lucky you might find sanguette, which is a boudin made from the blood of rabbits rather than pigs. More common is good headcheese, sold either as fromage de tête or hure.

Fish & Shellfish

The long Normandy coastline makes this region one of outstanding fish and seafood, a natural and welcoming accompaniment to its butter and creams. Dieppe and Fécamp are the most important ports commercially, but others certainly repay a visit. Dieppe is renowned for its young mackerel (maquereau de Dieppe or lisettes), its scallops and its herrings. In history, it was the major supplier of fresh fish to Paris and famed for its relays of horses, always on the trot, which got fish packed in seaweed to Paris in less than 12 hours. This continued until the end of the 19th century when they finally converted to rail, something Boulogne had done decades earlier.

Fécamp is an important center for making salt cod (morue) and has salted herrings to sail up the Seine to Paris since the 10th century; they have been smoked since the 13th. Honfleur seems to have been ever more enterprising with such products; her merchants set up trading posts in the Far East where they exchanged their salt cod for spices. It's a charming place with 16th- and 17th-century houses around the harbor and excellent seafood restaurants. Le Havre specializes in importing products for the food industry - coffee, cocoa, sugar, spices and citrus - but if you really want to get among the buying and selling of fish, Cherbourg is your place, with a market in the middle of town.

The star of Normandy's fishy firmament is the sole, and even here you might find it called a Dover sole or sole de Douvres. The competition to do

something different with it keeps chefs amused and customers befuddled. Its firm flesh makes this possible, for it is one of the few fish that can stand being heated and reheated and then kept hot. To my mind, the best version of sole normande *is the old one,* simply poached in cream or in stock and served with a thick cream sauce, usually a velouté made with the fish stock, a roux, eggs and cream. Today the saucier may dispense with the roux and construct the sauce from reduced stock and cream mounted with butter. Restaurant chefs have ever felt they must add something to justify their prices and so this basic dish is often dramatized by mussels, shrimp and mush-rooms; in Dieppe, or in the style à la Dieppoise, the mussels are creamed to flavor the sauce and shrimp are used as a garnish. When you are feeling, or are, poor, lemon sole (limande) is easy on the pocket and so is vive, the weaver fish, highly rec-ommended for its sole-like flesh.

In the changing climate of today's restaurants it is difficult to predict what might be offered you, or in which way it may be prepared. Apart from those already mentioned, most of the shellfish are good, and whelks and winkles (buccin and bigorneau) turn up unexpectedly. Limpets (patelles), locally farmed clams (praires, palourdes and clovisses) turn up raw in seafood platters, the best way to start a meal, but only in a busy restaurant, to ensure fresh-ness. For important celebrations the Normans like turbot. It may be served with a sauce Vallée d'Auge, in which you can expect apples and hard cider, if not calvados as well, and cream. All Normandy on a plate, in fact. In summer, watercress from local beds, tarragon and sorrel are commonly used with both salt and freshwater fish.

WORTH FINDING

- *Anguilles*: Eels used in matelotes and pâtés.
- *Demoiselles de Cherbourg*: See scampi.
- *Huîtres*: Oysters. They are cultivated all along the coast with Courseulles-sur-Mer and St-Vaast-la-Hougue, Dives-sur-Mer and Luc all important centers. Because they are firmer and whiter than more famous types they are often offered cooked as fritters (*beignets*) or in sauces. Most are *creuses* rather than native *plates*. See also page 127.
- *Matelote/Marmite*: Inter-changeable names for a mixed fish stew. In Normandy it is almost always made of sea fish, the reverse of elsewhere. It uses hard cider rather than wine and its most important flavoring is chervil (*cerfeuil*), whose licorice bite is excellent here. There are exceptions to this, as to every rule, thus a *matelote* may well be of freshwater fish when you are inland. But in my experience, the *marmite*, indicative of the pot in which it is cooked, is always of saltwater fish; a *marmite Dieppoise* is an elegant thing in principal, including sole, turbot, monkfish, scallops when in season, fennel and tomatoes, shellfish and, naturally, cream. But look for someone else eating it before you order, for the inclusion of fennel and tomato clearly indicates this is a bastard *bouilla-baisse* with no firm founda-tions in local cooking and thus the general techniques seem guaranteed to cook any semblance of texture and nuance of flavor right out of the dish.
- *Moules*: Mussels. Among the many varieties, the most unusual and natural is the *caïeu d'Isigny*, from the bay of that name. It spends all its time underwater, growing beyond the low tide mark; it grows far bigger than most mussels and is harvested wholesale, by dredging. *Moules* are normally offered one of two ways in Normandy, conventional *marinière* or *à la crème normande*, in a cream sauce often with a dash of hard cider.
- *Omelette normande*: When you see this offered as a first or a main course it should be stuffed with mushrooms and shrimps (*crevettes*) and might be topped with oysters, but it could also be almost anything else. (If it is a dessert it will be of apples.)
- Scampi: This is a deliberate mistake, for there are no scampi in these waters, but the name is used as a translation for *demoiselles de Cherbourg*. They are actually baby lobsters and quite as expensive as those allowed to grow up. If you get offered scampi, they will be from the Adriatic or the Irish Sea, *if* they are scampi.
- *Truite à l'estragon*: Tarragon is a popular herb in Normandy and well used when combined with local trout and a cream sauce.

Meat, Poultry & Game

It's likely that visitors unfamiliar with Normandy will nonetheless know of two of its great specialties, the Rouen duckling served in a sauce which includes its own blood and liver, and tripes à la mode de Caen. But there is another meat that is spectacularly good, and which I first ate in that most astounding of places, Mont-St-Michel, which manages to be only just in Normandy. Its bay is the mouth of three rivers, the Seine, Selune and Couesnon on the border with Brittany. There are immense expanses of salt marsh over which the tide creeps, iodizing and salting the herbiage. Sheep and lambs that graze here develop a delicately salty flavor. These are the pré-salés, the salt-meadow lambs. As well as enjoying lamb simply roasted with a little garlic or onion (and no gravy), you might find it served accompanied by apples, as in côtelette de pré-salé aux pommes. Pré-salé may also be called agneau des grèves (lamb of the shores). Isigny claims very special pastures.

Caneton Rouennais (stuffed duckling with a red wine sauce) is one of the few dishes from the classic repertoire that really may have been bad in the good old days. Its fame is based on the ruddy flesh and gamey flavor that ducks from Yvetot and Duclair develop when they are strangled or suffocated, so that their blood remains in their flesh. An unbled duck deteriorates with great speed, within hours in hot weather, but refrigeration assists here. It is fitting that it does, for it was from Rouen that La Frigorifique set sail in 1876, returning four months later with the world's first cargo of frozen meat. Pressed duck, more a Parisian dish, is based on this Rouen recipe and today, canard Rouennais can be seen on many menus à la presse.

A particular feature of the two types of duck preferred - the Rouen clair and the foncé - is their long body, allowing the chef to cut attractive fillets (aiguillettes).

There is a Normandy breed of pig whose flesh is commonly served with cream and apples (often caramelized) or with prunes, and a race of white geese (oies blanches) to complement the numerous types of chicken around, particularly in the Vallée d'Auge. Beef is more likely to be veal if it is genuinely local.

Game was once common, particularly game birds, but when Prince François de Broglie walked me on the grounds of his wife's château, he told me that his shooting parties never expected great bags these days. Pheasant and some partridge were all they might find, otherwise it had to be pigeons or crows. Wild pigs do exist in Normandy, but they are usually on their way somewhere else; if any do remain for some time, it is because a sow has farrowed.

TRIPE A LA MODE

Tripe is commonly cooked in Normandy and in this dairying country consists of ox stomachs. Tripes à la mode de Caen should properly be cooked in a tripière, a variation of the local marmite. The prepared pieces of stomach are layered with onions, leeks, carrots, a good bouquet garni, cloves, pepper and a couple of split calf's feet . . . and then comes the discussion. There is a belief, supported by some practice, that the liquid should consist only of hard cider with a touch of calvados. This is not now common - and may not ever have been - as cider can darken unacceptably the color of offal. It is more likely to be water with a good glass of calvados. The pot must then be sealed with a paste of flour and water and cooked, according to the books,

anything from a few hours up to 48 hours, hence a further point of dispute. There is no argument about the fact that a favored Norman time to eat tripes is still mid-morning, especially on market days.

In Coutances tripe is wrapped around fingers of petit-salé ham hock and the tripes aux brochettes of Ferté-Macé are worth ordering for they are packages of gras-double and pieces of cow or veal foot wrapped in more gras-double and secured with little sticks. Gras-double indicates the use of only three of the cow's four stomachs; tripes should mean that all four are employed. It is no dishonor not to cook your own. Tripes have always been very much food cooked by professionals for the public to buy.

Fruits & Vegetables

Apples and pears dominate Normandy. Together with spectacled cows and half-timbered houses, orchards are the most common sight. The varieties of cider apple are myriad, but the best hard cider and calvados du pays d'Auge should include the sweet Bedan, the acidic Noël des champs and Binet rouge, and the sweet Doux mouen. In other départements, the same apples may have different names. The varieties of pear grown are more generally for eating, with the Louise Bonne d'Avranches (September and October) and the later Passe-Crassane notably superior, as are the Calville apples.

Autumn is the time to enjoy the figs of St-Vaast-la-Hougue, where there are big auctions of dried fruit in October. Honfleur, surrounded by orchards, had an ancient reputation for its cherries (often found accompanying duckling) and its melons. Lisieux, too, is an important center for fruits. Berries grow extremely well in Normandy and the crop is increasing annually (especially from Caen). The varieties harvested at present yield strawberries (fraises) from June to mid-October, raspberries (framboises) from July to mid-August, red currants (groseilles) during July, give or take a week, and black currants (cassis) from mid-July to mid-August. Gooseberries (groseille à maquereau) are as often called gades or gadelles.

One of the least-known harvests of Normandy is samphire (cristal-marine), a salty, crunchy green plant that grows along the coastline and is collected

LOCAL PRODUCE

- **CABBAGE** *choux*
  Green: December to April
  White: December to March
  Red: Mid-December to mid-April
  Dep: Manche, Calvados

- **CARROT** *carotte*
  Var: *Nantaise, Amélioré, Nandor, Tancar*
  October to April
  Dep: Manche, Calvados
  The biggest and the best area for carrots in France; Créances and Mont-St-Michel are among important production zones.

- **CAULIFLOWER** *choufleur*
  Varied local and hybrid
  October to December and mid-February to May
  Dep: Manche

- **CELERIAC** *céleri-rave*
  September and October
  Dep: Calvados

- **CELERY** *céleri-branche*
  September to March
  No special center

- **LEEKS** *poireaux*
  Var: *gros de Rouen*
  October to April
  Dep: Manche - locally also

- **LETTUCE/ENDIVE** *laitue/chicorée*
  Var: green cabbage, iceberg, endive, frisée, etc.
  May to October
  Dep: Calvados

- **ONIONS** *oignons*
  Small production mid-July until mid-March
  Dep: Calvados

- **PARSLEY** *persil*
  Var: *Le Commun* - hardy and very perfumed; *Le Frisé* - vigorous and curlier
  Mid-November to February, December is peak season
  Dep: Manche
  The second most important parsley-growing area of France.

- **POTATOES** *pommes de terre primeur*
  Var: *Orne, Ostara*
  Mid-June to mid-July
  Dep: Orne

- **RADISH** *radis*
  May to September
  Dep: Manche
  In the second rung of important production zones.

- **SHALLOTS** *échalote*
  Var: medium long and round types
  Harvested June, July, August
  Dep: Manche

- **TURNIPS** *navets*
  Var: *Nancy, Saint-Benoît, Jaune, Boule d'Or*
  Some primeurs but mainly autumn
  Dep: Manche

mainly around Créances. It is used with seafood by creative restaurants and can be bought preserved in bottles, but loses much of its seaside tang that way.

Pastries, Desserts and Confectionery

Butter-bright brioches are claimed here as the invention of the people of Gournay, who make them both sweet and savory (see also St-Brieuc, Brittany), but they are made wonderfully almost everywhere in Normandy. The most noticeable variation is the gâche, made from the same dough but baked rather flatter (add some raisins and you have the kokeboteram of Dunkerque).

You will find few pâtisseries or restaurants without their version of a tarte normande, each a variation on the theme of apples, pears, almonds and custards. Sometimes the filling will be a thick purée of apples cooked with butter, some might be baptized with calvados, some will be open, some closed, some covered with lattice or other patterns. The best time to eat them is in the autumn or winter. After the apple harvest the superlative Reine des reinettes will be used, but ask in September and October about apples called Calville - the rouge tastes of raspberries and is used in glorious tarts. (Having proudly been exported to the USA, the Calville rouge is now reimported as pomme de Californie). If you can't find a tart of the Calville rouge, explore markets for the Calville blanc, a big ivory-yellow apple, whose high perfume and flavor is akin to that of pineapples.

Apples, pears and sometimes cherries will turn up in galettes, which may be lots of things, but in Normandy are usually tarts or layers of filled puff pastry. Those of Dieppe and Le Havre have always enjoyed a high reputation. Bourdelots, douillons, rabottes and chaussons are all names for whole pears or apples baked in pastry and are more likely to be found in the windows of cake and pastry shops than in restaurants.

The pectin content of apples means they lend their setting qualities to a great variety of confitures, pâtes (like apple butter) and jellies. Sucre de pommes is associated with Rouen and you might well also find a sucre des cerises. Chocolates flavored with calvados are common; this is a variety of French confectionery I recommend with gusto, for somehow calvados shows through in a way few other spirits or liqueurs do. One that matches the assertiveness of calvados is also from Normandy - Bénédictine. Inside the building in Fécamp where it is made, the shop offers a range of flavored confectionery, much of it chocolate based. But verify that you like the herb-medicinal flavor before you lay out your money.

Cheese

There are over 30 important Norman cheeses. Most of them are of the soft, white-coated style, the most renowned of which is camembert (brie is actually from Île-de-France, closer to Paris). The most prolific area for mass-produced cheeses is the Pays de Bray; if you are looking for artisan varieties, you are likely to find the Pays d'Auge more satisfying. Washed-rind cheeses are to be found in Normandy too, including Pont-l'Evêque.

- Bondard *(Pays de Bray):* Its name derives from the word for a cider barrel bung, bonde. *This is a really rich double-cream cheese (60% fat). Evening milk is used and it is cured for 4 months. Late autumn is the time to eat bondard, accompanied by a full-bodied red wine.*
- Bondon: *Related to neufchâtel. The name refers to its shape, as in bondard.*
- La Bouille: *Invented at the beginning of the century by Monsieur Fromage (sans blague!) and related to fromage de monsieur. A soft double-cream cheese made from enriched cow's milk, cured for 2 to 3 months. Richly flavored.*
- Bricquebec: *From the abbey of Bricquebec in the Manche, a washed-rind disk*

weighing about 1.5kg/3lb. Mild, eaten year-round. Not unlike Saint-Paulin (see Brittany).
- Brillat-Savarin: *Invented by Henri Androuet between the two World Wars. This triple-cream (75% fat) disk of cheese has a slightly sour milky flavor to it. Eaten year-round.*
- Camembert: *An AOC cheese first mentioned in 1702 but apparently perfected by Marie Harel after the Revolution with the aid of a priest from Meaux who was hidden on her farm. A Monsieur Ridel invented the little boxes for it in 1880 and so enabled it to travel and become famous worldwide. Made from raw cow's milk with a 45% fat content, it is cured for at least 21 days, six of which are at the place of manufacture. The curd is allowed to drain naturally after being laid in four or five slices in the molds. The body should be firm and evenly textured but not runny and if preferred, it can be eaten young when the center looks chalky. It has a farmlike smell and a rich, rather sweet flavor. Although camembert* pasteurisé *is produced in around 67 départements in France, authentic Normandy (raw milk) camembert is limited to a few départements in Normandy: Calvados, Eure, Manche, Orne and Seine-Maritime.*
- Carré de Bonneville: *See Pavé de Moyaux.*

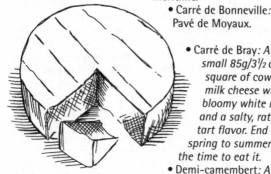

- Carré de Bray: *A small 85g/3½ oz. square of cow's milk cheese with a bloomy white rind and a salty, rather tart flavor. End of spring to summer is the time to eat it.*
- Demi-camembert: *A*

half-moon version of camembert.
- Demi-pont-l'Evêque: *A smaller-cut version of the pont-l'Evêque.*
- Demi-sel: *A small mild cheese created in the 19th century, uncured and packed in foil. The name refers to the low salt content (1.5%).*
- Dreux à la feuille: *Made from partly skimmed cow's milk. See feuille de Dreux, page 106.*
- Excelsior: *A distinguished Normandy cheese. High fat content (72%) made from enriched cow's milk. A mild creamy flavor. Particularly good in summer and autumn.*
- Fin-de-siècle: *Very similar to excelsior, another double-cream cheese from the Pays de Bray.*
- Fromage de monsieur: *From the Roumois area. Invented at the end of the last century. A rich, strong tasting brie/camembert–style cheese.*
- Gournay: *Typical Pays de Bray cheese with white-molded rind and a mild taste. Small, usually only 100g/4oz. Almost a small camembert.*
- Livarot: *One of the oldest Normandy cheeses and more popular than any other from the province in the 19th century. It has been described as smelling like town drains running down into the sea. An AOC cheese made only in a limited area - the Pays d'Auge straddling Calvados and Orne. The rind is washed and matured in a cave for at least a month after hand cutting and mixing of the curd. The cheese has acquired the slang name le colonel because the bands of sedge (used to keep the cheese in shape while it is maturing) are said to look like military stripes. It has a shiny,*

reddish-brown crust colored with rocau and typically a sweaty feet smell, but a surprisingly delicate, sweet flavor. (Rocau or roucou is a dye from the Caribbean tree of the same name.)

• Lucullus: A factory-produced triple-cream cheese from Normandy and the Île-de-France with a mild, nutty flavor.

• Magnum: A less mature version of the brillat-savarin, cured for only three weeks. A triple-cream cheese.

• Malakoff: An old brand of fresh gournay.

• Mignot (Pays d'Auge): Possibly the most recently invented of farm cheeses still made in Normandy. A thick disk of cow's milk cheese (40-45% fat) with a strong nose and a very fruity flavor. Best enjoyed in autumn and winter and usually eaten with sweet cider.

• Neufchâtel: From Neufchâtel-en-Bray, an AOC-protected cheese that probably dates back to the 10th century. Made from cow's milk, it is matured for between 10 and 20 days and comes in six different shapes, including a heart shape (coeur de neufchâtel). A farmhouse neufchâtel will always be presented on straw, those dairy-made are wrapped in paper. The rind should be white and bloomy and the body have a mousse-like texture. The aroma should be somewhere between mushrooms and mold. It has a delicate, lingering flavor, excellent with soft fruits and often eaten rather ripe. Thought to be best from August to November when the cows are eating the rich, second-flush, late summer and autumnal grasses.

• Parfait: Known also as fin-de-siècle (qv), a typical double-cream cheese from the Pays de Bray.

• Pavé de Moyaux: A washed-rind cheese in a square or slab, spicy and strong. Perhaps the original ancestor of pont-l'Evêque. Also known as pavé d'Auge.

• Petit Lisieux: Known also as demi-livarot, this is one of the oldest Norman cheeses and probably another of the ancestors of pont-l'Evêque. It has a 40-45% fat content and is shaped as a flattened cylinder. Strong smell, spicy flavor and best accompanied by a robust wine.

• Pont-l'Evêque: An AOC cheese that dates back to the Middle Ages. Originally called angelot and then augelot until the 16th century, but known since the 17th century by its present name, meaning Bishop's Bridge. Today produced in five départements of Normandy. It is a square cow's milk cheese (50% fat) with a washed or brushed rind, always matured in wooden boxes. The rind should be yellowish-orange to orange and the smell and flavor seem not in balance - the smell can be rather ripe but the flavor is always surprisingly sweet. It should not be eaten runny. Best from summer to winter.

• Saint-Paulin: Famous mild washed-rind cheese. See Brittany.

• Suprême: A double-cream cheese like fin-de-siècle, from the Pays de Bray.

• Trouville: The trade name of the famous old farm-made pont-l'Evêque.

Calvados & Cider

The slopes of Normandy are too fertile to grow useful grapes, so hard cider, apple brandy and calvados are the locally produced drinks which accompany Normandy's rich, creamy cooking.

There are three different grades of apple brandy. The lowest grade, which is not calvados, is made in a continuous still (as is grain whisky in Scotland) and called eau-de-vie de cidre. Do not be misled by the superior sounding name; it bears little relation to the wonderful fruit brandies of Alsace. Calvados, Appellation Réglementée is the next quality level, distilled either in continuous stills or in the superior pot stills used in the distillation of Cognac. The cider from which it is made must come from one of ten carefully specified areas.

The most aristocratic calvados comes from the eleventh of these regions, the Pays d'Auge. Calvados du Pays d'Auge must be made from Normandy's best cider, cidre de la Vallée d'Auge, and must be double-distilled in pot stills.

Like all the best brandies, calvados can be wonderful, capturing the essence of Normandy apples in its dry, intense fruit. It is aged in oak casks and improves enormously if it is left in these for five years or so. Look for VSOP (five years old, four of which will have been spent in barrel) and Napoléon, Hors d'Age or Age Inconnu (at least six years old, five in barrel). Calvados improves remarkably with age and it is worth seeking out some of the more sophisticated producers, such as Pierre Huet at Cambremer, to try some of their superbly refined Hors d'Age (at a corresponding price).

When you are in Normandy you will be offered calvados at the end of a meal, but may encounter it on two other occasions as well. Café calva is the local variant of the café cognac, the Frenchman's breakfast pick-me-up, a small cup of coffee, usually black, with a good slug of calvados to wash it down. Even better known, the trou normand (Norman hole) is a calvados drunk in the middle of a substantial meal, said to excavate more room for subsequent courses. Incidentally, the name calvados is supposed to come from some folk memory of the wrecking of a Spanish ship called Salvador on the coast; well, it is only a memory . . . Hard cider is produced all across Normandy - and increasingly in Picardy and Brittany as well - but the nature of the trade and the product varies from area to area. The Seine-Maritime is the site of France's largest commercial cider producers, such as Duché de Longueville (not, confusingly, in the town of the same name but in nearby Anneville-sur-Scie, 15 kilometers south of Dieppe) which offers guided tours and tastings as organized as those in any Reims champagne house.

Opportunities to buy direct from farms though are surprisingly few. As well as Livarot, Camembert and Pont-l'Evêque cheeses, the Pays d'Auge, Normandy's richest agricultural region, between Caen and the Seine Valley, is generally held to produce the best ciders, with plenty of fruit but nevertheless beautifully subtle. Here there's no mass production but some

producers are lush domaines with neat farm shops; others are very much farms, where if you drive into the yard some time may idly pass before anyone emerges and notices you are there. Fine ciders can be obtained from both. Further west again, in the Manche and the Orne, small farm producers predominate and even the larger cider manufacturers in the area are pleasantly sleepy and rustic.

There are hundreds of cider producers throughout Normandy and their products can be highly individual, making tasting all the more interesting. The Pays d'Auge has an appellation contrôlée for its ciders and producers of recognized quality on the local tourist board's Route du Cidre, in the north of the area around Cambremer, are identified by a sign with an apple and the words Cru de Cambremer placed at their gates. Elsewhere things are less organized, but the map J'irai gouter ma Normandie, produced by the region's Chambres d'Agriculture and available from most tourist offices, is a useful introduction to reliable producers.

Apples are usually harvested from late September to November. The longer the cider ferments in the barrel the drier it is, but once it has reached the chosen point and been bottled – after a few months – it does not change

much with age and is best drunk quite fresh. Most Normandy drinking cider is lightly pétillant and comes in a corked bottle (cidre bouché). Some very sweet cidre nouveau is produced each year for Christmas but most of the region's ciders become available in the spring, first the sweet (doux) and then the brut. The best time to visit farms and sample ciders is between April and August; by September the largest producers will still have some in stock but the smaller farms may well have sold out for the year. Calvados, on the other hand, is usually available at all times.

A great many producers now also offer cider vinegars, cider jams, Pommeau (the cider-and-calvados combination that's a satisfying liqueur) and poiré (pear cider). The latter can be very sweet but can also be very pleasant and it's pretty much potluck whether you find one or the other.

A very good guide to addresses in the Pays d'Auge is Produits du Terroir, available from Syndicats d'Initiatives or direct from CIPPA, 8 rue du 11 Novembre, 14100 Lisieux, or the Chambre d'Agriculture, 4 Promenade Mme-de-Sévigné, 14039 Caen.

SHOP 'TIL YOU DROP

In Normandy it is possible, with a little planning, for market enthusiasts to find good markets in different towns on every day of the week. This is in contrast to more industrialized regions such as the Pas-de-Calais, where they are concentrated around the weekends. Town markets can be large or small, strictly local or known over a wider area. Among the most impressive city

markets, constantly growing, is the one in the center of Caen, held every day except Monday but busiest on Fridays and Sundays. Traditional markets begin early in the morning and will already be packing up by 12:30 PM; more urban models may carry on into the afternoon.

One of the most exciting to the eye and tastebuds is the market beneath the trees alongside the River Touques in Trouville, on Wednesday and Sunday mornings. From June to August there are also a few stalls open every day. Trouville's status as a seaside town and its proximity to still-chic Deauville means that there is a high-spending clientèle with a taste for luxuries. Consequently, many of the best artisan food producers in Normandy go to sell there, bringing farm-made cheeses, ciders, andouilles, terrines and even tergoule rice puddings of wonderful quality. This is also a fish and seafood market where the catch is literally put ashore on one side of a building and put on sale on the other – and if you have any means of cooking them, the crab, lobster, mussels and rarer crustaceans are not to be missed.

At the same time however, this remains a local market, where you can buy tacky leather jackets, plastic bowls, boot laces, hip CDs and old furniture. Prices also are often surprisingly reasonable, even for the luxury foods.

Not hip at all but perhaps more spectacular is the huge market in St-Pierre-sur-Dives every Monday. The Pays d'Auge is Normandy's richest agricultural area and St-Pierre is its oldest and most important market, held since the early Middle Ages. The

town grew up around it and it fills two large, shapeless town squares. At its center is the giant medieval covered market, the Halles, first built in the eleventh century and completed in the sixteenth. It was severely war-damaged in 1944, but its magnificent oak-beamed roof has been faithfully restored down to the last detail, and the hall is now as much in use as it ever has been.

The market is entirely traditional. Inside the hall there are mostly chickens, ducks and ducklings, geese, rabbits and other creatures, all very much alive. Watching a well-dressed woman buy a live chicken is something you may find appalling, or you could take it as an indication of just how much effort some French people are prepared to go in the cause of fresh food.

Outside, around the hall, is a bank of stalls offering excellent prepared meats and local charcuterie, and many others with glossy fresh vegetables, fruit and cheeses (*Pont-l-Evêque, Pavé d'Auge* and farmhouse *Camembert* in particular) and truly free-range eggs. This being a market that caters primarily to country people, there are also stands with chain saws and tractor parts amid the usual denims and leather jackets. Wandering around St-Pierre market, one can easily begin to think that France is still a predominantly rural country, where the inhabitants really are in touch with their particular *terroir*.

Bon Marché

Below is a selective list of markets plus some fairs (*foires*) of special interest. Check with the local Syndicat d'Initiative (SI) for precise locations and time changes.

MANCHE

Agon Coutainville *Tue, Thur, Sat;* Avranches *Sat;* Barneville-Carteret *every Sat in summer;* Beaumont-Maque *Sat;* Bréhal *Tue;* Bricquebec *Mon;* Canisy *Fri;* Cérances *Thur;* Cerisy-la-Salle *Sat;* Cherbourg *Daily ex Sun (fish);* Coutances *Mon;* Créances *Sun;* Ducey *Tue;* Gavray *Sat;* Ger *Thur;* La Haye-du-Puits *Wed;* La Haye-Pesnel *Wed;* Isigny-le-Buat *Mon;* Juvigny-le-Tertre *Mon, Tue after Easter and Pentecost;* Lessay *Tue;* Marigny *Wed;* Montebourg *Sat;* Mortain *Sat;* Octeville *Sun AM;* Percy *Sat;* Periers *Sat;* Picauville *Fri, 29 April, 1 Dec;* Les Pieux *Fri, bigger market 2nd Fri of month;* Quettehou *Tue;* Sartilly *Fri;* Sourdeval *Tue;* St-Hilaire-du-Harcouret *Wed;* St-James *Mon;* St-Lo *Tue;* St-Martin-de-Landelles *Sat;* Ste-Mére-Eglise *Thur;* St-Pierre-Eglise *Wed;* St-Saveur-Lendelin *Thur;* St-Vaast-la-Hougue *Sat;* Tessy-sur-Vire *Wed;* Valognes *Tue, Fri;* Villedieu-les-Poêles *Tue.*

CALVADOS

Argences *Thur;* Aunay-sur-Odon *Sat;* Balleroy *Tue;* Bayeux *Daily PM (fish);* Le Bény Bocage *Thur;* Bernières-sur-Mer *Wed;* Blonville-sur-Mer *Daily in season;* Cabourg *Wed, Fri in winter, daily in summer;* Caen *Daily ex Mon;* Caumont l'Eventé *Thur;* Condé-sur-Noireau *Thur;* Courseulles-sur-Mer *Tue & Fri;* Creully *Wed;* Deauville *Daily AM;*

Hérouville-St-Clair *Wed;* Honfleur *Sat;* Isigny-sur-Mer *every 2nd Sat;* Molay Littry *Thur, Wed if hol;* Orbec *Wed, Tue if hol;* Pont-l'Evêque *Mon;* St-Jean-de-Blanc *Sat;* St-Martin-des-Besaces *Sat;* St-Sever Calvados *Sat;* Thury Harcourt *Tue;* Trévières *Fri;* Trouville-sur-Mer *Wed, Sun, daily from Easter to Sept;* Vassy *Tue;* Vire *Fri.*

SEINE-MARITIME

Auffay *Fri AM;* Aumale *Sat PM;* Bacqueville-en-Caux *Wed AM;* Barentin *Sat PM;* Blangy-sur-Bresle *Fri AM, 3rd Wed of month;* Bois-Guillaume *Tue, Fri;* Bosc-le-Hard *Wed AM;* Buchy *Mon AM;* Canteleu *Sat AM;* Caudebec-en-Caux *Sat AM;* Caudebec-les-Elbeuf *Fri AM;* Criel-sur-Mer *Thur and Sun AM;* Darnétal *Sun AM;* Déville-les-Rouen *Sun AM;* Dieppe *Tue, Wed, Thur AM, Sat;* Duclair *Tue AM;* Elbeuf *Tue, Thur, Sat AM;* Eu *Fri AM;* Fécamp *Sat, bigger market last Sat of month;* Fontaine-le-Dun *Thur AM;* Forges-les-Eaux *Thur;* Gaillefontaine *Wed PM;* Goderville *Tue AM;* Gournay-en-Bray *Tue, Fri, Sun;* Grand-Couronne *Fri AM;* Harfleur *Thur AM;* Le Havre *AM Tue, Thur, Sat;* Lillebonne *Wed AM;* Longueville-sur-Scie *Thur AM;* Malaunay *Sat AM;* Maromme *Sat PM;* Mont-St-Aignan *Wed AM;* Montvilliers *Thur AM;* Montville *Sat AM;* Neufchâtel-en-Bray *Tue AM, Sat AM;* Notre-Dame-de-Gravenchon *Fri AM;* Pavilly *Thur AM;* Le Petit Couronne *Fri AM;* Le Petit Quevilly *Tue, Thur, Sat, Sun AM;* Rouen *Tue, Wed, Fri, Sat;* Sotteville-les-Rouen *Thur, Sun AM;* Ste-Adresse *Tue, Fri AM;* St-Etienne-du-Rouvray *Tue, Wed, Thur and Sun AM;* St-Martin-de-Boscherville *Sat AM;* St Nicholas-d'Aliermont *Sun AM;* St-Romain de Colbosc *Sat AM;*

St-Saens *Thur AM;* St-Valéry-en-Caux *Fri, Sun AM June-Sept;* Le Trait *Sat PM;* Valmont *Wed AM;* Verville *Tue AM;* Yvetot *Wed AM.*

EURE

Les Andelys *Mon;* La-Barre-en-Ouche *Wed;* Bernay *Sat;* Beuzeville *Tue;* Bourg Achard *Mon;* Bourgtheroulde-Infreville *Sat;* Brionne *Thur, Sun;* Broglie *Fri;* Cormeilles *Fri;* La Croix-St-Leufroy *Wed;* Damville *Tue;* Ezy-sur-Eure *Sun, Thur;* Fleury-sur-Andelle *Tue;* Gaillon *Tue;* Garennes-sur-Eure *Wed;* Gisors *Mon, Fri, Sun;* Ivry la Bataille *Wed, Sat;* Louviers *Wed, Sat;* Lyons-la-Forêt *Thur;* Montfort-sur-Risle *Tue;* Montreuil-l'Argillé *Tue;* Nassandres *Sat;* Le Neubourg *Mon, Wed;* Pacy-sur-Eure *Thur;* Pont-Audemer *Mon, Fri;* Pont-St-Pierre *Sat;* Quillebeuf-sur-Seine *Sat;* Romilly-sur-Andelle *Sat;* St-André-de l'Eure *Fri;* St-Georges-du-Vièvre *Wed;* Thiberville *Mon;* Tillières-sur-Avre *Fri;* Le Vaudreuil *Sun.*

ORNE

L'Aigle *Tue AM;* Alençon *Fri and Sun;* Argentan *Tue;* Bognoles-de-l'Orne *Wed;* Bellême *Thur;* Brouze *Mon, Easter Wed;* Domfront *Sat;* Ecouché *Fri;* La Ferté-Macé *Thur;* Flers *Wed;* Gacé *Sat PM;* Longny-au-Perche *Wed;* Le Mele-sur-Sarthe *Wed;* Le Merlerault *Mon PM;* Mortagne-au-Perche *Sat;* Nocé *Tue;* Passais-la-Conception *Tue AM;* Pervenchères *Tue;* Putanges-Pont-Ecrepin *Thur;* Rémalard *Mon;* Le Sap *Tue PM;* Sées *Sat;* Ste-Gauburge-Ste-Colombe *Wed;* Le Theil *Wed;* Vimoutiers *Mon PM.*

SHOPPING AROUND IN CAEN

Where and when: St Saveur *Fri;* St-Pierre *Sun; the right bank at* Cygne de Croix *Wed and Sat;* Chemin d'Authie *Tue and Thur.*

CHAMPAGNE & THE NORTH

PORTS, BEER & CHAMPAGNE

"In which we ...
• Enjoy beer and herrings on the coast, and sorbets of marc in Champagne ...
• Discover the only vine leaves eaten in France and that champagne isn't cooked in Champagne ...
• Learn why brasseries always made the best charcuterie and how juniper flavors stews and genièvre ...
• Find a Little Venice growing for Britain, and try to tell the locals a thing about their sugar ...
• See an air-conditioned growth industry, sample unpasteurized butter and choose a quieter champagne ...
• Eat chocolate seafood in Le Touquet - but pâté almost nowhere ..."

L a Champagne - the place - isn't classic France at all, not the luscious, sunny, ripe France of the posters and topless sunbathing. And neither are the other areas I've included with it here - Flanders and Picardie, Artois and Ardennes. French is spoken of course, and they drink wine and eat garlic, but by the time Mediterranean France has pushed up to border other countries, the French have become distinctly different and, well, northern. They drink beer, and eat lots of cabbage, and pickle and smoke herrings. Most noticeable, the countryside is relentlessly flat - boring, most say as they speed south. But the great plains of northern France are precisely what have shaped its history, much of its food and all of its present prosperity. The answer lies in the soil.

From the lively ports of Boulogne, Calais or Dunkerque you can, if you wish, visit the manicured horror of the graves of thousands of young men who muddied further the dank fields of Ypres and Mons and other villages. There are more unmarked graves, too, in the older battlefields of Agincourt and Crécy. For these plains have always been the place where invading armies, from north or west, were first resisted and men have ever been their greatest crop.

The north is a brighter, prosperous region today, where crops and fortunes have flourished unhindered for almost 40 years; but the crops are hardly traditional, in the way that leeks or the ubiquitous cabbage might claim to be.

Since the Revolution, the potato has been at home here. Sugar beet was established by Napoléon and, now that American strains guarantee bigger harvests, wheat. Once the north's western border, the Channel, dropped its defences to welcome armies of day trippers, today's battles are with customs officers and in the aisles of supermarkets.

It is especially true in the north that regional food is what you get served in the region, for those continuously tramping armies made continuity of anything culinary impossible, and forced the area to serve what it could get, wherever it could get it. Truly traditional food will be based only on things wild - frogs and pigeons, trout or eels, herrings, and game large and small from whatever forest was left standing. And thus it is you find also quickly made waffles and a grateful reliance on the cabbage and potato, which might have survived in frozen trampled fields. The pig and its products, too, were sensibly important - if the winters didn't get you war did, so it behove you always to have something in the larder just in case.

In good times there was also lamb, and superlative vegetables grown in intricately irrigated areas. But it is sugar beet, of all things, that has most added to the crop of seemingly traditional foods. All across northern France there is a plethora of confectionery, pastries, breads, biscuits and cakes which celebrate the twin blessing of local sugar and wheat, and which also appreciates the additional modern bounty of Normandy's eggs, butter, cream and milk with which to mix and bake them.

As you move from the undoubted - but catholic - highspots of eating on the coast you will find extraordinary cheeses to eat with beer or juniper-flavored spirit, and game, if you are there at the right time. You will enjoy, perhaps, visiting a vast charcuterie factory in Lille, the market place of Arras, and searching for the pork and lamb products of Troyes, once seat of the counts of Champagne. But you will need to work hard if you want to find out if there is still an Ardennes pâté that isn't simply rubbish made to look like an Ardennes pâté. For most of the commercially made junk-pâté that is exported is made in this region, so much that it is difficult to imagine any is left behind; but it is and it is just as disgusting and dishonest here as anywhere.

Is it possible to have food adventures in the north? Of course, but you are more assured of them if, after a nod and a visit to such places as Arras, you head for La Champagne, and if you are also very clear as to whether you are eating in starred establishments, which serve much the same food wherever you are, middle-of-the-road places, which do the same with less style, or one of the few that makes genuine effort to reflect the area in which they are plying their trade; the real boon is that you will benefit from a wide choice of still and fizzy champagnes.

I started my travels at the top, on a Saturday evening - when I dined in the lofty dignity of the pale *boiserie salons* of Les Crayères, once the *hôtel-particulier* of a Princess de Polignac of the Pommery family.

Sunday morning was spent happily under the high trees of the promenade opposite Reims station, where a vast flea market offered copperware and local waffle irons and those uniquely French art-deco sets for *farine, riz, sel* and *poivre*. At the restaurant Le Continental, lunch started with a *ratafia*, of course, then a gratin of frogs' legs, and chicken in champagne, a description more geographical than of what constituted the sauce; the finale was a triumph of modern Champagne (and something now difficult to avoid), a sharp sorbet of *marc de champagne*.

A truer taste of Champagne is found on the short menu of Le Vigneron, just behind Reims Cathedral. Has it ever occurred to you to wonder why the French do not eat vine leaves? It must only be that there was no need to do so - yet in Champagne they were eaten, a clear illustration, as are the presence of *andouilles* and *andouillettes*, that life was particularly hard here. The stuffing of vine leaves at Le Vigneron was based on lamb, a neat package that was, even more surprisingly, fried.

What happened after lunch turned a memorable occasion into an unforgettable one. I wasn't allowed to see the bottle that came in an ice bucket, but the color and the honeyed flavor meant I was drinking an old champagne. Is it '59 I asked? The bottle was turned to reveal the date ... 1921. It was extraordinary, a champagne from the tiny house of Frederic Leroux that had been *en pointe* for over 50 years and degorged only two years beforehand. Its sensational color and maderized flavor, still brightened with robust columns of bubbles, was more that of a champagne cocktail. And the full story lent even more enjoyment, for 1921 was the Victory vintage, the first sign of normality and hope after World War I, as well as being one of the century's greatest vintages. Champagne needed such encouragement, for it was also recovering from the devastation of *Phylloxera* blight: at its height it was not unusual for growers to harvest only enough grapes to make a single *tarte aux raisins*.

With the champagne we enjoyed bread made of untreated flour baked in wood-fired ovens and a farmhouse *cendre de champagne*. This is a rare cheese akin to a *camembert* but aged in wood ash, traditionally that left over from the long cooking of pigs' trotters

in the style of Ste-Ménéhould. The apparently bizarre combination of champagne and cheese worked, because both, I was told, were authentic reflections of the same soil. It was all blissful until my too generous host revealed the rough diamond amidst his treasure chest of culinary gems. Once, he told me, these cheeses were aged not in wood ash but in *urine feminine;* it was particularly the custom of those who lived in Châlons-sur-Marne; they called it *fromage de cul.*

It made no difference when my host revealed this to have been a custom of the 13th century. I had, by now, drunk almost two bottles of Champagne's wines of one type or another; their effect was instantly doubled by the thought of what might have been done to the cheese, and by the awful similarity of the Lerous's color to that with which it would have been done. I left shortly, abandoning a final *flûte*, to shiver my way back to Paris in an unheated first-class carriage; it was better to travel than to imbibe ...

THE CHAMPAGNE METHOD

• Never ask for a *verre* always *une coupe* of champagne. Choose a tulip-shaped glass *flûte*. As a last resort, take a saucer with a hollow stem: the shape is supposedly based on a mold taken from Mme de Pompadour's bosom; the hollow stem was originally needed to drain off the debris which all champagne bottles contained until modern methods were perfected.

• Champagne should never pop vulgarly when you open it - unless you are a racing driver ...
* Do not lever the cork out with your thumb-tips: grip the cork firmly and turn the bottle.

• Champagne will never fizz out wastefully if you hold the bottle at about 45° when opening and hold the glass at a similar angle.

• Don't feel forced to drink all the champagne once the bottle is open; reseal for later with a *bouchon-champagne.*

Charcuterie

The importance of beer drinking in the north is an indication of a tradition of charcuterie. For it was the brewers, or *brasseurs*, who kept the best pigs, fattened on the grains of their trade, and from which were made the snacks which attracted drinkers and nibblers at any time of the day - hence our modern round-the-clock expectations of a decent brasserie. But the damp weather of the country meant that *saucisse*, or salami as some call it, was not commonly made; instead a distinct excellence in pâtés and terrines developed.

Today one of France's biggest manufacturers of a range of charcuterie is based in Lille, and there are countless others who, together with their proximate Belgian neighbors, swamp the world with a product they shamelessly call pâté. Some small shops still make their own pâtés, usually indicated by a lack of Disney-decoration and simple, uncolored bowls and dishes. If you are a convert to the bland, fatty modern products, you have been conned if you think them simple or in any way authentic. A quick look at the list of ingredients will tell you that. Yet, being aware of the caveat, a good eye and nose can still lead you to honest specialties of the area. Amiens, for instance, still has a high reputation for its pâté de canard en croûte.

WORTH FINDING

•*Andouilles/andouillettes*: The best-known and most reviled of pork products. Americans and the squeamish call them chitterling sausages, which means they are made from pigs intestines, sliced or layered inside more of the same. Andouilles are based on the large intestines, and to fill them other innards are included, such as tripe. They are boiled up in a savory broth flavored with cabbage, onions, potatoes or other local vegetables, but are more likely to be served sliced as a cold first course. Andouillettes are made from the small intestines and are a common lunchtime feature in brasseries, where they will be freshly grilled and served with mashed potatoes and something sharp - pickled cabbage, mustards and the like. One or the other or both have at times been famed from Arras, St-Pol, Cambrai, Douai, Lille, Troyes and Armentières, but the variations of herb and spice content which once gave individuality are beyond the palates of the uninitiated - and beyond mine, for both large and small versions have an underlying sweetness that I find unnerving.

•*Boudin*: Where there are pigs there are blood puddings; much rarer is a *boudin de lapin*, which is more likely to be found in Champagne; *boudin à la flamade* is served with semolina, almonds and raisins.

•*Jambon*: In Reims, locally cured hams are often baked in pastry; the more famous Ardennes hams are usually smoked and eaten raw.

•*Langues fourrées*: A famed dish of Valenciennes was tongue stuffed with slices of foie gras, which was also called *à la Lucullus*. You might have the luck to find it.

•*Langues fumées*: Smoked tongues are much more likely to be found. In Troyes they will often be sheeps' tongues.

•*Pieds de cochon*: Pigs' feet are big news, but no style is more famed that that of Ste-Ménéhould, over Champagne way. They are first cooked for 24–36 hours in a stock with white wine, cloves, herbs, etc., so that even the bones are soft enough to eat. Then they are chopped into large pieces, dribbled with butter, wrapped in breadcrumbs and grilled. The real thing is not served with a sauce. (The town was also the birthplace of Dom Pérignon and is therefore a place of pilgrimage for all true champagne lovers.)

•*Petits pâtés*: Small pies of pastry surrounding pâté mixtures, with flavorings of spice, liver and wine; the Champenoise are good at these.

•Potje flesh/vleesch: A Flemish pâté of veal, chicken and rabbit, also called *terrine flamande*, something rather more spoken of than seen, in my experience.

Fish & Shellfish

A surprise to most is the importance of herring (*hareng*) along the coast. Many simple but good bars and restaurants offer salted or pickled herrings, usually with potato, as an appetizer, but it is the smoked varieties I go for, especially the *bouffi* or *craquelot*. These are lightly salted and smoked ungutted herrings – what the British would call a bloater. Around Boulogne they are smoked over oak and beech, but in Dunkerque it is said that walnut is used. Though reputedly at their peak in October and November, when they are best served hot with a pat of butter, I've bought them and enjoyed them a lot in April and (cold) in May. Even a comparatively inland town like Abbeville has its distinctive marinade for them.

Sprats, often called *harengues de Bergues* or *harranguet*, are smoked too and, as with the herrings proper, often are consumed as a snack with juniper-flavored spirit, *genièvre* - a real treat on a cold wet day.

With one third of all fish landed in France coming through Boulogne, it's no wonder hundreds of British families hover across the Channel for Sunday lunch. It's not just fish from local vessels - rascasse and red mullet (rouget) and violets de Toulon from the Mediterranean will be just as fresh. When you drive or walk over the bridge from the ferry walkway, turn immediately left and explore the fish stalls on the harbor's edge, an ideal detour on your way to the Place Dalton market on Wednesday and Saturday. The marshes of the River Somme breed especially delectable frogs (the Artois are said to be the first whom the British called 'frogs'). For the uninitiated, you eat only the fleshy back legs of frogs (grenouilles) and they are not unlike chicken wings in texture and flavor. They are popular in Champagne, and often used in a pot-au-feu instead of more expensive meat. One could spend weeks traveling up and down the coast sampling each restaurant's apparently original way of serving sole, but most are simply garnished with different proportions of shellfish (noticeably shrimp and mussels), mushrooms and cream. Good

restaurants will do something with sorrel too.

As well as superlative sole, cod (cabillaud), and ling (lingue) that is a revelation, it is the mussels (moules) which are a special attraction, again especially in and around Boulogne; bouchots are very small ones and barbues rather large ones. Moules are usually served marinière, steamed over a little wine with shallot, or leek or onion, but here and there you might find this done with beer. Cockles, a specialty of the Picardie coast, are more likely to be called hénons.

In many of the busier resorts along the coast you find something called bouillabaisse du nord, a mixed fish stew, usually with something unnecessary like a lobster to justify the price; fish soups are also made the same way as they do down south with the fish from the rock bottom (pêches du rocher). A chaudière or chaudrée is a most traditional saltwater fish soup.

Inland, the fish stews are likely to be more authentic or, at least, localized; there are the matelotes, cooked in red or white wine and including eel, carp, perch, pike or whatever other freshwater fish has been caught. Beauvais makes good ones, and also specializes in trout cooked with black pepper (au poivre bouilli). Waterzooi, a soup of Belgian/Flemish origin, uses the same freshwater fish, but adds vegetables and cream. Beware, however, as the term waterzooi is used also for a chicken and leek dish.

Eel is a special joy of the north and with the Flemish

influence is found au vert or à la flamande, jellied in wine and herbs; it is often cooked in beer, the acid of which balances the fattiness nicely. Around Peronne it is made into pâtés.

It's worth remembering that the beautiful Vallée de la Course produces not only trout but also large-leaved watercress, and that its sharp greenness goes wondrously well with winter's great seafood treat, the scallop. But of all my memories of fish eating here, one stands out - seeing freshly caught fish being delivered to restaurants just before they opened on a Sunday morning. Definitely worth the crossing . . .

Meat, Poultry & Game

Within the area almost every type of meat, game and especially poultry is raised. Traditionally, the pig used to dominate towards the west, and sheep towards the poorer eastern Champagne area, supported by a wide range of birds, from geese to guinea fowl. The modern production of beef occurs only in pockets, noticeably between Boulogne and Le Touquet, and was probably as much stimulated by the need to feed smart French tourists as anything else. Over the last fifteen years, there has been a growing interest in goat-keeping, essentially for cheese-making, which means that around Easter you are likely to find suckling-kid (cabri).

Here and there, an enterprising shop or restaurateur will sell local produce or some of the small amount of boar or venison still at large. The most likely food of this kind is excellent wild duck from the Somme estuary. More important is to find and enjoy some of the styles and signature-flavors, the most noted of which is juniper berries, often in combination with beer. Equally important but harder to find is the medieval, Crusade-influenced idea of combining dried fruits with meat. Lapin aux prunes is relatively common, but in Flanders dried apricots might be used, the mix spiked with a little vinegar.

Although recipes for stuffed thrush, snipe, etc., are often mentioned in connection with the area, songbirds are no longer allowed to be shot in Europe and local game is quite rare.

WORTH FINDING

- **Carbonnade**: Beef, braised with onions and beer, originally Flemish.
- **Coq à la bière**: Casserole of chicken in beer flavored with juniper or the juniper spirit genièvre.
- **Coq en pâté**: A Champenoise specialty, which I've noticed particularly in Troyes; stuffed chicken baked in pastry. The flesh should be sliced and put back into the pastry; once the head would be left on for effect.
- **Ficelle picardie**: A savory crêpe stuffed with mushrooms, ham, maybe chicken as well, and baked in a cheese sauce. Standard throughout Picardie, served as an appetizer, and good winter comfort food.
- **Hochepot**: A soup-stew usually of pigs' ears, tails, etc., and with other bits of other animals too; oxtail makes a very rich version. The meats must be browned in fat and flavored with juniper berries.
- **Lapin à la flamande**: Rabbit marinated in red wine and vinegar, cooked with prunes.
- **Pepperpot**: An unusual Flemish combination of mutton and pork with vegetables, braised or stewed in beer.
- **Pieds de mouton**: Sheeps' feet, prepared in a similar way to pigs' trotters and more likely to be found towards the east of the area and in Arras.
- **Pot-au-feu**: Basically the same contents as a hochepot, but the meats are never browned. A real one is served as two dishes, first the broth and then the meat and vegetables. Regional and daily variations.
- **Tripée**: Pigs' offal cooked in white wine, usually in Picardie.
- **Veau flamande**: The most commonly found dish in which meat is combined with dried fruits, usually apricots and raisins or prunes.

VISITING RIGHTS

Visits to the underground caves of the great champagne-making houses in Epernay, Ay or Reims - Moët et Chandon alone have 16 miles - are unavoidable, and I urge you not to avoid several. The bas-reliefs carved for Madame L Veuve Pommery, the inventor of dry (brut) champagne and the great Pommery stairways and deep storage cellars cut into the chalk by the Romans will stimulate you quite as much as the cold will numb you. Only Moët will give you a sample, usually, but only one and so you still won't know the taste of a brut sauvage exactly or whether to agree that only the very driest champagne shows the skill of the blender and quality of the house. I am certain that a slight sweetness, as with a sec, enhances the finesse and multiplies the savor of the wine, as sugar does to all fruit. You will have to search for a restaurant and taste the wines there, and what a treat it will be to find a sweeter and less sweet champagne, and still champagnes and red ones and pink ones . . . but you will usually look in vain for food that is truly from Champagne or for food to which the sparkling wine of Champagne has made an appreciable difference. It

Fruits & Vegetables

Vegetables have saved the north again and again. Not just cabbages, which are life blood, but leeks, potatoes, beet root, carrots and cauliflower, everything you associate with slightly chillier climates. Soups have always been basic and still do abound, often right through summer, sometimes made of a simple vegetable, leek or pumpkin for instance. Just as often they are jumbled into a rich mixture; with pieces of salt or fresh pork they become the potée, a dish every region of France makes now for festivals, but which once might have been all you knew for weeks on end.

Picardie has been a famous region of market gardening for centuries. The biggest center is Amiens, where the canal-irrigated gardens hortillonnages,

is daft, pretentious even, to cook out the bubbles and finesse that so much time and money has put there. It is as indefensible as cooking with Stilton or with caviar ... what's more, the Champenoise only ever use still wine – if any!

Crémant wines are champagne, but less sparkling, and many think them more suitable for the morning – less noisy, I suppose.

For advice about visiting houses, routes, dates and times write or telephone: Comité Interprofessionel du Vin de Champagne (CIVC), 5 rue Henri-Martin, BP135, 51204 Epernay. Tel: (26) 54 47 20.

prompted Louis XI to call it his Little Venice. Much of its produce is grown specifically for export abroad.

The most common vegetables are familiar to most people: cabbages, leeks and potatoes. Cabbage is served as often as in Britain and as plainly, but is equally likely to be bathed in butter or bacon fat and flavored with juniper berries (genièvre) a great local favorite; modern chefs wrap other foods in its leaves. The best way to eat leeks is the flamique of the Artois, called flamiche in Picardie, and often particularly confusing; in Lille for instance, flamique can simply be hot rounds of bread dough sprinkled with butter and brown beet sugar (cassonade), or with just butter in Flanders. But the leek version is best and should be a purée of leeks and butter set with a little egg on a base of bread dough or, these days, of pastry. It's noticeable that although plenty of onions are grown in the region they rarely appear in the fish dishes of the coast, being considered far too strong a flavor - it is leeks you find instead.

You'll not find any particularly special potato dishes but Montdidier (Somme) is a place of pilgrimage for lovers of the South American tuber. It is the birthplace of Parmentier, who persuaded Louis XVI to patronize the potato, thereby setting a royal precedent for its eventual

acceptance as a staple food.

Among the less familiar vegetables grown here, haricot beans are the most important, with Soissons (Aisne) considered to grow some of the very best there are: the white or yellowish lingot type is harvested during September and October in the Pas-de-Calais, Nord and Aisne. The importance given beans in the French diet is matched by an even newer industry, that of sugar beet grown on huge sheets of land. White beet sugar (vergeoise) is exactly the same as that from sugar cane, pure or almost pure sucrose, and any difference in flavor or appearance is due to the manufacturing process. What you cannot make from sugar beet is natural brown sugars and thus cassonade, the local brown, has been flavored and colored with syrup from canes ... but the locals won't believe you.

Fruit is grown, of course, especially apples, and is sold locally, but none is important enough to be considered a commercial crop.

And those mysterious windowless huts are not some relic of a World War, but the homes of the Belgian endive, the white blanched crisp endive, that is, if you'll excuse the expression, one of the biggest growth industries here.

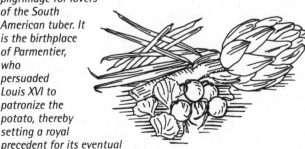

LOCAL PRODUCE

- **CABBAGE** *Chou*
Var: round and curly
October to end
December high season
Dep: Nord, Pas-de-Calais,
Lille, St-Omer and
Dunkerque are major
markets; but most
cabbage grown here
is for commercial use,
choucroute, etc.

- **BEET ROOT** *betterave*
Var: changing as crop
increases
Mainly an autumn crop
Dep: Nord, Pas-de-Calais

- **BRUSSELS SPROUTS**
chou de bruxelles
Var: no native ones now
Mid-November to end
December
Dep: Nord, Pas-de-Calais.
Somme Nord is the
premier production
zone in France, supplying
30% of the crop. St-
Omer, Lille and Aubers
are market centers.

- **CARROT** *carotte*
Var: *Nataise, Amelioré*
September/October is
mid-season
Dep: Somme, Nord, Pas-
de-Calais, Aisne

- **CAULIFLOWER** *choufleur*
Var: *Malines*
Best July to September
Dep: Nord, Pas-de-Calais

- **CELERIAC** *céleri-rave*
Var: *Excelsior, Neve,
Monarque, Alba*
Main crop September/
October
Dep: Nord, Pas-de-Calais,
Lille and Dunkerque
produce almost 20% of
the national crop, which
is increasing as the
vegetable becomes more
popular.

- **ENDIVE** *endive*
Var: *Zoom, Bergère*
December to March, mainly
Dep: Nord, Pas-de-
Calais, Somme, Aisne
Between the Nord and

Picardie 80% of the French
production is grown here,
although Finistère in
Brittany has a much longer
season. Generally grown
now in air-conditioned
sheds so that the requisites
of dampness and darkness
can be controlled.

- **LEEKS** *poireaux*
Var: many; summer, autumn
and winter types
September to March
Dep: Nord
The Nord is the biggest
French production by far,
but most goes for commerce,
freezing and the like rather
than fresh market.

- **LETTUCE** *laitue*
Var: *frisées* curly and
round, mainly
May to October
Dep: Nord

- **ONION** *oignon*
Var: F1 hybrids only
Usually harvested
September
Dep: Pas-de-Calais,
Somme, Ardennes, Aube

- **PEAS** *petis pois*
Var: dozens
May, June, July main season
Dep: Pas-de-Calais, Somme,
Aisne, Nord
This is 50% of the national
production but virtually all
is processed in some way;
fresh ones from Brittany or
Provence.

- **SHALLOT** *échalote*
Var: *Longue* and *demi-
longue*
Harvested June to August
Dep: Nord, Pas-de-Calais

- **SPINACH** *épinards*
Var: *Samos Symphonie*
Main crop September/
October
Dep: Nord, Somme

- **TURNIPS** *navets*
Var: *Nantais, Croissy, Milan*
Late winter and spring
Dep: Nord, Pas-de-Calais

Cheese

Here cheese falls essentially
into two categories: the
smelly, washed-rind cheeses
personified by maroilles, and
rich, fresh cream cheeses; but
recently goats' milk cheeses
have started to appear. The
lush grasses of the region are
not really ideal for goats, as
their milk and cheeses are
much better for being based
on the drier feed of the south.
Nonetheless, many are good
enough to be stocked by
Phillipe Olivier in Boulogne,
and that is recommendation
enough. He believes spring is
the best time, and some-
times adds extra flavor and
savor to locally made chèvres
by rolling them in, for
instance, pink peppercorns.

•Baguette Laonnaise
(Champagne): A washed-rind
loaf, with very high
ammoniacal nose and flavor,
developed since World War II.
Close relation to maroilles
(qv). Similar cheeses are the
baguette de Thiérache,
losange de Thiérache, coeur
d'Arras, coeur d'Avesnes, pavé
carré d'Avesnes.

•Barberey: A soft cheese
with a tangy flavor made
from skimmed cow's milk;
also known as fromage de
Troyes or Troyan cendré.

•Belval: From the abbey of
Belval in Picardie, a pressed
disk of mild cow's milk
cheese. Can be enjoyed year-
round.

•Bergues: A washed-rind
cheese from the village of
Bergues, close to Dunkerque.
It is low fat (15-20%), and
washed with beer daily.
Originally an imitation of
18th-century Dutch styles, it
is usually found at Monday
markets.

•Boulette d'Avesnes: A
Flemish cheese made in

farmhouses with buttermilk included, or industrially with fromage blanc and herbs, as le dauphin (qv). Cone-shaped and very strong, so that genièvre is the recommended accompaniment.

•Boulette de Cambrai: Herb-flavored cheese but fresher and shaped by hand.

•Boulette de Prémont: Richer and gentler than la boulette d'Avesnes; named from a village in Aisne.

•Caprice des dieux (Bassigny): A pasteurized cow's milk cheese, distinctively shaped to a small oval loaf. Made with enriched milk (60% fat content); delicate but characteristic flavor.

•Carré de l'Est: A small square cheese made in Champagne (and also Lorraine) that is mild and bland; really a commercial, lesser brie.

•Cendré de Champagne: Like a small ash-covered camembert; the ash reduces the fat content as it matures. Only 3 or 4 farms still make them.

•Chaource: An AOC cheese from Champagne; known since the 14th century. Made from the milk of three types of cow - the Alpine Brown, frisonne and tachetée de l'Est. It has 50% fat content. Very white crust, perhaps with a blush of pink. Should be finely textured and not grainy, smell a little of cream and mushrooms, and taste gentle and nutty. Best in summer and autumn.

•Chaumont: A washed-rind cow's milk cheese with a strong, spicy flavor, shaped to a tall, truncated cone.

•Coeur d'Arras: A heart-shaped version of a rollot from Picardie and Artois.

•Dauphin: Another relation of maroilles but one which has traditionally been

flavored with pepper and tarragon since the 17th century. A high smell and flavor. Molded into heart, shield, crescent or fish shapes.

•Ervy-le-châtel: A soft cow's milk cheese. Bloomy rind and milky flavor; shaped to a truncated cone.

•Fromage d'Hesdin: A monastery-made washed-rind cheese, sometimes known as Belval, where the monastery is actually situated. Relatively new but very highly regarded by restaurateurs interested in regional food.

•Gris de Lille: Also called vieux puant, vieux gris ("old stinker"). A strong, spicy, salty slab of cheese, clearly the strong man of the maroilles family. From Artois, Flanders and Hainaut, and best in autumn and spring.

•Igny: Made by Trappists at the monastery of Igny in Marne. A mild, washed-rind cheese best eaten end of spring to autumn.

•Langres: A strong, washed-rind disk from Champagne which is good from spring through autumn.

•Larron d'Ors: Also fromage d'Ors, one of the least-known cheeses of the area. A low-fat, washed-rind square cheese with the expected robust smell and flavor. Usually, it is considered best in winter and spring. Ors is a village close to Cateau (Nord).

•Maroilles: An important AOC cheese from an area of luxurious pastureland between Hainaut and the Ardennes. Invented over 1,000 years ago at the abbey of Maroilles, it is a washed-rind cheese with the usual reddish-orange crust. The exact area of manufacture is "the part of la Thiérache in the south of the

arrondissement d'Avesnes and in the north of the arrondissement de Vervins in l'Aisne." It should be shiny without being sticky, supple but not runny. The smell is definitely that of unsavory feet but the flavor is delicious, earthy, spicy and nutty-sweet. Good in all seasons other than spring. Goyère is a flan made with this cheese. It is often confused with gougère, a cheese-studded choux pastry made both in the south of Champagne and most of Burgundy.

•Mimolette: A Flemish cheese also called boule de

FROMAGE TO GO

Phillipe Olivier is one of France's most famous maître fromagers, and in his three cellars, each with a different humidity and temperature, is a selection of cheeses that even the French dream about but rarely find: roquefort made with breadcrumbs rather than being injected with bacteria; farmhouse-made camembert and brie from unpasteurized milk, bethmale artisanale from the Ariège. He also sells unpasteurized Normandy butter, either in bulk or packets. You simply cannot go to the north of France without visiting this exceptional shop, which now supplies a number of restaurants outside France with their cheeseboard, and you can't come home without cheese and butter from Monsieur Olivier (43-45 rue Thiers, Boulogne).

With notice, the Boulogne Chamber of Commerce can arrange a cheese tasting for a minimal charge per head, or even better, a combined cheese and wine tasting in central wine cellars.

Lille *and* vieux Lille. *This was the favorite cheese of General de Gaulle. An orange-fleshed ball related to Gouda and Edam. Its ideal age is between 15 and 16 months, but it is available younger and older. It must be aged with great care, as the rind needs regular brushing for the mites to keep their distance. A special mallet is used to determine if the cheese is properly conditioned.*

•Mont des Cats: *From Godewaersvelde, close to Bailleul, this is a typical Trappist cheese, a thick pale disk with a washed-rind and lactic flavor. Made only since 1880 and commonly eaten for breakfast.*

•Quart maroilles: *See* maroilles.

•Les Riceys *(Aube): A soft cheese made in small dairies from skimmed cow's milk. A very fruity flavor; rind coated with ashes.*

•Rollot: *A washed-rind cheese from the Arras area, made in a disk or heart shape and with the expected rich smell and flavor.*

•Sorbais: *A variation of* maroilles; *it takes its name from a small village in Aisne which holds an important cheese fair early in September each year.*

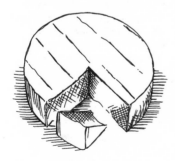

Pastries, Desserts & Confectionery

War has strange and lasting effects on diet. Britain's early 19th-century blockade of France encouraged Napoléon to commission the chemist Delassert finally to perfect the extraction of sugar from beet. The climate and soil of the north suit it admirably.

The most conspicuous example of lavish enjoyment

of sugar is the tarte au sucre, also found under many local names, which is a round yeast dough baked with a crust of sugar - a sort of sugar pizza. Chocolate and chocolate-making seem universal, and most villages have somewhere that makes it on the premises. Le Chat Bleu in Le Touquet makes clever chocolate cockles (hénons). In Champagne you will find chocolate molded into champagne-bottle corks (bouchons).

Confectionery is pandemic with such wondrous names as bonbons à la sève de pin, sottises *(Valenciennes)*, quinquins *(Lille), and* pailles au café *(Soissons). Pastries, croissants and open tarts of apples, prunes and pears are universal. You may find sweet pâtes of fruit, barley sugar (*sucre d'orge*) or, in Amiens, sucre de pommes. People in Provins may still make their confiture de roses and in Picardie look for* raisiné picard, *pear jam cooked with grape juice.*

Of course, before either cane sugar or local beet sugar, honey was the queen of sweeteners; that from Ste-Ménéhould went mainly to make the nougat de miel of Langres. Honey gingerbread (pain d'épices), was and is made here and so was a sort of almond bread, pain d'amandes.

CAMBRAI'S MISTAKES

A *Bêtise de Cambrai*, literally a Cambrai Mistake, is a boiled candy flavored with mint and given a light, slightly bitter touch by the use of caramelized sugar and by having plenty of air whipped into the mix. They have made the name of the town known all over France, even receiving the ultimate honor of appearing in an Astérix adventure, but there are only two manufacturers: Afchain, in Cambrai itself, and Despinoy, just to the west in Fontaine-Notre-Dame. Both resolutely claim that it was on their premises and nowhere else that, sometime between 1830 and 1850, a boy made the felicitous mistake of burning the sugar and adding an overdose of mint while preparing the mix for the family candy business.

An important market had been held on the 24th of every month in Cambrai for centuries and one of Europe's oldest confectionery industries had developed in the town to cater to the unsatisfied sweet tooth of the farmers, traders and other country people who flocked there for the day, providing fairly crude, sugary sweets. According to one side, it was Grandmère Afchain, the old dear who now appears on all their packaging, who after severely scolding her grandson for his stupid *bêtise* actually tried one of the spoiled candies and then told everyone how good they were. The Despinoy version is more prosaic: the boy who took the punishment was only an anonymous apprentice, and it was the prompt action of Monsieur Jules Despinoy in stirring the mix that stopped it from becoming an utter mess and led him, still accidentally, to come upon the delicious new creation. Either way, once the "mistakes" were put on sale, they immediately became more popular than any of the other

Cambrai sweets and a new business was born. Each company religiously refuses to recognize the other or even, it seems, to mention their name. Despinoy actually sued its rivals in the 1880s with a claim that they had lured away the famous apprentice and got him to give up the secrets of the family's recipe. Despinoy lost the case, a decision that still raises hackles in Fontaine-Notre-Dame. Today, accordingly, the august *Inventaire du Patrimoine Culinaire de la France* also gives the accolade to Afchain, which labels all its candies "*vraie Bêtises de Cambrai*". They are by far the largest company, recently acquired by a Spanish foods conglomerate. They have introduced chocolate and fruit flavored *bêtises* to complement the traditional mint and now market their products throughout France and in Germany, the USA and Japan, sometimes under the cringe-inducing label French Cancan. At their sizable factory in Cambrai there are free guided tours (mornings, Monday to Thursday) and even a *bêtise* museum.

Despinoy, meanwhile, is a much smaller operation, where the current head of the company, François Campion, still makes candies himself virtually by hand. He states trenchantly that he is "the last true artisan of the *bêtise*," and stresses that he uses only entirely natural ingredients in his products. Not to be outdone, though, he too has introduced a new line, a *sirop de bêtise liqueur*, and this time has ensured he has a patent to go with it. Should this sugary dispute ever be settled, which is unlikely, the winner could perhaps enter into a final battle to the death with the English mint humbug.

Bon Marché

Below is a selective list of markets plus some fairs (*foires*) of special interest. Check with the local Syndicat d'Initiative (SI) for precise locations and time changes.

PAS-DE-CALAIS

Aire *Mon, rummage sale 2nd Sun in May;* Arques *Tue;* Arras *Thur, Sat, Sun AM;* Auxi-le-Château *Sat;* Avion *Thur, rummage sale 5 Sept;* Berck Plage *Wed, Sat AM;* Béthune *Mon, Fri;* Boulogne-sur-Mer *Wed, Sat;* Brebières *Sat;* Bully-les-Mines *Thur, Sat;* Calais *Wed, Sat, Sun;* Carvin *Sat AM, rummage sale last Sun Sept;* Corbehem *Fri PM;* Courrières *Wed;* Desvres *Tue;* Etaples *Tue, Fri;* Fauquembergues *Thur;* Fléchin *Wed;* Frévent *Tue;* Grenay *Tue AM, rummage sale last Sun April;* Harnes *Thur AM;* Hénin-Beaumont *Tue, Fri;* Hesdin *Thur;* Isbergues *Thur, rummage sale last Sun Sept;* Lens *Tue, Fri, rummage sales 1st Mon June & 1st Sun Oct;* Licques *Mon, Turkey Fair 2nd Mon before Christmas;* Liévin *Wed AM;* Lillers *Sat;* Marquise *Thur;* Méricourt *Sat;* Montreuil *Sat AM;* Noeux-les-Mines *Fri AM, Tue PM;* Outreau *Mon & Thur AM;* Pernes *Thur;* Le Portel *Tue, Fri;* Sallaumines *Mon AM, Sat PM;* Samer *Mon, Strawberry Fair Sun nearest 20 June;* St-Omer *Wed, Sat;* St-Pol-sur-Termoise *Mon;* Le Touquet- Paris Plage *Thur, Sat (& Mon in summer), Easter Mon, Pentecost;* Vimy *Sat PM;* Wissant *Wed.*

SOMME

Abbeville *Thur, last Wed in month;* Airaines *Fri;* Albert *Sat, 2nd Wed in month, rummage sale June;* Amiens *Daily (except*

Sun), Picardie Exhibition June;
Ault Wed, Sat; Bray-sur-Somme
Thur, 1st Wed in month;
Cayeux-sur-Mer Tue, Fri, Sun in
season; Corbie Fri; Crécy-en-
Ponthieu Mon; Le Crotoy Tue,
Fri; Doullens Thur; Ham Sat,
rummage sale 1st two weeks
Sept; Harbonnières Tue;
Hornoy-le-Bourg Thur;
Montdidier Sat, rummage sale
Sun before 11 Nov; Oisemont
Sat; Péronne Fri (fish), Sat;
Poix-de-Picardie Tue; Rue Sat;
St-Valéry-sur-Somme Sun,
rummage sale May, Villers-
Bretonneux Wed.

OISE

Andeville Fri; Beauvais Wed,
Sat; Breteuil Wed PM, rummage
sales 1st Sun July, Sun before 25
Nov; Chambly Wed, Sat AM;
Compiègne Wed, Sat; Creil Wed,
Thur, Sat; Chestnut Fair 1st Sun
Nov; Crépy-en-Valois Wed AM;
Estrées-St-Denis Tue PM;
Liancourt Wed AM; Marseille-
en-Beauvaisis Fri AM; Méru Fri
& Sat AM; Montataire Thur &
Sun AM; Neuilly-en-Thelle Fri
AM; Noailles Thur AM; Senlis Tue,
Fri AM; Ste-Geneviève Fri AM;
Verneuil-en-Halatte Fri PM.

NORD

Armentières Fri AM, rummage
sale 2nd Mon Aug; Aulnoye-
Aymeries Tue AM, Sat PM,
rummage sale Easter Mon;
Avesnes-les-Aubert Sun AM, Fri
AM (Oct-March) (fish), Thur AM
(veg); Avesnes-sur-Helpe Fri AM;
Bailleul Tue AM; Bassée Thur &
Sun AM; Bertry Tue; Beauvois-
en-Cambresis Thur AM;
Bourbourg Tue; Busigny Thur
AM; Cambrai Daily except Mon,
rummage sale 1st Sun July;
Cassel Thur AM; Le Cateau Tue,
Thur & Sat AM; Caudry Fri & Sun
AM, Tue AM (fruit & veg); Denain
Tue, Thur; Douai Daily, rummage
sale 2nd Sun Oct; Dunkerque
Wed, Sat, rummage sale 15 Aug;
Faches-Thumesnil Thur & Sat
PM; Flines-lez-Raches Thur PM,
rummage sale Mon (AM) after

29th Sept; Formies Sat AM;
Hautmont Tue & Fri AM;
Hazebrouck Mon AM;
Hellemmes-Lille Wed AM, Sat;
Lambersart Tue AM, Fri & Sat PM;
Landrecies Sat AM; Lille Daily,
grand rummage sale Mon after
1st Sun Sept (midnight-1PM);
Loos Sun AM, Thur, rummage
sale 1st Mon in Sept; Marcq-
en-Baroeul Tue, Wed, Thur, Sat
PM, rummage sale 1st Sun Sept;
Maubeuge Sun, Mon, Wed, Sat;
Merville Wed AM; Nouvaux Tue,
Wed, Sat AM; Roubaix Mon AM,
Tue, Wed AM, Thur, Sat, Sun;
Solesmes Thur AM; Steenvoorde
Sat AM; St-Amand-les-Eaux
Wed, rummage sale 4th Sun
Sept; St-Pol-sur-Mer Sun AM;
Tourcoing Daily exc. Sun;
Wallincourt-Selvigny Tue AM;
Wattrelos Thur, Fri, Sun,
rummage sale Monday after
Pentecost & 3rd Mon June.

AISNE

Bohain-en-Vermandois Fri;
Château-Thierry Tue, Fri;
Chauny Tue, Fri; Crécecy-sur-
Serre Mon; Guignicourt Fri;
Guise Sat; Hirson Mon, Thur;
Láon Tue, Wed AM, Thur, Sat PM,
rummage sale 4th Mon June;
Marle Fri; Le Nouvion-en-
Thiérache Wed; Rozoy-sur-
Serre Wed AM, Soissons Wed,
Sat; St-Gobain Sun; St-Quentin
Wed, Thur, Fri, Sat.

ARDENNES

Carignan Fri; Charleville-
Mézières-Théatre Tue, Thur, Sat;
Fumay Wed, Sat.

MARNE

Avize Thur; Bazancourt Fri;
Sermaize-les-Bains Sun;
Suippes Fri; Ste-Ménéhould
Mon; Vertus Tue; Vitry-le-
François Thur; Warmeriville
Thur.

AUBE

Aix-en-Othe Wed, Sat; Bar-sur-
Aube Sat AM, Wines of
Champagne Fair (2 days) 2nd
Sun Sept; rummage sale Sat
mid-June; Brienne-le-Château

Thur, Choucroute & Champagne
Fair 3rd weekend Sept; Chaource
Mon AM, Cheese Fair 3rd Sun
Oct, Lily-of-the-Valley Fair May
1st; Ervy-le-Chatel Fri AM;
Nogent-sur-Seine Sat, Wed AM;
Pâlis Thur; Les Riceys 2nd & 4th
Thur in month; Romilly-sur-
Seine Mon, Thur & Sat; Ste-
Savine Tue & Fri AM, Sun AM
(flowers); St-André-les-Vergers
Wed; Troyes Daily, Maundy Thur
(hams), Champagne Fair 12 to
20 June.

HAUTE-MARNE

Bourbonne-les-Bains Wed, Sat;
Chalindrey Thur; Chaumont
Mon & Sun AM; Châlons-sur-
Marne Wed, Fri, Sat; Châtillon-
sur-Marne Wed; Dormans Sat;
Epernay Tue; Orbais Sat;
Pargny-sur-Saulx Sun AM;
Reims Daily; St-Dizier Wed, Sat;
Wassy Thur.

ALSACE
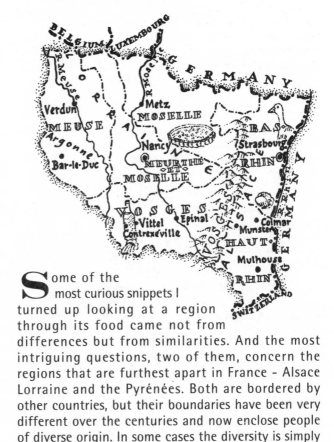 LORRAINE

BOUNDARIES OF TRADITION

"In which we...
•Eat mixed meats with
chilled red wine and
discover where a
deposed king played
sweetly...
• Take pretzels for tea
and find how Jewish
spice merchants talked
amongst themselves...
•Decide about
squirrels, taste the
waters that got brewers
hopping and meet the
Doyen of pâté de foie
gras...
•Find an artist of puff-
pastry, grapple with the
problem of rose hips,
enjoy beavers' tails and
meet a sweetheart...
•Dragées through
Verdun, bake a rhubarb
tart, get into pickles
with turnips...
•Discover winstubs and
a hot tip for going cold
on fruit brandies..."

Some of the most curious snippets I turned up looking at a region through its food came not from differences but from similarities. And the most intriguing questions, two of them, concern the regions that are furthest apart in France - Alsace Lorraine and the Pyrénées. Both are bordered by other countries, but their boundaries have been very different over the centuries and now enclose people of diverse origin. In some cases the diversity is simply that associated with border change, but it is equally the result of refugee settlement of decimated border areas after conflict, the dispossessed moving into the deserted.

A feature of the Basque and the Pyrénéean region of France directly in contact with Spain is dishes that contain the flesh of more than one animal, or that mix meat and fish. There is the *garbure* of Gascony and the *cassoulets* of Carcassone or Toulouse; *paella* is the best-known Spanish example. In Flanders, another area with historical borders different from its contemporary ones, they have a pepperpot, which mixes mutton and pork, but it is not that common. In

Alsace, though, even the casual visitor can eat winter's *baeckenoffa* - large chunks of lamb, beef and pork marinated in fragrant but dry Alsatian Riesling and traditionally cooked with potatoes and onions in the baker's oven while housewives did their Monday morning washing. The inclusion of beef indicates the dish to be less than a century old, and thus was developed and accepted into the local ethos at the time of most identity confusion, when Alsace was swung from France to Germany four times between 1870 and 1945.

I discovered *baeckenoffa* in a noisy, old restaurant by the river, near 16th-century Petite France in Strasbourg. It was a place of wood and low ceilings and shared tables that felt and looked German. When my order came, it was enormous and steaming in a brown earthenware casserole. I thought there had been some mistake and that it was intended for two people. But it was indeed for one. The mixed meats and wine had created a savoriness far greater than expected from such simple ingredients, and they had blended their individuality to the point that only differing textures allowed you to be certain which you were eating. In a properly made *baeckenoffa*, the meats are never jumbled together but given their appropriate and consistent place in the casserole; families will disagree over whether the pork should be left, right or center, or whether it might be better if the shoulder of lamb were always in the center - but that is the way of such dishes. Those who were clearly regulars accompanied their *baeckenoffa* with carafes of chilled red Alsatian wine, notwithstanding sub-zero December temperatures outside. They knew what they were doing in combining winter food with a summery-seeming wine: I enjoyably finished mine with the *tarte du jour*, of *merises* (wild cherries),

before starting my exploration of the pockets of junk market between the river and the cathedral.

The special element of my enjoyment was that I had eaten as traditionally as could be asked for in Strasbourg but with great ease and in the center of what, in other cities, would be a tourist kingdom. And I had not needed to consult a specialist guide to find a restaurant serving local dishes. Here is the second mirror image this northern region has with the southern. In both, the visitor is able easily to eat those specialties and traditional foods which elsewhere are the fodder only of foodwriters' pens. Perhaps the coincidence is some manifestation of the problems of being borderline cases? Lacking any sense of continuity in culture, government or language, they defiantly opted instead for the tangible and comforting security of identifying, and then identifying with, the food they ate. Now, untrusting of modern history, they stick with it.

There may be other reasons why Alsace Lorraine and the Pyrénées alone remain areas where the casual visitor might most easily taste dishes truly of that area and which are enjoyed at home as much as in restaurants, but no one has ever offered any to me.

Driving or flying across the rugged, blue Vosges mountains that divide Alsace from Lorraine, you are bound to wonder why we say Alsace Lorraine instead of Lorraine Alsace, or why they should be linked at all. Lorraine is very much bigger than Alsace, and in history has been rather more seriously French that Alsace. Joan of Arc was born here, in Domrémy. For a while it even had its own duke.

Lorraine's food is gentle, elegant even, when you move on from the soup-stew *potée* to pretty *dragées*, lots of eggy things, and sweet and savory dishes using pastry, like quiches, of course. And hence come the spa waters of Vittel and Contrexéville, Baccarat crystal and Bar-le-Duc red currants.

Alsace has always been more German, and serves you *spaetzli*, ravaged tatters of noodle dough, sausages and fruit-heavy cakes. It has a reputation for Jewish influence (and thus for chocolate and foie gras), for wine and for superlative game. The currency of spice, cumin particularly, is explained by that Jewish presence. Jewish businessmen were always the merchants of Venice throughout the spice-loving colder countries of Middle Europe and Russia; until the 16th century all spice reached Europe exclusively in the trading ships of Venice. So, when the same men escaped pogrom, war or famine and crossed the Rhine into Alsace, they brought with them both the taste for and the access to spices. The question I wanted answered was why they had stayed here. Why didn't they move further from their memories, deeper into France? It wasn't as though the towns and villages here were that much safer - Jews had been massacred in Alsace, too, although unusually the miscreants were often executed in their turn. The talking during a wine tour unraveled the reason, as I compared *vendanges tardives* in company with the 12th and 13th generations of the Hugel family who make wine in that walled masterpiece of a town, Riquewihr. Both the Alsace dialect and Yiddish have the same 8th-century German roots. Thus whatever their homeland, a new Jewish immigrant could understand and be understood here and settle into life and business without having to learn a new language or retire into a ghetto.

It is war that has so linked Alsace and Lorraine, uprooting them often enough to forge them inseparably in the common consciousness. They have also the Vosges as a common denominator. In summer now you can stay at the dairying farms folded into their valleys where munster cheese and its relatives are made. The summer woods offer the pleasure of gathering the wild berries that are made into tarts or fruit brandies to be drunk iced in winter and, in early autumn, rich, rare mushrooms to enjoy with the game that panics ahead of you as you drive or walk. And you'll meet families out walking, for the somewhat alpine-like hamlets, spas and health centers of 19th-century life are once again fashionable retreats from the city. The Vosges mountains divide as much as they stitch together, for the peaks are just high enough to protect Alsace from Atlantic weather, so it is one of the sunniest areas of France, pleasantly warm rather than baking hot.

Alsace and Lorraine and the Vosges are not any part of the general received view of France and French food. There may be croissants for breakfast, but pretzels for tea and noisy suppers in *winstubs*, a cross between beer cellar and wine bar. Perhaps you will have a thickly creamed slice of chocolate and cherry cake, less of a catering cliché here, when the Black Forest for which it is named can be visited for the day. Alsace Lorraine is the more refreshing because of this individuality, and more rewarding for the generosity with which you are welcome to share hospitality that is their own, rather than a posturing of nouvelle, hamburgers and french fries. There is true tradition in food to appreciate here but, paradoxically, the wines are like none other in the world precisely because they have no truck with tradition . . .

Charcuterie

The pride of every hamlet, village and town will be its charcuterie, for both Alsace and Lorraine cling to the old reliance on pork products, though few families now rely for survival upon a pig. Like their neighbors in Champagne, brewers (brasseurs) fattened pigs on the by-products of their brewing to make sausages and snacks to attract customers to their beer, creating some of the best brasseries. The combination of reliance and ancient excellence of produce means every possible variation of charcuterie is here, even the air-dried sausage in sunny Alsace. Most universal are the saucisses de Strasbourg, showing their Germanic influence by being bigger, thicker versions of the frankfurter, and thus just as likely to be seen under their other name knackwurst.

The complication of French, German and dialect names for most produce makes attempts at precise guidance a nightmare, so this is a region in which to use your eyes and good sense as your guide. To my mind the most important sausages are the finely textured ones like knackwurst, and cervelas, a name that indicates that pigs' brains (cervelles) were once an important ingredient. These and all the variations upon them are likely to be spiked with pistachio nuts, whole spices, truffles and such, the variations based on individual flair and interest rather than tradition. Tongues and livers are also used as sausage ingredients, indeed there is a boudin à la langue, a blood pudding with cubes of tongue, very common over the border

in Germany. Nancy is particularly associated with blood puddings, and includes in its repertoire a soup and an omelette based upon the boudin.

With the abundance of both wild and commercially reared pork, a favorite dish is kalerei, fromage de tête or hure, what we would call headcheese. Look for excellent laxschinken and kassler, salted loin of pork and salted cooked and smoked loin. Schifela is smoked shoulder.

There are pâtés of sorts all through the year, but come autumn and winter the range multiplies to embrace every imaginable combination of pork and game; you will even find squirrel (écureuil). Alsace and Lorraine also have plenty of veal, thanks to their dairying.

This sweet, light meat adds a sophistication and rich elegance to the pâté mixtures missing elsewhere. Many dishes are presented en croûte. And so, of course, are the tourtes; coarsely chopped combinations of veal and pork (usually) baked into large, pastry-covered pies and sold by the slice. Sometimes small versions will be made, not unlike lesser versions of the British pork pie. I find them tastier than most pâtés, and their honest farmhouse origins are often revealed in the names given them, linking them to this or that valley on one or the other sides of the Vosges. Perfect picnic and party food. There are also hams, sometimes poached (such as Colmar ham), usually smoked and in spring combined with asparagus. Andouilles and andouillettes are found here as well.

TERRINE OR NOT TERRINE?

Foie gras and *pâté de foie gras* should not strictly be found in a charcuterie, but in a *traiteur* if cooked and in a *boucherie* or *volailleur* if fresh. But in small towns and markets, the boundaries are now blurred.

To the outsider the thought of Alsace instantly conjures up *pâté de foie gras en croûte*, and you will certainly find it here. This was probably invented in Strasbourg by Jean-Pierre Clause around 1780 for the table of le Maréchal de Contudes, governor of Alsace, who sent some to Louis XVI. Later, Nicolas-François Doyen is believed to have perfected the recipe and to have introduced truffles. It's probable that the Romans, who fattened

geese with figs for foie gras, made a type of pâté and that pâtés of goose liver were already known in France, particularly in Périgueux. The pâté is properly foie gras in a farce mixture baked in pastry. Unless made with exceptional skill, the pork flavor of the farce will draw away and dilute that of the liver. Fois gras or *terrine de foie gras* should be nothing but fattened goose liver. On today's budgets, therefore, you are better advised to go for a slice of nothing but foie gras, or as many a restaurant with a good kitchen will offer you, several scoops of its own recipe from a large earthenware pot.

Fish & Shellfish

With the Rhine and its major tributary the Ill in Alsace, and both the Moselle and Meuse in Lorraine, as well as countless streams and brooks rising on both sides of the Vosges mountains, freshwater fish have always played an important part in local culinary traditions. The exceptional modern restaurants throughout the region, especially in Alsace, are today tending towards lighter dishes featuring fish, and frogs' legs are served in mousses and mousselines where once they would have been gratinéed, sautéed with Riesling or found in soups. Frogs are measurably less popular than before.

You will regularly be offered salmon. In spite of stories of salmon, salmon trout and even sturgeon nosing their way so far inland, it is unlikely to be local. Instead, enjoy the countless variations offered with carp, bream, perch, tench, pike, eel and the confusingly naked pike-perch or zander: respectively carpe, brème, perche, tanche, brochet, anguille and sandre. Butter, cream and wine will be employed, with the occasional use of an unexpected spice. It will often be cumin. Any of these fish may be found in a matelote, a superior stew of such fish in Alsatian white wine or a Lorraine vin gris, plus cream.

The abundance of trout means you might be offered a real truite au bleu, for which the fish must be plunged into boiling, vinegar-spiked stock the very second it expires. The best recommendation I can give is to take advantage of the Jewish tradition and try carp. It will often be offered with a stuffing based on ground almonds, but simpler and better is the renowned carpe à la juive, or Jeddefesch which, typical of many Jewish dishes, is prepared so that it can be enjoyed cold on the Sabbath, when cooking is forbidden.

EMINENCE ROUGE

The fabled freshwater crayfish (*écrevisses*) have all but disappeared since the start of this century; in the 15th century they were a cheap way to feed the horde of workers who suspended the great bell of St George's in Haguenau. Lorraine has more of its *écrevisses* left than Alsace, where those you eat are more likely to have come from the Black Forest. Cooked in wine, they may be described as *cardinalisées*. The appeal has been also to poets, as this neat three-liner demonstrates.

Du ruisseau, l'écrevisse
est l'eminence grise
Qui changeant couleur,
sortant d'un feu d'enfer
Prend l'habit éclatant
d'un price d'église.

Out of the stream, the crayfish is an eminence grise
That changes its colors going through hell-fire
To emerge in the brilliant robes of a prince of the church.

Meat, Poultry & Game

There have always been cattle here, but they were mainly in the valleys of the Vosges, and raised for their milk - and that was used for cheese. Thus neither beef recipes nor cooking with butter was common until tastes started to change about 100 years ago. Even so, rendered pork fat is as likely to be found in savory dishes as butter. For the large Jewish community, neither was permitted, hence their special interest in raising geese for schmalz (grease). But beef tongue (langue) with a Madeira sauce is considered a local triumph, and stews à la mode alsacienne or supperfleisch are not uncommon and often served with noodles. Vinegar is often used to point beef dishes, and rather than tripes, all four stomachs, look for dishes with gras-double, which indicates only the three superior stomachs are used. You might even find estomac de boeuf farci, a stomach filled with fat, onions and starch and boiled. I should ignore it if you do, and go instead for veal dishes, notably stuffed breast

(poitrine farcie) or anything to do with calf's liver.

Pork was the mainstay of rural life, and so good was it that Ancient Rome imported much of her requirements from the peoples living on the left bank of the Rhine here. As well as the vast array of charcuterie, Alsace and Lorraine both enjoy fresh pork, especially suckling pig (cochon de lait), served hot in Alsace but, more often, cold in a jelly of its own juices in Lorraine. In such an important fruit-growing area, expect to find pork combined with fruits and berries, too, perhaps the famous currants of Bar-le-Duc.

The two greatest - but by no means commonest - meats of Alsace and Lorraine are goose and game. The locally reared chickens and turkeys are excellent, mainly because there is so much wheat and barley grown in the area. You'll find them in cream sauces, often with wild mushrooms, morels (morilles) especially. Jewish ways of stuffing, or with casseroles containing no dairy products,

COOKING YOUR GOOSE

Geese are fresh and ready to eat about the same
time game makes its appearance, but, if you can bear the richness, fat-preserved goose confit will be around at most times of the year. The Jewish ways with goose are the best; stuffed necks (cou d'oie farci/ganshalsel) and a stew of neck, wings and gizzards (ragoût d'oie/ gansvoresse).

are excellent, usually bright and fresh with parsley and made interesting with ground ginger. And no celebration is complete without bouchées à la Reine, puff pastry cases crammed with chicken or ham - brie, it is said, for the original - in a creamy sauce attributed, as are so many elegant dishes, to the court of Stanislas.

Game, notably in Alsace, is considered outstanding even by those living in other areas of France. It runs the gamut from wild pig (sanglier) and venison (cerf) or (chevreuil) to the pigeons of Toul and Vaucouleurs (Lorraine). Marcassin is the sweeter, younger wild pig; as its youth prevents it from having developed any singularity of flavor, it is often indistinguishable from ordinary pork. Pheasant, partridge, (en chartreuse - in cabbage) and hare will all be outstanding and, depending on the skill of the chef, vary from simple to complicated. A civet is the most common way to cook all of them, and is a slow-cook stew (properly thickened with blood but this is not now common); when game is not in season, lapin de garenne (wild rabbit) will be used. Most such dishes will be cooked in local white wine, but as it is always fermented out to be bone dry it works extremely well. Equally it is a revelation to drink dry Alsatian Riesling wines from a carafe with game dishes. What red wines there are are served chilled but I think they are less robust than the whites. St Hubert often appears in the name of game dishes for he was from Lorraine and is the patron saint of hunters.

Fruits & Vegetables

In the 17th century, Lorraine alone grew 83 varieties of pears, 36 of peaches and 33 of apples. Today there are fewer but the ways you are served them, and the other fruits of the plains, mountains and forests, are ever increasing. In summer and autumn, fruits and berries are fresh in tartes, strewn over and through pancakes and cakes of all shapes and sizes; then and in other seasons, they'll be in syrup, in chocolates, or made into eaux-de-vie. Dried apples, plums and pears (schnitz) are served with meat and game, or cooked fresh in autumn or winter to accompany blood pudding, especially the exquisite Reinette apples. Pickled plums (prunes) are often served as a first course or appetizer at home. Don't be passive, expecting the fruits to come to you in menus; one of the best souvenirs is as many pots of jams, preserves and confitures as you can manage to take home. Even the most ordinary super-market offers undreamed-of treasures and experiences.

Apart from the gorgeous greengages (reines-claudes), promoted since the 15th century, this is the top area in France for quinces (coings), wonderful as the oldest of all preserves, quince cheese (pâte de coings). The Portuguese and such call it marmelada, and its antiquity gives some sense to the French calling most jams marmelade. Bar-le-Duc is famous for its ways with red and white currants, all of which are seeded by hand.

THE BOTTOM LINE

One of my most vivid shopping experiences happened in a Colmar supermarket after a slightly too wonderful lunch. My interest in local alcohols being - how can I put it? - somewhat awakened by the lunch, I went to explore others. It was December 6th, St Nicholas was distributing gingerbread men, and much to the obvious discomfort of some elderly shoppers, Tannenbaum was playing relentlessly through the shop's sound system.

Disorientation heaped itself upon festive confusion, first before the jams then the fruit alcohols offered... *sureau, alissier, houx, genièvre, gentiane, sorbier, épinessapin, cumin, mûres, myrtilles, pousse-églantiers, airelles* - you get the idea - elderflower, whitebeam berries, holly, juniper, gentian, rowan berries, pine needles, cumin, mulberries, bilberries, dog-rose buds, and a sort of cranberry. There were also more familiar alcohols of pear, cherry (*kirsch*), peach (*persicot*), quince (*coing*), apricot and wild cherries (*merises*). But the one which stopped further alcoholic intake that day was *gratte-cul*, translated for the excitable as rose-hip (which it is), but which actually means "itchy-bum." That was one cultural shock too much. Wimpishly, I bought only apricot jam, and hurried through the festively lit snow to an overdue siesta.

LOCAL PRODUCE

VEGETABLES
- **ASPARAGUS** *asperges*
  Start of April until end of May
  Dep: Haut-Rhin, Bas-Rhin

- **CABBAGE** *chou*
  Var: every type, red, white and green
  September to April
  Dep: Haut-Rhin, Bas-Rhin
  Best choucroute variety is *blanc d'Alsace/quintal*.

- **CUCUMBER** *concombre*
  all under cover
  February until October
  Dep: Meuse, Moselle, Meurthe-et-Moselle

FRUITS
- **APPLE** *pomme*
  Var: mainly foreign
  September until December
  Dep: Haut-Rhin, Bas-Rhin

- **CHERRIES** *cerises*
  Var: *Montmorency* (clear juice), *Chattelmorelle* (colored juice)
  June until last days July
  Dep: Haut-Rhin, Bas-Rhin, Meuse

- **PLUMS** *prunes*
  Var: local ones, mirabelle and quetsch especially, also greengages (*reine-claude*)
  Mid-August to start October
  Dep: Bas-Rhin, Haut-Rhin, Moselle, Meuse, Meurthe-et-Moselle, Vosges
  Almost all mirabelles and quetsches are used for confectionery, conserves and distilling.

There are many individual pockets of specialty; either broadly, such as the strawberries of Metz, or specifically, such as the toupie, a pear unique to Colmar.

It would be hard to miss altogether the region's most famous vegetable, cabbage, either as choucroute, or as a garnish to some cooked dish. It might be red, green or white, with or without chestnuts or other goodies, but it will be there. In winter it is essential to the potée and pot-au-feu; any difference between the two is purely of interest to academics, for both are rich mixtures of meat and local vegetables in broth, and no single ingredient affects the result enough by inclusion or omission to render either worthless of enjoying.

In the north of Alsace you'll find the hop fields and barley fields which succor the breweries. So it's here you are more likely to find hop shoots (jets d'houblon), perhaps in a soup. Long white radishes, very dark red beet root, cucumbers or morilles in a cream sauce are all indigenous but relatively unexported. Spinach appears a lot; one bouillon combines it with eggs, raisins and spices in a clear reminder of the eastern origins of many of Alsace's people. The mix of influences is clearly illustrated in the little town of Stosswihr, famous for its painted easter eggs but also for brou de noix, made by soaking green almonds in eau-de-vie in the sun with cinnamon, anis, nutmeg and sugar, once the products only of Araby.

After the cabbages, the most generally encountered

CHOUCROUTE
CABBAGE AS A KING

Steaming yallery-greenery, glistening with newly forbidden fats, jewelled with spices and topped with dribbling slices of pink-gray sausage and hunks of pork, *choucroute* is essentially salt-pickled cabbage, what we know better perhaps as *sauerkraut*. It is thinly sliced and layered with salt when there is plenty for the times when there is not. Some authors suggest its popularity throughout Northern France is dropping alarmingly, but a quick turn through a village High Street will quickly dispel this. Choucroute may not be being made at home much, or eaten in restaurants so often, but it is sold in huge amounts to be enjoyed at home. And not just in Alsace or Champagne - you'll find it steaming fresh in markets in Paris and Bordeaux, *Traiteurs* and charcuteries all over France organize special choucroute nights, and it is a mainstay of many a brasserie, for beer is a proper accompaniment. Even Colmar organizes chou-croute days in September, presumably to remind people of it as summer disappears. If you've never eaten it, thinking it heavy, salty, sour and fatty, do not continue to desist.

For even though it can be all those things, and like most of the best northern dishes, belongs to the mists and gray skies of autumn and winter, it is usually lighter and more delicious than you can imagine.

Choucroute garnie

indicates the pickled cabbage has been drained, washed and cooked for several hours, and will be served piled with a variety of meats and charcuterie, commonly a thickly sliced sausage (it would be *knackwurst* in Strasbourg or Colmar), pickled (salted) pork and fresh belly of pork. The reality is infuriatingly more complicated - and infinitely more fun. For some will use goose fat and some oil or lard, some will cook the cabbage in stock, others will use beer or, and this is the most common, dry white Alsatian wine. Whatever is used, one of the few agreed points is that the choucroute should be cooked until the liquid has all but disappeared. Onion, usually used very sparingly in choucroute, may be increased and some will use juniper, some coriander seeds, some both. Some cooks will include vegetables, others cook them separately, but a firm tradition is always to serve potatoes *en robe de chambre,* baked or steamed, very mealy and dry potatoes in their skins. And when it comes to the garnie part, well, anything can appear. Blood pudding might be here, some tongue there, different sausages or parts of the pig or some *confit* of goose. There have been garnishes of snails and in a reliable restaurant a choucroute with smoked fish is light enough to be perfect summer food.

And then there is *choucroute royale,* in which

a bottle of champagne or Alsatian crémant is poured through the dish just before it is served. To me this is crass beyond words, an insult to the wine. Cook choucroute in champagne if you must - the champenois and anyone who actually likes champagne wouldn't, but don't pour it in after cooking.

Rather harder to find are *navets confits,* salted turnips used in the same way as pickled cabbage. Even fewer people make this at home, and only few shops now sell it, but they are one of the highlights of my discoveries, and worth pursuing. Jean Hugel, of the Riquewihr winemakers, told me how he remembered it being made. Only white turnips were used: each was impaled on a spike and turned against a blade to cut it into a single long thread. These were layered with salt, juniper and pepper in stoneware jars, and left for three to four weeks, with the liquid and scum formed by the fermentation removed regularly. Each time you ate some, the linen cloth and weighted wooden lid which fitted inside the jar, and together kept out the air and prevented putrefaction, had to be changed.

Navets confits turn up in unexpected places, humble and grand. I was introduced to them by Monsieur Hugel as an accompaniment to the superlative pheasant, baked inside a farce of its legs, I ate at the Auberge du Schoenen-bourg in Riquewihr. "That," he said of the combination, "is all Alsace on a plate."

vegetables are the onion, used liberally in more than the onion tart served so universally as an appetizer, and the potato. Lorraine was growing it and incorporating it into potées by 1665, a good century before Parmentier was nagging Versailles.

Horseradish (raifort) is a favorite condiment, a suitably wild flavor to serve with the fabulous game. Equally likely to be wild are dandelion greens (pissenlits) for sping salads, or sorrel (oseille) and nettle (ortie) for spring soups. Those who stay in the chalets of the Vosges may find both fruit and vegetables have been collected from nature; most beguiling are the wild mushrooms of autumn, sometimes in spring too, or the elusive wild strawberries (fraises des bois). In Alsatian Hoedt, it is sophistication that brings brief annual fame. Its asparagus, cut from beds of 800 ha/1,600 acres and most often served with local hams, is typical of the cosmopolitan influences of the seeming backwater. Asparagus was introduced by the town's pastor - who had come from Morocco - in 1873. There is a small monument to him on the old presbytery, as well there might be.

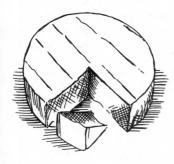

Cheese

The celebrated munster dominates the scene in this region on both sides of the Vosges mountains. The few other cheeses available are also made from cow's milk and have the usual yellow-orange- to red-colored rind typical of washed cheeses.

•Fromage blanc/ Bibbeleskas: Fresh cheese used in cheesecakes and tarts. Also eaten with horseradish and herbs.

•Gérômé and Gérardmer: The same cheese type as munster, but made only on the Lorraine side of the Vosges mountains. Gérômé is a corruption of the longer name.

•Gureyin: A domestically made fromage fort fermented in a crock until creamy and yellow. In the Pays Messin (Lorraine) you may find it in markets or village shops.

•Munster: A well-known AOC cheese made in farms high up on the Vosges slopes of both Alsace and Lorraine. Originally of monastic origin (munster is a contraction of the Latin monasterium), it has been in existence since the Middle Ages. Faithful to tradition, munster is made with rennet-curded milk, put into molds with neither washing nor mixing; it drains slowly and matures for 21 days (14 for a petit munster).

QUICHE SERA SERA

When Elizabeth David first wrote of them, a quiche was a delicate, pale and trembling thing, a simple savory custard of cream and eggs and a little bacon, baked in pastry and served lukewarm on every upwardly mobile pine table. Today the word is used for anything savory in pastry without a lid, even in France. The battle for its proper use is lost. Although more associated with Lorraine, the name quiche seems to be based on the Alsatian word kuche. Be that as it may, the quiche was indeed once just cream and eggs baked with a little bacon in puff pastry, justifying by this last detail the description "Lorraine." Once onions, cheese and other ingredients were added to the custard mixture, you had a féouse. The féouse was basically simpler and cheaper, often a flavored, flour-thickened white sauce on a bread dough base, and thus clearly related to tarte flambée/ flammekueche. Today, féouse is considered archaic, and tarte is more commonly used - or would be if quiche didn't sound better. The appearance of the bouchée à la Reine - white sauce with chicken or ham in puff pastry cases - at the court of 18th-century Nancy, was not a culinary breakthrough but a refined puff pastry base of quiche, two established dishes of the people, which explains the alacrity with which those vol-au-vents were universally accepted. Few celebrations, even today, are complete without them.

Munster fermier *is best eaten in summer and autumn when the cows are out to pasture on the thick grass of the Hautes Chaumes, which adds particular savor to the cheeses. The commercially made dairy cheeses,* munster laitier, *are much the same all the year round. The cheese, a flat disk in shape, has a smooth surface varying in color from yellow-orange to red and has the typical strong washed-rind odor. Mild when very young, it becomes spicy with a sweet, rich flavor as it matures.*

•Munster au cumin à l'anise: *A farm-made munster flavored with cumin seeds or anise (sometimes caraway) seeds. When you buy munster cheese, you sometimes get a small sachet of cumin to sprinkle on it as you eat.*

•St-Rémy: *A factory-made cow's milk cheese from Lorraine; square in shape and weighing about 240g/8oz. It has a smooth, light red-brown rind, very strong smell and somewhat spicy flavor. Best eaten from late spring through to autumn.*

•Thionville: *A processed cheese, made from* mattons, *a Lorraine-made whey cheese; see* mettons *(Burgundy.)*

•Oelenberg: *Made in the traditional way by Trappist monks in the monastery of Oelenberg in Alsace; a mild, lactic-flavored cheese with a smooth, light-yellow rind.*

RESPECT YOUR YOUNGSTERS

Despite his comparative youth, Strasbourg-based Thierry Mulhaupt is one of France's leading *pâtissiers*, a sweet tonic for the ills of the country's industrialized pâtisserie concerns where everything is brought in ready made and further processed with high-tech equipment to produce the right shapes and patterns but the wrong quality. In contrast, Dalloyau-trained Mulhaupt's range of delectables is adjusted throughout the year to reflect the fruits of the changing seasons. The *compôtes* and jams used in his cakes are freshly made on the premises to maximize the flavors of high-quality fruits, not sugar.

Some may say his consistent application of the highest standards is idealistic, a characteristic as consistent with youth as inventiveness. Long may it continue, for it is precisely these youthful qualities that have secured his reputation among France's pâtisserie élite. Recommended is the *abricot en macaronnade*, slices of almond macaroon sponge topped with pine nuts and layered with cream, *apricot compôte* and an intriguing rosemary pastry.

The *Belle d'Eté* features genoise sponge soaked with carrot juice and filled with saffron mousse and fresh red currants. On top are pieces of candied carrot.

Such creativity however does not preclude the inclusion of traditional pâtisserie items in Mulhaupt's range. An important aspect of his widespread acclaim is that he is reviving regional specialties, such as the *Bordeaux Cannelé*, and introducing them to a younger, thoroughly chic market. His apricot tart, made from fresh apricots, features a light pistachio custard. The *tarte au chocolat* is a simple but intense construction of crisp pastry shell, bitter chocolate *ganache* and a topping of crunchy cocoa beans. The crisp, delicate pastry of Mulhaupt's *mille feuille* is enhanced by its extortionate butter content and baking the pastry on the hot-tiled floor of a bread oven.

Try also his selection of chocolates. Flavors range from the popular Islay malt and fruit flavors to the unusual coriander and Sichuan pepper varieties.

Pastries, Desserts & Confectionery

To hear some, you'd think nothing sweet or delicious or frothy was ever baked here until Louis XV sent his father-in-law, King Stanislas of Poland, off to Nancy to be Duke of Lorraine. But Alsace and Lorraine needed no regal patronizing, for the abundance of milk and cream

WORTH FINDING

• *Baba*: Another reputed invention, or intervention, this time by Duke Stanislas himself, by the simple expedient of dipping some rather dry *kugelhopf* (most of it is) into syrup. Now made rather lighter and more yeasted, often with rum in the syrup (*baba au rhum*) and served with fresh fruit and cream.

• *Bredle/petis fours à l'Alsacienne*: Rich, buttery little cookies brought out on every special occasion, and so named in French because they were cooked in a special small oven (*petit four*).

• *Bretzel/pretzel*: Sweet and savory pretzels of every size are a visual trademark of Alsace and Lorraine.

• *Bergamotes*: Square candies made with honey, which are reckoned to taste like a local pear of the same name; associated especially with Nancy.

• *Chocolates*: There are many reasons for good chocolate here. Jews from Spain who settled in Alsace brought knowledge of this New World luxury to the rest of Europe. With the later proximity of sugarbeet fields plus the abundance of fruits, liqueurs and spirits, how could they go wrong? They didn't. There are special specialties, like the *carreaux en faïence* of Sarreguemines, but each *chocolatier* has something to recommend it.

• *Crêpes Alsaciennes/ pfannekueche*: Yes, pancakes, but not thin bitsy crêpes. The ones I ate were always enormous, flat and thick, smothered with berries from the Vosges, fresh or preserved, and with rivers, or mountains, of cream. There are

savory ones, too. *Schankelas* are small ones, made with ground almonds, to accompany creamy desserts.

• *Dragées*: Sugared almonds have been made in Verdun since 1220 at least, and have been commercialized since 1660. The almonds were always imported – mainly from Spain and Italy; today the hard crisp case may also enrobe nougatine, chocolate, liqueurs or an almond paste.

• *Kaffeekrantz*: Brioche-based, large or small iced confections to enjoy with coffee.

• *Kugelhopf*: Although almost certainly not originating in the region, this yeasted cake with a hole in the middle has become one of its icons. It's also found as *kuelhopf*, *gugelhupf*, *kugelhopf*, *kougelhopf* and more. With or without raisins and a surface scattering of flaked almonds, it is best baked in earthenware rather than metal molds.

• *Lebkueche*: Sweet gingerbread biscuits made from a recipe of considerable antiquity, the name coming from ancient German for sweet, *leb*. Thick, thin, soft, crisp, iced or uniced, they are usually tongue or heart shaped. Large *hertzlebkueche*, decorated with flowers of icing, were once more important. Men sent them to sweethearts, who found their names iced upon them plus a verse and a small piece of mirror, so the beloved could see herself in her lover's heart.

• *Linzertorte/Tarte à la Linz*: A sweet tart of pastry which should include almonds and *kirsch*, be filled with jam, and covered with a lattice-work of pastry. Raspberry, cherry,

strawberry or red-currant confections are the most popular and authentic fillings.

• *Macarons (des Soeurs)*: Macaroons have been made in Lorraine since at least the 12th century. After the Revolution in 1789, dispossessed nuns went into business making them, hence the suffix.

• *Mendiant*: Also called *bettleman*, this is a terrific cake/dessert, made from stale brioche, kugelhopf, or breadcrumbs, mixed with egg, spice, *kirsch* and cherries or apples. Extremely good served warm with custard sauce. A big brother of the *gâches* of Normandy.

• *Mirabelles*: These fêted gold-yellow plums are made into numberless examples of sinfulness. In Metz they are preserved in a very rich sugar syrup, in Strasbourg they are crystallized, and they and other such plums as the quetsch may also be stuffed (*fourrée*), either with a mixture based on ground almonds or with a purée of themselves.

• *Tartes*: One of the simplest but most special joys of Alsace and Lorraine, particularly so in summer. Rhubarb, believe it or not, is enormously popular in Alsace. The rhubarb is usually drained of liquid by being cut and sprinkled with sugar before baking. As well as the expected apples and pears, you'll find cherries (*cerises*) and wild cherries (*merises*), every type of plum and all the berries of the mountains, bilberries and blackberries, whortleberries and blueberries. Raspberries and strawberries too.

also meant butter if you wanted, the plains grew wheat for flour, and you had to do something with all the luscious fruits of summer, the cascade from trees, bushes and vines.

Fruit pastes, jams and

confitures, spirits and liqueurs were all embraced, as they were invented, as ways to use the harvest and enjoy it later. Bar-le-Duc became famous simply because its people bothered - and do still - to extract individually the large

seeds from red and white currants before they cooked them up. Everyone else cheats by making jellies, so they can strain out the seeds after the cooking.

Pastry is featured because the region has the ingredients,

and because it claims the invention of puff pastry. Well, Claude Lorraine the painter is given the credit, but he may have brought back the idea from the time he spent in Italy. He started working life as a pastry cook there in 1613. It is a claim with substance, and there is little of the counterclaim there is with brioches, for instance. Because poultry is important, there are meringues; as honey was abundant, beignets may still be served with this natural sugar rather than a syrup of refined beet sugar. There are some especially unusual names amidst cakes and confectionery for you to find - biberschwanz de Haguenau, *beaver's tails*, cailloux de Rhin *(Rhine stones)*, and the like.

Bon Marché

Below is a selective list of markets plus some fairs (*foires*) of special interest. Check with the local Syndicat d'Initiative (SI) for precise locations and time changes.

MEUSE

Bar-le-Duc *Tue AM, Thur, Sat;* Bouligny *Wed PM;* Commercy *Mon, Fri AM;* Ligny-en-Barrois *Tue & Fri;* Stenay *Fri AM;* St-Mihiel *Sat AM;* Tronville-en-Barrois *Thur AM;* Vaucouleurs *Sat AM;* Verdun *Tue, Wed, Fri.*

MEURTHE-ET-MOSELLE

Audun-le-Roman *1st & 3rd Wed in month;* Baccarat *Fri AM;* Blamont *Fri AM;* Bouxières-aux-Dames *Thur & Fri PM;* Crusnes *10th & 25th of month,* Custines *Tue AM;* Dameslevières *Fri PM;* Dombasle-sur-Meurthe *Thur AM;* Giraumont *10th & 25th (PM) of month;* Herserange *Wed AM;* Joeuf *Tue, Fri AM, rummage sale 1st week June;* Liverdun *Tue PM;* Longuyon *Fri AM, Gastronomic Fair 1st Sun Sept;* Longwy *Tue, Thur & Sat AM;* Lunéville *Tue, Wed AM, Thu, Sat;* Moutiers *Wed AM;* Nancy *Daily exc Sun;* Pagny-sur-Moselle *Thur AM;* Pont-à-Mousson *Sat, rummage sale 25 Aug;* St Nicholas-de-Port *Fri AM;* Saulxures-les-Nancy *Fri AM;* Tomblaine *Mon AM;* Tucquegnieux *Thur PM;* Valleroy *Fri PM;* Varangéville *Wed AM (veg);* Villerupt *Tue & Fri to 11 AM (veg).*

MOSELLE

Algrange *Fri, rummage sale begin Sept;* Ars-sur-Moselle *Fri AM;* Audun-le-Tiche *Thur AM, Sat PM, rummage sale May;* Behren-les-Forbach *Sat;* Bitche *Tue, Fri;* Boulay *Wed, Fri;* Bouzonville *Tue (pigs, veg);* Château-Salins *Thur AM, Quiche Fair 1st Sat Sept;* Clouange *Tue, Fri;* Créhange *1st*

& 3rd Fri in month; Creutzwald *Thur AM;* Dieuze *Mon, Fri AM, rummage sale 1st Fri Oct;* Faréberswiller *Thur AM;* Forbach *Tue, Fri, rummage sale Sept;* Freyming-Merlebach *Wed, Thur AM;* Guénange *Tue & Sat PM;* Hagondange *Tue AM & Fri;* Hayange *Tue, Thur, Fri PM, Sat;* L'Hôpital *Sat AM;* Maizières-les-Metz *Thur;* Metz *Daily exc Sun;* Moussey *Wed;* Moyeuvre Grande *Wed, Thur, Sat, rummage sale June/July;* Ottange *Thur;* Petite Rosselle *Wed, Thur;* Phalsbourg *Fri;* Puttelange-aux-Lacs *Sat;* Sarralbe *Thur;* Sarreguemines *Fri AM;* Sierck-les-Bains *Tue;* Stiring-Wendel *Wed, Thur, Sat;* St-Avold *Tue, Fri;* Thionville *Tue, Thur, Sat;* Woippy *Tue AM, Fri, Strawberry Fair second to last Sun June.*

VOSGES

Arches *Pastry Fair June;* Bains-les-Bains *Fri AM;* La Bresse *Sun AM;* Bruyères *Wed AM;* Charmes *Fri AM;* Châtel-sur-Moselle *Fri AM;* Contrexéville *Tue & Fri AM;* Darney *Fri AM;* Epinal *Wed, Thur, Sat;* Fraize *Fri AM;* Gérardmer *Thur, Sat AM;* Golbey *Thur PM;* Liffol-le-Grand *Thur AM;* Lamarche *Fri;* Mirecourt *Sat AM;* Moyenmoutier *Thur AM;* Neufchâteau *Sat AM;* Monthureux-sur-Saône *2nd Mon of month, Pudding Fair 2nd*

Sun Oct; Plombières-les-Bains Fri (Oct to April), Tue, Fri & Sun (May to Sept); Rambervillers Thur; Raon-l'Etape Sat AM; Remiremont Tue & Fri AM; Saulxures-sur-Moselotte Wed; St-Die Tue, Fri AM; Thaon-les-Vosges Thur AM; Thillot Sat AM; Val d'Ajol Sun AM, Andouille Fair 3rd Mon in Feb; Xertigny 2nd and 4th Thurs of month; Vittel Wed, Sat AM, Frog Fair, 1st two weeks April.

BAS-RHIN
Andlau Wed; Barr Sat; Benfeld Mon AM; Bischheim Fri; Bischwiller Sat; Bouxwiller Mon; Brumath Wed; Chatenois Wed; Dambach-la-Ville Wed, Sat; Erstein Thur AM; Fegersheim Thur; Haguenau Tue (pigs), Fri; Hochfelden Tue; Illkirch-Graffenstaden Sat AM; Lauterbourg Tue, Fri; Marmoutier Onion Market 2nd Sun Sept; Mertzwiller Thur; Molsheim Mon AM (pigs); Mutzig Fri AM; Niederbronn-les-Bains Fri; Obernai Thur; Pfaffenhoffen Sat (pigs); Reichshoffen Thur AM; Rhinau 1st & 3rd Tue of month; Rosheim Tue, Fri; Sarre-Union Fri AM (pigs); Saverne Thur (pigs); Tue, Sat (veg); Schirmeck Wed; Sélestat Tue, Fri; Seltz Thur & Wed (pigs), Soultz-sous-Forêts Tue (pigs); Strasbourg Tue, Thur, Wed, Fri, Sat; Vendenheim Mon (pigs), Wed; Wasselonne Mon (pigs); Wissembourg Tue, Thur (pigs), Sat; Woerth Wed (pigs).

HAUT-RHIN
Altkirch Thur; Bartenheim Fri; Bergheim Mon; Colmar Thur, Sat; Dannemarie Sat AM; Guebwiller Tue & Fri AM; Ingersheim Wed AM; Kaysersberg Mon; Lapoutroie Fri; Lutterbach Wed, Sat (fruit); Masevaux Wed AM; Mulhouse Tue, Wed, Thur, Sat; Munster Christmas Market, 15 days before Christmas; Brisach Fri AM; 1st Tue of month; Orschwir Thur AM; Ribeauville Sat, Wine Fair last Sat & Sun July; Riquewihr Fri; St-Amarin

---

A DRINKER'S GUIDE

Wines of ordinary Alsace AOC quality should usually be drunk young. Alsace wines of *resérve* quality, made in good years, benefit from bottle age. *Grand crus*, *vendange tardive* and *sélection de grains nobles* wines should be kept for a minimum of five years.

RECENT VINTAGES
1994: Early pickers made reasonable wine; later pickers made good late-harvest wines due to rain.
1993: Patchy vintage. The rieslings are the best.
1992: A long hot summer produced some excellent wines but not uniformly.
1991: Late rains again spoiled the vintage party.
1990: A great year, perhaps one of the very best. Quality wines will age for long-term maturation.
1989: A good big vintage of no better than good wines. Serviceable.
1988: More rain led to average wines, although the best are good.
1987: Very selectively, there were good wines made, although the general standard was ok.
1986: This vintage is fully mature now and should be drunk.
1985: A great year, to keep for a long time yet or drink if self-control is not your forte.
1984: Ignore.

PREVIOUS GREATS
The top wines of 1983 are now great and will mature further although the lower-quality wines were not so successful. 1981, 1979, 1978, 1976 and 1975 were also good years. Réserve wines from 1973 and 1971 may be worth trying if you can find them. Drink older wines only on recommendation.

SPIRITS AND LIQUEURS
Alsatian *eaux-de-vie*, colorless fruit brandy, can be made from practically any fruit and the best are exquisitely perfumed, but more unusual is *marc de gewürztraminer*, made when the debris left after pressing gewürztraminer grapes is turned into wine and then distilled. This fiery, chocolate-flavored spirit is the perfect restorative after an autumn visit round the vineyards but like all white spirits must be served freezing cold into a cold glass to be appreciated. Lorraine produces very much the same range of spirits as Alsace and, less commonly, *ratafias* of many fruits, combinations of the fresh fruit and a related or natural *eau-de-vie*. *Ratafia de noyau* is made from the kernels of peaches and apricots and thus has an almond-like flavor. Good *marcs* too.

Mon AM; Ste-Marie-aux-Mines Sat; Thann Wed AM, Sat; Turckheim Fri, Wine Fair Aug; Willer-sur-Thur Thur; Wittelsheim Thur, Fri AM; Wittenheim Fri AM.

BRITTANY

SAINTS, SARACEN WHEAT & PANCAKES

"In which we...
• Learn of iodized potatoes and how Crusaders went against the grain...
• Taste the dumplings of ancestors, and fight about brioches...
• Find a lard with shallots and decide on a lobster dish's origin...
• Look for vintage sardines, test a northern bouillabaisse, fish for spring whitebait and sail to stone-tethered sheep for a salty treat...
• Enjoy an upscale lardy cake, look for a bread of oats and cream, and drown in wells of love..."

There's only one proper way to reach Little Britain from Great Britain, Bretagne from Grande Bretagne. Go the way of the ancients and nobles, directly by sea, with your head filled with stories of magic and mystery, of King Arthur and Merlin, and the Corsairs, those good pirates, who robbed only on behalf of others. The precedent you follow is remarkable.

Other than overusing words like fresh and simple, it has been virtually impossible for anyone to define the Breton table. The most accurate view I found was from Gault Millau, which says that although it ranges from the *galettes* of grain and iodized potatoes of the extreme west through commercial market gardens on to the creamy lavishness of Rennes in the east, Brittany actually divides into only two culinary regions: the northern coast, Haute-Bretagne, which is influenced by the cider-based cuisine of Normandy, while the south, Basse-Bretagne, is allied to the wine-based food of the mouth of the Loire. It makes sense, especially when you know that Normandy and Brittany have always squabbled over who claims Mont-St-Michel in the north and that Nantes in the south was considered part of Brittany until bureaucracy took it to one side and said it should now consider itself in Loire-Atlantique. It also makes sense that the cuisine of these two neighbors should have seeped along their proximate coasts, mingling only on the eastern border in Rennes. West of Rennes and in the wooded wilderness that divides the two coastal areas, fashion and style seem to have made few inroads.

In between remained most independently Breton, for here there was little chance for most men or influence to reach. Grains and vegetables were more particularly the basis of diet; cider, wine and cream were much the same, nice when you could get them. It is that last, cream - and butter from it - which must be the single ingredient that might be considered a unifier. Yet there can never have been much cream left once the better-keeping butter had been made, for Brittany has virtually no historic tradition of eating or of making cheese.

The strongest modifiers of Brittany's food have been the climate and the landscape, ever more relentless and windtorn as you travel westwards towards the Atlantic. Fully to appreciate how rugged life remains even today, visit one of the offshore islands, an island like Île de Seine, off the southwestern tip, Pointe du Raz. Here beneath the lighthouse which lords it over the single square kilometer of the island, the rule which once dominated all Brittany's coast remains the only way to survive: "*La mer aux hommes, la terre aux femmes* . . . the sea is men's work, the land is women's." While men fish or hunt seabirds or gather things that live in shells to make stews, women hack with shovels and picks at the poor thin layer of sand and guano. Not much will grow but grain of one sort or another, and potatoes that taste of iodine because of the guano at their roots and the spray on their leaves.

On the mainland, grain was the only reliable staple and remained so here longer than in other regions. Pork and other meat was too valuable to eat more than once a week, or as salted accompaniment to something else, wherever you lived. On the coast you could hardly rely on daily fish with such unreliable seas at your doorstep. So the grain crops needed to be hardy, reliable and warming, like the crops of Scotland and Wales and Ireland. This means barley, oats, rye and, once the

Crusaders began returning, Saracen's wheat (buckwheat, *sarrasin* or *blé noir*), actually grass seeds rather than a true grain. These are all good crops for poor land, but none of them contains enough gluten in its flour to make a light, yeast-risen loaf, and so they were made into the most ancient and universal of foods, grain porridges (*bouillies*). Sometimes the porridges were made extra thick and boiled in a cloth to make savory or sweet puddings, the *fars* and the *noces*. Only in Brittany are they still part of today's diet.

Visitors driving quickly through to some other region may be able to taste these, especially such savory boiled puddings as the *kig ar fars*, more of a buckwheat dumpling, and glimpse through it the culinary world of northern Europe's ancestors. But *bouillies* and *fars* took time to make and cook, and neither was a substitute for bread. So the Breton household made *galettes*, large pancakes, and when buckwheat arrived from the Middle East, it became the favorite.

Originally these large, griddle-cooked pancakes were simply made to bulk out, as bread would have, simple food - eggs, salty bacon or a little meat, a few vegetables. As wheat became more generally available, towards the end of last century, white and wholegrain wheat flour began to be used to make sweet pancakes, a treat for better times and another way to use cream. Today *galettes* have become the symbol of Brittany. There seems nothing savory that cannot be served in or on a buckwheat *galette*, and nothing sweet that is not good with wheaten pancakes. In Rennes, they eat *galettes* with *tripes*. The current interest in eating fish has made Brittany a foodlover's must, but to be honest there is as much criticism of holiday resort junk food as there is elsewhere. Its market gardens provide superb vegetables, even though the great majority are for canning and freezing, and the survival of old yeast-raised cakes, especially on the north coast, makes an adventure even of wandering from pâtisserie to café . . .

Charcuterie

It is the central regions of Brittany that produce superlative pork flesh, and thus the best charcuterie. The range is as broad as you will find anywhere, enhanced by local entrepreneurs as much as by modernism and copying. The products with the best reputation come from opposite ends of the charcuterie business, but the same end of the pig – andouilles/andouillettes and hams (jambons).

But for a guaranteed reflection of true Breton taste and cooking, it must be the baked combinations of meat - usually pork - and vegetables to which you should turn your palate's attention. You might, for instance, find haricots rouges puréed with sausage meat and salt pork. Some of the really famous pâtés - of horse and of cormorant - seem to have disappeared from Concarneau, among other places, but you can still get pâté de lièvre (hare).

WORTH FINDING

• *Andouilles*: Large slicing sausages made of the large intestines and other pieces of innards of pigs. If you like both the idea and the flavor, those from Guéméné, Auray, Ancenis and Carhaix are known to be the best.

• *Andouillettes*: Grilling sausages made from the small intestines, usually served hot with onions and potatoes. Quimperlé has a reputation for such sausages.

• *Boudin noir, boudin blanc*: Black (blood) and white sausages. These are a great tradition in inland Brittany. In Rennes where the *blancs* include the town's famous poultry, you are likely to find them served with haricot beans or, naturally, apples. In Brest they may be made with cream. My favorite, and another taste of antiquity, is the *boudin aux pruneaux* associated with Dinard and Beauséjour, worth visiting also just for its name, which means "nice stay."

• *Caillettes*: Rissoles or faggots, often with a mustard sauce.

• *Casse*: A terrine of ham baked in a caul, often that of calf, but also chunks of veal baked with other bits in an earthenware pot called a *casse*.

• *Jambon*: There are many locally produced hams, and it's likely you will find them cured with some proportion of *eau-de-vie de cidre*. The most famous Breton ham is from Morlaix, where butter, and thus baking, is also outstanding.

• *Lard*: There are three lards here. Basically you have pork fat or bacon (not rendered lard, which is *saindoux*). The next most general is *lard recet*, a rendered mix of salt-pork fat and shallots. Either one, but especially the latter, is important to Brittany's most famous soup made with buckwheat. The third, *lard Nantais*, is a dish of pork chops cooked with wine, most often a Muscadet, on a bed of almost every type of edible offal.

• *Terrine*: Seemingly a catch-all name, but used most for baked combinations of meat and vegetables.

Fish & Shellfish

Brittany has more important fishing ports than any other part of France and, after Boulogne, the biggest. There are few places on the wind- and sea-tortured coastline that do not make some contribution to the haul. The largest ports are St-Malo, Douarnenez, Loctudy, Lorient, Port de Keromen, Quibéron and Concarneau.

The catch is varied enough to keep a serious eater enthralled for weeks. Anything in shells is marvelous, including scallops, winkles, whelks and oysters. Two great attractions are, for the rich, lobster (homard), and for me, clams (palourdes), particularly when they are stuffed. The continuing dispute about the origin of homard à l'Armoricaine has three protagonists: one group which feels it is a recipe from Brittany (Armorica); a second that says it was simply invented by someone who came from St-Pol-de-Léon in the region; and a third who maintain that it is all a dreadful misunderstanding and that it was first called à l'Américaine. It seems likely that the inventor was Pierre Fraysse from Sète in Languedoc. After working in Chicago he opened a restaurant in Paris called Peter's. He modified a dish from his own region, which used oil and tomatoes, substituting whisky for eau-de-vie and flattering his guests by calling it à l'Américaine. Subsequently gastronomes such as Briand and Montagné, perhaps in praise of the lobster rather than its sauce,

WORTH FINDING

•*Anguilles*: Eels. The rivers of the Côtes du Nord and the Loire at Nantes are the most obvious sources. Might be grilled or served in cream; sometimes smoked and grilled over apple wood or soaked in milk and sautéed in butter, which they are prone to do in Lamballe.

•*Brochet*: Pike. Found everywhere and the most likely of fish to be served *au beurre blanc* but it will also be pounded with cream and eggs and shaped into *quenelles.*

•*Cabillaud, Morue*: Cod and salt cod. St-Malo is the most important for both. The related ling is known recognizably as *lingue* but also as *julienne.*

•*Carpe*: Carp. From the Côtes-du-Nord particularly, and also the Loire and Nantes. Usually grilled, often on skewers. The roes (*laitances*) may be found combined with tuna in an *omelette bretonne.*

•*Civelles/pibales*: Tiny eels, deep-fried like whitebait or served in omelettes. Fished from the river weeds in March and April. Although a specialty of Nantes, they are found throughout Brittany.

•*Coquilles St-Jacques*: Scallops. More than half the French catch comes from St-Brieuc, where they have only been redeveloped as a catch since 1960.

•*Crabe, tourteau*: Crab. Served many ways but only St-Malo has a tradition of serving cold boiled crab with mayonnaise.

•*Grenouilles*: Frogs. Found most places, served with *sauce poulette*, a rich cream sauce with wine and mushrooms.

•*Homard*: Lobster. Even if you solved the problem of where or what *homard à l'Armoricaine* is or should be, they wouldn't sell you one cheaply, even in places where it is common, such as Concarneau, Quibéron, Roscoff and the mouth of the Loire.

•*Huitres*: Oysters. A very special speciality of Brittany. *Belon* are the best known and get their special flavor from the rich mixture of fresh and sea water that swirl together at the mouth of the Belon river. As is common, the oysters are not actually bred here but come only to be flavored and fattened for 8-10 months. Other important centers are Cancale, Auray, Prat-Ar-Coum. Oysters from Lannilis are said to have the saltiest flavor. The large oyster park between Pointe de Pardic and the Îles-St-Quay takes its seed oysters from the Morbihan, as do most of France's famed types. There is little to see for the tourist, for the action is underwater most of the time. Paimpol is another good oyster center. (See Bordeaux for more oyster information.)

•*Lotte*: Monkfish or angler fish. Sweet firm-fleshed fish with lobster-like flavor; also called *baudroie.*

•*Morue*: See *cabillaud.*

•*Mulet*: The gray mullet, usually served roasted or grilled, sometimes on skewers, and also with beurre blanc.

•*Ormeaux*: Abalone. In Dinard made into a *ragoût* with Muscadet, or put into the unusual *civet de pêcheur*, fish in red wine.

•*Oursin*: Sea urchins. A speciality of St-Brieuc, where the roe is eaten spread on garlic bread.

•*Poulpe, minard*: Octopus. Easily found, but no common method or preparation prevails.

•*Raie*: Skate. Most often served classically with *beurre noir*, browned or burned butter, and capers.

•*Sardines*: Fished almost everywhere and especially important at Quibéron and Douarnenez where there are over 50 canners. Fresh ones are grilled, of course, but also put into soups – and may even turn up in cream, it being Brittany. Connoisseurs will look for cans with date marks, for vintage sardines in oil are a rare treat indeed. Gravier Aîné Cie is a revered brand. All must be 1 year old before sale, improve another 6 years in the tin and must be turned very 6 months.

•*Thon*: Tuna. There are two types, *thon blanc* and *thon tropical.* The *blanc* is the most likely one to be found fresh and you could find it baked, marinated or, most unexpectedly, combined with carp's roe in an omelette. The tropical is usually frozen, and the fishermen of Concarneau make this one of their specialties.

determined it should be à l'Armoricaine. *This seems silly to me, for nothing based on oil and tomatoes could possibly be thought Breton. In any case, I'm not convinced this is what should be done to* the fine, sweet flesh of any lobster.

Don't leave the region without buying and trying Brittany's most important contribution to the tea tables and picnics of the world –

sardines in oil. One of the most important sardine-preserving centers today is Concarneau, and in its Musée de la Pêche you can see the original glass containers used for sardines in oil. On the last

Sunday in August there is a festival commemorating the time when sardines were the sole lifeblood of the port, an opportunity to see folklore in the streets.

For both sporting and culinary pleasure, it is important also to turn your attention inland, for Brittany is equally a paradise of freshwater fish, the Côtes-du-Nord alone having almost 2,200 km/1,400 miles of trout streams, 126 km/80 miles of fishing canals and hundreds of reservoirs, ponds and pools. There's every famous type of fish, excluding it seems, the shad, but including salmon. Salt and freshwater fish are generally simply cooked - grilled mostly, or poached - and served with cream or sauces with cream and butter in them. In the southeastern regions of Morbihan and Ille-et-Vilaine, where they border the Loire regions and are close to Nantes, the voluptuous sauce beurre blanc will be more noticeable, but not necessarily more memorable.

Beware of any salt cod (morue) dishes unless you are certain you like it. Brandade de thon is a curiosity, and must be a relatively new one, for it is a mixture of tinned tuna fish and the local haricot beans, clearly influenced by Italy's tonno e fagioli. It's nice, but once I was presented instead with tuna accompanied by Russian Salad in a distinctly individual mayonnaise, which seemed also to have come from a tin. And it was served in a scallop shell! Caveat emptor . . .

COTRIADE: BOUILLABAISSE DU NORD

Of all the fish dishes, I suppose there is only one you really should try more than once, cotriade. Like the better-known bouillabaisse of the south, this is a fishermen's soup, originally made by them from their share of the catch. Variety of fish is more important than the exact ingredients, but a balance between oily coarse fish and firm white fish is the ideal. It always includes potato, but sophisticated ingredients like wine, eau-de-vie de cidre or saffron are the fancifications of food writers. Cream is commonly used to finish it, and in summer sorrel is a delicious addition. Although traditionalists don't include any shellfish, the bright gleam of mussels is becoming quite common. As with bouillabaisse, don't waste your money on any version that contains delicate langoustine or lobster, and even if served it, do not use rouille - well, you can, but it will no longer be cotriade.

GARLIC, SHALLOTS & ONIONS

An old culinary rule used to be that garlic (ail/aulx) started popping into pots only once you crossed the River Loire, and that the further south you went, the more was used. That remains broadly true today, but now that France imports so much garlic from abroad - mainly South America - it is used more generally. Don't be confused or put off simply by the amount used in any dish - the further south you grow it, the sweeter and milder garlic becomes. That is why the Languedociens use it in whole cloves and why they'll cook chicken and lamb with handsful. Thus, if you've had Provençal-style food that lost you friends because of garlic contents, it either was not truly Provençal or the garlic had probably come from another area, and gave a much stronger taste than the recipe actually demanded. Even onion should not be recognizable in a true Provençal dish. Onions (oignons) remain the great standby of the north and as far south as the Lyonnais; generally the French do not use them as lavishly as, for instance, the British. So, with fish, for example, it is more likely that leeks (poireaux) are used. And if not leeks, then the shallot (échalote).

Shallots are actually a distinct member of the onion family with a mild flavor something between onion and garlic. They come in a variety of shapes and sizes, including a long, wine-flushed one which is astonishingly sweet and found only in the south. They are not spring onions or small pickling onions, and neither of these is a substitute for them, whatever cookbooks say. Garlic is rarely used in the same dish with shallots; but if you cannot get shallots, some mild onion and a touch of garlic will give a better, sweeter and more authentic solution than simply substituting onion.

Meat, Poultry & Game

The obvious importance and attraction of Brittany's seafood should not divert the visitor from the undoubted attractions of its other products. In 1689, Madame de Sévigné was asking for "une aile de ces bonnes poulardes de Rennes." Strictly speaking aile means wing, but the word is often used to mean breast in poultry cooking, with aileron used for the wing proper. Whatever part you eat, they are excellent, for there is more to French poultry than the poulets de Bresse. Cooked in white wine, often with prunes, the local breed is called coucou, and has eggs with a rather yellow shell. Other parts of Brittany produce other types. You should find a number of pigeon dishes in inland places, and farm-raised ducks, especially canetons Nantais.

Brittany has a good reputation for charcuterie and there is a lot of pork. Porché is a soup-stew of trotters, skin and bony pieces of pig, cooked with sorrel overnight in the village baker's oven.

With so much dairying, there are also plenty of veal dishes, noticeably more than of beef. The most important meat is pré-salé lamb, raised on salty marshes of fields exposed to sea breezes, both of which Brittany has a surfeit. You should eat this as plainly as possible, ideally as a roasted leg - gigot de pré-salé - with or without haricot beans. If you ever see roasted forequarter or shoulder (épaule) of pré-salé you may more easily understand what all the flavor fuss is about; shoulder is also as likely to be stewed and served with artichokes.

Perhaps a place to experience this is the Île d'Ouessant, a short sail into the Atlantic west of Brest, where the small sheep have to be tied together and tethered to stone walls as protection against the strong, salt-laden winds which so flavor their feed. It is the epitome of the Breton maxim of work, for only the women tend the sheep.

Game is not very varied. Hare (lièvre), and wild rabbit (lapin de garenne) are probably tops and both are used for terrines and pâtés. If you find local wild duck (canard sauvage), make the most of it. That from La Brière has a reputation.

SALT SELLERS

With all that sea around, one could reasonably expect that there would also be plenty of sea salt. Indeed, the question that pops into my mind is why don't other seaside areas make as much of this potential "crop" as Brittany?

The salt marshes of the Guerande peninsula have been farmed for more than 1,000 years by the French salt makers (paludiers), who also work to maintain the region's ecological balance. 1992 saw the marshes, a haven for birds, granted official protection by the French government and Guerande salt awarded the Label Rouge.

This salt is harvested by hand in the traditional way, manufactured without additives, clay or impurities and screened to ensure top quality.

Intriguingly, the flavors of the different salts produced vary according to the part of the salt bed they come from. Fleur de sel is the "cream" of the crop, but literally the "flower." The wind whips the crystals off the top of the salt bed and they subsequently settle in a mound on the water, from where they are scraped and dried. The result is a delicate violet color, a salt mild and delicious enough to eat in its own right. Try it sprinkled generously on ripe tomatoes.

Coarse salt for cooking (and bathing) comes from further down the bed and is known as sel gris. It is grayer in color than the fleur de sel and has a moister texture. Very finely milled table salt is also available, as is sea salt flavored with seaweed and herbs.

To maintain these superlative salts at their peak, keep them in natural clay or wood containers; these allow the salt to breathe.

Fruits & Vegetables

I harbor two enduring pictures associated with Brittany. One is of Roscoff - or Onion - Johnnies, Bretons on bicycles with the new crop of onions flung over the handlebars. The other is of narrow Breton roads jammed with the tractors and anger of farmers protesting about the derisory prices received at Dutch auctions for their artichokes and other produce, which was then sold at high prices in cities around France and Europe. Both are seen less today, the first as a result of what farmers did about the second. Dynamic leadership organized the growers against their exploiters, then ensured access to newly created markets abroad by providing their own transport - the Brittany Ferries.

A lot of produce you see cultivated in the fields of Brittany is not for fresh consumption but for canning, freezing or drying. Haricot beans, petits pois, spinach and brussels sprouts are the most important, I suppose. Other products flourish although they are not native to the area; garlic in North Finistère, cider apples in Ille-et-Vilaine and South Finistère, apples and pears generally and, rather surprisingly, marrons in Redon. This center in Ille-et-Vilaine takes its chestnuts very seriously, serving them with potatoes, with sausages and, of course, with its buckwheat galettes.

Although the haricot bean is linked insolubly with the culinary view of Brittany, this has only been so since the ancien régime. Before the haricot, the broad bean (fève) was the staple. According to Gault Millau there are two distinct garnishes called bretonne, one just of beans, the other a white sauce with finely sliced leeks, onion and celery but definitely no beans, an old sauce for things white - poultry, eggs and fish. Other beans here include the native coco paimpolais, and the chevriers, haricots dried a special way to keep their fresh green look, a technique perfected at Arpajon in the Essonne, where there is an annual beano, foire aux haricots. Chevriers must not be confused with flageolets.

Beans and virtually every other vegetable grown here and elsewhere turn up in the potées and potages of the region, including a delicious pumpkin (potiron), and thick mitonnée, of onions, bread and milk. Such heavy, simple food is rarely the lot of the visitor to enjoy.

Rennes is interesting for the summer eater. Asparagus has been officially encouraged as a crop since 1585, and her artichokes have been famous for quite as long, eaten raw, quartered and fried or boiled and served with a cream sauce. Best of all are the petit gris: not snails, but tiny melons of perfumed pink flesh, a delicious complement to the fruit from the extreme opposite end of Brittany, the strawberry of Plougastel. It was here in about 1800 that Monsieur Freziers brought back plants from Chile and Virginia, crossed them with European varieties and began the modern love affair with the fragrance and flavor of strawberries. Before then, they were as boring as many of the modern commercial varieties have become.

Angelica (angélique) is candied, and mint is used in berlingots, but on the whole herbs are not an important part of traditional Breton cooking. Modern chefs, of course, use their perfumes more readily. The only dish generally mentioned is chicken à la Nazairienne, from St-Nazaire, with tomato, tarragon and cream sauce.

BRETON BUCKWHEAT

Haute Bretagne gave the world the buckwheat galette, called a gaoff when it is at home. Traditionally, they were made only with buckwheat but in these feebler times, wholewheat or white flour may be added. Make your own with a couple of eggs, half a liter of milk, 450g/10oz buckwheat flour and 100g/4oz melted butter. Fry in butter in a large pan, better still on a griddle.

NO WINE TODAY: A DRINK PROBLEM

Nantes and thus the closeby wines of Muscadet and Gros Plant were once part of Brittany, but today's Brittany can claim no wine making within its borders. Hard cider is the drink here, but it would be dishonest to expect too much of it. It is better the newer and fresher it is, some has sparkle (cidre bouché) through being allowed to complete fermentation in the bottle. Once distilled into an apple brandy, it is sold as eau-de-vie de cidre, but this is not calvados.

LOCAL PRODUCE

- ARTICHOKE *artichaut*
  Var: *Camus de Bretagne*
  Mid-May until October
  Dep: Finistère, Côtes-du-Nord
  With 65% of French production, and rising, Brittany dominates Europe.

- BEAN *haricots à écosser*
  Var: *Coco paimpolais*
  Harvested August/September, but sold semi-dry until November
  Dep: Grown only around Paimpol
  Unique to Brittany, this bean has a speckled pod and white seeds. *À écosser* means "in the pod" or "to be podded" and these are a hybrid product, a semi-dry bean but remaining in the pod. They can be podded and further dried or used as "almost fresh."

- CABBAGE *chou*
  Var: Winter king
  Reds and whites grown locally
  Mid-January/mid-March
  Dep: Finistère, Ille-et-Vilaine

- CARROT *carotte*
  Var: *Nantaise, Nandor*
  Primeurs start in October, season continues until following May
  Dep: Finistère, Ille-et-Vilaine

- CAULIFLOWER *choufleur*
  Peak, January to May
  Dep: Finistère, Côtes-du-Nord, Ille-et-Vilaine. 70% of national production comes from Brittany, and there is always one variety or another being harvested throughout most of autumn, winter and spring.

- CHICORY *endive/witloof*
  Var: *Zoom, Bergère*
  October until April
  Dep: Finistère

- CUCUMBER *concombre*
  May to October
  Dep: Finistère

- LEEKS *poireau*
  Var: *Briand tardif, Armor*
  December until April
  Dep: Ille-et-Vilaine

- LETTUCE *laitue/chicorée*
  Var: White and green cabbage types plus icebergs increasingly now.
  May until December, with icebergs May/June and September/December.

- ONION *oignon*
  Var: *Rose de Roscoff*
  Freshly dug end July to start October
  Dep: Finistère

- POTATO *pommes de terre* nouvelles/primeur
  Var: *Duke* from Paimpol region is exclusively for British market; *Ostara, Brittany Prince*
  Mid-May until end June
  Dep: St-Malo, Paimpol, St-Pol de Léon

- SHALLOT *échalote*
  Var: long, medium and roundish types
  Dep: Finistère
  The medium length ones are most productive, the long ones the sweetest and best for cooking; Britain usually gets the round ones . . . Freshly dug June and July, stored for year-round use. Brittany grows 70% of France's production, but these are very different from the wine-red and white, long shallots of the south, which are less commercialized, and one of the few oniony things delicate and sweet enough to include raw in food.

- SPINACH *épinard*
  May/June and October
  Dep: Finistère, Morbihan
  The biggest producers in France; 33% of the total crop.

- STRAWBERRY *fraise*
  Var: *Belrubi, Gariguette Favette, Kid Gauntlet, Gorella* (good)
  May until mid-September
  Dep: Finistère (Plougastel)

- TOMATO *tomate*
  Var: *Marmande, Montafanet, Quatuor*
  May until end November
  Dep: Finistère and around Rennes.

Cheese

The washed-rind cheese holds its own in Brittany. Saint-Paulin, *the best known, is quite typical. Virtually no other varieties of cheese are produced.*

•Campénéac*: A typical Trappist or Saint-Paulin style cheese, except this one is made by nuns. Although very smelly, it is gratifyingly mild of flavor.

•Crémet Nantais*: A fresh cow's milk cheese from Upper Brittany with mild creamy flavor, often eaten as a dessert with fresh fruit or compôte.

•Fromage du curé*: A factory-made, washed-rind cheese with strong nose and taste. Invented by a curé from Nantes in the 19th century; also called Nantais.

•Meilleraye de Bretagne*: Large, tangy washed-rind Trappist cheese you can buy by the portion.

•Nantais*: See Fromage du curé.

•St-Gildas-des-Bois*: A soft triple-cream cheese with bloomy white rind. It has a faint smell and a creamy flavor. Beaujolais is a suitable accompaniment.

•Saint-Paulin*: The daddy and momma of all the washed-rind cheeses of this type, also the mildest. Made year round from pasteurized milk in Brittany and elsewhere.

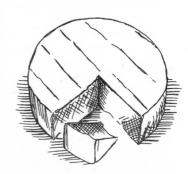

Pastries, Desserts & Confectionery

St-Brieuc on the favored northern coast claims the invention of the brioche, one of the most perfect of all amalgams of butter and wheat flour. It is a claim hotly disputed by neighboring Counouaille, by the people of Brie (who reckon brioches are so called because they once contained their cheese), and by the inhabitants of Gournay in Normandy. The very name would seem to give the claim to the St-Briochains; or is that why they claim it? There are long brioches called cornes in Nantes and cornics, a sort of croissant in Douarnenez. The most interesting though is kouign'amann. The name is dialect for cake and butter. It is a yeast dough folded and rolled about in butter and sugar - an exceptionally upscale version of English lardy cake.

Just as famed and far easier to find made well, perhaps because it is simpler to make, is gâteau breton, a rich pound cake which should include almonds and dried fruits. According to Gault Millau, it was invented only last century in Paris, as was the Paris-Brest, a ring of choux pastry sprinkled with almonds and stuffed with cream. Both have been convincingly embraced in the interest of profit and tourism – and why not? Quatre-quarts, though, seems a more authentic thing, a classic pound cake of equal weights of eggs, butter, flour and sugar. In late summer look for gâteau aux figues fraîches. Although almost all of Brittany ripens wonderful figs, this cake is especially associated with St-Briac.

In the extreme west and center of Brittany, where both soil and weather combined to defeat the growth of the old strains of wheat, other grains have fought and defied the elements, particularly nutty buckwheat, sarrasin or blé noir. You are most likely to meet it as a galette, indeed it would be difficult not to do so, but these are usually savory. It is more unusual to be confronted with far breton, a bouillie or porridge of buck-wheat (or of oats - avoine), sweetened with dried fruits, raisins or prunes usually. Noce is always a sweet version, boiled in a cloth like the original British suet puddings, and may be sliced for serving. Far breton is most easily found in the southwestern Pays de Léon. Fars of other types, and even far breton, might well be savory, as is the kik am gaz.

Now that there is more wheat available, bakers have increased the palatability of some of the lumpen breads once made with alternative grains, notably pain de seigle (rye bread), pain d'antan (a mixture of wheat and rye flour, cooked very slowly) and my favorite, the naturally sweet pain d'avoine (oaten bread). Of course the Bretons have long appreciated the affinity of oats and cream and many places make oat bread with cream, pain d'avoine à la crème.

Most cream is used as is or is made into butter for baking, but there are many puddings based on milk curds, including junket (jonchée).

Dol-de-Bretagne makes a sweet, light pickle of pears for dessert, poires au vinaigre.

WORTH FINDING

- *Berlingots:* Peppermint boiled candies especially made in Morbihan.
- *Craquelins*: Basically a rather dry biscuit thing, but also found stuffed with apple or cherries.
- *Crêpes dentelles*: Literally "lace pancakes." The super-thin, crisp, rolled pancakes made commercially in Quimper since 1897 are quite the best crunchy accompaniment to frozen or creamy or fruity desserts. Savory filled versions are also available.
- *Crêpes (de froment)*: Wheat-flour pancakes, white or wholegrain, almost always served sweet, and sold from crêperies virtually everywhere, with cream an obligatory accompaniment.
- *Maingaux, mingaux, migots*: The epitome of high-summer sumptuousness. Today it is whipped cream or a very light cream cheese with raspberries, strawberries or cherries, but it once was a complicated mixture of creams of different ages to give a desired slight sharpness.
- *Mamgoz*: Associated with Quimper, these are apples baked with jam and butter.
- *Puits d'amour*: "Wells of love." Seductive pastry shapes stuffed with summer's soft fruits, especially strawberries. There'll be a lake or mountain of cream nearby, too - or perhaps some *maingaux . . .*

Bon Marché

Below is a selective list of markets plus some fairs (*foires*) of special interest. Check with the local Syndicat d'Initiative (SI) for precise locations and time changes.

FINISTÈRE

Brest *Mon, Fri;* Carhaix-Plouguer *Sat;* Châteaulin *Thur;* Concarneau *Mon, Fri;* Crozon *4th Wed of month;* Douarnenez *Mon, Fri, Sat;* Le Faou *Sat;* Guerlesquin *Wed;* Huelgoat *2nd & 4th Thur of month;* Landerneau *Sat, 1st Mon each month;* Landivisiau

---

SHOPPING AROUND IN RENNES

Where and when: Les Valles (daily); Cleunay, Maurepas, Thorigné-Landel (Tue); St-Thérèse (Wed); bd A-Carrel, sq Sarah-Bernhardt (Thur); Villejean (Fri); parking lot between rue d'Isly and esplanade du Général-de-Gaulle (Fri & Sat); pl des Lices (Sat); Thorigné-Landel (Sat AM).

Tue (auction of animals for slaughter); Lesneven *Mon;* Loctudy *Tue;* Morlaix *Sat;* Ploudalmézeau *Mon;* Pont-Aven *Tue;* Pont-l'Abbé *Thur;* Quimper *Wed, Sat, (cattle);* Quimperlé *Fri;* Rosporden *Thur;* St-Pol-de-Léon *Tue.*

CÔTES-DU-NORD

Binic *Thur;* Broons *Wed;* Callac *Wed;* Châtelaudren *Mon;* Corlay *Thur;* Etables-sur-Mer *Tue;* Guingamp *Sat;* Lamballe *Thur;* Jugon-les-Lacs *Tue, Fri;* Lancieux *Tue;* Lannion *Thur;* Lanvollon *Fri;* Lézardrieux *Fri;* Merdrignac *Wed;* Paimpol *Tue;* Plancoet *Sat;* Pléneuf-Val André *Tue, Fri (June-Sept);* Plestin-les-Grèves *Wed;* Pleouc-sur-Lie *Thur;* Ploubalay *1st & 3rd Mon of month;* Plouha *Wed;* Pontrieux *Mon;* Quintin *Tue;* Rostrenen *Tue;* St-Brieuc *Wed, Fri, Sat;* St-Cast-le-Guildo *Tue, Fri (June to Sept);* St-Quay Portrieux *Mon, Fri;* Trégastel *Mon;* Tréguier *Wed (pigs);* Uzel *1st & 3rd Wed of month.*

MORBIHAN

Allaire *Fri;* Auray *Fri, 2nd & 4th Mon of month;* Baud *Sat;* Elven *Fri;* Gourin *Mon;* Hennebont *Thur;* Josselin *Sat;* Locminé *3rd Thur of month (breeding cattle), Mon PM (beef cattle);* Lorient *Wed, Sat;* Malansac *Fri (only in chestnut season);* Malestroit *Thur;* Muzillac *Fri;* Ploermel *Mon, auction every Tue.*

ILLE-ET-VILAINE

Bain-de-Bretagne *Mon;* Betton *Sun AM;* Cancale *Daily;* Dol-de-Bretagne *Sat;* Domagne *Mon;* Fougères *Sat, Fri AM (cattle);* Grand-Fougeray *Thur;* Guerche-de-Bretagne *Tue;* Loheac *2nd Sat of month;* Louvigne-du-Désert *Thur;* Maure-de-Bretagne *Thur;* Médrèac *Tue;* Melesse *Thur;* Mordelles *Tue, Wed;* Noyal-sur-Vilaine *Tue;* Pipriac *1st Tue of month;* Pleurtuit *2nd Wed of month;* Redon *Daily;* Rennes *Daily;* Sens-de-Bretagne *Mon;* St-Brice-en-Coglés *Mon;* St-Just *Thur Oct & Dec (chestnuts);* St-Malo *Tue, Fri, (St-Malo town), Mon, Thur, Sat (Rocabey);* St-Méloir-des-Ondes *Daily (potatoes in summer, cauliflower in winter), Fri (pigs);* St-Ouen-des-Alleux *Wed (cattle);* St-Servan-sur-Mer *Tue, Fri;* Tinténiac *Wed;* Vitré *Mon.*

MARKET WISE

Wandering around in markets is the best way to discover what makes the heart of a region beat. I don't want to load you down with so much information that you are unable to respond spontaneously to what you find or to make your own memorable mistakes, but here are a few tips and useful words.

• *Braderie*: A kind of huge rummage sale, held annually or more often and lasting for a day or as long as a month. Think of all those authentic kitchen things *d'occasion*, as used by *grandmère*, even if it is not your own.

• *Comice*: Not a pear fair but an agricultural show.

• *En gros*: Wholesale - you'll want *detail* (retail).

• *Forain*: Un marché forain is an itinerant market, so you may meet it several times in one region. *Une fête foraine* is a fun fair.

• *Marché au cadran*: A traders' auction conducted against the clock by tight-lipped, ruthless wholesalers. Incomprehensible but worth watching at a distance. Don't join in.

• *Poulain*: Don't be fooled by assonance, association and expectation that this has anything to do with chickens; a *poulain* is a colt. *Foires aux Poulains* are regularly held.

Remember that not all markets take place in les Halles or la place du Marché. You may be directed to cité, lotissement, or Z.U.P. (zone d'urbanisation priorité), all of which indicate a large housing estate or new town development. They too have their regular market days. What could be less *touristique*? Also keep in mind that France has many religious and public holidays, and market days that clash with these may be postponed or moved up. Check with the local Syndicat d'Initiative.

☙ THE LOIRES

A MUSHROOMING TRADITION

"In which we...
- *Share a mistress's comforts, squabble in markets and steam in seaweed...*
- *Find a regal affinity and learn the truth about Loire-abiding recipes...*
- *Sorrow for missing vegetables and learn not to reject rillons...*
- *Discover saffron gardens, a birthplace of dispute and what was hatching in Amboise...*
- *Unpeel a Chateaubriand mystery, local pears with a Down Under connection and an undercover tart...*
- *Join arguments about sandy biscuits...*
- *Draw pistoles and make a divertissement to a rhapsody in Blois...*
- *Learn the Roman way with honey cakes and just where the men are most doué..."*

Bed of the royal river, *le fleuve royal*, playground of the *ancien régime* and Garden of France, the Loires are a combination of the fabulous and the commonplace. It is strangely comforting to know, as you wander through the great galleries and gardens of the magnificent châteaux, that outside is the region of Muscadet and Sancerre wines, of familiar logs of goat cheese from Ste-Maure, of strawberries, and of Golden Delicious apples that someone will slice to make a caramel-rich upside-down tart. But this familiarity of the table can mislead visitors into dismissing the food of the Loires as predictable and uninspired. How wrong they are, for this very predictability is the Loires' proud insignia of authenticity and tradition.

The most common style of sauce, other than the velvet warmth of *beurre blanc*, is of cream and mushrooms, regarded by many as stateless à la francaise food. But this sauce is centuries old and, far from being any reflection of boredom, is an illustration of how the region's food so impressed its visitors it was relentlessly copied and devalued, familiarity breeding an ill-deserved contempt. Those mushrooms have been a specialized local crop ever since men hewed caverns into the hills to carve building blocks for the châteaux, and then used the caverns' darkness as a new source of income.

If you plan only to see the châteaux and then to move elsewhere for culinary pleasure, I should reconsider and stay much, much longer, exploring the modern Loires' food and the perfumed red wines with names of châteaux, Chinon for instance. For although a new epithet, its reputation as the Garden of France is well deserved, something more than proved when I stayed once in medieval Loches, well off the château route.

The streets, markets and ancient bent-walled buildings of Loches are a great place for the culinary romantic. There lived Agnès Sorel, first of the great royal mistresses of whom we know who made a career of giving a king the comforts that queens, crowns and ermine could not. Her speciality was ministering to the stomach, and she is said to have created *salmis* of

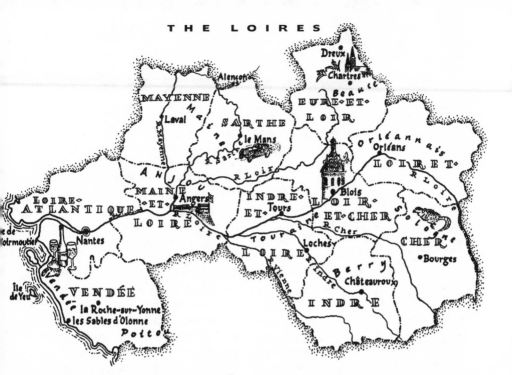

woodcocks (*bécasses*) and *petits timbales* for King Charles VII. It must have been easy if the markets of Loches were only half as good as I found them.

Even well inland, as Loches is, the tight, noisy market smelt of the sea, with a choice of oysters and wet, bright fish, fresh enough to seem slumbering rather than dead. Pungently competing for the nose's attention were the open-sided trucks selling goat's cheese from the Touraine, rich camemberts from Normandy and farmhouse brie from the Île-de-France.

Beyond them were parked the more colorful sellers of sausages and hams, black (blood) and white sausages, *andouillettes* and the local passion, *rillettes*, most vendors wearing the black, wide brimmed hats and startling neckerchiefs of Bretons and Auvergnats.

I was cooking to earn my board at the time and was quickly taught the secret of shopping in markets - to adopt the discipline of shopping with no list other than of the number of guests that must be satisfied. Lists for shopping pinch the imagination and close the eyes to what is on display. Once I had started,

my confidence quickly grew enough to compete with the locals, feeling the breasts of the live chickens and squabbling with the best of them as I protected my turn to be served. I poked and pried at boxes of snuffling brown-furred rabbits, pigeons, ducks and guinea fowls (*pintades*). It was only the eyes of the chickens I managed to avoid, so we had chicken for dinner. But I lacked the confidence to take them home privately to wring their necks or chop off their heads, and had to have them executed for me there and then, much to the amusement of the locals. They (the chickens) were delicious, stuffed with blood pudding and local apples.

We began that meal with a whole fish cooked in seaweed so fresh that only the clinging remains of a vermouth marinade needed to be added to the casserole. Steamed in a distillation of the sea and studded with salty-fresh oysters warmed in cream and the seaweed's juices, it made us believe we were dining on the sea's edge.

We ended with a confection of ice cream and sorbet from Monsieur Couturier of rue de la République, a master *glacier*. Had you imagined there would be a guild of master ice cream makers? There is, as part of *Les Maîtres Pâtissiers de France*, and you can find them in most towns and villages of any size, displaying their badge on the window. Each has his or her specialities, and Monsieur Couturier names some after Agnès. But that night we ate his *Pompadour*, pear and *poire William* sorbet inside raspberry ice cream on a meringue base, a fruity affinity of regal magnificence I had not imagined. And neither would Agnès, for the growing and eating of vegetables and fruits had little real significance in her time.

When Catherine de Medici came later from Italy to marry the heir of King François I, she added a few vegetables including artichokes to the gardens and encouraged a lighter touch to the food she found. She was not tampering with the food of France, barely even with the food to the Court. Her chef's pretty concoctions were for special occasions, for parties and fêtes; most courses of most aristocratic and courtly meals were still of flesh. Meat was the main meal of the rulers: grains and cheeses and whatever grew that was edible, that of the ruled.

Just as Catherine's contributions to the foundations of haute cuisine have only little place in the history of French food, the glorious châteaux of the Loire Valley contribute the thinnest threads of gold to the fabric that wove itself into France. But the château of Villandry at least offers a glimpse of a true picture of past life, through the tiniest culinary chink. Villandry is not set in a manicured hunting park and I cannot remember anything of its rooms except for the views from them of descending terraces of Renaissance knot-gardens, the lowest of which is a kitchen garden (*potager*). It had been restored to its 16th-century state, planted only with vegetables and fruit trees that were contemporary, and thus fascinating for what was not there, most noticeably potatoes.

What a shame Monsieur (Louis XIV's brother) and his catamites, or the huntress Diane de Poitiers, or the inventive Agnès Sorel and their glittering friends did not know the pleasure of squashing the floury body of baked or roasted potatoes into the juices from the haunches and ribs and skewers of game and game birds and poultry. I feel much more sorrow for them for that lack than I feel envy of them living in the gilt salons of those hunting-lodge châteaux. Just think of those smoky fires, and the draughts, and the stone floors - and all that meat and no potatoes.

Charcuterie

The Touraine precisely, and the Loires generally, offer a singular opportunity to decide what you really think about rillettes, which claim this as their home. The name is a diminutive of the rarely used rille. Not that this will make any difference, for diminished or otherwise, rillettes are either an unctuous, spreading essence of sublimity (to their devotees) or a bland, stringy and pallid paste (to everyone else). After much consideration in the establishments of Tours and about, I have come down fairly heavily on the side of the dissenters.

You, or rather they, make rillettes by taking moderately fatty pork - neck is considered best - reducing it to small pieces, and cooking it with the addition only of salt over gentle heat for many hours, stirring as often as practical. To even out the texture, the exhausted meat is further harried into threads by being pulled apart with two forks. To the true enthusiast the fork is still new-fangled, and there are only inimitable throat sounds and operatic appeals to heaven at the mention of how factories whisk the stuff. Other than salt, no seasoning is allowed (more's the pity). To me the exercise is pointless, for the interminable cooking emasculates whatever flavor may have been present in the threads of meat, and I have never spread rillettes upon bread without thinking the flavor to be that of over-boiled, underseasoned meat. Rillettes or rille d'oie (the same product but made from goose) and rillettes de lapin de la garenne (made from wild rabbit), are even more highly considered. As some measure of excellence for the basic product, the suffix de Tours, plus some indication that the product was actually made in that city, usually works. But there is no legal protection of the claim. All of Anjou makes rillettes; Blois, Vendôme and Saumur are regularly mentioned for theirs.

Be careful not to reject rillons, thinking they are chunky rillettes. Rillons, often called grillons elsewhere, are pieces of pork cooked in fat until most of their own fat is rendered and they are very crisp and crunchy; Tours makes them well, too, and Vendôme does the same with ham (jambon).

The Orléannais has an ancient reputation for its pâtés, but the disappearance of most (not all) game on four legs and legislation banning the taking of most on wings means the varieties are reduced considerably. Only the old or the intrepid attempt today to make the famous pâté de Pithiviers stuffed with whole larks. Most reliable for a taste of genuinely wild local produce is probably that of hare (lièvre). The Sologne and the Gâtinais and the Beauce alike have some reputation for pâté and there is some chance of it being of venison (venaison). The most famous pâté center must be Chartres.

It is said that a hare pâté offered to Attila the Hun so calmed his warriors that they settled here peaceably to become farmers in the Beauce.

If you have just one stop you can make in the area, and you are enamored of charcuterie, I think you should choose Tours. There you can lunch with more assurance upon rillettes and andouilles or andouillettes. You will then be a man or woman who knows what they like.

After that, or instead, I should head for Nantes, which does everything well, or for Le Mans in the Maine, where white sausage (boudin blanc) of onions, eggs, fat, herbs and spices is usually grilled. That I recommend. Tripe, too, is a popular dish, and often it will be just the choicest of stomachs, the gras-double, and will come finished with much cream. (Neither is strictly charcuterie, but there are more ways to enjoy eating large amounts of fat than rillettes.)

WORTH FINDING

- **Lard Nantais**: Sometimes petit lard; pork rinds, liver, lungs and flesh prepared in small pieces and, usually, served with pork chops.
- **Jambon**: Ham. Amboise hams are specially delicious.
- **Jambonneau**: Small cone-shaped ham, usually just the hock. Perfect for picnics. Also served boiled with potatoes, cabbage and chestnuts.
- **Saucisses au muscadet**: Porky sausages with a modicum of wine included and sometimes served with a chestnut purée (purée de marrons/châtuignes).

Fish & Shellfish

For me a valley presupposes the presence of water somewhere in its twisted lengths. But until I first drove into the Loire Valley while researching my book on delicatessen foods in 1978, I had no idea quite how much there was throughout the départements. For as well as the Loire and its best-known tributaries - the Cher, Indre, Vienne and Loir - there are a good half dozen more streams of note, plus the countless lakes of the Sologne, the puddles of the marais you find here and there, and the man-made étangs. Thus the inhabitants have a special regard for freshwater fish, of which they have not just the fullest range, but also a wide repertoire of ways to prepare them.

As with meat, simple cooking was traditionally favored. So a friture or mixed fry-up of perch and gudgeon (goujon) and tench (tanche) is basic. When shad (alose) arrives with spring, often as early as February, it may be stuffed with sorrel (oseille) and baked or, in special restaurants and private homes, served with mousserons, the most delicate of wild spring mushrooms, fresh and bright. Yet it is as likely to be simply served with plain butter, or with beurre blanc, the sauce which most perfectly combines the contradictory sources of the finest foods - art and science. You might find pike (brochet) in quenelles, but it, too, is just as likely to be roasted with plain butter.

Loire salmon is not extinct

as it is claimed, but not very common. Remember it will be fatter and tastier for being caught nearer the sea, as salmon does not feed in freshwater.

After beurre blanc or plain butter, mushrooms and cream are probably the most common ingredients of sauces, nudged into individuality by the use of this or that local white wine, or wild mushrooms. It is a shame if you make the mistake of thinking such dishes the result of modern influence or to be "international" cooking. But of course, they will only be simple, honest reflections of local food if the establishments cooking them are the same. It is easy to dismiss as a modern affectation the offer of shad or pike with chives, but this is a proper and local way, owing nothing to the fashion for replacing parsley with chives willy-nilly.

In the Beauce, and perhaps elsewhere, the same mistake may be made when these and other fish are offered with saffron, but saffron is, surprisingly, a crop of Boynes in that region.

Most books, and everyone you ask, of course, say the banks of the fleuve royal are the real birthplaces of matelotes, stews of fish in wine, that may or may not be finished with cream. Eels and lampreys were once the basis of the Loire version. The latter

is less common these days, but in Chinon they have a distinguished method of frying it in walnut oil. Eel is perhaps the most popular of freshwater fish, and as well as in pâtés, braises and casseroles, it might be found served with prunes. (I cannot imagine why there is so much antipathy towards eating eel, shared sometimes by me, for it has the cleanest, clearest flavor and succulent juicy flesh.)

In March and April Nantes celebrates the appearance of civelles or piballes, minute elvers which are cooked whole in omelettes or made into a sort of pâté. They are delightfully nutty and have none of the large-eyed horror of whitebait. Although not a major fishing port, Nantes was once the most important commercial port, certainly in the 18th century, when sugar, rum and spices were imported from Africa and the Americas. Many of the industrialized food products of Nantes and neighboring Lower Brittany are based on the older requirement of producing victuals for the crews of the merchant navy.

There are small fishing ports along the coast of Loire-Atlantique of course, whence come scallops (coquilles), oysters (huîtres), lobsters (homard) and a variety of crabs. There are mussels, too, but they are more a speciality of the coast of Vendée, with L'Aiguillon-sur-Mer as the acknowledged center.

Mussels have been cultivated around here since at least the 13th century. Its bay is protected from the fiercest Atlantic winds by the Île-de-Ré, and irrigated by sweet water from the land. It takes two or three years

before the mussels are big enough to sell, and it is estimated that there must be more than 6,000 bouchots, wooden posts on which they are raised. Naturally the area uses them every which way, including the mouclade associated with the Charente-Maritime. This is an upside-down éclade, in which the mussels are grilled on a bed of pine needles rather than under them (see Bordeaux).

La-Tranche-sur-Mer has mussels and oysters too, raises beef in the marais (marsh) and, according to Gault Millau, claims its potatoes are the best in the country. You may see men slashing their way dangerously through the river growth from boats in the marais de Goulaine. They are not fighting off killer eels but harvesting souche, a tough swamp grass that makes terrific litter for animal stalls.

WORTH FINDING

• *Bouilliture*: Essentially a *matelote* of eels in red wine, but with prunes as well as onions and mushrooms.
• *Fritures*: Often means mixed fry-up, but in spring might indicate a mixture of gudgeon (*goujon*) with shad roe (*laitance d'alose*) and anything with a good beurre blanc.

Meat, Poultry & Game

You need little more than the operatic trumpets of Rameau in your car to summon up thrilling tableaux of past days as you drive through the Maine or the Orléannaiss. Skeletons, or in some cases, whole limbs, of a countryside dedicated to la chasse are still easy to find. These are forests, elegant and light in an unmistakably French way. Meat, its hunting and eating, was the basis of life for court and country. But except for small pockets of hare (lièvre), some quail (caille) and perhaps partridge (perdreau) and the deer of the lake-laced Sologne, the natural game which even 30 years ago made this area France's most reputed for hunting, has gone, or gone elsewhere, or is artificially reared, like the pheasants. But to complement or replace hunted meat, there are luscious domesticated alternatives. Even they have roots in the past. Not everyone enjoyed earning their dinner on horseback. Not everyone had a horse.

Veal and beef are among the best, grown succulent and fat enough to be served simply. For the pasturage, particularly of the Touraine, is so rich that dairying animals are uncomfortable and goats overwhelmed. A small part of Normandy's Perche, the Petit Perche, juts into the Loires and produces beef you'll often find deliciously braised. Choplet is perhaps more generally known for beef; Montsoreau and Saumur are more associated with excellent veal.

Veal is just one of the specialties of Le Mans, a most interesting center for flesh eaters; its race of chickens, poulets gris, traditionally fattened on the local produce of wheat and milk, are particularly worth seeking. Capons (chapons) were the most highly prized, but these are not popular with our EC masters and may no longer be found. La Flèche was the biggest supplier of chickens to the ancien régime, but it was at Amboise that the western world's first incubator for artificially rearing chickens was installed - in 1496. It was a surprise to me to find in several books, but in no restaurants, reference to oeufs en meurette, the Burgundian dish of eggs in a red wine sauce, being enjoyed here. Still, Burgundy is only across the border, and turkeys and guinea fowls are also reared here, so I suppose they do everything possible with eggs. Chicken is also likely to be called géline.

All poultry, and the wild ducks taken from the river banks, can be found cooked in red wine, but the singular herb-flavored red wines of Bourgueil and Chinon make extremely interesting daubes, civets and every other kind of stew, including coq au vin.

Vendée, especially its marais (marsh), drained to become pasturage centuries ago, produces excellent beef and, incidentally, snails; those of Lucon are the most famed.

Lamb and mutton of the charmoise breed are the product of Montmorillon, and the coast of Vendée will offer good pré-salé lamb in spring. Château-Gontier (Mayenne) is perhaps more for those interested in the living animal: it is the registration center for pedigree bleu du Maine, a breed of sheep distinguished by steel grey markings on their legs and face. In the Beauce, Châteaudun is a major sheep raising center and mutton market. Of pigs, the craonnais are the oldest repute.

Indre-et-Loire includes Ste-Maure, famous for goat's milk cheeses and walnut oil. Only here are you likely to be offered kid (cabri) at spring time, or a gigot de chèvre, for its pastures are already drier and more suitable, like that of Poitou.

FOIS GRAS CANARD

The charming village of Palluau-sur-Loire, about 25 km/15 miles from Blois, is where Catherine and Didier Urso make and sell recommended fattened duck livers. They are the only people for hundreds of miles who do so and their shop, Le Canardière, is on Place de L'Eglise, in the shadow of a mainly 16th-century castle restored lavishly by Paco Rabanne. The ducks are fattened in the château's old stable block. Their livers are cooked with as great care as the ducks are and also made into pâtés. Take home confits, confits de gésier (giblets), or gressons, cubes of duck fat not quite rendered down and wonderfully wicked on hot toast.

Fruits & Vegetables

The countryside close to the rivers of the Loire is riddled with the man-made caves, originally the birthplace of the walls of 15th- and 16th-century châteaux but now the site of a gigantic cultivated mushroom industry, a commercial under-taking, incidentally, which has existed since at least 1600. The expression de Paris associated with mushrooms means they are cultivated, for originally Paris was virtually the only market for what was then a luxury. Langeais and Chênehutte-les-Tuffeaux are places to look for mushroom caves. Saumur is one of the most important centers for drying them. In Marboué (Beauce) the bigger heads are stuffed with snails and baked with garlic.

The wild and cultivated marvels of the garden of France are beyond listings, for lists suggest inevitably some degree of finite knowledge. This is impossible when a region too glibly associated only with the broad bean (fève) includes also the Beauce, one of France's granaries (Châteaudun is its center) and the Gâtinais, famed for walnuts, honey, saffron and mushrooms, and Orléans, maker of the world's best wine vinegars, pickles and mustard. It was Orléans, not Dijon, that stimulated a huge increase in the French mustard crop in the 1940s.

The Loire Valley is where St François de Paul created the Bon Chrétien pear 500 years ago - it is said to have disappeared from French markets, but survives in Australasia, I believe. In 1849, the Comice horticultural gardens in Angers developed the Comice pear, and if you are in Amanlis in September, its own summer pear, Beurre d'Amanlis, should be ready. The better known Williams is ripe about mid-August and is finished by the end of September. The huge Louise-Bonne pear is a speciality of Les Essants.

Whence, too, came the queen after whom the French call their greengage reine-claude. Claude, wife of François I, was born in Romorantin in the Sologne, home of excellent apples, of strawberries and, for those who look, the medlar (nèfle). Strawberries, incidentally, are often served in red wine hereabouts.

Reinettes (little queens), are a French variety of apple considered as good as the British Cox; the Loire grows a number of local strains, including the Reinette d'Orléans - and plenty of the superb Reine de reinette (queen of reinettes), considered one of the world's best apples and thought to have come first from Britain. Azay-le-Rideau has rather special apple orchards. Upside-down apple cakes or tarts are commonly found. They are known sometimes also as tartes renversées or solognotes, and appear sometimes in an expected variation using pears rather than apples. Use good Golden Delicious apples or Cox's to make this as special at home as the original.

Olivet is another pear center, and makes those bottles of Williams eau-de-vie with a whole pear inside. There are great cherry orchards too, as in Vineuil, but her cherries, mainly guignes, tend to be used to make guignolet (cherry

LOCAL PRODUCE

VEGETABLES

- **ARTICHOKE** *artichaut*
  April until October
  Dep: Maine-et-Loire, (Angers),
  Vendée (Sables d'Olonne)

- **ASPARAGUS** *asperges*
  April until June.
  Dep: Loir-et-Cher,
  Maine-et-Loire
  After the Gard, Loir-et-Cher
  is the second biggest grower;
  markets include Saumur,
  Chinon, Orléans, Blois,
  Selles-sur-Cher.

- **CABBAGE** *chou*
  Var: *Tête de Pierre,
  Roi d'Hiver*
  September until February
  Dep: Loire-Atlantique,
  Vendée, Maine-et-Loire,
  Loiret, Sarthe.

- **CARROT** *carotte*
  July until following May
  Summer crops May until July

- **CAULIFLOWER** *choufleur*
  Mid-October until May
  Dep: Loire-Atlantique,
  Vendée, Maine-et-Loire,
  Indre-et-Loire

- **CELERY** *céleri-branche*
  End April to July covered
  Mid-August to November
  open air
  Dep: Loire-Atlantique,
  Maine-et-Loire
  Tours has a celebrated
  celeri-violet. Nantes, Angers
  and Saumur are important
  market centers - biggest
  overall grower in France.

- **CUCUMBER** *concombre*
  May until August
  Dep: Loiret, Loire-Atlantique,
  Maine-et-Loire, Loir-et-
  Cher, Indre-et-Loire, Vendée
  The Loiret is France's biggest
  producer: 14% of national
  crop. Orléans, Nantes and
  Angers are the biggest markets.

- **FENNEL** *fenouil*
  Autumn-ish
  Dep: Maine-et-Loire
  A traditional crop of the
  Loire valley.

- **LEEK** *poireau*
  Var: *Briand, Artaban,*

Malabare (giant winter variety)
Year-round
Dep: Loire-Atlantique,
Vendée, Maine-et-Loire
Loire-Atlantique is biggest
producer in France after the
Nord.

- **LETTUCE** *laitue/chicorée*
  Round batavia, curly endive,
  etc., varieties:
  Covered from March. Open
  air from June to autumn.
  Dep: Loire-Atlantique,
  Maine-et-Loire, Vendée
  Among France's most
  important production zones.

  Cabbage and iceberg varieties:
  Main season April until
  September. September to
  November has almost no crop.
  Dep: Loire-Atlantique, Loiret,
  Maine-et-Loire, Vendée

- **ONION** *oignon*
  All year, but mainly
  August-May
  Dep: Loire-Atlantique,
  Maine-et-Loire
  By far the most important
  production zone in France.

- **RADISH** *radis*
  Year round
  Dep: Loire-Atlantique,
  Maine-et-Loire, Vendée

- **SHALLOT** *échalote*
  Var: short and long varieties,
  including *Grise* and *Jersey*
  Harvested June and July,
  available year-round
  Dep: Maine-et-Loire, Vendée,
  Loiret, Loir-et-Cher

- **TOMATO** *tomate*
  Var: *Beefsteak*
  Mid-April until mid-November
  Dep: Loire-Atlantique,
  Maine-et-Loire, Loiret, Vendée

- **TURNIP** *navet*
  Var: red/white and violet/white
  February until October
  Dep: Loire-Atlantique, Loiret
  Loire-Atlantique is one of
  the 4 biggest producers.

- **ZUCCHINI** *courgette*
  Var: *Diamant* (open air),
  Seneca (covered)
  Mid-June until mid-October
  Dep: Loiret, Vendée

FRUITS

- **APPLE** *pomme*
  Var: *Reine de reinettes,
  Clochard, Belle de Boskoop*
  Harvested September to mid-
  November for selling
  September to July
  Dep: Maine-et-Loire, Loiret,
  Cher, Loire-Atlantique,
  Sarthe, Indre-et-Loire,
  Deux-Sèvres
  A very important crop, which
  also includes English, American,
  even Japanese varieties.

- **BLACK CURRANTS** *cassis*
  Var: *Noir de Bourgogne*
  July
  Dep: Maine-et-Loire, Loir-et-
  Cher, Sarthe, Loire-Atlantique.

- **HAZELNUTS** *noisettes*
  Main harvest October to
  November
  Dep: Loiret, Indre
  From July you can buy green
  noisettes, (cobnuts in English);
  the dried ones are mainly
  sold for chocolates and cookies
  but as the Loiret, together
  with the Dordogne, produces
  50% of the French crop,
  there should be some around
  in the shell (*en coque*) for you.

- **MELON** *melon*
  Var: *Charentais*
  May/June until September
  Dep: Deux-Sèvres, Loire-
  Atlantique, Vendée

- **PEAR** *poire*
  Var: *Beurre Hardy, Comice,
  Passe-Crassane* (winter),
  Williams
  Harvested from end-August
  to mid-November, sold
  August to April
  Dep: Maine-et-Loire, Loiret,
  Sarthe, Indre-et-Loire

- **RASPBERRY** *framboise*
  Mid-June to mid-July
  Dep: Loire-Atlantique

- **STRAWBERRY** *fraise*
  Var: mainly *Belrubi*
  April until early August
  Dep: Loir-et-Cher,
  Main-et-Loire
  Based in the Loire Valley and
  the Sologne but very much
  aimed at the Parisian market:
  centers include Angers,
  Saumur, Romorantin, Vallée
  du Cher, Contres, Soings.

THE VINEGARS OF ORLEANS

Just as all brandies are not cognac, all vinegars are not Orléans vinegars. Modern techniques make modern vinegars in less than 24 hours, but Orléans vinegar is made in two stages. First, the wine is slowly turned to vinegar over three weeks, promoting the development of bouquet and perfume. Once considered ready, it is drawn off into oaken casks and kept another 3 or 4 months to mature fully. It's really worth comparing Orléans and ordinary vinegar at the same time. There's a sharp difference.

brandy), and the real fame of Vineuil is her asparagus.

Dried plums (prunes) turn up in any number of sweet or savory dishes, but not perhaps as much as they used to do. Tours was once known as a city of towers (tours) for there were dozens, where plums (originally from Damascus, i.e., damascenes, hence damsons) were dried and stored for winter use. Blois also dries its golden plums (mirabelles) into prunes and calls them pistoles (as does Brignoles in Provence because their shape and color is reminiscent of old gold coins).

Expect lots of sorrel (oseille) in spring and early summer, with freshwater fish generally, or specifically, in an omelette beauceronne combined with bacon and potato. Sorrel may also be cooked with chestnuts. The prepons is a sweet melon, cardoons (cardons) are popular, pumpkin, amazingly for France, is eaten in pies, and the Touraine has a peach/apricot they call alberge.

Although not used noticeably, saffron (safran) is an unexpected harvest of Boynes (Loiret); it takes more

than 200,000 of the hand-picked stigmas from the saffron crocuses to make 500g/1lb, hence the astronomical expense. Saumur, like many wine centers, grows luscious strawberries and Cholet makes many of hers into jam.

If you miss the asparagus of spring, you might better wait until autumn when wild mushrooms, especially from the forest of Orléans, abound. Cèpes and other types of bolets predominate, but the forest also breeds excellent parasol mushrooms (courmelles/coulemelles). Summer visitors may be compensated for unseasonal dampness by the earlier appearance of the apricot-perfumed girolles/chanterelles. Vilainer-les-Roches is the traditional center for making the wicker baskets into which you gather them or send your harvests of fruit to market.

Angers has a broccoli named for herself, Sully-sur-Loire harvests the oriental crosnes, tiny tubers, Nantes and Angers grow macres (water chestnuts), Chemille grows enormous amounts of mint and camomile for vermouth. Le Mans has a local hazelnut, culroux (redbottom), a local chestnut nouzillard, and also grows the important walnut variety franquette. Nut oil is every bit as important and famous here as in the Dordogne; Tours makes it well, and so does Ste-Maure.

In short, the orchards and gardens that stretch either side of the Loire and its tributary rivers fairly bristle with opportunities for good eating. With its own good butter and cream, and that of neighboring Normandy and the Charentes, with which to make lakes of beurre blanc, only those who are slow of learning, or too fast of driving, will fail to eat well.

Cheese

Farm-produced goat cheeses abound in the green valleys of the Loire: some are mild, like chavignol, others far more goaty, such as the distinctive pyramides. This is France's capital of goat cheese manufacture, producing around 500 tons per annum. Although chèvres predominate, you can also find a good selection of small flavorsome cow's milk cheeses in the valleys, the olivet being perhaps the best known.

•Bondaroy au foin: From the Orléannais, a soft cow's milk cheese with a tangy flavor that is cured for five weeks in hay-filled bins.

•Chavignol-Sancerre: A small flattened ball of mild chèvre eaten as a dessert. It does not become a crottin (qv) until quite black and brown.

•Crezancy-Sancerre: Similar to chavignol, a mild goat's cheese from the southern Loire area.

•Crottin de Chavignol: An AOC cheese with a reliable regional tradition and flavor, this has been made by the peasants of Sancerre since the 16th century. Made from full-cream goat's milk, these cheeses are small, white or ivory in color and have a fine white mold. Best from March to November, the characteristic taste gets stronger with age. It is a favorite snack, may be grilled or marinated in white wine. Made in most parts of Cher and in small areas of Loiret and Nièvre (Burgundy), these cheeses were not called crottin until 1829, and the origin is a supposed reference to a small oil lamp with the same shape. When they are allowed to age and become black and horrid they are then the crottin referred to in the dictionary - horse droppings.

•Entrammes: A typical unpasteurized washed-rind, cheese made in the monastery of Entrammes in Maine which made the original Port Salut.

•Frinault: A small, strongly flavored disk of cow's milk cheese, best in summer and autumn. 50% fat content. The frinault cendré is cured in boxes of wood ash for four weeks, which creates a waxier flavor and texture.

•Gien: A chèvre or mi-chèvre made only on farms in and around Gien in the Orléannais region. Nutty flavored; may also be cured in leaves or ashes.

•Gracay: A recently invented goat cheese from the Arnon valley; truncated cone weighing about 500g/1lb with dark blueish coating and dusted with powdered charcoal.

•Laval: Made by Trappists at the monastery of Laval in Maine, a washed-rind disk of cow's milk cheese. The body should have lots of tiny holes, pale rind and sharpish, somewhat unexpected flavor.

•Levroux: A Valençay-style cheese made around the fortified town of Levroux.

•Ligueil/Loche: Commercially made chèvres, similar to a Ste-Maure.

•Montoire: A fruity flavor to this small chèvre from the Loire valley, shaped into the classic truncated cone. Troo is a variety.

•Oléron: A pure white fresh sheep's milk cheese from the Île d'Oléron. Mild creamy flavor and 40-45% fat content. Made in whatever shape and size

attracts on the day. Mainly available in spring.

•Olivet bleu: Small disk of blueish-skinned blue cheese; cured for a month in chalk caves of Olivet. It has a full but not sharp flavor and is made from cow's milk.

•Olivet cendré: An olivet matured in wood ashes, and thus lower in fat (40%).

•Pannes cendré: Low-fat (20%-30%) cheese of skimmed cow's milk from the Orléanais. Strong flavor after curing three months in wood ashes. Seen mainly in late summer and autumn.

•Romorantin: See Selles-sur-Cher.

•St Benoist/St-Benoit: From St-Benoit-sur-Loire, a farm-made disk (about 350g/14oz) made from partly skimmed cow's milk. Perhaps of monastic origin, but the pale rind has not been brushed or washed; fruity flavor.

•Ste-Maure fermier: A popular chèvre with a goaty smell and strong taste. Cylindrically shaped and made on the farm, this cheese has straw running through it, said to indicate where the cheese broke and was stuck together again after unmolding.

•Ste-Maure laitier: A commercially produced version of fermier with no straw. Often called a log. Verneuil is another brand name.

•Sancerre: A commonly used catch-all name for such chèvres as chavignol, crezancy and santranges.

•Santranges-Sancerre: A tangy goat's milk cheese produced on farms in and around Santranges in Berry; shaped like a small flattened ball.

•Selles-sur-Cher: Said to recall the sweetness of life in the valleys of the Loire and

Cher (which enjoy a fine climate), this is one of the well-known goat's milk cheeses that are covered with powdered charcoal. Lightly renneted curd is placed in molds - unbroken curds are the secret to this cheese - and it is then salted and coated with ash and left to mature for 10 to 21 days. Mild in flavor it is best enjoyed from the end of spring until autumn. Protected by an appellation contrôllée, the manufacture of these cheeses is limited to a few départements of Loiret-Cher, l'Indre and Cher. Also known as Romorantin.

•Tournon-St-Pierre: A mild, nutty chèvre from Tournon, made on the farm. Tallish trimmed cone, and good in summer.

•Valençay fermier: A mild goat's milk cheese produced on farms in the Loire area. Shaped as a low truncated pyramid, dusted with charcoal; best eaten from late spring to autumn, although locals also macerate it in crocks for use in winter.

•Valençay laitier: Known also as pyramide, a well-known goat's milk cheese made commercially all year using frozen goat's milk curds and powdered milk. A strong nose and slightly rancid taste. Levroix is the same thing. Chabris is a brand name of commercial valençay and levroux.

•Villebarou: A cow's milk cheese from the Loire that is fast disappearing. Distinguished by its appearance - a thin flat disk not wrapped but sitting on a leaf.

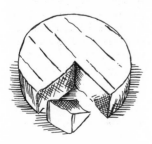

Pastries, Desserts & Confectionery

When it comes to the end of a meal, you've probably read it already, in the Fruit and Vegetable section, for with such luscious abundance of almost every fruit, you don't have to try hard to find delicious and simple desserts.

It is the tarte that rules, with enough variations of pastry and of fillings to keep you amused differently each day. Local prunes (pruneaux) feature quite as much in tartes as fresh fruits, sometimes whole, sometimes as rich purées, or stuffed with almonds or other dried fruits. Prunes soaked and then simmered in wine are a special favorite and are usually served teamed with one or other of the dairy products so featured - cream, cream cheese, junket (jonchée) or thicker curds (caillebotte).

Almonds have a special role here, for they flavor one of France's most famous pastries, that of Pithiviers and which is called just that or gâteau de Pithiviers feuilleté. The filling is frangipane, an almond pastry cream additionally flavored with rum, and this is one case where I did bother to travel to the eponymous town to try a specialty and where just being there enhanced the flavor, I'm sure. Puff pastry is seen in millefeuilles as specialties in almost every pastry shop.

Plenty of honey traditionally found its way into cakes in the past and still does in pain d'épices (gingerbread). Interestingly, the idea of putting honey into cakes is only a few centuries old; when the ancient Romans and Greeks spoke of honey cakes, they meant cakes which had been soaked in a honey syrup, as they still do in Greece and the Middle East. Honey also flavors a number of sweets, of which rigolettes are probably the ones most worth trying.

Blois, already mentioned for its pistoles, has also a reputation for chocolates and, unusually, makes a chocolate cake con brio - gâteau chocolat de Blois. When you get to the borders of this large area you find other influences creeping in, especially that of Brittany into Anjou. Pancakes and crêpes become more common, filled, naturally, with fruits.

And then there are the cookies. Nantes invented the petit beurre biscuit. Illiers seems to have made madeleines since the Middle Ages; it was one of the stops on the long pilgrimage to Santiago de Compostela in Spain, the sign of which journey was a scallop shell, and the shape of these biscuits remembers that. Sablé-sur-Sarthe argues with all of Normandy about who invented those other almost universal cookies, the sablés. The choice everywhere will probably calm most argument, but should you want a single center in which to eat pastries, cakes and confectionery, the craftsmen of Le Mans have the Gault Millau accolade of being specially gifted doué.

SWEET GIFT OF NATURE

Although he trained as a lawyer, René Renou is the seventh generation of his

A DRINKER'S GUIDE

As a rule, drink all Muscadet, Sancerre and Pouilly Blanc Fumé as young as possible; avoid bottles over three years old. This holds true, too, for all other basic dry Loire whites. Only Vouvray and Savennières will repay keeping. The very best Chinon and Bourgueil will last for ten years, most reds will not improve after five. The best sweet white wines made here are stunning - every now and then. Coteaux du Layon is the finest.

RECENT VINTAGES
1994: A poor year. The Coteaux were the best but the reds will disappoint.
1993: An excellent year with most of the region (unusually for the Loire) producing good wine.

1992: A large crop of middling quality.
1991: The weather was so bad that there was very little wine made in Muscadet, and many other regions were similarly affected. Quality was average.
1990: A great year. Stunning sweet wines and excellent reds. Wines that will mature over the long term.
1989: A great year. The sweet wines are compared with the 1947s, which are said to be the best ever. Another vintage to keep and dream about drinking.
1988: A good year for Sancerre wines, which are just at their peak now, and an excellent year for the reds which are also very ready.

1987: A middling year, although the sweet wines were poor.
1986: A very good year in Sancerre and reasonable in the rest of the Loire.
1985: A great year for reds and sweet wines, one of the best, with reds likely to stay at their peak for a while.

PREVIOUS GREATS
1983 produced excellent sweet wines, 1982 good Vouvrays and Bourgueils. The sweet wines of 1976 have had a long and glorious life.

SPIRITS AND LIQUEURS
Anjou makes an *eau-de-vie* and *marc* plus spirits and sweet liqueurs from its many fruits, so do all the côteaux of the Loires.

---

family to make sweet white wines in the Loire Valley. Indeed, the Renous have proudly worked the soil of their vineyards and the presses in their ancient cave, Domaine de Terrebrune, since before the Revolution.

René, who is active in the French AOC system, believes the sweet white wine he makes is the best expression of the Loire Valley.

Anjou, Touraine, Saumur and Sancerre are the local wines familiar throughout France and beyond. Two and a half million bottles are produced annually, accounting for ten percent of all French Appellation Controllée wines.

Domaine de Terrebrune sits in the heart of the small village of Thourace, some 30km/18 mi south of Angers.

The eastern side of the village square is dominated by the cellars of the Domaine de Terrebrune.

The soil of Thourace is a heavy dark-brown mixture of clay and shiste, a blue slate unusual to the areas close to the hills of Brittany, hence the name Terrebrune, meaning brown soil. The best grapes always come from vines grown in poor soil. The roots grow deeper in search of water and build stronger plants. "This may yield fewer grapes," says René, "but it is the intensity of flavor for which we strive."

The grape variety is chenin, which René allows to mature on the vine until noble rot concentrates the sugar to well over 20 percent. For weeks leading up to harvesting, René watches the weather closely, waiting for the right combination of sunshine and rainfall. Each grape is hand picked during the afternoons when there is no moisture to

dilute the sugar and only those grapes that have yellowed to the maximum concentration of sweetness are selected; those still green must wait until the next picking.

Even at the pressing stage, René again hand selects every grape. The sugar content of a grape can vary by as much as two percent from another picked from the same vine on the same afternoon and it is this concentration that gives the special cuvée, the great vintage. "The best vintages are a gift of nature not made by man," says René. "The miracle we hope for every year is to combine sweetness with freshness. If it goes wrong, all you get is a wine like jam."

His grapes are grown in three locations close to his cave. Each vineyard lies on southwest-facing slopes for maximum sun. In poor years,

AN OLD TART

Lamotte-Beuvran in the Sologne is the home of the tarte Tatin, the upside-down caramelized apple pie that bears the name of the hotel-keeping sisters, les demoiselles Tatin, who invented it in the 19th century.

A happy accident or triumph over adversity? The town's tarte Tatin obsessives prefer to believe it was the latter that inspired their heroines Caroline and Stephanie. It is said that late one day at l'Hotel Tatin, an aristocrat hunting in the area demanded a dessert with his meal but the sisters had nothing left in the kitchen except apples, butter, sugar and flour. They had a go and - Voila! - a legend was born.

A less popular theory is that these noble ladies were flirting and while distracted, accidentally burned an apple pie. It was not until they tipped it into the dustbin that they realized what a treat had been created and the new tart was hastily retrieved.

Today l'Hotel Tatin still stands and in the bar, the sisters' oven is decorated like a shrine with tarte dishes and photographs of the ladies. The tradition is perpetuated by La Confrérie des Lichonneux de Tarte Tatin, formed to protect the dessert from adulteration and compromise. To wit they conduct lectures, festivals, street processions and dinners as well as an annual competition to find the best maker.

One of these is the local Michelin two-starred chef Bernard Robin who uses equipment once owned by the Tatin sisters. He recommends only two varieties of apple for the tart, reinette or le golden blush, and suggests cooking it in a chimney - apparently a method introduced by the sisters some time after the tarte's invention - for the characteristic smoky flavor.

At investiture ceremonies the confrérie wear the ritual pale-blue farming smocks and large black hats. On red ribbons around members' necks hang various sizes of medallions in the shape of tarte Tatins. Of course, the larger the necklace the more prominent the personage. Yes, size does matter, terribly. And in case you're wondering what kind of person is attracted to such an organization, the leader of the group sells shower equipment.

---

when the noble rot has been thwarted by bad weather, he consigns the grapes to production of the local sparkling wine. His total output rarely exceeds 25,000 bottles and if much of it is sparkling wine, he fails to generate the revenue needed to cover his costs.

For the 1987 Montagne Terroir, which René describes as a difficult vintage, the rot was not good. The wine hints of quince, acacia and a distinct honey finish. René describes it as lacking elegance but it has a freshness unusual in most sweet wines. The 1989 Montagne Terroir is far richer but nevertheless delivers freshness and a longer finish than the '87.

The 1990 is described by René as the best vintage since 1947, which is to date the best this century. It tastes of honey balanced with young fruit and the strength of the noble rot is evident.

René regularly drinks vintages from the 1920s, and within his cellars, he stores bottles dating back to 1869. In tasting the 1990 vintage, one is conscious that this wine is unlikely to achieve its best until beyond one's own lifetime. "For the first ten years, the wine tastes of fresh fruit," René explains. "After that, it starts to develop flavors more like dried fruit. As the decades roll on, the color deepens and the flavors concentrate to create a wine best drunk like a sherry."

Bon Marché

LOIRE-ATLANTIQUE

Bernerie-en-Retz Fri; Châteaubriant Wed; Coueron Thur, Fri; Donges Thur; Guémené-Penfao Fri; Loroux-Bottereau Sun, Wine Fair 1st Sun Mar; Nantes Daily especially Sat; Rezé Tue, Fri; Savenay Wed; St-Brévin-les-Pins Thur, Sun; St-Etienne-de-Montluc Fri; St-Nazaire Daily exc Mon, Onion Fair 15 Sept; St-Sebastien-sur-Loire Tue, Fri; Trignac Wed; Vallet Sun, Wine Fair 3rd week Mar.

MAYENNE

Ballée Wed; Château-Gontier Thur & Sat AM; Cuille Thur;

Fougerolles-du-Plessis *Fri;*
Gorron *Wed;* Lassay-les-
Châteaux *Wed;* Laval *Tue & Sat*
AM; Mayenne *Mon;* Montsurs
Tue; Port Brillet *Tue;* Pré-en-Pail
Sat; Renazé *Fri;* Villaines-la-
Juhel *Mon.*

SARTHE

Allonnes *Sat;* Aubigné Racan
Sat; Beaumont-sur-Sarthe *Tue;*
Bonnetable *Tue;* Bouloire *Tue;*
Cérans Foulletourte *Tue;* Conlie
Thur; Coulaines *Thur & Sat AM;*
Ecommoy *Tue;* La Ferté-Bernard
Mon; La Flèche *Wed, Sun;*
Fresnay-sur-Sarthe *Sat;* Loué
Tue; Le Lude *Thur;* Mamers *Mon;*
Le Mans *Daily except Mon, Fri*
most important; Marolles-les-
Braults *Thur;* Noyen-sur-Sarthe
Sat; Parcé-sur-Sarthe *Thur;*
Sablé-sur-Sarthe *Mon, Wed;*
Savigné-l'Evêque *Thur;* La Suze-
sur-Sarthe *Thur,* St-Calais
Thur.

EURE-ET-LOIR

Arrou *Fri;* Auneau *Fri;* Authon-
du-Perche *Tue;* Bonneval *Mon;*
Brezolles *Wed;* Brou *Wed;*
Chartres *Wed, Thur, Fri, Sat;*
Châteaudun *Tue, Thur, Sat;*
Châteauneuf *Wed;* Dreux *Sun,*
Mon, Fri; La Ferté-Vidame *Thur;*
Illiers-Combray *Fri;* Janville
Wed; Maintenon *Thur;* Nogent-
le-Rotrou *Sat;* Senonches *Fri;*
St-Remy-sur-Avre *Sat;* Toury
Wed; Voves *Tue.*

LOIRET

Beaugency *Sat;* Châtillon-sur-
Loire *Thur;* Courtenay *Thur;* Gien
Sat AM, Wed AM (poultry);
Malesherbes *Wed;* Montargis
Wed AM, Sat; Orléans *Tue, Wed,*
Thur, Sat; Puiseaux *Mon;* St-
Denis de l'Hôtel *Sun AM, Cheese*
& Junk Fair 1st Sun June; St-
Hilaire-St-Mesmin *Mon, Wed &*
Fri (May to Sept), daily in cherry
season; Sully-sur-Loire *Mon;*
Tigy Asparagus Fair 3rd Sun in
May.

CHER

Aubigny-sur-Nère *Sat;* Baugy

Fri; Bourges *Daily;*
Châteaumeillant *Fri;* Culan
Wed; Dun-sur-Auron *Sat;*
Graçay *Thur;* Henrichemont
Wed; Mehun-sur-Yèvre *Wed;*
Sancerre *Sat, Tue (Mar to Nov);*
Sancoins *Wed;* Savigny-en-
Sancerre *Thur;* St-Amand-
Montrond *Wed, Sat;* St-Florent-
sur-Cher *Fri;* St-Germain-du-
Puy *Thur;* Vailly-sur-Sauldre *Fri;*
Vierzon *Tue AM, Wed, Sat.*

INDRE

Argenton-sur-Creuse *Tue, Sat;*
Bélabre *Fri;* Le Blanc *Wed, Sat;*
Buzancais *Fri;* Châteauroux *Mon*
(cattle) Sat; Châtillon-sur-Indre
Fri, Sun; La Chatre *Sat;* Cluis *Fri,*
Sun; Issoudun *Wed, Sat;*
Levroux *Mon, Fri;* Luant *Wed;*
Mézières-en-Brenne *Thur;*
Neuvy-St-Sepulchre *Fri, Sun;*
Neuilly *Fri;* St-Benoit-du-Sault
Thur; St-Gaultier *Fri;* Tournon-
St-Martin *Tue;* Valençay *Tue;*
Villedieu-sur-Indre *Wed.*

INDRE-ET-
LOIRE

Amboise *Wed (glass), Fri, Sat,*
Melon Fair 1st Wed Sept; Azay-
le-Rideau *Wed, Wine Fair last*
weekend Feb, Apple Fair last
weekend Nov; Bléré *Tue, Fri,*
Melon Fair 2nd Fri Sept;
Bourgueil *Tue, Wine Tasting 2nd*
Tue Sept, Chestnut Fair 4th Tue
Oct; Celle Guenand *Wed, Melon*
Fair 1st Sun Sept; Chambray-les
-Tours *Thur, Sun;* Chinon *Thur,*
Sat, Sun; Joué-lès-Tours *Sun,*
Wed, Thur, Fri; Ligueil *Mon;*
Loches *Wed;* Montlouis-sur-
Loire *Thur, Wine Fair 3rd*
weekend Feb; St-Branches
Onion Fair 2nd Wed April, Melon
Fair 29 Aug; Ste-Maure-de-
Touraine *Fri, Cheese Fair 1st Sun*
June; St-Pierre-des-Corps *Tue,*
Wed, Fri, Sat, Sun; Tours *Daily*
(poultry Wed & Sat), Garlic &
Shallot Fair 26 July; Vouvray
Wine Fair 2nd weekend Aug.

LOIR-ET-CHER

Blois *Daily, Sun AM;* Contres
Fri; Droué *Tue;* Herbault *Mon;*

Mondoubleau *Mon;* Montoire-
sur-le-Loir *Wed;* Montrichard
Mon; Neung-sur-Beuvron *Tue;*
Romorantin-Lanthenay *Wed,*
Sat; Salbris *Thur;* Savigny-sur-
Brave *Tue;* Selles-sur-Cher *Thur;*
St-Aignan *Sat;* St-Amand-
Longpré *Thur;* Vendôme *Fri.*

MAINE-ET-
LOIRE

Angers *Daily;* Avrillé *Tue;*
Beaufort-en-Vallée *Wed;*
Beaupreau *Mon;* Candé *Mon;*
Chalonnes-sur-Loire *Tue, Fri;*
Champigné *Tue;* Châteauneuf-
sur-Sarthe *Fri;* Chemillé *Thur;*
Cholet *Tue, Wed, Thur, Fri, Sat;*
Combrée *Fri, Sat;* Fontevraud
l'Abbaye *Wed, Sat AM;* Jallais *Fri;*
Lion d'Angers *Fri;* Montjean-
sur-Loire *Thur;* Montreuil-
Juigné *Fri;* La Pommeraye *Mon;*
Les Ponts-de-Cé *Fri;* Pouance
Thur; Rochefort-sur-Loire *Wed;*
Romagne *Mon;* Saumur *Tue,*
Wed AM, Thur, Sat; Segré *Wed.*

VENDÉE

Aizenay *Mon;* Beauvoir-sur-Mer
Thur; Challans *Tue, Fri;*
Chantonnay *Thur, Sat;*
Châtaigneraie *Sat;* Coex *Sat;*
Les Epesses *Fri;* Les Essarts *Wed*
(eggs & butter), 1st Wed
(poultry), Fontenay-le-Comte
Sat; La Gaubretière *Mon;* Les
Herbiers *Thur;* Luçon *Wed, Sat;*
Montaigu *Tue, Thur, Sat;*
Moutiers-les-Mauxfaits *Fri;*
Notre-Dame-de-Monts *Sun AM,*
Thur, Sat; Les Sablés d'Olonne
Daily in summer; St-Gilles-Croix
de-Vie *Tue, Wed, Thur, Sat;* St-
Hilaire-de-Riez *Thur, Sun;* St-
Jean-de-Monts *Daily at beach,*
Wed, Sat; St-Michel-en l'Herm
Thur; Talmont-St-Hilaire *Tue,*
Sat; La-Tranche-sur-Mer *Tue,*
Fri, Sat & Sun in season;
Vendrennes *Wed (butter).*

✿ PARIS

NOT MY CITY – BUT YOURS

"In which you will discover...

• *Kitsch for kitchens and a street of chopped liver...*

• *Virgin choices, ice cream queues on an island and the best cookbook shop in France...*

• *Bread that is art, haunted bars and the world's finest cookery schools...*

• *Madeleine glitz relief and Maxi-Minims snacks...*

• *Grand Mother Goose's bargains and a paradise of tableware...*

• *Engadine amid Abbesses..."*

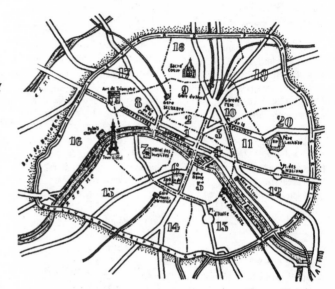

On countless visits to Paris I learned, as millions of others must have done, that the pleasure of seeing a famous painting, revisiting a favorite royal apartment, or simply sailing on the Seine is only complete if you blend it into contemporary life rather than viewing it as an obligatory set lesson in history or tourism. People rarely go home to boast of seeing the Eiffel Tower or the Mona Lisa; it is taken for granted.

A well-traveled gentleman once said: "I've visited many fascinating places in my lifetime. For one reason or another, I never made it to Paris. When I eventually did, it was as if I'd saved the best until last." What enticed him? The Louvre, a trip on a Bâteau Mouche, a night at the Opéra - yes, but that and more. He had delved beneath the postcard-Paris surface and not only seen but experienced another art form, the very essence of France, food.

To truly discover Paris and to take home a lasting memory, you must come closer and enter into the spirit of the city by painting your own culinary portrait. The memories we will share are of discovering a sumptuous new ice cream flavor or a creamier pastry, taking home a jar of Fauchon's passion-fruit syrup to store for a quickly made sorbet, serendipity in a Russian tea shop that serves cheese scones, perhaps joining a cookery class at one of the world-famous schools. Stand in line outside the Poîlane on rue du Cherche-midi, shop in the marché Europe, the city's smallest covered market, warm up with a dreamy hot chocolate at La Charlotte-en-isle, visit the oldest confectioners on rue du Faubourg Montmatre or taste regional cooking at Café Parisien. Any one of these will mean that we have slipped under the skin of Parisian Paris and are no longer onlookers.

There is something else about Paris. As capital and seat of kings it has more than its own glory to reflect. It must dutifully mirror the produce of all the ancient or forgotten fiefdoms and kingdoms within France's modern borders. Transport, commerce and nationalism make this more likely than ever, and the interested and discerning may, through Parisian markets, shops and restaurants, build up a culinary portrait of the whole country. This is why I have broken the even mosaic of this book and devoted this section more to the discovery of Paris than to the Île-de-France which surrounds her.

The guidelines I have chosen are based on my beliefs and experience - that food is the best and most universally interesting way to discover any city. So I have taken 11 of the central *arrondissements* of Paris, combined them to make six areas, and produced a guide to their most important or interesting food establishments, from open and covered markets to department stores, from tiny tea shops and butchers to antique shops, cheese shops, bakers and ironmongers.

The maps accompanying each section are purposely simple so you can, say, after reading the guidance given, work out a route for yourself either to cover it all, or to pander to your special interests. Restaurants are intentionally fairly limited - there is an ocean of advice on the subject and you probably already have a guide and enough sense to paddle your own canoe.

One tip for those not enamored of cities, who are speeding through to elsewhere or who are marooned in Paris by time or funds: take advantage of the huge range of regional foods offered here to learn and to prepare yourself for journeys elsewhere in the country. For comparison is the finest way to learn anything and you can't compare without some basis. Also, be bold. The addresses I have given are but a framework upon which to build your own adventures. Turn left or right, linger longer or hurry past. It is not my Paris I want you to discover, but yours . . .

DEATH OF THE BISTRO

The sneer of the *garçon*, the thick wafts of Gauloise, the ridiculously priced *café crème* - *oui*, you are in a typical Parisian bistro. But have you noticed that the lovers around you are really Michelle and Brian from Norwood and Bob and Pat from Santa Fé? The Parisians are at home watching television because they can no longer be bothered with rude waiters, dirty smoke-filled rooms and overpriced coffee. When Parisians need a snack and a drink, they'll head for McDonalds, Burger King or one of the new breed of clean, professional sandwich bars.

In 1960 there were around 200,000 bistros in France. Today this figure has been quartered and it is estimated that bistros are closing at a rate of 3,000 a year. In 1994, half this number closed in Paris alone. In the towns and villages outside the capital, this loss can be more obvious: where once you may have had a choice of five cafés in a village of 500 people, now there may be none.

But perhaps the death of the bistro was inevitable. In practice, the term is largely interchangeable with café but is possibly derived from *bistrouiller*, which means to blend inferior wines.

France's National Federation of Cafés and Brasseries has composed a quality charter encouraging bistro owners to offer good products at good prices, to clean up their premises and be pleasant to customers. The general response of owners? Why, a sneer of course.

THE SPIRITUAL HOME OF CHOCOLATE

TEA FOR DEUX

The British drink their tea as the French drink their coffee: hot, very strong and always with milk. When it comes to *thé*, the French are *sympatique* with the Japanese, preferring a bit of delicacy and no milk or sugar, thank you.

The irony is that in France, tea's association with Britain gives it snob-appeal and hence the market is well-served with high-quality, premium-priced products. More irony: two of the most important names in French tea are Mariage and Betjeman and Barton (ok, so that's three names), all originally Dutch.

Didier Jumeau-Lafond of Betjeman and Barton (23 bd Malesherbes) reminds us that tea does not fare well if served hastily or in badly chosen utensils. To this end, the store offers a choice of bags, filters, caddies and other paraphernalia important to the art of tea making. He believes they are not just simple accessories, but an essential part in preserving "this noble art of living that we are proud to pass on to customers."

For mornings, Didier suggests Ceylon OP or Darjeeling tea (light), the breakfast blend, Grand Yunnan or Assam (strong) or Lapsang Souchong (savory). At lunchtime, he recommends Yunnan or Darjeeling, and in the afternoon, Keemun or Caravan (light), or any of the fragrant flavored teas. Formosa Oolong is Didier's choice for evening.

Betjeman and Barton stocks a formidable range: smoked and unsmoked China teas, classic blends, teas from Ceylon, India and Kenya, unfermented green tea, and a range of more than 30 flavored teas including spice, fruit and flower blends, even caramel. Smell before you buy.

The Mariage Frères shop and café is at 30 rue du Bourg-Tibourg. It boasts 450 types of tea, beautifully packaged and displayed.

Over the last ten years, Paris has increasingly become a playground for lovers of fine chocolate. Indeed the spiritual home of chocolatiers throughout France and around the world must be La Maison du Chocolat at 225 rue Faubourg Saint Honoré. Owner Robert Linxe speaks of chocolate in the loving, poetic manner you would like to imagine all artisan food producers use (they don't). This, combined with his expertise and constant dedication to developing the art of fine chocolate in France has made him the most admired chocolatier in the world, the master with whom most beginning chocolate makers would like to train.

La Maison du Chocolat began in 1977, although Linxe has been working as a pâtissier chocolatier since the apprenticeship he began in 1949 at the age of 18. The business now has several outlets but it is the flagship store opposite the concert hall Les Salles Pleyelle which has proven the inspiration for many of his musically named products. Production has been moved to premises on the outskirts of Paris and Linxe now employs 18 staff members, including ten fulltime chocolatiers.

Specialities of La Maison du Chocolat include Rigoletto, a silky caramelized butter enrobed in milk chocolate that explodes on the taste buds "like the heroes of Rigoletto," says Linxe. Garrigue is a fennel-flavored ganache enrobed in dark chocolate, Othello a chocolate ganache perfumed with mountain honey and enrobed in dark chocolate, Yoko a tea-perfumed ganache with a

smoky taste. Andalousi is named after the country where lemon is king: the ganache is infused with fresh lemons and contains three different grand crus of cocoa. Bacchus contains rum-flambéed raisins in dark chocolate and Liselotte is described as a harmony of high-quality chopped praline with milk chocolate - "Think of Clair de la Lune by Werther de Massenet," says Linxe.

Michel Chaudun, once a student of Robert Linxe and also trained in Switzerland, has been making chocolate for 30 years. His store (149 rue de l'Université) is the place to go for chocolate sculptures, the most famous of which is probably the prize-winning replica of Tutankhamen he constructed in 1965.

The work of Christian Constant (26 rue du Bac) is particularly interesting, and more so given that he has been officially recognized as the best traiteur in France and has opened a restaurant. He is typical of modern French chocolatiers in that he works with teas and spices but it is his use of flower oils (ylang ylang, rose, Yemeni jasmine and orange blossom among them) that have won him acclaim. Look also for Constant's range of haute couture Easter eggs, made in collaboration with some of France's leading fashion designers. Should you become addicted, there's always the worldwide mail-order service.

In 1994 Jean-Paul Hévin (3 rue Vavin) was voted the second best chocolatier in France - after Robert Linxe - by the Guide Juillard des Croqueurs de Chocolat. Hévin has worked under chef Joël Rebouchon and specializes in

HOW DO YOU LIKE YOUR EGGS?

The roaring twenties, as we commonly call them, are known in France as *les annés folles*, the mad years. It was during this period that the brothers Melkoum and Moucheg Petrossian arrived in Paris, having decided, like other aristocrats, that revolutionary Russia was not the place to be. Perhaps it was the revolution however that made everything Russian fashionable in the French capital. The Petrossians decided to introduce caviar to Paris and immediately, France became the world's largest consumers of the prized sturgeon roe.

The French have a law stating that only roe from the sturgeon may be called caviar. Although France has its own sturgeon roe from the Gironde, French people want to believe caviar is a rare, expensive product imported from very far away. If you want to enjoy the real thing and all the luxury associated with it, Paris is where you must come.

Because of their connections back home, the Petrossians have enjoyed a privileged business relationship with Russia for the last 70 years and were the first to hand-pick caviar direct from the fisheries of the Caspian Sea. The Caspian is fished twice a year, in March and October, and it is the roe acquired during the spring season that is thought to provide the fresher, cleaner taste.

The largest sturgeon, which take 18 to 20 years to mature, weigh 1800 lb. and grow up to 20 ft. long, and there are only three breeds of sturgeon from the Caspian known for their fine caviar: beluga, osetra and sevruga.

Sevruga, with its light to dark gray eggs, is the strongest caviar, more intense in flavor than the others but nevertheless considered delicate. Osetra has golden brown eggs and a fruitier, nuttier flavor. The eggs of beluga, probably the most famous, are the largest, but they are also the most fragile. It is the fragility of caviar, its rarity and the difficulties associated with its storage and transport, that make it so expensive.

Of course you want to enjoy the real thing at its freshest, so purchase from a reputable dealer who is knowledgeable, such as Petrossian or Caviar Kaspa (17 place de la Madeleine), which also has a caviar restaurant on the premises.

It is best to purchase caviar in closed tins of a size you will finish in one sitting. Unopened, it will stay fresh for up to four weeks but once it's open, you'll have to finish it - as if you wouldn't want to!

Keep fresh caviar in the refrigerator until serving and when that happy moment arrives, first, smell the eggs. They should remind you of the sea, salt and sweetness. Salt preserves the caviar and helps release its flavor however the roe should never taste too salty. Nor should it be tough or hard, which is a sign that the eggs may have been pasteurized.

Using a spoon made from mother of pearl, ivory or gold (silver taints the flavor) take a small portion and press the grains against the roof of your mouth - their flavor will burst across your taste buds. Feeling naughty? You're getting 30 percent pure protein and a gobful of vitamins A, B, C and D, we'll just ignore the cholesterol content.

The proper accompaniment to first-grade caviar is vodka or champagne. Forget lemon, forget chopped eggs, forget sour cream and in particular, don't even think of onion.

---

delicately flavored dark chocolates.

La Fontaine au Chocolat is famed for precisely that - a chocolate fountain in the store at 101 rue Saint Honoré. The company, whose internationally available and respected brand is Michel Cluizel, is family-run and still makes its own chocolate from scratch. This is a small industrial-scale business but not the worse because of it, although whether or not you enjoy or find indelicate their highly roasted, 99 percent cocoa bean chocolate bar is a matter of personal taste. If you want to acquire the French habit of eating chocolate with a piece of dry bread, this is probably the one with which to try it. Also look out for Fouquet, a fourth-generation family business with two outlets in the 9e and 8e. This company imports its own cocoa beans directly from Venezuela.

LOCAL PRODUCE

Parisian markets are great places to buy regional produce at low prices, or simply to observe the colorful merchants as they banter with customers. There are over 58 open air markets in Paris, 12 covered markets and an increasing number of organic markets. In addition, Paris has market streets and these retain a provincial air. In the arrondissements guide, I've indicated some of the markets, but below is a check list for the market lover in a hurry.

2e ARRONDISSEMENT
• Rue Montorgueil (market street), between Rue Réamur and Rue de Turbigo. Bustling street in the heart of Paris full of quality produce. Chefs from top Parisian restaurants shop here. Plenty of cafés for a pick-me-up coffee or beer.

3e ARRONDISSEMENT
• Rue de Bretagne (market street) Wander through the Marais to this lively street. Although there is a considerable flow of traffic, it manages to retain a village atmosphere. Small shopkeepers line either side of the street. Good fromageries, fruits and vegetables and bakeries.

5e ARRONDISSEMENT
• Maubert (uncovered), place Maubert, open 7AM to 2:30PM Tuesday, Thursday and Saturday. Busy market with friendly merchants. Enter into the spirit and if you're stuck for recipe ideas, they will willingly give you some tips.
• Monge (uncovered), place Monge, open 7AM to 2:30PM Wednesday, Friday and Sunday. Small market with high-quality produce, especially bread.

• Port-Royal (uncovered), bd Port-Royal beside the Val-de-Grâce hospital, open 7AM to 1:30PM Tuesday, Thursday and Saturday.
• Rue Mouffetard (market street) Rue Mouffetard takes on a country feel as it descends towards the church St Médard. In contrast to the pushy restaurateurs at the upper end, the mood here may make you feel more inclined to buy.

6e ARRONDISSEMENT
• Saint-Germain (covered), between rues Lobineau, Clement and Mabillon, open 8AM to 1PM and 4 to 7:30PM, Sundays 8AM to 1:15PM. Built during Napoléon's reign. Pristine market selling good fish and meat as well as Vietnamese and Greek products.
• Raspail (uncovered), bd Raspail, between rues du Cherche-Midi and de Rennes, open 7AM to 2:30PM Tuesday and Friday. Locals are impressed with the standard of meat and fish. There is an organic market in this area on Sunday morning.

7e ARRONDISSEMENT
• Saxe-Breteuil (uncovered), place Breteuil, where ave de Saxe meets ave de Ségur, open 7AM to 2:30PM Thursday and Saturday. Colorful and uncluttered market. Plenty of ripe fruits and vegetables attractively displayed alongside blocks of roquefort and St Nectaire.
• Rue Cler (market street) Comparatively sedate market street in Paris's most expensive residential arrondissement. Good poultry and game at number 36.

8e ARRONDISSEMENT
• Europe (covered), rue Corvetto, between rues de Maleville and Treilhard, open 8AM to 1:30PM and 4 to 7PM, Sundays 8AM to 1PM.

9e ARRONDISSEMENT
• Rue des Martyrs (market street) Steep street climbing from Notre Dame de Lorette towards Montmartre. Relaxed atmosphere during the week, hectic on Saturday and Sunday morning. Don't miss the charcuterie Chez Terrier at number 58.
• Rue Cadet (market street) Animated small street with plenty of delights to choose from. Mediterranean fishmonger sells swordfish and mullet, while the charcuterie at number 18 cures its own hams.

10e ARRONDISSEMENT
• Porte St-Martin (covered), 31 and 33 rue du Château d'Eau, open Tuesday to Saturday 8:30AM to 1PM and 3:30PM to 7:30PM, Sundays 8:30AM to 1PM. Four of the original 1879 doorways were retained when this market was reconstructed in 1979. Good balance of produce, fish, meat, dairy, Italian, oriental and organic.
• St-Quentin (covered), 85 onwards on bd Magenta, open 8AM to 1PM and 3:30PM to 7:30PM, Sundays 8AM to 1PM. Exhilarating atmosphere at this large market comprising over 40 merchants offering a diversity of produce.
• Alibert (uncovered), rue Alibert to rue Claude Vellefaux, open 7AM to 2:30PM Thursday and Sunday.

11e ARRONDISSEMENT
• Bastille (uncovered), bd Richard Lenoir, from rue Amelot to rue Saint-Sabin, Tuesday and Sunday 7AM to 2:30PM.

LOCAL PRODUCE

This market stretches nearly the full length of the boulevard. Marvelous vegetables, regional charcuterie plus a variety of international produce.

12e ARRONDISSEMENT
- Beauvau (covered), pl d'Aligre, Tuesday to Thursday 8AM to 1PM and 4PM to 7:30PM, Friday and Saturday 8AM to 1PM and 4PM to 8PM, Sunday 8AM to 1:15PM. 18th-century market retaining many features including a drinking trough transformed into a fountain. Witty merchants attract the trendy Bastille clientèle.

13e ARRONDISSEMENT
- Auguste Blanqui (formerly Gobelins) (uncovered), bd Auguste Blanqui, between rue Barrault and pl d'Italie, open Tuesday, Friday and Sunday 7AM to 2:30PM. Cheerful merchants and colorful stalls make this market well worth visiting.

14e ARRONDISSEMENT
- Rue Daguerre (market street) Lively market street near the Montparnasse cemetery. Pleasant Saturday afternoon shopping. Excellent fishmongers include Daguerre Marée at number 9. There's recommended *andouillette* in the terraced café opposite.

15e ARRONDISSEMENT
- Rue du Commerce (market street) A hive of activity in the evenings and at the weekend. A good Monoprix supermarket is nearby.
- Grenelle (uncovered), bd Grenelle, between rue Lourmel and rue du Commerce, Wednesday and Sunday, 7AM to 2:30PM. Especially good on Sunday morning. Towards the Metro Dupleix there is a poultry man who sells exquisite chicken wings.

16e ARRONDISSEMENT
- Passy (covered), rue Bois le Vent, Tuesday to Saturday 7:30AM to 1PM and 4PM to 7PM, Sunday 7:30AM to 1PM. Here the fish is reputed to be the best in Paris and there is an astounding selection of Italian specialities.

17e ARRONDISSEMENT
- Batignolles (covered), 96 bis rue Lemercier, Tuesday to Saturday 8AM to 12:30PM and 4PM to 7:30PM, Sunday 8AM to 12:45PM. The largest covered market offers a wide variety of produce. The cheerful merchants chat away for hours with customers. A ritual for the locals.
- Batignolles organic market (market street), on the boulevard between rue des Batignolles and rue Puteaux, Saturday 7AM to 2:30PM. Good dairy products plus an impressive selection of tarts and other prepared dishes.

18e ARRONDISSEMENT
- La Chapelle (covered), rue de l'Olive, open Tuesday to Saturday 8AM to 1PM and 4PM to 7:30PM, Sundays 8AM to 1PM. Built in 1858, this market has remained intact and is a listed building. Some stalls have been there for more than three generations.
- Ornano (uncovered), bd Ornano between rues Mont-Cenis and Ordener, open 7AM to 2:30PM Tuesday, Friday and Sunday.
- Crimée (uncovered), 4 to 30 bd Ney, open 7AM to 2:30PM Wednesday and Saturday.
- Barbès (uncovered), contre-allé of bd de la Chapelle, opposite Lariboisière Hospital, open 7AM to 2:30PM Wednesday and Saturday.
- Ney (uncovered), bd Ney between rues Jean-Varenne and Camille-Flammarion, open 7AM to 2:30PM Thursday and Sunday.
- Ordener (uncovered), rue Ordener between rues Montcals and Championnet, open 7AM to 2:30PM Wednesday and Saturday.
- Rue du Poteau (market street) A taste of old Paris. Take a couple of hours to wander along the narrow streets around rue du Poteau and find some of the best bread and cheese in Paris.

19e ARRONDISSEMENT
- Riquet (covered), 36-46 rue Riquet, open Tuesday to Friday 8:30AM to 12:30PM and 4PM to 7:30PM, Saturday 8:30AM to 1PM and 4PM to 7:30PM, Sunday 8:30AM to 1PM. The most recent of the covered markets with merchants meticulously setting up their stalls on market days. Sweet smelling fruits and vegetables fill the air of this "new look" market. Foreign specialities are from Greece, Italy and Asia.

20e ARRONDISSEMENT
- Telegraphe (uncovered), to the right of Belleville cemetery, Wednesday and Saturday 7AM to 2:30PM. Small market in which you won't find many tourists but there will be plenty of good regional produce.

RUNGIS AND THE MARKETS OF PARIS

The transferral of the Parisian wholesale food market, Les Halles, from central Paris to Rungis, just beside Orly airport, was as devastating to Parisians as losing a vital organ: Les Halles was the stomach of Paris and for a while there was a feeling of starvation, or at the very least, unfamiliar gnawing hunger pains. But the new freedom of movement in the ancient central streets, the creative developments above and below ground, and the obvious success Rungis has made in maintaining traditional choice and freshness of produce has finally won the hearts and stomachs of the suspicious Parisians.

For the visitor, however, it means the demise of one of the great Parisian experiences: you can no longer share onion soup early in the morning with men who have already done a hard day's work (probably unloading the onions). Rungis is one of the largest wholesale markets in the world and does not have much time for the casual rubber-necker; you might find that you are only seeing rather more of what is everyday in the street markets of Paris.

In central Paris alone there are over 80 markets, covered and uncovered, for you to find and enjoy. Some 70 of these are food markets (*marchés alimentaires*). Some are permanent, some are peripatetic, but you'll most enjoy those stumbled upon serendipitously. If you are a marketomane, contact the Mairie de Paris (tel: 276 49 61) for their special free leaflet *Les Marchés de Paris*. Even with the leaflet, it is better to check with your hotel first.

It is not all food either. Don't forget the flower market on the Île-de-la-Cité or the fabulous flea market (*marché aux puces*) at Clignancourt, still with sensational treasures and junk and some delicious steamy bistros and restaurants where you can listen to a Piaf imitator as you eat your *moules* (mussels).

BRASSERIES

Brasseries are loud, colorful places, ideal for an evening in the company of friends, an after-theater meal or a business lunch. The food is nourishing, although not of a particularly high standard, prices are low and the ambience convivial.

• *Le Vaudeville, 29 rue Vivienne, 75002*
Beautiful 1920s interior. Cheerful waiters glide across the main dining room with platters of shellfish and choucroute. Reserve a table on the terrace on a warm day.

• *Chez Jenny, 29 Boulevard du Temple, 75003*
Huge 1930s Alsatian brasserie where waitresses in traditional costume serve steaming plates of choucroute, plump sausages, bratwurst and jugs of Riesling. Try the kugelhopf (Alsatian cake with almonds and raisins), that is, if you still have room. Menus in French, English and German. Expect to pay between 100F–160F per person.

• *Bofinger, 5 rue de la Bastille, 75004*
Paris's oldest and most glamorous brasserie. Try to reserve a table under the magnificent belle-époque dome. Traditional choucroute, lamb cassoulet and seafood platters are among the better choices. Draught beer and pitchers of wine are good accompaniments.

• *Île-Saint-Louis, 31 rue Saint-Louis en île, 75004*
With a view of Notre Dame, this is a favorite weekend gathering place for Parisians and tourists alike. Hearty Alsatian specialties at low prices.

• *Ma Bourgogne, 19 place des Vosges, 75004*
This brasserie is located under the arches of the oldest square in Paris. Absorb the architectural beauty from the terrace, or enjoy an evening meal or an afternoon hot chocolate in the cosy interior.

• *Balzar, 49 rue des Ecoles, 75005*
This Latin Quarter mini-brasserie serves traditional dishes such as choucroute, steak tartare and.

grilled meats throughout the day. Lively atmosphere and quick service.

• *Lutetia, 21 rue de Sèvres, 75006*
Mix with the Parisian in-crowd at this chic brasserie. Good value lunch menu at 95F.

• *Lipp, 151 Boulevard St Germain, 75006*
This is known as Paris's literary brasserie. Writers, poets and artists used to spend hours on end here. Keep one eye peeled for celebrities. Go for the atmosphere, as the food is nothing special.

• *Le Boeuf sur le Toît, 34 rue Colisée, 75008*
For an authentic Parisian atmosphere, this is a wonderful place to visit. Try the warm foie gras with apple. If you come after 10PM, there is a set price menu at 112F, "Faim de Nuit."

• *Flo, 7 cour des Petites Ecuries, 75010*
This is the original Flo brasserie built in the 1900s. Don't be discouraged by the perpetual line in the evenings - it moves quickly and once you're installed, you won't regret it. Foie gras, choucroute and shellfish are among the specialties.

• *Julien, 16 rue du Faubourg Saint-Denis, 75010*
It is rather surprising to find this elegant brasserie in a rundown district, but Julien oozes charm and beauty with its large, bright 1890s dining hall, art nouveau mirrors and murals. Try the crêpes flambés au Grand Marnier.

• *Terminus Nord, 23 rue de Dunkerque, 75010*
1925 brasserie beside the Gare du Nord (Eurostar terminus). Oysters and other shellfish are displayed out front to entice you inside.

• *La Coupole, 102 Boulevard du Montparnasse, 75014*
An essential Parisian experience. This listed building offers quality brasserie food at average prices and the opportunity to soak up a 1930s atmosphere. Traditional brasserie fare such as oysters and curry d'agneau.

DEPARTMENT STORES: LES GRANDS MAGASINS

It's tons of fun to find specialty shops and to see and taste new things, but unless you go to something more ordinary as well, you've not actually been to France and you remain a tourist - what's worse, a tourist with airs. Markets are a start and a very good one, but they aren't always in the next street and even if they are, you may have hit the wrong day or time. What do you do? Make sure you know where the department and chain stores are.

France's provincial towns have kept their department stores, deliciously fading though some of them are. A quick swing through their food departments shows what people like to cook, eat and drink locally, the china, glass and cookware show how fashion-conscious they are, and the clothes and furniture indicate the inroads designers have or have not made.

More universal, and most definitely not to be missed, are the self-service chains of Prisunic and Monoprix (self-service or *libre-service*). They sell marvelous plates, cups, glassware, Provençal pottery, super French crystal and kitchen gadgets at ridiculously low prices - important to remember if you are unable to raid a hypermarket. Most have excellent food departments if you are self-catering or simply want something to munch on your way past. Good for basics to bring home, too - jam, coffee, oils, etc.

Most visitors go to Galeries Lafayette and Au Printemps and think they've done the department stores. No, they haven't. Monoprix and Prisunic are all over Paris and they really are worth making time for. Here are some others worth tracking down:
• Bazar de l'Hôtel de Ville, 55 rue de la Verrerie 4e
Quincaillerie is probably my favorite French word. It means hardware and ironmongery and BHV is renowned for the most complete range possible. Good book section and kitchen goodies too. There is another big branch at 119 rue de Flandre 19e.
• Au Bon Marché, 38 rue de Sèvres 7e
Two great buildings divided by the rue du Bac and called the *doyen de nos grands magasins* by Gault Millau. A specially good food department on the ground floor of Magasin 2.
• Galeries Lafayette, 48 bd Haussmann 9e (main shop) and Tour Montparnasse, 17 rue de l'Arrivée 15e
Important and influential for fashion and style - in everything.
• Au Printemps, bd Haussmann 9e (main store), other branches at République, 63 rue de Malte 11e; Nation, 21 cours de Vincennes 12 e; Italie Centre Commercial Galaxie, pl d'Italie 13 e; Ternes, 30 ave des Ternes 17e.

The Ternes store is one of the most interesting - it has an excellent food department but behind and beside it is one of the best permanent food markets in Paris and ave des Ternes has outstanding branches of the chain stores, bars, cafés, restaurants, traiteurs and charcuteries of note.
• La Samaritaine, rue du Pont-Neuf 1er
Two huge buildings with some amazing internal architecture that whisks you back to the days when nice men wrapped parcels with brown paper and string that came never-endingly from hidden spools. You can buy everything, living or dead, and there are amazing views of Paris from the 10th floor of Magasin 2, but the terrace there is closed from October to March. It's especially exciting when they have their sales, but I'm mad about it any time.
• Aux Trois Quartiers, 17 bd de la Madeleine, 1er
As its position might lead you to expect, very traditional and classic in atmosphere, especially in its twinset and tweed clothes. It feels somewhere between London's Harvey Nichols and Harrod's, and has a nice tea salon on the 4th floor where you can lunch lightly and, usually, elegantly.

Arrondissements 1, 2 & 3

In the vicinity of the Tuileries, Louvre and Palais-Royal, Comédie-Française, Les Halles, Bibliothèque Nationale, Bourse, Archives Nationales and Temple.

It's too easy to saunter through the Tuileries, gasp at the Impressionists in the Jeu de Paume, hit the high points of the Louvre and then head back to the place de la Madeleine - so I've started you at the other end of these arrondissements. As you explore the culinary attractions, you'll find the cultural and civic sites listed above in somewhat reverse order. When you finish though, you'll have seen some of the crustier side of Paris, perhaps explored a food market or two and found where Les Halles used to be and, I hope, be more in a frame of mind to view the Louvre and Palais-Royal as grand but living houses rather than just museum buildings. You'll enjoy what they have to show much more; the Musée des Arts Décoratifs, entered from the rue de Rivoli, is a stunning collection of authentic rooms from every period of French domesticity, grand and otherwise.

This part of the route starts at the upper eastern corner of the 3e arrondissement (métro Temple or République). Much of it is through areas which are not at all grand, but in which old Paris is still visible.

- **Brocco, 180 rue du Temple**
Pâtisserie and tea salon. Amazing art deco temple, marble walls, high painted ceiling, with a superb façade showing excellent cakes and pastries including charlotte aux poires and tartes aux framboises. Go for the decor and be doubly pleased that the goodies are good too.
- **Souche Laparra, 157 rue de Temple**
Cutlery very good value and craftsmanship in silver and silver plate of all styles.
- **Comptoir du Chocolat et des Alcools (CCA), 108 rue de Turene**
Alcohols and chocolates. Dark, forbidding shop with old fashioned displays and surly sales people. Excellent prices for quality wines and fine chocolates compensate. There is a minimum purchase required.
- **Confroy, 34 rue Saintonge**
Bakery. Wholewheat baguettes and every other grain-bread baked in a wood-fired oven. Modest assortment of pastries including almond tartelettes and prune

turnovers. Nicely restored interior. Highly recommended for quality.
- **Cannelle, 10 rue de Bretagne**
Natural products, interesting artisan soaps, oils and herbs, also biscuits. Extravagant display window.
- **Bassaguet Morin, Charcuterie Fine, 17 rue de Bretagne**
Prepared food. Small square room filled with delicious things, such as egg in smoked salmon aspic, pork in aspic, cooked meats, well-prepared salads.
- **J. Durand, 25 rue de Bretagne**
Pastry and ice cream. Strawberry tarts overflowing with fruit, beautifully decorated coffee & walnut cake, boxes of sweets and miniature cream puffs. Enormous weekend lines.
- **Cours des Halles, 29 rue de Bretagne**
Fresh produce. Lovely fruit attractively presented.
- **Marché des Enfants Rouges, 39 rue de Bretagne**
Small covered market of around 30 stalls including fish mongers, butchers and fruit and vegetable stalls. The fish mongers sell salt cod, spider crabs, tiny live crabs and smoked fish kebabs. The coffee shop Le Café Torrefié at 35 rue Charlot in the market roasts on the premises. Teas also.
- **Caves de Betagne, 40 rue de Bretagne**
Opposite the market entrance. Beers, cidre bouché, wines and spirits from all over France. Fauchon luxury tinned and bottled goodies. Good range of Champagnes and Calvados as well. Friendly.

If you turn up rue Picardie or the streets either side of Mairie, you will find the covered Marché du Temple.

- **L'Oustal, 68 rue des Gravilliers**
Prepared foods and regional products from the Auvergne and the Rouergue. A tiny shop with specialities produced on farms including confit de canard, marrons glacés, sausages, homemade brioche with candied fruit. Whole cured hams hang from the ceiling.

- **Ambassade d'Auvergne, 22 rue du Grenier-St-Lazare**
Restaurant, rustic and warm with exposed beams and consistently good regional food. Start with cabbage and bacon salad, then try one of the daily specials like duck stew or cassoulet with lentils accompanied by wine from the area, perhaps a St-Pourçain.

- **Durand, 147 rue St-Martin**
Grocery, worth a detour for the belle-époque decor. The front window is framed by a milkmaid painted on tiles and the interior is colorfully tiled as well, with marble work surfaces. Stocks essentials like eggs, tea, jam and also goat cheese and walnut bread from Poilâne.

- **Duthilleul & Minart, 14 rue de Turbigo**
Professional clothing. Uniforms for butchers, bakers, chefs and waiters. Excellent source for aprons and dishtowels and some of the natural-fiber garments can be quite chic out of their normal context.

- **Central Union, 28 rue de la Grande-Truanderie**
Gifts. Super-creative modern kitsch objects that look like something else, but enormous good humor and French style.

- **Jounna, 45 rue Montorgueil**
Butcher. Narrow shop with high marble altar in the front displaying meat on one side and poultry on the other.

- **Le Founil de Pierre, 49 rue Montorgueil**
Wide range of breads.

- **Stohrer, 51 rue Montorgueil**
Pastry and chocolate. Stand opposite to appreciate the building: business began in 1730. Tall display cases packed high with bonbons and pastries. The Ali-Babas are a house speciality, as are buttery pains au chocolat and sparkling strawberry tarts. Delightful original decor with Louis XV-era ladies cavorting on the walls and ceiling.

- **Rue Montorgueil Market, 80 onwards rue Montorgueil**
Gutsy, noisy and sometimes bloody remnant of the days when Les Halles was just across the street. Americans living in Paris tend to be sniffy about it, but they usually can afford to shop at Fauchon or the markets of the Left Bank. Visitors may be astonished at the butchers, for instance, but they should be entranced, knowing that here, along with rue de Montmartre, they will be more in touch with Paris than the Beaubourg center, slick (and virtually uncleanable) though it is. Chefs from some fairly smart restaurants shop here daily, so it's good enough for me.

- **Aux Vrais Produits d'Auvergne, 98 rue Montorgueil**
Regional products from Auvergne including ham, sausages and farm cheese. The place for a terrific cantal, laguiole or, midweek, fresh Auvergnat cheeses. Extraordinary charcuterie from exotic pieces of the pig.

- **René Collet, 100 rue Montorgueil**
Bakery and pastry shop with huge croissants, pretty apricot and strawberry tarts. The small square pound cake, le Weekend, is a speciality.

- **Detou, 58 rue Tiquetonne**
Speciality ingredients. Important shop for pâtisserie ingredients packaged in bulk including chocolate, flour, candied violets, bags of salted nuts, boxes of cookies. Also sells smoked salmon roe and pickled herring along with a good selection of wine and champagne. Good prices.

- **La Bovida, 36 rue Montmartre**
Restaurant supplies. Spices in bulk, aluminum molds in many shapes and sizes, dishes, glassware and cooking vessels.

- **Breizh da Guenta, 34 rue Montmartre**
Cider specialists with a range of snacks.

- **A Simon, 21 rue Montmartre**
Restaurant supplies including wine glasses by the dozen, huge lucite salad bowls, stainless steel or silver-plated cutlery, china in myriad patterns, all restaurant quality at wholesale prices. You must buy in quantity. Also further down the road, on the corner.

- **Foie Gras Luxe, 26 rue Montmartre**
Commercial prepared foods. Raw foie gras or a mixture of duck and goose livers. Known also for prosciutto, Bayonne ham, rillettes, Ardennes smoked ham and inexpensive choucroute.

- **MORA, 13 rue Montmartre**
Restaurant supply store since 1814. Portable ovens and professional-size food processors. A fantastic range of molds and cake pans and almost everything else, including books and video tapes of cooking demos.

- **Marguerite Dorlin, 11 rue Montmartre**
Fish market. Large shop, good quality and an interesting assortment of fish including skate cheeks and baby salmon.

Labeyrie, 8 rue Montmartre
Speciality foods including foie gras raw, mi-cuit or conserves and mushrooms and truffles under the distinctive red, gold and black label. The deluxe tinned foods are not as good as expected.

• **Le Pavillon Baltard, 9 rue Coquellière**
Alsatian restaurant with numerous varieties of choucroute, although it is most famous for its fish version.

• **Alsace aux Halles, 16 rue Coquillière**
Alsatian restaurant. Oysters and choucroute in a quaint-looking half-timbered place. The proliferation of restaurants in Les Halles dates from the era of the old market.

• **Dehillerin, 18-20 rue Coquillière**
Cookware and kitchen equipment heaven. A huge selection of everything - individual tart molds in every size, every conceivable shape and design of dessert molds, copper bowls and balloon whisks. Go early in the day if you want a civil reception and don't expect advice.

• **Boucherie Coquillière, 32 rue Coquillière**
Butcher with meat neatly presented and a chance to compare Charollais beef with Angus from Britain.

• **Tchin-Tchin, 32 rue Coquillière**
Traiteur Chinois. Takeout food including hot spring rolls. Smells so good you can't walk past.

• **Emilio Robba La Maison, 20 rue Hérold**
Modern furniture and housewares. Stunning gold furniture. Lucky you, if you can afford it.

• **Au Panetier, 10 pl des Petits Pères**
Lovely old bakery with ceramic murals on parrot theme. Strawberry tartlets

and onion turnovers, wood-oven bread including poppy seed and pepper.

• **Lucien Legrand, 1 rue de la Banque**
Wine specialists where the decor hasn't changed for two generations. Excellent selection of inexpensive regional wines plus spirits, port, etc. of great age. Confectionery and spices too.

Detour into the covered shopping area Galerie Vivienne (one entrance is up rue de Banque past Lucien Legrand) to step back into another time.

• **Willi's Wine Bar, 13 rue des Petits-Champs**
Restaurant and wine bar offering light meals, salads, hot daily specials with an unmatched selection of Côtes-du-Rhône. Cheerful, chic and sometimes snobby in spite of (or perhaps because of) the English owner. At least the staff speak your language. There is another branch at 18 rue des Halles.

• **Tachon, 38 rue de Richelieu**
Cheese shop. Unprepossessing established specialists with unusual and fine farmhouse cheese. Labels give fascinating information. The époisses is particularly good here. Nearby neighborhood specialty shops and fruit and vegetable stands make this detour most enjoyable.

• **Chez Pauline, 5 rue Villédo**
Restaurant with absolutely classic French food, including regional and seasonal favorites in a setting that is almost a cliché of what you expect a bistro to be. Tons of fun.

• **Jean Gabart, 14 rue de la Michodière**
Bakery with whimsically shaped loaves in display cases flanking the door. Individual lemon curd tarts and huge fluffy meringues in the window. Sandwiches and a

few essential groceries like eggs and milk.

• **La Tour de Jade, 20 rue de la Michodière**
One of the best Chinese-Vietnamese restaurants in one of Paris's oldest buildings. Economical set menu, large selection à la carte, first-class takeout too.

• **Paul Corcellet, 46 rue des Petits-Champs**
Condiments, exotic food. Always something new at this shop. Wondrous jams, including green tomato, fruit vinegars, flavored mustards, unusual rums and liqueurs, house wines and champagnes. I defy you to walk out empty handed.

• **Coin Cuisine, 5 rue Danielle-Casanova**
Cheap housewares, novelty bottles of martini, aprons and enameled cookware.

• **Giorgio Lapri, 6 rue Danielle-Casanova**
Italian cuisine.

• **Cacao & Chocolat, 13 rue Danielle-Casanova**
Hessian-walled chocolate temple, pâtisserie, chocolate wafers, bonbons and chocolate drinks.

• **Flo Prestige, 42 pl du Marché St-Honoré**
Prepared foods. Imaginative and tasty dishes of class, for which you may pay accordingly. Also offers pastry, ice cream and wine. Associated with Brasserie Flo, one of the best and most authentic in Paris.

• **Le Central St-Honoré**
Restaurant, 12 pl du Marché St-Honoré
Traditional dishes including moules (mussels), steak tartare, and chèvre chaud roti aux noisettes.

• **Chèdeville, rue du 18 Marché St-Honoré**
Commercial butcher and charcuterie. Substantial choucroute and hearty potato salads, Corsican sausages and

recommended andouillettes. *They supply well-known restaurants.*

• **Max Poilâne, 42 rue du Marché St-Honoré**
Fabulous pâtisserie and solid breads.

• **Le Rubis, 10 rue du Marché St-Honoré**
The local bar for this neighborhood has been invaded by the young, smart set. Simple meals of tripe, sausages, blood pudding, etc. Sandwiches and snacks anytime. An interesting wine selection.

• **Au Jardin d'Espagne, 8 rue du Marché St-Honoré**
Large fruit and veg shop, attractively arranged.

• **Au Ducs de Bourgogne, 4 rue du Marché St-Honoré**
Burgundian products including smoked duck breast, andouillette, croustades, regional wines and liqueurs.

• **Jean Danflou, 36 rue du Mont-Thabor**
Unique alcohols and equally hard-to-find premises - at the left rear corner of the courtyard, go up to the first floor and ring the bell. There's a small tasting room to try the full range of eaux-de-vie, marcs and cognacs of great distinction. No obligation or pressure to buy, but you will.

• **Le Soufflé, 36 rue du Mont-Thabor**
A restaurant that's a bit touristy, but isn't that what you are? The soufflés are very good, which is the important thing.

• **WH Smith and Son, 248 rue de Rivoli**
A bookshop but not like the one on your high street. There's a food book section with menu dictionaries and guides to French regional food among the cookbooks. Extensive array of guidebooks too.

While in the rue de Rivoli, find time to explore the marvelous department stores: La Samaritaine, between rue de l'Arbre and rue de la Monnaie, Magasins du Louvre on the pl du Palais Royal and La Belle Jardinière between rue du Pont Neuf and rue des Bourdonnais.

• **Godiva, 237 rue St-Honoré**
Belgian chocolates. A treasure cave of foil-wrapped bonbons twinkle under crystal chandeliers in large glass display cases. Expensive but appreciated.

• **Aux Beaux Fruits de France, 304 rue St-Honoré**
Neat, orderly, artful displays of perfect fruit and vegetables.

• **La Fontaine au Chocolat, 201 and 101 rue St-Honoré**
Michel Cluizel chocolate, lovely packs of bonbons, loose chocolates and carraques. See page 78.

• **Gargantua, 284 rue St-Honoré**
Known for giant croissants and pastries, enormous array of prepared salads, roasts, desserts, good charcuterie and a few tables for a quick meal.

• **Verlet, 256 rue St-Honoré**
Coffee and tea salon. A mecca for serious lovers of tea or coffee, for here you can buy the lot. Tea or coffee will also be blended to your taste and you can get a light meal. A goodie for the enthusiast and stimulating for the amateur.

• **Delamain, 155 rue St-Honoré**
Wonderful old bookshop that moved here from the Palais Royal in 1990. Pretty glass canopy over the door and a small selection of French cook books among the treasures.

• **Louvre des Antiquaires, pl du Palais-Royal**
Antiques market with a well-organized, self-administered alliance of about 250 reputable antique dealers displaying their treasures in a renovated former storage hall of the Louvre. Of particular culinary interest is l'Herminette - tureens and terrines, tools and scales, on the ground floor. Other shops offer Moustiers and Quimper pottery, Rose Medallion porcelain, pewter plates and steins, crystal and silver decanters, antique silver cutlery and beautiful old wooden platters, bowls and implements. Not cheap but convenient, and warmer than the flea markets in winter!

• **Maison Micro, 144 rue St-Honoré**
Greek products and ingredients, drums of olives and capers, sacks of lentils, pistachios, chickpeas, olive oil, Greek wine.

• **Ragueneau, 202 rue St-Honoré**
Pâtisserie, traiteur and salon de thé. Sit under the red umbrellas to relax and imbibe.

• **Pepeterie Moderne, 12 rue de la Ferronerie**
Marvelous sign shop and great place for stationery freaks. Crammed with all sorts of signs that are part of Parisian daily life - butcher's tickets, cheese tickets with names of common cheeses, innumerable others including WC "mixte" and the perennial chien méchant (beware of the dog). Great souvenirs.

• **Forum des Halles, rue Ste-Opportune**
Shopping center that is cavernous and variable but worth an expedition, particularly to see the museum shop, which boasts a collection of the most fashionable and classic modern homewares at various price points.

Arrondissements 4 & 5

In the vicinity of the Pompidou Center, Marais, Hôtel de Ville, Tour St-Jacques, the Jewish Quarter, Place des Vosges, Bastille, Notre Dame, Île-de-la-Cité, Île-St-Louis, the Quais, the Latin Quarter, Sorbonne, Polytechnique, Musée de Cluny, Musée National d'Histoire Naturelle and the Panthéon.

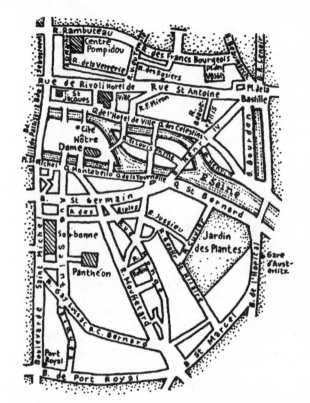

All seafood lovers should touch their cap at the Tour St-Jacques, in the place St-Jacques on the border with the 1e arrondissement. This was the gathering point for the tens of thousands of pilgrims who annually walked in penance wearing scallop shells to the shrine of St James at Santiago de Compostela in Spain, for whom the first travel guide was written and for whom coquilles St-Jacques were considered cheap and easy nourishment.

Domestically, these two arrondissements include the single-but-special-friends households of the fast-refurbishing Marais, the student hangouts of the Latin Quarter and the great silent town houses of Île-St-Louis and of the President himself. So the food available is particularly wide ranging. You can eat falafel in pita or corned beef and cheesecake, watch the breaking of the bread at Notre Dame, line up for the best ice cream of your life on rue St-Louis-en-Île, shop in expensive places for antiques or oils, dawdle down the slope of the rue Mouffetard market or find one of the best cookbook shops in France, which will send you regular newsletters on request.

• **Laurence Roque, 69 rue St-Martin**
Tableware and china, tablecloths, placemats and everything else in every imaginable color, design and cloth, or so it seems. Tea things and pine furniture confirm the British origin of lots of the wares.
• **Bazar de l'Hôtel de Ville, 55 rue de la Verrerie**
See Department Stores p. 83.
• **Lescene-Dura-Eurocave, 63 rue de la Verrerie**
Wine paraphernalia including grape presses, casks, corks, bottles, glasses, corkscrews, wine coolers and a wide range of wine racks. Also volcanic rock to balance the humidity if your cave is too damp.
• **A la Ville de Rodez, 22 rue Vieille-du-Temple**
Products from the Auvergne.

As well as the expected hams, fouace (sometimes with cédrat (citron) among its glacé fruits) and cantal cheese, here will be more homely things such as salaisons and andouillettes and other internal piggy bits.
• **Maison des Colonies, 47 rue Vieille-du-Temple**
Coffee merchant. A spacious shop with wooden floors and an excellent, inexpensive range of coffees from almost everywhere, plus blends. The teas are just as varied and include both classic mint, jasmine and rose plus modern mango, blackberry and the like. Honey, jam and biscuits to accompany. Building was once the home of the ambassadors from Holland.
Rue de Rosiers is the ancient center of Jewish life in

the Marais. The quarter is typically confusing, with wonderful buildings on winding streets. If touring is getting too much, head to number 27 or number 7 for sustenance, or to number 4 for no-nonsense relaxation.

• **Le Roi du Falafel, 34 rue des Rosiers**
Exotic grocery, a reminder that Jews have their roots in the Middle East. Olives, nuts and everything else from that part of the world. Try falafel, hot cakes of chick peas or beans in a pita bread with salad, almost the national dish of Israel.

• **Finkelsztajn, 27 rue des Rosiers**
Pastry shop specializing in central European goodies but with a Madagascan proprietor. Poppy-seed loaf, fruit-filled pavés, strudels. And have they got a cheesecake for you!

• **Jo Goldenberg, 7 rue des Rosiers**
Restaurant and delicatessen, a real Jewish community center and a lovely noisy place to go for Sunday lunch whatever your faith. Chopped liver, corned beef, cheesecake.

• **Hammam Saint Paul, 4 rue des Rosiers**
Nothing to do with food unless you have overeaten, but a wonderful old-fashioned steam bath and sauna with a restaurant overlooking the plunge pool. Men Thursdays and Saturdays, women Wednesdays and Fridays. Beauty treatments plus healthy food.

Now that you are here, you might like to detour to the rue de Sévigné and the Musée Carnavalet, 400 years of Parisian history in Madame de Sévigné's house. A little further up at 5 rue de Thorigny is the Hôtel Salé, home for Picasso's collection of Picassos. The hôtel was built by Monsieur Aubert with the proceeds of his salt tax collecting for Louis XIV, hence the name.

• **Autour du Monde, 8 rue des Francs-Bourgeois**
Interior-decorating shops laid out like a country house. Stripped furniture, cluttered dressers, neatly folded bed linen and low classical music create a cosy, rustic ambience. Smaller items include kitchen utensils, pottery, olive oil soap and flowerpots.

Good poking about too in some of the shops of the arcades of place des Vosges, built in the 17th century for Henri IV's royal spectacles and surrounded by magnificent town houses. Look for the trompe l'oeil brickwork.

• **Clichy, 5 bd Beaumarchais**
Tea salon, pâtisserie and chocolates with frescoed views of the Marais right beside the Bastille. Painted by Monsieur Bugat, who also gets praise for his croissants, pastries and his lavish chocolates and seasonal window displays.

• **Brasserie Bofinger, 5 rue de la Bastille**
The oldest and one of the most wonderful belle-époque restaurants in all Paris. Specializing in Alsatian food, like a brasserie should, but also outstanding seafood and good house wine. You can order until 1AM every morning. A favorite of Jean Cocteau.

• **Caves des Pyrénées, 25 rue Beautreillis**
Wide range of wines from all over France but particularly the lesser known ones from the southwest and Pyrénées, with such names as Tursan and Irouleguy.

• **Au Sanglier, 49 rue St-Antoine**
Charcuterie. There is a large wooden boar that sits on the street, so you'll know when you've arrived. This charcuterie has been owned by the same family for three generations. They sell regional produce: andouillette, boudin noir and blanc, Toulouse sausage. One of the specialties is quenelle de brochet maison (pike dumpling).

• **Les Fils Peuvrier, 43 rue St-Antoine**
Spotless white-tiled dairy shop selling cheese, butter, cream, crème fraîche and eggs. The chèvre are usually excellent. It has a slight atmosphere of yesteryear.

• **Caves St-Antoine, 95 rue St-Antoine**
Wines and spirits. A vast but cramped emporium specializing in clarets but with grand names from every region plus vin de pays bottled on the premises. Terrific selection of beers too.

Here you should cross the border into the 11e - actually you simply turn left out of rue St-Antoine into bd Richard Lenoir to the Marché de la Bastille, but only on Thursdays and Sunday mornings. It is a huge neighborhood market with over 150 stalls of noise and banter. Mainly fruit and vegetables but look for homemade cream cheeses that sit dripping in pottery molds, the mushroom stall that has just *girolles* and *petits rosés* in July but overflows with varieties in autumn, fish stalls and butchery and charcuterie sellers with sausages-galore from the regions. At the Bastille end, Arab traders predominate. If your French is good, look for A La Poule d'Or, where poultry is sold live. This stall sells over 15,000 eggs on Sunday as well as rabbits, quails, really good homemade pâtés, ducks, geese, all sold with humor and lots of advice. You'll really feel you are in France here.

• **Suba, 11 rue de Sévigné**
Hungarian charcuterie. The place to buy a supply of both hot and sweet paprikas, whole or ground, so you can make your own flavors. Hungarian wines, meats and sausages and unusual savory strudel rolls. Not open Sundays.

• **Confiserie Rivoli, 17 rue de Rivoli**
Sugared almonds of some variety and in many different packs, plus sweet regional specialties such as calissons d'Aix *to look at.*

• **A l'Olivier, 23 rue de Rivoli**
Truly fabulous smells assail you as you discover virgin olive oils, sesame and nut oils and every other type of oil. Plus fruit vinegars, essential oils for aromatherapy and super-succulent Breton sardines in olive oil - the best present ever for elderly relatives. Closed Monday.

• **Izraël (le Monde des Epices), 30 rue François Miron**
Speciality and exotic foods. In business over 50 years and overflowing with sacks of nuts, grains and legumes. Imported canned specialties, especially from the Middle East. You may find Egyptian white truffles, relatively tasteless but cheap and good for impressing others. Prepared foods and baskets for sale.

• **La Poussière d'Or, 11 rue du Pont-Louis-Phillipe**
Secondhand tableware, linens and laces of the best quality plus tea sets, glasses and food-related items.

• **Foucher, 12 rue Jean-du-Bellay**
A sugar shop with an enormous array of sugars of all sorts, colors and flavors, plus fantasy shapes. Chocolates, dragées, honey and fruit jellies too. A real sweetie.

• **Brasserie de l'Île-St-Louis, 55 Quai de Bourbon**
See Brasseries, p. 82.

Rue St-Louis-en-l'Île is one of my favorite Parisian streets, not least because it is the local, for some of the most exclusive addresses in town yet retains a neighborhood feel. Bakeries, cheese shops, traiteurs and antiques, with glimpses of the Seine down the side roads. Some shops work the old way, with Monsieur doing the work and Madame sitting hawklike at the cash register. After 9PM, the Angelis restaurant at No 31 has jazz and you can't get much more Parisian than that.

• **La Ferme St-Aubin, 76 rue St-Louis en-l'Île**
Cheese shop, very good for the rich, creamy fresh cheeses of the Île-de-Paris, bries, fontainebleaus, that sort of thing. Excellent chèvres in spring. Every cheese matured on the premises.

• **L'Epicerie, 51 rue St-Louis-en-l'Île**
A delightful stop for any food lover. Jars are stacked in an orderly fashion from floor to ceiling. Preserves made from chablis, muscadet and Bourgogne aligoté are among the more enticing items. A wide range of vinegars, oils and mustards at reasonable prices. Simple and traditional.

• **Boucherie Jean-Paul Gardil, 44 rue St-Louis-en-l' Île**
Butcher with prize-winning andouillettes, poulets de Bresse, happy veal (veau de lait fermier) with certificates to prove it and free-range guinea fowl. Small, family-run establishment you can trust.

• **Le Moule à Gâteau, 47 rue St-Louis-en-l'Île**
A fabulous range of breads including ryes with walnuts and raisins. Savory tarts and quiches, cheesecake, fruit tarts and pretty creations. Arabella comprises red currants on a sponge base topped with meringue.

• **Lefranc, 38 rue St-Louis-en-l'Île**
Cheese shop. The farmhouse bries and other wonders are aged in the 17th-century cellars beneath the shop. I like to watch the aristocratic men who carefully choose two or three cheeses as their contribution to their nearby lunch and dinner tables. Excellent selection of chèvres.

• **La Charlotte de l'Isle, 24 rue St-Louis-en-l'Île**
It is impossible to walk past this tiny tea salon without taking a closer look. Works of art made of chocolate are on display in the window. If you can get a table, try the scrumptious hot chocolate. Open from Thursday to Sunday, 2PM-8PM.

• **Berthillon, 31 rue St-Louis-en-l'Île**
Best ice cream in Paris and hence some of the longest queues. Think of a flavor and it will be there, especially seasonal fruits, which may alternatively be made into sorbets. I like the bittersweet chocolate ice cream and the marrons glacé - what's better is some of each. Also sold around the corner at Restaurant Cadmios (17 rue des Deux Ponts) and at Le Flore-en-l' Île if you need a rest.

• **Haupois, 35 rue des Deux-Ponts**
Bakery considered one of the best in Paris for traditional breads. Small loaves offer the chance to experiment. Formidable cakes, sablés, florentines and so on.

• **Le-Flore-en-l'Île, 42 quai d'Orléans**
Tea shop and café. A good spot for Sunday brunch with a corner site overlooking Notre Dame. Sit and dawdle over a Berthillon ice or a cup of tea, or both. Classical music soothes too.

• **Lerch, 4 rue du Cardinal-Lemoine**
Alsatian baker with kugelhofs year-round, wondrous fruit tarts according to what is seasonal, and traditional gingerbreads for Easter and Christmas.

• **Boulangerie St-Germain, 18 bd St-Germain**
Bakery with good baguettes and fruit charlottes recommended by the locals.

• **Aux Produits de Bretagne et des Pyrénées, 42 bd St-Germain**
Regional produce. Business must be booming for this shop is closed from June to mid-October. When open, it is a tumble of wonders of exceptional quality, especially for air-dried hams, fresh sausages and confits. *Hard cider from Brittany.*

Place Maubert is the scene of a busy and good market on Tuesday, Thursday and Saturday mornings. The high presence of police does not mean dishonest traders - the President lives just around the corner at 22 rue de Bièvre. No 33 is Yorgantz, a Russian-American piano bar with blinis, stuffed eggplant and kebabs. When the market isn't there, the high-class locals are still served well. In one corner, at 31 and 35, are Vietnamese shops with exotic herbs, vegetables and fruits, oriental teas, dried squid and at No 35 there are also cooking utensils and cookbooks. In between the two is a Vietnamese restaurant if you want to try before you buy.

• **Charcuterie St-Germain, 47 bd St-Germain**
Charcuterie and traiteur with a really superb selection of dishes plus individual savory tarts and quiches, croques-monsieur and genuine flamiche, *the leek tart from Picardy.*

• **Thanh Binh, 18 rue Lagrange**
A branch of one of the Vietnamese food stores on Place Maubert.

• **Madam Bardon, Box 11, quai de Montebello**
Recommended for old French cookbooks if you can cook in that language. Not usually there on Sunday or Monday.

• **Gibert Jeune, 4 pl St Michel**
Books and records. You may have to search a little over several floors but there are plenty of cookbooks and food books in the huge shop. Good records too.

Rue de la Harpe is tourist-oriented - sometimes pushily so, with constant admonitions for you to eat here or there. Mainly Arabic or Greek, nonetheless it's fun and the pastry shops are better and more authentic than the restaurants.

• **Au Gargantua, corner of rues de la Harpe and Huchette**
Another spot for oversized croissants and sandwiches plus terrific speciality breads, salads and prepared foods.

• **South Tunis, 17 rue de la Harpe**
Ethnic pastry shop, perhaps the most authentic of the many syrup-dribbling and sometimes brightly colored pastries here. Those with rosewater and orange flower water syrup and an almond or pistachio filling are the most voluptuous.

• **Piccadilly Pub, 92 bd St-Germain**
Le pub Anglais à la Parisienne, - I thought you'd like to know where it was . . .

• **Aux Gourmets de Cluny, 86 bd St-Germain**
Pâtisserie and café with good apple turnovers. They seem to like to do unusual things with meringue.

Rue de la Montagne-Ste-Geneviève is a nice neighborly street with a touch of the east

as you enter at one end, but a more solid French regional ambiance at the other.

• **Apple Tarte, 50 rue de la Montagne-Ste-Geneviève**
Small bakery from which a localized clientèle enjoys crusty breads and fruit flans and tarts.

Place de la Contrescarpe is close to the Ecole Polytechnique and thus a popular student hangout. Swing through it and rue Rollins to rue Monge, one of the best local haunts in Paris.

• **Aux Ducs de Gascogne, 111 rue St-Antoine**
Charcuterie and traiteur, part of a nationally franchised chain of shops specializing in Gascon produce. All the goose and duck products including foie gras are from their own stock rather than imported. Nice canned sauces and one of the places to buy genuine magrets. *Excellent recipe sheets.*

• **M Grivet, 28 rue Monge**
Pâtisserie and baker. Sweet specialities from the regions such as pruneaux d'Agen, grisettes de Montpellier, castilles de Perpignan, etc. Fascinating but too many taste boringly similar or are based on almond. Best go for his own chocolates unless you are writing a thesis.

• **Au Cochon d'Auvergne, 48 rue Monge**
An attractive charcuterie that tries hard to have a good range of regional produce and one of the few in which I've found goose rillettes.

• **Mon Kraemer, 60 rue Monge**
Large cheese shop with marble counters and unmistakable but not unpleasant odor. Lots of raw milk cheeses from the regions plus fromage frais, jams and honeys.

• **Blondel, 70 rue Monge**
Pâtisserie. I like the bavarois best, especially the black

currant and the raspberry. Other goodies to tempt include hand-dipped chocolates.

Wednesday, Friday and Sunday mornings you'll find a market in place Monge. Stall 61 sells particularly good whole rye breads from the Vendée, but they are not the sort of thing to pop into a suitcase. Le Villefranche on Place Monge features Niçoise specialities.

• **Pharmacie, 74 rue Monge**
Herbal pharmacy with over 2,000 medicines available, most seeming to be laxatives, antirheumatic or for weight loss - or a combination. Interesting display details medicinal properties of herbs.

• **La Mosquée de Paris, pl du Puits-de-l'Ermite**
It's well worth taking a stroll beyond the Jardin des Plantes to visit this mosque. An excellent address for afternoon tea but be prepared to wait for a table on a Sunday afternoon. A good range of Moroccan pottery in the shop.

Rue Mouffetard has been a stronghold of *le petit commerce* and a food market since the 14th century. Once closely associated with horse trading, in the 19th century this was a street of artisans. Its partly cobbled climb is changing again as small shops and cafés become discos, boutiques and tourist traps. Yet there is tremendous atmosphere and as Paris constantly changes, the Greek, Spanish, Brazilian, Lebanese and Martiniquais restaurants at the Contrescarpe end merely reflect this. Make sure you have enough time to explore the side streets and discover far more than can be listed here. Much of the criticism of produce or service is simply part of the Parisian act. But as a visitor, do you care? It's village life.

• **Traiteur Ara, 106 rue Mouffetard**
Arabic and Eastern specialities with many homemade by the Turkish-Armenian owner. Cheeses in oil, labna, poutargue, Russian and Turkish wine and raki.

• **Le Moule à Gâteau, 111 rue Mouffetard**
Pastry shop chain that usually turns up in busy market streets. Everything baked with butter and sold by the portion. Good and honest and much preferred by me to the overdecorated and glazed creations of some smarter-looking places.

• **Les Panetons, 113 rue Mouffetard**
Modern bakery with a range of breads of different grains plus savory tarts and quiches - the watercress one is excellent. Fresh pasta too.

• **L'Huître et Demie, 80 rue Mouffetard**
Reasonably priced fish restaurant with specialities including bouillabaisse and fruits de mer. There is a fixed price menu at 57F at lunchtime and in the evening 88F or 145F. Pleasant atmosphere.

• **La Masion du Fromage, 105 rue Mouffetard**
Impressive array of cheese from the regions. Try the Saint Nectaire fermier, brebis fermier or the brie aux herbes.

• **Aux Vrais Produits d'Auvergne, 37 rue Rambuteau**
Regional produce. An enormous selection of air-dried sausages and outstanding hams hanging from the ceiling. So much else to sell, including fascinating cheeses, that both produce and customers spill onto the street.

• **La Librairie des Gourmets, 20 rue Daubenton**
Bookstore. Every type of cook book imaginable with a distinct international flavor.

Plus books on wine etiquette for the specialist and colorful atlases.

• **La Tuile au Loup, 35 rue Daubenton**
Provençal gifts and books, handicrafts, ceramics and such. Good for gentle research before you head south.

• **Quincaillerie, 24 rue des Patriarches**
Hardware. An Aladdin's cave of economical cookware, reasonably priced pottery bowls, casseroles, cheese molds, baskets and the like.

• **Les Délices d'Aphrodite, 4 rue de Candolle**
Greek restaurant and traiteur. Fun place that really bustles at lunchtime, plus everything you need for Greek cooking.

• **Porcelaine Blanche, 119 rue Monge**
Tableware including seconds, discontinued styles, and overstocks among the stylish china, cutlery and glassware.

• **La Ferme du Périgord Restaurant, 3 rue des Fossés-St-Marcel**
Regional specialities from the Périgord including confits and truffles in season. Menu Gastronomique available.

• **Jadis et Gourmande, 88 bd de Port-Royal**
Sweets and chocolates of almost every kind, from caramels to peppermints and wonderful fruit jellies including quince. Great for nicely packed, pricey presents.

• **Camoli, 202 rue St Jacques**
Italian traiteur featuring fresh pasta, Parma ham, parmesan and plenty of other Italian treats attractively displayed both inside and out.

Arrondissements 6 & 7

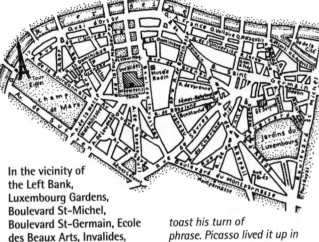

In the vicinity of the Left Bank, Luxembourg Gardens, Boulevard St-Michel, Boulevard St-Germain, Ecole des Beaux Arts, Invalides, Napoléon's tomb, Musée Rodin and the Eiffel Tower.

Here you'll find some of the most expensive food shops and markets in all Paris and no one dare spoil the produce there. Or perhaps it is because no one can afford to eat regularly in Le Drugstore or on the glittering terraces of the cafés either side of ever-fashionable Boulevard St-Germain, which locks the sometimes self-conscious 7e into the livelier and more literate 6e. White Russians still seem to rule, Napoléon's empire is striking at Le Récamier and names like Petrossian, Christian Constant, Barthélemy, Lenôtre and Poujaran supply the fashionable with luxurious or perfect foods, and the observer with entertainment and a bittersweet taste of life led by politicians, aristocrats and Americans in Paris.
The 6e seems more public and has better places to eat and drink. Indeed, Le Procope is where coffee was first sold in Paris in 1686. Oscar Wilde ended his life in Hotel le Bélier and its bar is a terrific place to

toast his turn of phrase. Picasso lived it up in the Café de Flore and Hemingway gave readings at Aux Deux Magots, where Sartre was a regular. Definitely not to be missed is Poilâne the baker, if only because someone once described the place as being "where art meets baking." Very Left Bank, that.

• **Comtesse du Barry, 1 rue de Sèvres**
Specialty food store famous for mail-order foie gras, magret de canard, terrines. Other stores at 13 rue Taitbout 9e and 88 rue Mozart 16e.

• **La Grand Epicerie de Paris, 38 rue de Sèvres**
Thought by many to be the best store in Paris. This is the future of French food halls – clean, tastefully decorated, cosmopolitan food, friendly and fast service. Attracts young modern families and celebs.

• **Vigneau Desmarest, 105–107 rue de Sèvres**
Caterers. Everything is beautifully presented but pricey. Handmade ravioli and pasta, pain Poilâne; the charcuterie is their pride.

• **Eurasia, 52 rue de Sèvres**
Oriental market offering takeout. Breaded shrimp, spring rolls and pot stickers.

There is a very good street market on Tuesday and Friday on bd Raspail between rue du Cherche-Midi and rue de Rennes. Rue du Cherche-Midi dates back to the 15th and 16th centuries when cherche-midi meant someone who begged for food at midday, the time of the day's main meal. Antique shops and discount designer shops are at the lower end; the upper end by Sèvres-Babylone is very trendy and pricey.

• **Chez les Filles, 62 rue du Cherche-Midi**
Tastefully decorated tea salon with a touch of Morocco. Try one of their tagines at midday or the Marco Polo salad. A pleasant place to rest your feet mid-afternoon. Open from 12-6PM.

• **Puyricard, 106 rue du Cherche-Midi**
Chocolate shop with an impressive display of tempting chocolate delights all handmade in Aix-en-Provence. The marrons glacés are not to be missed.

• **MA Dauliac, 112 rue du Cherche-Midi**
Antique shop specializing in furniture and objects mainly from the 1930s and 1940s. Tableware, glassware, bathroom fittings and much, much more. Well worth a visit.

• **Casa Pascal, 15 rue d'Assas**
Economical china, mainly French and mainly white. An opportunity to buy such items as pierced dishes for radishes.

• **Café Parisien, 15 rue d'Assas**
Small, cosy bistro on the corner of rue d'Assas and rue de Rennes. On a cold winter's evening this address will warm the cockles of your heart. The reasonably priced menu changes every day.

• **Poilâne, 8 rue du Cherche-Midi**
Boulangerie set in a 14th-century Gothic abbey and

probably the best known in France. Owned by Pierre Poilâne, who is famed for his bread designs, of which the most famous is the cluster of grapes. It is rumored that Salvador Dali commissioned him to make a bedroom out of bread after he saw a bread chandelier in Monsieur Poilâne's office. The wheat used in baking is grown to Monsieur Poilâne's secret specifications. The sourdough bread is baked around the clock in wood-fired ovens, in kitchens hewn from rock 500 years ago. It is now flown all over the world. Look for the 2kg pain de campagne, apple tarts and pain aux noix. Closed Sundays.

• **Hélène Fourner-Guérin, 25 rue des Sts-Pères.**
Antique shop specializing in 18th-century porcelain from Strasbourg, Rouen and Sceaux. Delft tiles and 18th-century faïence.

• **Debauve et Gallais, 30 rue des Sts-Pères**
Chocolate shop that began life as a pharmacy. Monsieur Gallais, believing they were a beneficial tonic, began manufacturing chocolates in 1818. Black squares of praline and croquettes of bittersweet chocolate. The shop is protected by the Beaux Arts Society.

• **Le Bélier, 13 rue des Beaux-Arts**
The hotel where Oscar Wilde met his end. An overpriced restaurant but visit the bar for an apéritif and drink to the spirit of the '90s . . .

Down rue Mabillon you'll find the covered St-Germain market, surprisingly warm and neighborly and with generally high standards of produce, knowledge and welcome. The rue de Seine is especially noted for its art galleries and art supply shops.

• **Bar de l'Institut, 21 rue de Seine**
A wine bar and the oldest establishment in the quarter. Wine by the glass and sandwiches served at the rear.

• **La Palette, 43 rue de Seine**
Another bar and popular with the local artists. Excellent coffee and sandwiches made with pain Poilâne.

• **Fournil de Pierre, 64 rue de Seine**
Boulangerie with excellent tarts and a choice of pizzas daily. Bread by the kilo and good cheese and charcuterie. Also on the corner of rues de Sèvres and St-Romain.

• **La Table d'Italie, 69 rue de Seine**
Italian food store with sandwiches and pizza to eat at the counter. Good spot for lunch after visiting Buci market or the Latin Quarter. Homemade pasta and a complete selection of Italian hams and cheeses.

• **Boulangerie Carton, 6 rue de Buci**
This site has been known since 1950 for fougasse made with puff pastry instead of bread dough and its cheesecake.

• **Vieille France, 14 rue de Buci**
Pâtisserie with good chocolat de maison, merveilles (puff pastry with honey and jam), tamousse roquefort and palet cognac.

• **Bonbonnerie de Buci, 12 rue de Buci**
A mâitre pâtissier with tea salon upstairs. Mousse aux pommes sold with caramel sauce and Black Forest cake (forêt noire).

• **Boutique Butard, 25-27 rue Buci**
Traiteur and catering service where prepared foods can be bought, but it's best just to look!

• **Aux Vrais Produits d'Auvergne, 32 rue Buci**
Charcuterie specializing in products from the Auvergne and one of several such shops throughout Paris. Tomme fraîche d'Auvergne, confits, walnut bread.

• **Le Petit Zinc, 11 rue St-Benoît**
Restaurant open until 3AM. 1900s decor and trendy clientèle. Southwest and Aveyron cuisine including choucroute de poisson.

• **Taverne de Nesle, 32 rue Dauphine**
Bar that won the award for best mug of beer in Paris in 1977. Over 400 beers from around the world, including Zywiec from Poland, Tsing Tao from China, Macabé from Israel.

• **Charcuterie Coesnon, 30 rue Dauphine**
Charcuterie run by the Coesnon family from Normandy. Fifteen varieties of blood pudding as well as boudin blanc and andouillettes.

• **Charcuterie du Pont-Neuf, 12 rue Dauphine**
Charcuterie and winner of the Concours National du Boudin Blanc. Also has andouillettes de Troyes.

• **Axis, 18 rue Guénégaud**
Specializes in whimsical objets d'art, bistro ashtrays and glove-shaped vases.

• **L'Ecluse, 15 quai des Grands-Augustins**
Wine bar that lets you sample superb Bordeaux by the glass and the first of this chain. Gas lamps and belle-époque posters. Good for a late night snack such as foie gras with some Sauternes or filet d'oie and St-Emilion.

• **Côté Seine, 45 quai des grands-Augustins**
A favorite spot for Parisian theater-goers. On the menu you will find traditional dishes such as foie gras, escargots, salade landaise, magret de canard. Very pleasant surroundings and friendly staff.

• **A la Coeur de Rohan, 59-61 rue St-André-des-Arts**
Nonsmoking, country-style tea salon with classical music and the occasional live concert. Scones au fromage!

• **Allard, 41 rue St-André-des-Arts**
Touristy restaurant and bistro nevertheless awarded Les Lauriers de Terroir for good regional cuisine.

• **La Lozère, 4 rue Hautefeuille**
Restaurant doubling as tourist information center for the Lozère. Serves excellent dishes and charcuterie including saucisse de Lozère.

Note that No 15 rue Hautefeuille was where Charlotte Corday stabbed Jean Marat in his bathtub.

• **Le Procope, 13 rue l'Ancienne-Comédie**
Café and restaurant dating back to 1686, the oldest in Paris. It was here that a young Sicilian, Francesco Procopio dei Coltelli, who had arrived in the city to seek his fortune, began selling the new beverage, coffee. A gold plaque commemorates its most notable patrons - Voltaire, Diderot, Rousseau, Ben Franklin, Danton, Marat, Robespierre and Bonaparte. More interesting from a historic point of view.

• **La Pinte, 13 carrefour de l'Odéon**
Bar with over 500 beers. Usually crowded, sometimes rowdy, or is the word hearty?

• **Brûlerie de l'Odéon, 6 rue Crébillon**
Coffee shop selling 15 freshly ground coffees plus a complete range of Fortnum and Mason teas.

Rue Monsieur-le-Prince combines two great French enthusiasms, the Orient (and its food) and the cinema. Quite an experience.

• **Chez Maître-Paul, 12 rue Monsieur-le-Prince**
Restaurant awarded Les

Lauriers du Terroir. Small rustic interior, wines from the Jura and excellent morbier and vacherin cheeses.

• **Polidor, 41 rue Monsieur-le-Prince**
Unpretentious home cooking in art-deco surroundings. Closed Sunday and Monday.

• **Estrella, 34 rue St-Sulpice**
Coffee shop whose owner refuses to blend beans. Colombian and Kenyan coffees are a specialty.

• **Chez George, 11 rue des Canettes**
Bar with a reputation for typical bistro atmosphere but popular only with tourists.

• **Guy, 6 rue Mabillon**
Brazilian restaurant. Feijoada, the national dish, is served Saturday lunchtimes.

• **La Foux, 2 rue Clément**
Restaurant with a reputation for good Saturday luncheons. Lyonnais dishes in winter and Provençal dishes during summer.

• **Caves Miard, 9 rue des Quatre-Vents**
Wine store that used to be a crémerie. 1850 decor has been retained. Specialties include Château Pech-Redou, Côteaux de la Clape and 1900 Port Greyhound Colheita.

• **Brasserie Lipp, 151 bd St-Germain**
Fashionable designer brasserie. See Brasserie panel.

• **Aux Deux Magots, 6 pl St-Germain des Prés**
Famous brasserie and bar with a literary and philosophical history. See Brasseries, p. 82.

• **Café de Flore, 172 bd St-Germain**
Equally famous brasserie and café.

• **Michele Aragon, 21 rue Jacob**
Antique shop with 19th-century tableware and cutlery, furniture and linen. Afternoons only.

• **Tiany Chambard, 32 rue Jacob**

Antique shop specializing in art deco and items from the '30s, '40s and '50s. Tableware too. Afternoons only.

• **Maison Rustique, 26 rue Jacob**
Bookshop specializing in gardening and how-to books on beer and cheese. Plant and vegetable books. French- and English-language publications.

• **Culinarion, 99 rue de Rennes**
Kitchen shop specializing in molds and decorative objects. Pricey.

• **FNAC, 136 rue de Rennes**
Chain store with a book section containing one of the largest and most comprehensive collections of food and wine books.

• **La Vaissellerie, 85 rue de Rennes**
Good-quality porcelain at low prices. The small shop is also packed with good gift ideas such as escargot dishes, crème brûlée irons, coffee bowls, unusual tea strainers, bread knives in the shape of a baguette. Also at 80 bd Haussmann in the 8e, 332 rue St Honoré in the 1e and 79 rue St Lazare in the 9e.

• **La Closerie des Lilas, 171 bd du Montparnasse**
Restaurant and brasserie that draws film stars and the BCBG (bon chic, bon genre). An old haunt of Henry James and Hemingway. Piano bar, brasserie reasonable, restaurant overpriced.

• **Galerie Michel Sonkin, 10 rue de Beaune**
Antique shop specializing in folk objects of wood. Bread stamps (from when villages and families put their seal to bread loaves) and wooden butter molds.

• **Tan Dinh, 60 rue de Verneuil**
Restaurant specializing in Vietnamese cuisine with a dash of French. Excellent wine cellar. Poulet au patates douces et cardamome and sweet and

sour veal are among the interesting dishes.

• **Les Glénan, 54 rue de Bourgogne**
A restaurant that under American chef Marc Singer won Les Lauriers de Terroir, *the* Gault Millau *award for exceptional cuisine.*

• **Pradier, 6 rue de Bourgogne**
Pâtisserie that has as its slogan "all pâtisserie made with butter" and the taste confirms it. Also handmade chocolates and very good savory pastries. Closed most of summer.

• **Barthélémy, 51 rue de Grenelle**
Cheese shop patronized by the famous. Tiny, chaotic and very "in," it also boasts cheeses of exceptional quality.

• **Surface, 16 rue St-Simon**
Tile shop specializing in Italian decorator and hand-painted tiles.

• **Diners en Ville, 27 rue de Varenne**
Antique tableware shop, particularly known for pieces produced 1880-1930. Glasses, barbotines, whisky flasks, silver.

• **A La Ville de Cremone, 76 rue du Bac**
Italian food shop dedicated to a small village in Cremone. Panettone perugina, salami de cremone and cicillo, a mild Milanese cheese shaped like a pear.

• **Lenôtre, 44 rue du Bac**
Pâtisserie and caterer, part of the Lenôtre empire, which includes several Paris shops, a school and a factory. Chocolate is a speciality; Concorde is a meringue filled with chocolate mousse.

• **Christian Constant, 26 rue du Bac**
Pâtisserie and tea salon that also makes some of the best chocolate. Attracts the BCBG clientèle to its white contemporary rooms. Nineteen teas to have either with acacia

honey or five different sugars.

• **Lefèbvre Fils, 24 rue du Bac**
Tableware shop including 18th-century trompe l'oeil serving dishes in the shape of plates of olives, cabbage, etc.

• **Boucherie d'Orsay, 20 rue du Bac**
Butcher specializing in veau fermier.

• **Jean Saffrey, 18 rue du Bac**
Ice cream shop where fun-seekers buy made-to-order busts of Marilyn Monroe, or Giscard d'Estaing. Or you could pick up an off-the-freezer-shelf President Mitterand. Boy, do I want to party with these dudes!

• **Au Bon Marché, 38 rue de Sèvres**
Department store. See page 83.

• **Le Récamier, 4 rue Récamier**
Empire-style restaurant frequented by government ministers. Outdoor dining too. Burgundian cuisine and one of the best wine cellars in Paris.

• **Peltier, 66 rue de Sèvres**
Pâtisserie with frozen fruit soufflés , mango-flavored charlotte and excellent croissants.

• **Cremier le Quatre Homme, 62 rue de Sèvres**
Cheese shop that supplies grand restaurants. All the cheeses are cave-aged. Rare fermiers such as livarots, reblochon and beaufort. Raw-cream butter from the Charentes, usually.

• **Marché Breteuil, ave de Saxe, from ave de Ségur to pl de Breteuil**
Market selling fish, produce, cheeses, flowers and some clothing. One of the moving markets, here Thursday and Saturday. It's a nice street to wander in.

• **François de Broglie Cooking School, 18 ave de La Motte-Picquet**
Cooking school with courses in English, French and Spanish. Recommended.

• **Le Petit Boulé, 16 ave de la Motte-Picquet**
Russian tea salon owned by the Petrossian family. Piroshki, blinis, tarama on toast, chocolate cake. Also sells foie gras, honey and teas.

• **Marie-Ann Cantin, 12 rue du Champ-de-Mars**
Cheese shop with two cellars - one lined with damp rocks to keep the cow's milk cheeses moist, and a less humid cellar for goat's milk cheeses. Nearly 100 seasonal cheeses and a good selection of farmhouse chèvre. Owned by the daughter of Christian Cantin, who has a famed cheese shop in the 15e.

• **Dubernet, 2 rue Augereau**
Food store specializing in products from the Landes. Foie gras au torchon, chichons d'oie, cous d'oie farcis and cassoulet.

• **Marché rue Cler, ave de la Motte-Picquet to rue St-Dominique**
Expensive street market in an upscale area. Look for moussaka or coulibiac at Charcuterie Gorin at No 40 and the Italian market Davoli at No 34, which has exceptionally good produce. The market has more space than most and lots of American residents who are grateful for this.

• **Leonidas, 39 rue Cler**
Belgian chocolate shop; Belgian chocolates are sweeter than the French.

• **Rôtisserie du Champ-de-Mars, 145 rue St-Dominique**
Very special fish market specializing in langoustes, lobsters and trout, all direct from their own salt- and freshwater tanks.

• **Viandes du Champ-de-Mars, 122 rue St-Dominique**
Butcher with poulets de Bresse, canettes de Barberie and excellent beef and tripe.

• **Pâtisserie Millet, 103 rue St-Dominique**
Pâtisserie, caterers and tea salon. Owner Monsieur Millet is a maître pâtissier. Chocolate

Arrondissement 8

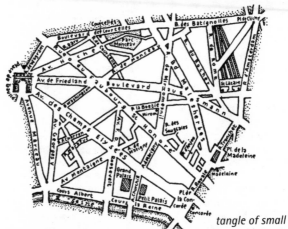

made for sale throughout France. Double-filled pain au chocolat, *kiwi or* fruit de passion charlottes. *All perfection.*

• **Gisquet, 64 rue St-Dominique**
Boulangerie dating back to 1900, decorated in earthernware tiles and pottery. Large round country loaves.

• **La Varenne Ecole de Cuisine, 34 rue St-Dominique**
Cooking school founded in 1975 by British cookery writer Anne Willan. Special one-week courses during the summer and Easter holidays plus courses in Burgundy. Demonstrations are open to the public between 2:30 and 5:30PM Monday to Friday and 10AM to 12:30PM on Saturdays. All in French and translated into English.

• **Petrossian, 18 bd La Tour-Maubourg**
Internationally acclaimed specialty food shop where for many years the Petrossian family has been supplying Parisians with caviar. Also smoked salmon, truffle, foie gras, vodkas - everything rare, expensive and stylish. See panel, p. 79.

• **Poujauran, 20 rue Jean-Nicot**
Pâtisserie and boulangerie becoming noticeably famous for its organic bread, especially the baguettes. Gâteau basque, pizzas, gingerbread and lovely pastries. Southwestern influence. Worth finding.

• **Puyricard, 27 rue Rapp**
Chocolate shop. Handmade chocolates arrive twice weekly from Aix-en-Provence. Particularly good are the chocolats fourrés and calissons d'Aix.
And now you're off to the Eiffel Tower . . .

In the vicinity of the Arc de Triomphe, Champs Elysées, Elysée Palace, Faubourg St-Honoré, Grand Palais, Petit Palais, Place de la Concorde, St-Lazare, Madeleine.

High fashion is now reduced to ready-to-wear in the rue du Faubourg St-Honoré, but the Elysée Palace and the grand mansions of the American and British embassies ensure they, and the food shops thereabouts, don't have to drop their prices. Rue Daru is a touch of Russia, the best Danish and German foods can be found here, and on the eastern borders are Androuet and La Ferme St-Hubert, the renowned cheese shops. For truffles and foie gras, dinner at Maxims, tea times of elegance, breathtaking silver and glass for tables, caviar on toast and anything else luxurious, you simply need never leave the 8e. Yet the great boulevards carved through medieval Paris last century left pockets of thin streets and high contrast. You'll easily find your own culinary routes once you've touched bases with these highlights. I especially like the
tangle of small shops and streets named after international cities between Boulevard Malesherbes and the Gare St-Lazare.

• **Boutique Danoise, 42 ave de Friedland**
Modern housewares and furniture. Glorious glass and massive crystal bowls in simple designs with clean contemporary lines. Also sleek leather furniture.

• **Flora Danica, 142 ave des Champs-Elysées**
Restaurant and traiteur specializing in a delightful range of Danish products, in particular stoneground breads, herring, smoked eel, and apple, almond or prune pastries. Right next door to Royal Copenhagen, the porcelain specialists.

• **Peter, 191 rue du Faubourg St-Honoré**
Exclusive tableware and cutlery. Solid silver or silver plate with handles of precious things or of plastic to suit dishwashers. China and serving pieces too.

• **La Maison du Chocolat, 225 rue du Faubourg St-Honoré**
Even the shop seems to be chocolate coated. See page 78.

• **Etoile d'Or, 260 rue du Faubourg St-Honoré**
Traiteur with boucherie next door specializing in regional foods.

• **A la Ville de Petrograd, 13 rue Daru**
Restaurant and traiteur. A log facade evokes its namesake. Sample fresh caviar, smoked salmon, blinis, coulibiac and borscht in the dining room or take some home.
Appropriately situated facing the gold domes on the Russian Orthodox church.

• **Daru, 19 rue Daru**
Russian traiteur and grocer with casual restaurant attached. Smoked fish, stuffed eggplant, shashlik, all to take out if preferred.

Go down rue de Courcelles and through the gilded gates onto ave Van Dyck, which gives access to Parc Monceau. Here you have a glimpse of Parisians at leisure. Walk on to the place Prosper Coubaux and down rue du Rocher, a market street.

• **Au Miel de France, 71 rue du Rocher**
A superb variety of flavors plus honey spice cakes, honey confectionery and good jams and jellies. See panel, p. 100.

• **Puiforcat, 131 bd Haussmann**
Tableware. Extravagant displays of sensational settings. Many designs reproduced from the original 19th-century collection of Monsieur Puiforcat, which is now in the Louvre. The place for important gifts for weddings or anniversaries.

• **René-Gerard St-Ouen, 111 bd Haussmann**
Bakery and café - they call themselves sculptors with bread and the windows are filled with fantasy bread creations.

• **L'Esprit et le Vin, 65 bd Malesherbes**
Mecca for the wine lover with a fantastic range of wine accessories.

• **Vernet, 65 bd Malesherbes**
Bakery and tea salon with cheese-wrapped frankfurters served on homemade rolls, croissants filled with chicken and ham, fruit tarts and chocolate macaroons.

• **Augé, 115 bd Haussmann**
Épicerie with luscious fresh fruit complementing many speciality ingredients. Once the place to go for polar bear steaks, elephant trunks or anything else intrepid.

• **Au Chat Bleu, 85 bd Haussmann**
Confectionery including bonbons, nougat, marzipan, chocolate nut clusters plus teas and cookies.

• **Au Lys Royal, 13 rue de la Pépinière**
Confectionery including marzipan tennis balls and good bitter chocolates in leopard-print boxes.

• **La Cigogne, 61 rue de l'Arcade**
A pâtisserie with some charcuterie. Alsatian specialties include puff pastry pretzels, cinnamon kugelhof, lovely real sausages, choucroute and smoked tongues.

• **La Carpe, 14 rue Tronchet**
Kitchen supplies. Several styles of knife rests to avoid washing dishes between courses, bar ware, kitchen equipment and small appliances.

Go back up rue Tronchet to where it intersects rue Vignon. A walk down rue Vignon is a feast. The even-numbered shops are actually in the 9e but are included here.

• **La Maison du Miel, 24 rue Vignon**
More than a dozen types of honey plus yogurt or granola cookies and honey spice cake. See panel.

• **Ferme St-Hubert, 21 rue Vignon**
Cheese shop and restaurant justly famed as one of the best. Raw-milk farm cheeses are matured on the premises but all types of French cheese are represented. Restaurant offers roquefort soufflé, cheesecake, raclette, fondue and homemade chèvre à l'huile.

While you are on the borders of the 1e and the 8e, stay a while and take a look at the classic department store Aux Trois Quartiers, 17 bd de la Madeleine.

• **Fauchon, 26 pl de la Madeleine**
One-stop luxury shopping. Totally reliable for foie gras and excelling in foie gras de canard. Syrups for sorbets, dried mushrooms, cheap wild rice, eccentric jams (jasmine blossom for instance). Masterful displays of fresh produce and an intoxicating traiteur. Bakery and coffee shop. Go, even if you are poor.

• **Hediard, 21 pl de la Madeleine**
Sharp competition for Fauchon and once seen as more exotic. Pistachio and pine nut oils, famous jams and jellies made in own kitchens, extraordinary range of vinegars and wines. Smart restaurant upstairs with elegant food.

• **Maison de la Truffe, 19 pl de la Madeleine**
Traiteur specializing in truffles. Fresh and preserved truffles, foie gras and good-quality prepared dishes.

• **Caviar Kaspa, 17 pl de la Madeleine**
Caviar shop and restaurant. Downstairs you can also buy smoked sturgeon, smoked salmon, eel and gravadlax. Restaurant serves caviars with thick blinis, melted butter and sour cream. Flavored vodkas. Bar for single diners. Wondrous, wicked escapism.

• **L'Ecluse, 15 pl de la Madeleine**
Wine bar and restaurant. Good chain offering vintage wines by the glass and foie gras by the slice.

Marché de la Madeleine is a tiny, secret market entered from 11 rue Tronchet or 7 rue de Castellane. I love the place, just for putting my feet on the ground or for putting together an economical lunch. But should I be telling you this . . . ?

• **Mémoires de Baccarat, 11 pl de la Madeleine**
Homewares. Incredible highball glasses and mad vases.

• **Odiot, 7 pl de la Madeleine**
Upscale cutlery, crystal and porcelain in the elaborate French style. Some cutlery patterns are pre-Revolution.

• **Au Verger de la Madeleine, 4 bd Malesherbes**
Fruits and liquor, a formidable selection of wines and whiskeys, fuzzy green almonds in summer, strawberries in winter, fresh truffles too.

• **Betjeman and Barton, 23 bd Malesherbes**
Selected teas individually blended, plus tea-making equipment. See p. 78.

• **Maison du Whiskey, 20 rue d'Anjou**
An array of sparkling decanters fills the window. Inside are mini-decanters in the shape of golf balls, bar ware and a huge selection of whiskeys, malts, Irish, Canadian and bourbons. Some are very old but what counts is when they were bottled.

• **Au Bain Marie, 10 rue Boissy-d'Anglais**
Tableware shop with excellent range of colorful plates and cutlery, linens and some older lines among the contemporary items. A must if you like to dress up your dinner parties.

• **Le Savio, corner rue Boissy-d'Anglais and rue de Surène**
Bar, tearoom and bakery with pristine petits fours, shimmering fruit tartlets, chicken or ham croissants, quiches and sandwiches. Food all day at the bar.

• **Jadis et Gourmande, 27 rue Boissy d'Anglais**
Confectionery. Specializing in fantasy form chocolates, bow ties for Father's Day and plaques to replace greeting cards. Every type of caramel, fruit jelly and bonbon.

Cross the street and continue down until you find Cité Berryer on your left through the archway under the Hotel d'Aguesseau. On Tuesday and Friday mornings it's a noisy, bustling market place.

• **Villeroy & Boch, 23 rue Royale**
Tableware famous and expensive, as chosen by top restaurateurs throughout the world. Cookware beautifully displayed with shelves of glittering glass.

• **Ladurée, 16 rue Royale**
Pastry shop and tea salon of mirrored Louis XIV distinction, overseen by the cherubim on the ceiling. Equally heavenly cakes, pastries and specialities such as filled brioches and royals, chocolate or coffee and almond cookies.

• **Christolfé, 9 rue Royale**
Elegant cutlery and glass, from soup tureens to nut crackers in plastic, porcelain or silver. Established in 1850 but very aware of trends and fashions.

• **Lalique, 11 rue Royal**
Crystal showroom, mostly decorated pieces. The wine glasses and glass plates are exquisite.

• **Maxims, 1 rue de Royal**
World famous art nouveau restaurant with flower shop alongside. Around the corner (quite a walk, actually) on 3

rue Durasse is the new branch of Minims, where you can buy the corporate foods, plates or enjoy the salon de thé.

• **Boucherie de la Présidence, 15 rue Montolivet**
Lively and stylish butcher a few yards from the Elysée. Particularly good veal and poultry, which you can also buy roasted. Pristine meat counter and amazing mosaics.

• **Boulangerie des Saussaies, 12 rue des Saussaies**
Bakery and restaurant. Fresh individual veal pâtés in puff pastry, hot daily specials served at stand-up counters. Good bread and palmiers.

• **Boucherie Dufour, 29 rue Miromesnil**
Butcher selling top-quality Normandy beef. Neat rows of chickens and chops, sawdust on the floor, sells a few pâtés and vegetables.

• **Bonbonnière St-Honoré, 28 rue Miromesnil**
Chocolates and confectionery. Display windows filled with sugared almonds, rich nut clusters and a selection of jams.

• **Au Petit Montmorency, 5 rue Rabelais**
Top restaurant long known for its fine foie gras de canard. You can also buy it to take out.

• **Dalloyau, 101 rue du Faubourg St-Honoré**
Salon de thé that has been successful for around 200 years. Features pastries, prepared foods, chocolates and highly rated croissants. Fine jams, mustards, jellies and other specialties. Upstairs enjoy ice cream sundaes, light salads (lobster and raspberry vinegar is very good), or the gâteaux, such as mogador, opéra and so on. The tea is brilliant too.

• **Little Pig, 73 ave Franklin D Roosevelt**
Grocery, traiteur. Very popular prepared dishes of meat, fish

or poultry, some to eat cold, some to reheat. Pig's trotters, seafood, sausages, salads, fruit and wine too.

• **J Julien, 75 ave Franklin D Roosevelt**
Bakery and restaurant featuring crusty baguettes and chewy macaroons, homemade ice creams, quiches, pizza and pâté.

• **Le Val d'Or, 28 ave Franklin D Roosevelt**
Wine bar and restaurant. A good place to stop for a glass of beaujolais and a plate of country ham and sausages. More substantial meals featuring daily specials available in the downstairs dining room.

• **Boutique Tong Yen, 7 rue de Ponthieu**
Takeout oriental dishes. Home delivery or you can enjoy your meal in the restaurant around the corner at 1 bis rue Jean Mermoz.

• **Fouquet, 22 rue François-1er**
Speciality foods, nicely boxed gift assortments of their own mustards and condiments, preserves and teas, handmade chocolates. Unusually, they have marmalades among the jams and confitures, good fruit syrups too.

• **Faquais, 30 rue de la Trémoïlle**
Speciality foods. Particularly good roast coffees roasted daily or you can buy green beans. Jams, foie gras, confits de canard, outstanding oils, teas, wines, spices. Quite simply one of the best stores in town.

• **Pavillion Christoflé, 27 rue Marbeuf**
Classic crystal, cutlery, porcelain, hampers and napery. Great for bargains when the sales are on.

• **Torréfaction Marbeuf, 25 rue Marbeuf**
Coffee and tea of the highest quality, both pure and

HONEYS

Paris presents a marvelous opportunity to taste a selection of regional flower and herb honeys from all over France. Two stores in particular are worth a special trip, La Maison du Miel at 24 rue Vignon in the 9e and Au Miel de France at 71 rue du Rocher in the 8e.

Varieties you may find include:
• **Sunflower honey from Aquitaine:** as sunny as its name, so yellow it looks more like lemon curd than honey. There is a distinct lemon-floral flavor to the thick, granular paste.
• **Chestnut honey from the Cévennes:** when spread thickly with butter, this strong and distinctively flavored honey tastes more pleasant than it smells. Rich caramel color, thick paste.
• **Fir tree honey from the Vosges:** looks like treacle, but runnier. Dark, sweet flavor reminiscent of the forests.

Hang on, maybe it is treacle . . .
• **Mountain honey from the Savoies:** so thick-set you almost have to crack the top with a spoon. Lovely caramelized flavor and color but an orangey floral tang.
• **Hill honey from Burgundy:** beige color, thick-set. Quite floral and light.
• **Acacia honey from the Loire Valley:** very runny, very sweet but more strongly flavored than Chinese acacia honey.
• **Lavender honey from Provence:** distinctly herby flavor. Pale color, thick set, solidifies quickly.
• **Forest honey from the Sologne:** Thick-set, crack-through-the-top kind of honey. Deep flavor of caramelized oranges.
• **Linden tree honey from the Auvergne:** Distinctive flavor of linden and forests, but is it a good match for honey? I'm not sure. Thick glass texture.

---

blended, plus regional jams and honeys.

• **Vignon, 14 rue Marbeuf**
Traiteur featuring roasts, stuffed and tied, veal with wild mushrooms or paella to heat up, prepared vegetables and salads, fruit, cheese and wine. Desserts too of course.

• **Cave de Georges Duboeuf, 9 rue Marbeuf**
The king of beaujolais but stocks others too, mostly under his own label. Sampler boxes of 6 splits or 8 half bottles of different beaujolais wines are available.

• **Maison de la Vigne et du Vin de France, 21 rue François-1er**
A wine boutique with tastings, books and objets du vin.

• **La Maison du Chocolat, 52 rue François-1er**
Another branch of this superb store.

• **L'Ecluse, 64 rue François**
Wine bar and restaurant chain in which you can sample wines by the glass and match them with foods such as foie gras and roquefort.

• **Maison du Caviar, 21 rue Quentin-Bauchart**
Restaurant in which you can toy with caviar or smoked salmon and blinis until 2 AM or take their specialties home and do it there.

• **Le Fouquet's, 99 ave des Champs-Elysées**
Bar and restaurant. In the same spot since the Champs-Elysées was a muddy country lane. A good place to stop and watch le monde go buy, if you enjoy the opportunity to pay 64F for two cups of coffee.

Arrondissements 9 & 10

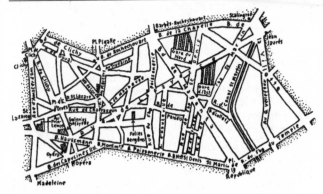

In the vicinity of Opéra, Casino de Paris, Folies-Bergères, Porte St-Denis, Porte St-Martin, Gare du Nord, Gare de l'Est, Canal St-Martin.

Here's a challenge for your culinary nose to lead you towards real exploring, to inspect the underside of Parisian high-life and haute-cuisine. For beyond Galéries Lafayette and Au Printemps on Boulevard Haussmann, the swagger of the Opéra and the famous theaters, north of the swirling boulevards and east of the railway stations, is working class life.

You quickly leave behind places familiar, yet the sights to be seen are more fascinating just for that. All has once been more fashionable and so there are abrupt surprises - some of the best and oldest confectioners in Paris, a magical Indian food shop, startling offers and Utrillo vistas in narrow rue des Martyrs, oriental Jewish shops, plus the most concentrated array of china, crystal, glass and a poster museum in a street nicely named de Paradis. Schmid is the best Alsatian charcuterie, Grandmère l'Oye sells the best foie gras. As ever, the streets around railway stations are vivacious with competition and emotion, but

they are blisters of intrusion, and there is the canal. Do you know about the Canal St-Martin, which bisects the 10e as it starts its watery way to Belgium? Once you cross it, pleasure spots and historical buildings must be of your own imagining, although there are details of Louis-Philippe lettering on shop fronts and elegant balconies to appreciate. It is vast, dilapidated and quietly self-sufficient, lived in by artisans and shopkeepers and immigrants, and an illustration of what is found in the provinces rather than what is expected in Paris. Maigret feels right at home.

From the high arched footbridges over the canal, you'll look down on barges with potted palms and televisions and chequered curtains, especially by the Pont Tournant, which opens every half hour. The 9e and 10e are not the places for the usual touring, and conspicuously expensive or scanty clothing would be stupid. To me the atmosphere is finely balanced between welcome and challenge; I feel I must not gawp or comment or take arty photographs, if any. Yet it is photogenic and it's raunchy here and triste

there, but the welcome in the cafés and bars is only as honest and sincere as you are. Of course, it's like working-class neighborhoods anywhere - they've seen a lot of living, but not a lot of tourists, thus I've not noted the neighborhood shops and bars and stalls across the canal. Those who will be interested will be capable of finding them on their own.

• Léonidas, 9 rue Auber
Belgian chocolates. You can choose both the pretty gift boxes and the assortment that goes into them.
• Zagori, 6 rue La Fayette
Although looking mainly like a self-service sweet shop, it's more important. You must sample their ice creams and sorbets, made for many of the grand restaurants. Only real, fresh ingredients are used and if you want to thrill a French host or hostess, ice cream cakes or vacherins can be made to order.
• Galeries Lafayette, 40 bd Haussmann
See Department Stores, p. 83.
• Au Printemps, 64 bd Haussmann
See Department Stores, p. 83.
• Brûlerie Caumartin, 71 rue de Caumartin
Coffee roaster and restaurant between the two buildings of Au Printemps. Very high reputation for pure coffee and blends. You can try one if you eat here.
• Baggi, 33 rue Chaptal
Simple surroundings for the oldest ice cream makers in Paris - father to son for over 130 years. Plain direct flavors or elaborate confections of ice cream and sorbet in cakes or sundaes. Often as many as 50 flavors in summer. Caresse combines hazelnut, cognac and walnut, Williamette is pear and black-currant sorbet.

• **Androuet, 41 rue d'Amsterdam**
Cheese shop and restaurant. Monsieur Androuet is revered in France for his knowledge, influence and books. The cheeses can be sensational and upstairs are a variety of menus with cheese in every course, from triple creams to blues. But to be honest, I'm not really sure that is the best way to enjoy cheese.

• **Bonbonnière de la Trinité, 4 pl d'Estienne-d'Orves**
Mainly chocolates. One of three shops with a reputation for old-fashioned respect for the customer and the product. Chocaholics swear by the blocks of supra-bitter or supra-amer, really dark and intense, in thick plain slabs or stuffed with everything imaginably wicked. Also honeys and teas.

• **JC Cornu, 82 rue de Clichy**
Specialty foods including olive oils of many flavors, more or less acidic, or as fruity as you like. Nut oils too, plus poultry from the Landes, teas and sardines in olive oil.

• **Shah et Compagnie, 33 rue Notre-Dame-de-Lorette**
Indian food and supplies. A riveting example of an ethnic food shop including fresh exotica imported direct. Spices and spice mixtures, unusual rices. The more you buy, the less you pay.

Rue des Martyrs isn't very touristy yet it is classically Paris. A narrow winding street with peeps of Sacré-Coeur over rooftops like Utrillo paintings. As you climb towards Pigalle, filles de joie in tightly belted raincoats ogle from doorways.

• **Chez Terrier, 58 rue des Martyrs**
One of the best sources of lyonnaise charcuterie in Paris. You should be able to sample a true rose de Lyon and burgundian specialties from jambon persillé to pike quenelles. Stock changes according to the season.

• **Molard, 48 rue des Martyrs**
Charming cheese shop with display of pots and molds not for sale. Usually a good variety of chèvres, homemade yogurt and crème fraîche. One friend found sheep's milk ricotta.

• **Bourdaloue, 7 rue Bourdaloue**
Another "olde worlde" sort of place with their own confectionery and chocolate, ice creams and sorbets to complement the range of cakes and pastries. Flavored macaroons, apple chaussons and a pain de gênes, an almond pound cake. A few tables for tea or coffee.

• **Fouquet, 36 rue Laffitte**
One of two shops specializing in confectionery of the utmost quality. Everything is special but particularly the raspberry drops, caramels and exceptional glacé fruits, although as usual these look better than they taste. Everything is prepared here. On another site the specially recommended vinegars are made. Other condiments are available, as well as preserves, jams and champagne.

• **A la Mère de Famille, 35 rue du Faubourg-Montmartre**
Confectionery and confitures are the prizes for finding this, the oldest confectioners in Paris, established in 1761. Wonderful dried fruits from the best areas of France plus chocolates and marrons.

Rue Cadet makes a fascinating detour. It's full of food shops and stalls, a butcher selling pale pré-salé lamb in spring, fish markets and the start of a Jewish orthodoxy, and surprise . . . especially when you wander back and along rue Richer to see the Folies-Bergères building on your way to lunch at Brasserie Flo.

• **Poissonnerie Moderne, 2 bis rue Cadet**
Fish shop specializing in Mediterranean fish, reflecting the sort of people who live here. You could find rascasse, mullet, tuna and salt cod.

• **Mon Porc, 18 rue Cadet**
Charcuterie and butcher that cures its own hams on the premises. Look for rillons, andouilles and fresh foie gras available most of the year.

• **Le Dessert Fin, 3 rue Cadet**
Exceptional cake shop. Bavarois of fresh fruits and whipped cream are their great pride - the passion fruit is my favorite. But marvelous gâteaux of all sizes and flavors. A find.

Intriguing rue Richer has Tunisian kosher shops (truly) and at No 51 a kosher shop selling Adolphe burgers - think about it. . . . Rue de Paradis is the street for china and glass, French and imported in every price range. But before you spend time and money, there are two little-known museums I earnestly recommend: The Baccarat Crystal Museum (No 30) is combined with a vast and impressive shop selling everything from magnificent chandeliers and glasses to animal sculptures. The fascinating museum has crystal dating to 1823 and ancient glass blowing instruments. Le Monde de l'Art (No 18) has extraordinary art nouveau mosaics in the passage and stairway. It was built around 1900 by the architect Jacottin.

• **Limoges Unic, 56 rue de Paradis**
Villeroy and Boch, Lafarge and others as well as a wide range of Limoges.

• **Editions Paradis, 29 rue de Paradis**
Famous marques of crystal like Baccarat and Lalique, figurines by Tallec, Lyadro and Wiertasca.

• **Arts Ceramiques, 15 rue de Paradis**
Traditional china and silver, reproduction faïence, good for gifts.

NO PAIN NO GAIN

The French have been crazy about wheat bread since the middle ages, when they began phasing rye out of the mix. Although French bread consumption has been decreasing this century, it was only 150 years ago that the average family spent half of its food budget on bread. If you've ever seen French people shaking visibly when bread is not at the table, you'll find it difficult to believe they are consuming less than half as much bread as they did in 1900, but more than 80 percent still eat bread daily or almost daily.

Some bakers say the world is divided into people who eat baguettes and people who eat flutes, which are longer, thinner and traditionally heavier than baguettes. In country areas, they tend to opt for the flute, which weighs on average 400g. The typical 300g baguette appeals to townfolk and city dwellers, but the baking techniques for both are the same.

I've been told that the secret to a good baguette is 52°C. That's not the temperature of the oven when it's cooked, but the sum total of the temperature of the flour, the kitchen and the water used in the mix. So, if early in the morning, the kitchen is at a temperature of 18°C and the flour is about the same (it usually is), that means the water used needs to be at a temperature of 52°C minus 18°C minus 18°C, equals 16°C.

The oven should be a high 300°C so that the dough effectively explodes when it hits the oven floor, creating the ideal golden colored, crunchy crust. Knock the base of your baguette and it should sound like a drum. Press a baguette lightly with your thumb and the crust should crack.

• **Tholoniat, 47 rue du Château-d'eau**
Monsieur Tholoniat fashions sugar into every imaginable shape with consummate artistry. A good variety of rich, classic cakes. Look carefully at those chocolates famed for their luscious centers and then look away - many are fashioned to represent the, ummm, droppings of this or that animal. It's a comment on what is thought of his competitors rather than of his own chocolates, I believe. Closed Wednesdays.

• **Marché St Martin, corner of rue du Château-d'eau and rue Bouchardon**
Opposite the local mayor's office, this old covered market is a genuine flavor of the way things used to be, but may be too much for some, especially the sight of produce being washed in the communal fountain. It survives as a protest against too much progress and if the locals like it, who are we to criticize or patronize? Open Tuesday to Saturday, closed 1–4 PM and on Sunday mornings.

• **Schmid, 76 bd de Strasbourg**
The most important and busiest Alsatian charcuterie in Paris. Wonderful choucroute and all the sausages you can imagine to go with it. Naturally enough, the fruit tarts of spring and autumn are terrific. Their other branch at 3 bd Denain has a smaller selection but you can actually eat there. Also at 36 rue Lévis in the 17e.

• **Marché St-Quentin, corner de Magenta and rue Chabrol**
This covered market has been restored and boasts as a focal point one of the Wallace fountains that used to grace most of Paris. An hour or two spent here tells you much of what is happening in Paris, for the choice ranges from fabulous Atlantic and Mediterranean fish to Asian takeout, health foods, Corsican ewe's milk cheese, a triperie, a volaillier with every imaginable bird, marvelous vegetables, regional charcuterie, wine, a café and frozen foods.

• **Aux Délices de la Table, 63 rue Chabrol**
A strangely out-of-place luxury food shop with produce from Fauchon including wines and spirits, chocolates and teas.

• **Mauduit, 12 bd Denain and 54 rue Faubourg St-Denis**
Really marvelous food to eat in or take out, prepared primarily at the second address. Confectionery, chocolates, pastries or something more substantial. The Denain address is somewhat belle-époque and has an upstairs tea salon.

Now here you can walk on to the canal St-Martin and cross it to do some real exploring. If you do, head for the revolving bridge and the Café du Pont Tournant on rue de la Grange-aux-Belles and watch this extraordinary world go by through fabulous 19th-century etched glass windows. Otherwise, head up to Montmartre by rue de Dunkerque, which is brash and touristy beside Gare du Nord, and thus with the advantage of good cheap eats and cheap hotels. Once over the junction with boulevard Magenta it narrows and becomes neighborly. You'll find plenty to interest you.

• **Grandmère l'Oye, 57 rue de Dunkerque**
Small shop specializing in foie gras, fresh and cooked, but which doesn't accept credit cards as their prices are considered lowest for value in Paris. Other goodies too.

Arrondissement 18

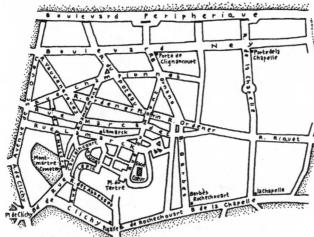

In the vicinity of Place du Clichy, Pigalle, Montmartre, Place du Tertre, Sacré-Coeur, Cligancourt.

I can't think of a better autumn morning I've spent anywhere. The sparkling, cleaner air and sudden high, gaping views down to the Seine dismissed the steep-stepped routes that make and mar Montmartre. A street fair enlivened further both the bohemian casualness and my enjoyment of picking over fresh cèpes and trompettes de la mort from overflowing panniers, and it assisted the weaker to walk past the dribbling stacks of heads, legs and haunches of wild boar. The fair's gallic disorganization melted the crowd into one, for while men with bagpipes and girls with clogs jigged regional dances in the streets, pop music blared from lamp posts; someone had forgotten to close the streets and cars hooted and drove cursing through the ribboned troupes. With two slices of nut-and-caramel-filled engadine from Le Moule à Gâteau, the sun on my back and a wondrous

array of fish and cheese, meat, poultry, game, charcuterie and confectionery to explore, it was pas de problème.

The drama of Montmartre's setting forces new views upon you on even the shortest walk. They are as potent as the paintings, even amid the busloads of gapers, and still infect hundreds of artists with the belief that they can emulate the imagery of their Impressionist predecessors. You can judge their success, and those who buy the works, in the Place du Tertre. But it is you who will have a finger - feet? - on the more valid pulse of Montmartre when you potter down rue du Mont-Cenis to the markets of rue du Poteau and rue Duhesme. If you've only a short time in Paris but want to balance the might of her monuments and art with some modern reality, this is probably the best place to do it. And you can combine the area with the Marché aux Puces at Cligancourt. There are other antique and junk markets, but you need to see this once at least. There are bargains in small things for

kitchens and in bigger pieces, if you look carefully.

• **Le Wepler, 14 pl Clichy** *Seafood restaurant specializing in oysters but also such regional specialties as confit de canard or andouillette. Daily until 1:30 AM.*

• **Pettier, 14 ave de Clichy** *Artisan boulangerie with traditional shapes and types of loaves plus walnut bread.*

• **Cochet, 20 ave de Clichy** *Pâtisserie with palmiers, sorbets, chocolates and excellent petits fours. Closed Wednesdays.*

The area where rue Lepic meets avenue de Clichy is a busy mixture of styles and cultures. At the corner of the two thoroughfares is Moulin Rouge, surrounded by sex shops, shops catering to transvestites and fast-food shops. The district has always been favored by artists and theatrical people. A large Arab and North African community has settled around Clichy, which has meant an influx of exotic foods into the shops and market. Don't be snobby and look only at the high-class shops - the supermarket on the left as you walk up is terrific and cheap for snacks, mineral water to sip and toiletries.

• **La Poularde, 10 rue Lepic** *Old poultry market with glass and wooden counter where poultry is cut to order. Poulets de Bresse delivered Wednesday and Friday, venison in season, barbary duck, guinea fowls, quails' eggs.*

• **Lux Bar, 12 rue Lepic** *Local bar with marble-topped tables and a tile mural of belle-époque Montmartre. Also serves food.*

• **Broquère, 22 rue Lepic** *Île de la Réunion specialties. Converted from an old* grainerie. *Plantains and okra, vanilla pods, peanuts, exotic syrups, pink peppercorns.*

• **Les Petits Mitrons, 28 rue Lepic**
Pâtisserie with old-fashioned tarts and tourtes, homemade jams and preserves, cherry clafoutis and cucumber and mint tourte.

• **Da Graziano, 83 rue Lepic**
Restaurant situated on the site of one of the three remaining moulins on the hill. 100 yards down the hill is the famous Moulin de la Galette. Tables in the garden. Carpaccio and panserotti are specialities.

• **Le Montagnard, 102 rue Lepic**
Specialties Campagnarde. *Decorated tables and beautiful lace tablecloths in this pretty street-side restaurant with garden out the back. Traditional French food such as onion soup and moules (mussels).*

One of the finest art deco metro signs can be found at Metro Abbesses. An art deco water fountain scintillates in the cobble-stoned and chestnut-lined place Emile-Goudeau, a walk up rue Ravignan. Abbesses market, rue des Abbesses, is a street market stretching from the corner of rue Lepic to metro Abbesses.

• **La Boutique au Fromage, 48 rue des Abbesses**
Cheese shop.

• **Chez Claude, 50 rue des Abbesses**
Sells every type of clam as well as ready-to-eat escargot prepared in butter.

• **Letellier-Volaille, 57 rue des Abbesses**
Resembles a hunting lodge where stuffed partridges and quails are traded beneath the stuffed heads of deer and boar.

• **Poissonnerie de la Butte,** corner rue des Abbesses and rue Lepic
Beautiful coquilles St-Jacques with corals, as well as tuna and live crab in this large shop.

• **L'Assommoir, 12 rue Girardon**
Restaurant named after Emile Zola's first realistic novel and full of the owner's cats, most of them china, plus a collection of African and Oceanic masks. Specializes in haddock, turbot and magret de canard.

• **Vineyards of Montmartre, rue des Saules**
Vineyard, of all things, producing a wine that is sold off once a year at a charity auction held at the Hôtel de Ville. A grape harvest festival in October.

• **Caves de Nîmes, 7 bis rue Tardieu**
Wine shop selling 160 kinds of crus d'appellation and 40 champagnes. Cheese platters on wicker prepared to order. Closed Wednesdays.

Now find Place du Tertre, teeming with artists good and bad, the stunning views of Paris from the Butte and Sacré-Coeur Cathedral. Plenty of places to eat and snack, but it's better to go on away from the crowd.

• **Beauvilliers, 52 rue Lamarck**
Smart, expensive restaurant that draws a very Parisian crowd and is filled with more flowers than any other establishment in the city. Specialities include ragonnade de veau aux truffes et à la crème de marsala.

• **Passa Temp Gallery, 54 rue Lamarck**
Stunning vases, platters and art glass.

• **Ferme Poitevine, 64 rue Lamarck**
Cheese shop with munster fermier and camembert.

Recommended charcuterie too.

• **Sadier, 43 rue Ramey**
Classic charcuterie and catering in the champenois style. Interesting range of champagnes and wines.

• **Meneau, 59 bis du Mont-Cenis**
Boulangerie specializing in health foods prepared by Abel Meneau and sold throughout Paris. Pain de campagne biologiques, cakes diététiques, wonderful almond macaroons. Closed Sundays. Honeys include raspberry flower.

• **Pâtisserie René Raveau, 81 rue du Mont Cenis**
Classic Pâtisserie with ganache chocolate cake and the gâteau maison of chantilly and chocolate-topped caramelized crème. Said to be one of the absolute best of this style in Paris.

Rue du Poteau is a busy working-class market street where every shop sells vegetables, fruit, meat, poultry, prepared foods or flowers. Shops in the surrounding streets are devoted strictly to food and food-related products.

• **Fromagerie de Montmartre, 9 rue de Poteau**
Cheese shop offering almost 250 cheeses including pérails fermiers, Corsican cheese, chantilly cream, bite-sized fromage frais covered with herbs, raisins, cinnamon, walnuts, etc. Heart-shaped cheese molds and fresh pasta also sold.

• **Charcuterie du Montmartre, 11 rue de Poteau**
Plats à emporter *such as canard a l'orange and stuffed zucchini. Whole glazed hams.*

• **Aux Vrais Produits d'Auvergne, 23 rue Lepic and 23 rue du Poteau**
Food shop specializing in products from the Auvergne.

- Jandré, 76 rue Duhesme
A maître pâtissier de France with particularly good peach and pear charlottes.
- Marché rue Duhesme, from rue du Poteau to rue Ornano
Many merchants still wear blue smocks. Serenaded by street musicians, buy vegetables, fish, poultry, cheese, meat, flowers and some clothing. Closed Sundays and Monday afternoons. Good prize-winning Bretonne charcuterie, excellent fish and Jean Barthélémy cheese.
- La Pêche Bretonne, 8 ave de la Porte-de-Montmartre
Fish shop which also supplies many fine restaurants. Mediterranean and Atlantic fish, fresh frog's legs, bouillabaisse. Closed Mondays and Tuesdays.
- Aux Ducs de Gasgogne, 123 rue Caulaincourt
Specialty shop with own brand foie gras products from Gascony (no imported livers used). Shops located throughout Paris. Wines from the region too.

From rue Caulaincourt, walk up rue Junot where the building at No 13 with its tile murals is a homage to *dessinateur* François Poulbot. Further on is rue Girardon, a delightful residential street lined with chestnut trees. The houses are of painted brick, an unusual sight in Paris. Walk up rue Tourlaque to le Fussains (at No 22), an artists' colony set in a maze of 16th-century buildings. Classic and modern sculptures are set in the flowering overgrown gardens.
- L'Escargot de la Butte, 46 rue Joseph-de-Maistre
Restaurant dedicated to escargots. They're also painted on the building, featured on posters and celebrated in sculpture. Closed Mondays.

CHEESES IN THE ÎLE DE FRANCE

As befits the cradle of France, this is the home of the cheese voted king - *brie de Meaux*. All the other cheeses made in the area are either variations of this round, flat, white-molded variety or are soft, creamy cheeses, some enriched further with double cream.

- *Brie de Coulommiers*: Also known as *brie petit moule* and related to *brie de Meaux*. It is rather rich and sharp and sometimes used to make cheese croquettes. Best autumn to spring. Weighs about 1kg/2lb or more. Note that it is not a *coulommiers* (qv).
- *Brie laitier*: Commercially produced in this area and other parts of the north. Made of pasteurized milk of differing fat content and the quality varies enormously. In France you should only eat the next three types of brie ...
- *Brie de Meaux fermier*: Officially voted "King of Cheeses" in 1815 by the 143 negotiators of the Congress of Vienna, who reorganized Europe after the Napoleonic wars. This cheese has an ancient and distinguished history. It was appreciated by Charlemagne, Henry IV and by Queen Marie Leczinska who used it in her famous *bouchées à la reine*. Made from raw cow's milk, the white crust should be slightly pigmented with red or brown, the body a firm, pale yellow, supple but not runny, and the flavor farmy and rather nutty. Best from July to March, but difficult to look after well in high summer. The most highly regarded is from Meaux itself. Made in the *département* of Seine-et-Marne and as well in nearby *départements* of Burgundy, Champagne and the Loire.
- *Brie de Melun AOC*: Another brie protected by an AOC, this is perhaps the oldest of them all. Produced in small dairies in the traditional manner and cured twice as long as other bries. Made from raw cow's milk and very like *brie de Meaux* but a little fruitier and earthier to the nose. Smaller too at about 1.5kg/3lb. Best July to March. May also be eaten fresh (*frais*) or sprinkled with charcoal (*bleu*).
- *Brie de Montereau*: A very fruity flavor to this brie made in traditional small dairies. Also known as *Ville-St-Jacques* and more the shape and size associated with Normandy *camemberts*.
- *Chèvru*: An ancient farmer's cheese that keeps well, cured on beds of fern for a month. Very similar to *brie de Meaux* in flavor and may be called a *fougère* or *fougèru*. Very delicious dinner party food.
- *Coulommiers*: Increasingly produced in factories, a smaller type of *brie de Meaux* on a bed of straw (usually plastic!). Sometimes made extra rich at 50 percent fat content.
- *Délice de St-Cyr*: From St-Cyr-sur-Morin, a triple-cream cheese (75 percent fat) with a mild, somewhat nutty flavour, excellent with light, fruity wines.
- *Explorateur*: Commercially made triple-cream cheese with creamy flavor and 75 percent fat content.
- *Feuille de Dreux*: Made from partly skimmed cow's milk, a low fat (30–40 percent) cheese with a strong, fruity flavor related to *brie de Melun*. An ancient house-hold cheese wrapped in six chestnut leaves.
- *Fontainebleau*: Fresh cheese curds mixed with whipped cream and thus an immature triple-cream cheese. Eaten with sugar as a dessert but needs to be chilled. It's simple to make your own.
- *Ville-St-Jacques*: See *brie de Montereau*.

- Schmid, 199 rue Championnet
Charcuterie specializing in food from Alsace, including choucroute and saucisson de foie.

- Chuet, 28 ave de St-Ouen
Corsican products including broccio cheese and charcuterie such as prisuttu, figatelli, lonzo and coppa.

BURGUNDY & FRANCHE-COMTE

A BROTHERHOOD OF COMMITTEES

"In which we...
• Go above the salt and below stairs in a palace...
• Learn of wet nurses and dry hams in the Morvan...
• Explore a lotte of confusion and see where boiling wine changed our life...
• Taste the produce of a fisherman's pouch and try to get an invitation to a genuine pig-out...
• Are told not to expect fireworks in Chambertin and learn how to lose heart...
• Enjoy the cream of the currant crop and perhaps a Japanese rarity, and cut into a gaude...
• Find which cheese should have holes, and which cheese isn't a cheese...
• Buy gingerbread and are introduced to a rock that should not be eaten...
• Meet unusual women and learn of one's connection with a monastery...
• Go to a fair and taste all day...
• Visit the town that cuts the mustard..."

Life at the domestic tables of Burgundy must be dreadfully confusing. The region eats and drinks under the burden of as many opinions as there are people, and under the scrutiny of more brotherhoods, societies, circles, guilds and the like per village and town than anywhere else in the world. *Les Chevaliers du Tastevin* have become an international institution; others are relentlessly local - the Chevaliers dedicated to protecting and eating pauchouse, the *Confrérie de l'Escargot, Les Chevaliers des Trois Cèpes* and the like. The epicenter of this earnest scholarliness is Dijon.

I went there in early November, knowing only that the city's name was on a lot of mustard and that the dukes of Burgundy had been envied for their kitchen. I traveled by slow-stopping train northwards from Lyon, with the Sâone on my right, and the gray skeletons of the last vintage on my left, through Chagny and Châlons and other towns with nothing but names to tell of their connection with wine. From trains you see little of the real life of a village, smell neither tang of acrid black tobacco nor the rich air of buttery baking, hear no hiss of a coffee machine, enjoy no sudden turn into a bright market or quiet shop where even old friends are addressed as Monsieur and Madame. At least on this route I knew they were there, for I had once driven open-topped through the harvesting villages. Now my backyard view from the carriage completed the picture, for behind the tall, bright-tiled village houses I discovered gardens growing herbs and tightly staked tomatoes, with next door here an ill-tempered goat bullying with yellow teeth a hedge, and there in the next, the last reddened apples on an old tree waiting their turn for the table.

The reason for this seemingly unseasonal visit is one that I urge all admirers of French food to copy, a visit to the Dijon Food Fair; and you can now get to Dijon from Paris by TGV in 1½ hours. It is different from most fairs, being for the public rather than for the trade. For two weeks, families from Dijon and *la toute France* cram the hall to taste *saucisses* new to them, compare oysters from Brittany with those of Aquitaine, eat in restaurants from other regions, try old and new gingerbreads from Mulot et Petitjean, and to sniff at specialities from the featured guest country. Few internationally known brand names are there, not even of wine, and thus it is an excellent opportunity to compare the products of champagne houses never seen in Britain and the U.S. Or perhaps to taste the wines of Arbois or of new plantations from the south. The Dijon fair is also the meeting place of distinguished bodies with long names; exceptionally learned and interesting culinary papers are delivered by *États Généraux de la Gastronomie Française et de l'Alimentation de Qualité*. Members of the press belonging to equally over-named societies come from all over France to hear what they have to say, and to attend the only other functions to which the public is not privy, the judging of alcohols and the awarding of the year's new ribbons by *La Commanderie des Cordons Bleus de France*.

If the food or the fair becomes too much to digest easily then you should return to the center of town and the duke's palace. Fully to appreciate its golden symmetry, delay your expedition until late in the evening, then circle the site so that you approach it by one of the arch-ended, narrow streets that empties into the subservient low semicircle of shops on the place de la Libération. Dramatically, the floodlit palace floats at eye level across a broad rise of cobbles, a grand country house come to town, with undertakers and gingerbread shops for its gardens and fountains. Only when you return the next day will you appreciate the irony of building such a palace around the lopsided Tower of Philippe le Bon.

Included in the palace is the *Musée des Beaux Arts*, housing the best art collection in France after the Louvre and mercifully open on Mondays when everything else is closed. Once you have walked to find favorites on the walls and appreciated some fine contemporary furniture in the grander rooms, return to the ground floor and to the room considered by many as the heart of Burgundy, the 15th-century kitchens of the palace. There is talk that the dukes entertained there, but a few minutes imagining the heat from the fires that burned under the six open chimneys should show this was no place for velvets and breeches. No, I think the meaning behind this view is that the dukes were here so overwhelmed by the food their fabulous wealth and power could command that their culinary hospitality was an important part of the influence they wielded. The kitchen became a symbol of Burgundy in a way it did nowhere else, perhaps explaining that rash of opinions and brotherhoods. Currency was given to the belief that in Burgundy everyone ate and drank like a duke. Of course, that simply wasn't the case.

The Burgundians are largely descended from bluff Vikings, the sort who came overland rather than by sea. They found things fairly well organized, thanks to the legacy of the Romans - decent vines, good grain crops and access to the produce of the north, east, west and south via river and easy land. The essentials of the Burgundian table today are much the same. The wine you know about, although almost no one can claim to understand the finessing of vineyard names on the bottles' labels. And today Burgundy grows three times more wheat than she can eat. With this long tradition of grain there is generally an excellent range of pâtisserie and of bread; the number of bread types is increasing according to a local baker, as the French demand more organic, whole wheat and mixed grain loaves. In the Morvan, pigs remain virtually free-range, but the other crop, of wet-nurses for Paris, is today harder to find.

Freshwater fish, small game, poultry and snails all played their part in the Burgundian diet of the less privileged majority, but the basic was that of most of France, a porridge, or *bouillie*, of whatever grain was available. Often it was millet, for this gives more bulk when cooked than any other grain, but this was universally replaced by corn when it came from the Americas. Today *bouillies* are eaten only by the old, but through choice rather than necessity.

The Burgundian's easterly neighbors, the Francs-Comtois have none of that culinary competitiveness. The very name of the region means Free Country and a palpable independence has been enhanced by extraordinary community spirit - and more committees. The cheese makers formed themselves into co-operatives before the end of the 13th century to make communal cheeses, the fruits of the mountains, in *fruitières*. The motto of winemakers some centuries later was: We Are All In Charge.

Franche-Comté, often confused with Jura, which is only its southern *département*, appears to have borrowed a number of foods from other countries - they have there a fondue of cheese like the Swiss, their *gaude* of cornmeal is often served like *polenta*, their *bresi* is thinly sliced air-dried beef, like that of the Alps, and such *vins jaunes* (yellow wines) as Château-Chalon taste like sherry. They serve a cheese flan (*flamusse*), and ramekins of cheese, with apparent ignorance of those of Burgundy. But it is as well if any such similarities you notice while visiting are kept to yourself, for in the Franche-Comté they are Francs-Comtoises.

You may, however, laugh as much as you like at the ineptitude of central governments and at royal madness in Arc-et-Senans (Boubs). Here you will find the extraordinary semi-classical buildings of the *Saline Royale*, Royal Saltworks. Built in the late 1770s, it planned to provide huge quantities of salt by the evaporation of water from local saline springs over fires stoked by wood from the forest of Chaux. But almost immediately, the salt level of the spring was found to be lower than thought, there wasn't nearly enough wood, and other more economical methods of making salt were mastered. The restored buildings and works are well worth seeing, and then you can go off to older, smaller, nicer Salins-les-Bains, a spa with salt mines and wells you can visit.

You will find much to intrigue you in Burgundy and Franche-Comté. Where it is most interesting you are most likely to find some supporting organization in the background. There are enough of them in Franche-Comté for there to be a *President des Societés Culinaires de Franche-Comté*. The men and women who bring their country produce to the narrow streets and huge covered market between Dijon's rue de la Liberté and Church of Notre Dame, will belong to one or have a relative in La Cousinerie de Savigny-les-Beaune, or supply something special to a rôtisseur. Thus anyone with French who enjoys a good argument on the relative merits of one chicken against another or the amount of garlic that should be in the butter of the snails prepared in Auxerre is in for a wonderful time. It's even more interesting because here, far more than in Lyon, supposedly famed for the influence of women on its food, I found successful and respected women in the food business, like Madame Porchevet, who has managed to winkle supplies of Cîteaux out of the monks who make it. Or Louise Mirbey, chef-patronne of Auberge du Vieux Moulin (Aubigny-70140 Pesmes), and President of the *Association des Restauratrices-Cuisinières*.

I can't guarantee you'll always eat wonderfully in Burgundy or Franche-Comté, but I can guarantee you'll have much fun doing it. You'll meet more enthusiastic shopkeepers, with hand-written labels in red ink on everything, more eccentric opinions and more newly invented specialties than anywhere else in France. The best way to cope with it is to do as the Burgundians. Form a committee of people who agree with you. You'll be welcomed to the fray . . .

Charcuterie

As with most foods, Burgundy and Franche-Comté have absorbed the best ideas from neighboring regions and adapted them to their superior produce. Even with such abundance, they make and enjoy boudins, andouilles, and andouillettes *in Arnay-le-Duc, Chablis, Clamécy and Mâcon. I like to snack wickedly on grillons and grattons, which are pieces of bacon or salt pork cooked until crisp and frizzled; they are also found in galettes. Sausages are great specialties, both air-dried saucissons, such as rosette du Morvan, and fresh or smoked saucisses which are usually enjoyed hot. The garlic ones - à l'ail - can be cut up to fatten a soup of cabbage and onion, and there are others flavored with cumin.*

Exceptional hams are a great boast of the area, especially those from Morvan and Luxeuil in Franche-Comté. Ham is often enjoyed hot, braised, with a cream sauce or as a saupiquet.

Fish & Shellfish

In this region of rushing streams, of brooks and rivers, I find myself thinking of Louisiana: her Cajun cray-fishers are descended from 17th-century French immigrants and the Acadienne swamps now produce 85 percent of the world's harvest of écrevisses (freshwater crayfish). There are persistent whispers that most écrevisses sold in France are actually Acadienne, imported through necessity in the same way as snails and foie gras. But considering the amount of fresh water available and the comparatively few visitors who patronize Franche-Comté, I feel more certain of getting a genuine local crayfish here than anywhere else in France. Just as well, for what is more luxurious than the rich sauce of puréed crayfish tails, cream and wine named after the epicenter of crayfish eating, Nantua, just across the way in Savoie?

In Burgundy and Franche-Comté you can dine confidently, assured of the best of virtually any

WORTH FINDING

• *Écrevisses à la nage*: Often called a *nage* of this or that. *Nager* means to swim and so these dishes are always crayfish, whole or just tails, in an aromatic liquid, not sauce, of wine and herbs, sometimes with cream or butter or both.

• *Meurette*: Burgundian red-wine sauce used for almost everything and excellent on eels, carp, perch and tench.

• *Pauchouse/Pochouse/Pochou*: One of the region's most famous dishes and still found easily. It is a stew of freshwater fish, a variation on the matelote of the north of the region. The essentials are eel and burbot (classically from the Saône or Rhône), white wine, onion and garlic. Some recipes will include bacon or salt pork, cream or marc; old ones insist that only carp, eel and pike should be used. Several villages claim the invention, and some say the word is a dialect corruption of *pêcher* (to fish), others that it is a corruption of a word for fisherman's Pouch. Certainly Verdun-sur-le-Doubs is one of the sources; inevitably they have a *Confrérie de la Pauchouse.*

freshwater fish you would expect to find inland. Rainbow trout is superb universally, and especially from the Cure and Cousin in the Yonne, from the Doubs in Franche-Comté and at Gray and Dôle, where Louis Pasteur began his experimenting by boiling wine. Smaller, quieter restaurants may offer the rare chance of a genuine truite au bleu.

Pike (brochet) is also found poached in white wine (those stories of the bones being difficult are a little over-dramatic). You will find carp, eels, perch and tench (carpe, anguilles, perche and tanche) en meurette among other ways, but not the rare char

(omble chevalier), which is cooked more simply and anyway is more likely to be found in adjoining Savoie. Butter, cream and wine, onions, mushrooms and garlic are all used extensively; but it may be a surprise to find lotte on the menu. This is not the monkfish or anglerfish of the deep ocean, but an abbreviation of lotte de rivière, which is burbot.

Naturally, with so much water around, frogs are common, and commonly eaten, especially in Franche-Comté where among the many famous soups is one made from grenouilles.

A RITUAL OF SNAILS

The snail most often eaten throughout France is the *petit gris* (*helix aspersa*), which is especially common on vineyards. It fattens itself through summer, when it is known as a *coureur* or runner, then becomes a *dormeur* or sleeper when it burrows under the ground to hibernate in winter. It is at this time that the snail is considered tastiest, and this is when snail hunts are, or were, common. Not very sporting.

In the chalkier regions of eastern France there is a bigger, fatter, juicier snail, the Burgundy snail, *escargot de Bourgogne* (*helix pomotia*). In the culinary world it is a star, but a waning one, for it is one of the few culinary specialties of national importance not protected by AOC legislation. Thus, even in Burgundy, your escargots de Bourgogne might be any species - what's more they may come from Turkey, and might well have arrived prepared and frozen.

The high general regard the French seem to give snails is less than a century old. Although the Romans cared

enough to provide artificial rain for the snails they raised, the French regarded them as food for the poor, or for hard times. But they have long been part of national custom surviving only in one festival in Burgundy, at Basou near Auxerre, an important center for snail preparation still.

All French snails are becoming rarer as a result of the increased use of agricultural chemicals, especially in vineyards, and the disappearance of hedgerows. Even though laws prohibiting the gathering of Burgundian snails during their breeding season (April 1st to June 30th) have been passed, the number actually harvested is remarkably small and few restaurants, anywhere, are able to offer the genuine product. Thus 95 percent of all snails consumed in France come from Germany, Hungary, the Czech Republic, Poland, Greece, Turkey, North Africa or Southeast Asia. Many of those countries have been forced to cut their quotas dramatically, some because drought has reduced their reserves, some because France is attempting to control the condition of snails arriving at the borders. Most are shipped live but often over 25 percent are dead on arrival, with many of the survivors diseased. Frozen ones avoid this, but are often tough and tasteless through bad feeding and worse processing. The combination of a shortage in France and reduced supplies from abroad is increasingly changing the role of the edible snail - reversing it indeed. The food of the poor may soon be the food only of the rich.

The average French person eats 600-800g/1lb-2lb of snails a year. A study of old cookbooks reveals the taste for snails with garlic-laden butter is very modern. Butter with a touch of garlic and a lot of parsley was considered the way really to enjoy the flavor of the snail, and when I was served an omelette of butter-smothered snails at a cognac distillery outside Jarnac, I understood why, and enjoyed the delicious nutty flavor of snails for the first time in my life. It is said in fact that the flavor is rather of *eau-de-vie*, or of cognac itself if they are genuinely local snails. A white wine is the best accompaniment if the garlic is restrained.

Among the myriad different ways of preparing snails, one of the most unusual is the *cargolade* of Languedoc-Roussillon, in which they are grilled over charcoal, and here is where you are equally likely to find them combined with a little salted ham/*petit salé*, anchovies or nuts. Elsewhere wild mushrooms, cream, herbs, anise and tomatoes will feature; *sausage* is part of Provence's *à la suçarelle* style where you suck the snails from their shells. On the west coast, Angoulême is the most re-nowned center; indeed people here are known as *cargouillards*, said to move as slowly as the *cargouilles* which they stuff and put into *ragoûts*.

Many modern restaurants eschew shells, and so also do some old ones, notably the fabulous-looking Escargot Montorgueil in Paris. Here they serve up to seven varieties of snail, and also create delicate gratins and casseroles. With fascinating mirrors and painted ceilings it's one of the most evocative restaurants in Paris and quite as old as it looks; it's equally famed for an almost professional lack of interest in you.

Meat, Game & Poultry

The great charollais *cattle* from Charolles produce the most famous meat of the region, to the outsider. The appeal is more to the breeder and producer than to the eater for the flavor of the huge amounts of flesh each animal produces is pretty inferior. But if you like looking at beef on the hoof, St-Christophe-en-Brionnais is the biggest market center for them. There is a variation called the charolles-nivernaise, and for more flavor the animals of Brezail and l'Auxois repay investigation. Any of them should be found grilled over sarments (vine cuttings). Naturally, with so much dairying throughout Burgundy and Franche-Comté, there is veal, usually served simply with cream-based sauces. Because so much grain is grown, almost every type of poultry bird is bred; they are particularly likely to be teamed with cream plus a seasonal green, anything from dandelion to tarragon.

WORTH FINDING

• *Boeuf bourguignon*: This is what it's called when you are not in Burgundy, where it is *boeuf à la bourguignonne*, which is beef in a *sauce meurette*.

• *Chaudrée de lièvre*: A hare stew flavored with wine from Jura; more likely to be found in Franche-Comté.

• *Coq au Chambertin*: The ultimate *coq au vin*, but to be authentic only fresh young wine should be used, so don't expect fireworks and don't pay huge prices; a white wine alternative might be *poulet au Meursault*.

• *Ferchuse*: You may like to avoid this, a *ragoût* of lights, that is, lungs, heart, etc.

• *Fondue bourguignonne*: Actually Swiss, a cheeseless fondue in which pieces of steak are cooked in boiling oil at your table.

• *Galimafrée*: Sounding Eliza-bethan, this is a Morvan roast shoulder of mutton stuffed with bacon and mushrooms and served with vinaigrette.

• *Jambon persillé*: Once served only at Easter, today it is perfect summer food, provided a decent ham is used. Should be generous chunks of ham in a parsley-packed jelly of white burgundy.

• *Lapin rôti*: Although implying a rabbit roasted simply, this is almost always one of the many ways the Burgundians find of combining their mustard and their rabbits, often by covering the rabbit with a mustard coating or sauce.

• *Petit-salé aux pissenlits*: Simple, peasant food cele-brating spring, the classic combination of salt pork and young dandelion greens.

• *Potée*: Hearty vegetable/pork soup/stew found in most areas, made local by the variety of vegetables; you might also find it here including oxtail (*queue de boeuf*).

• *Saupiquet*: The first dish I ever ate in Burgundy and something you should cer-tainly order if you see it. Classically it should be slices of excellent Morvan ham, with a creamy sauce based on a classic *espagnole* or brown sauce with extra butter, vinegar, pepper and, sometimes, juniper berries. Great when it is great, but the balance of creaminess and sharpness is not easy to achieve. Gault Millau point out that where it was once famed throughout France, it is now underrated.

Virtually unobtainable outside France is the poulet de Bresse which has an appellation contrôllée of its own; first time, eat it as plainly as you can to appreciate the flavor; à la crème is a favorite.

Burgundy's game, which runs the gamut from sanglier (wild pig) and marcassin (wild piglet), to venison, hare, pigeon and pheasant, is exceptionally good. What's bagged from the forests of Morvan at least equals the superlative quality of that from Alsace; certainly it's a persuasive reason for being here in autumn and winter rather than in summer. Lapin de la garenne (wild rabbit) is a great local favorite. Towards the south, where more goat's milk cheeses are made, you will find roast kid (cabri) around Easter. Although pigs are raised universally, their flesh is more likely to be found in charcuterie of some kind. Look for delicious tourtes which are rather like pâté baked in pastry, pie-shaped rather than loaf-shaped, and petit-pâtés, a sort of small hot pork-pâté pie. But in Franche-Comté, break a leg to get invited to a repas du cochon, which should be a progression from boudin, fromage de tête and andouilles to chops and roasts of pork . . .

An important flavor difference between the meat cooking of Burgundy and that of Franche-Comté is the type of wine used. The wines of Arbois and the sherry-like Château-Chalon of the Jura lend a distinct individuality to Franc-Comtois cooking.

POULETS DE BRESSE AOC

Contender for title of best chicken in the world, the White Bresse breed has white

EGG-BOUND

With so much poultry about, and so much grain to feed them upon, you are bound to find eggs offered often. Indeed, some spots have fancy names for dishes that turn out to be ham and eggs. Eggs turn up whisked into creamy sauces but are also featured as protein alternatives, hence that most famed Burgundian dish, oeufs en meurette, poached eggs in a robust thickened sauce of young local red wine, as important here as haggis to a Scot.

Eggs combine with milk and cream in a number of savory dishes; they are sometimes mixed into the cheese fondue of Franche-Comté; they set the Burgundian cream and bacon flan called fouée,

first cousin of the true quiche; they go into gougères and galettes and the crépiau (a dialect name for pancakes). But they are most commonly and deliciously used in omelettes, classic with bacon or salt pork but also with the simplest of local vegetables, herbs and greens, even cabbage. The omelette nivernaise of summer will probably combine ham and sorrel (oseille). More famous is the dramatic omelette au sang made with pig's blood; it's sometimes called omelette bourguignonne. Hard-boiled eggs are served with local hams, and are enjoyed with spring-fresh dandelion greens in the Morvan.

skin, flesh and feathers, smooth gray or blueish legs with four toes and a red wattle - any variation, even of feather color, means the bird may not be sold under an AOC label. Famous for centuries, fraud and substitution meant that some control of their production was mooted as long ago as 1591. It was only in 1936, however, that their production zone was first defined and it took until 1957 to agree legally on how they must be raised.

The most important centers within the 400 sq km/250 sq miles are Bourg and Louhans, whence Fernand Point went to Vienne to become famous. Seven breeders supply day-old chicks to some 1,000

farmers, who may raise only 500 at a time. The birds spend 35 days as chicks and then must be free-ranging, on grass, for 9 weeks in the open air. Their feed must be nothing but cereal, with corn predominating, and skim milk. Even the weight of each bird before and after dressing is defined and, although there are poulets, poulards and chapons, they are usually collectively referred to as poulets de Bresse. AOC of course.

The parvenu turkey from the New World has found a little paradise for its time on earth here, too. Much less common than the chicken, but just as revelatory to enjoy as long as you can trust the chef.

Fruits & Vegetables

Any talk of the fruits or vegetables of Burgundy brings to mind a strange contrast of favorites - the ancient crop of cassis, and the modern one of crosne du Japon.

Cassis (black currants) were recommended medically in Burgundy centuries ago, but were as likely to be administered as an infusion of the leaves as in a decoction of the berries. In the heady days of 18th-century "vapours," their reputation for efficacy was further enhanced and by 1750 the Dijonnais were encouraged to begin serious planting of the bushes, first at the Château Montmuzard. The gradually increased crops inspired another cassis medicine, that of berries macerated in alcohol. In 1841, they perfected crème de cassis, made by crushing berries into vats of alcohol, filtering the result and sweetening it, according to what are said to be secret techniques, but which use ordinary old sugar. If you are going to make some yourself, and there's no reason why not, use one part currants to three of plain eau-de-vie and don't sweeten until you've drained off the mash. As you can imagine, there is both alcohol and flavor in that mash, so strain out the seeds and include the juice when you cook up, or cook down, some pâte de cassis, made just the same way as an apple or damson cheese.

The quick success of the crème meant even more bushes were enthusiastically planted throughout Côte-d'Or, often between the grape vines. Thus when phylloxera destroyed the vines later in the century there was still a crop to produce income. The popularity of crème de cassis dropped dramatically during and after World War II, said to be a result of using saccharine instead of sugar. Miraculously, Mayor Felix Kir, who was also a canon of the church, announced his favorite drink to be a dilution of crème de cassis with chilled white burgundian wine of the aligoté grape. He was seen introducing "his" drink to Russian leader Nikita Khrushchev, Pope John XXIII, and any other dignitary who happened to be present contemporaneously with a reporter or photographer. The Kirs, drink and man, were a gift from God to the growers: one of the most needed, and most successful, marketing ploys of the age.

Beware when buying, that you are indeed buying an alcohol rather than a sugar syrup (the label will tell you) and don't be boring but go also for other flavors of the same idea. Vedrenne Père et

LOCAL PRODUCE

VEGETABLES

• CABBAGE *chou pommé*
Dep: Côte-d'Or

• CARROT *carotte*
August to mid-November
Dep: Saône-et-Loire,
Côte-d'Or

• CAULIFLOWER *choufleur*
Early varieties, mainly
for export
Around June
Dep: Côte-d'Or,
Saône-et-Loire

• CELERIAC *céleri-rave*
Harvest in summer, stored
for winter
Dep: Côte-d'Or

• CUCUMBER *concombre*
Mid-summer crop
Dep: Saône-et-Loire

• FENNEL *fenouil*
Autumnish, but stored
Dep: Rhône, Ain, Haute-
Savoie

• LETTUCE *laitue/chicorée*
Var: from curly endive and
batavia down to round
lettuces
Variable according to type
Dep: Saône-et-Loire

• ONION *oignon*
Mid-June harvest starts,
sold next April
Dep: Côte-d'Or

• RADDISH *radis*
Spring to summer
Dep: Saône-et-Loire

• SHALLOT *échalote*
Freshly dug mid-summer,
stored for use all year
Dep: Côte-d'Or
The second-largest
production zone after
Hérault

FRUITS

• BLACK CURRANTS *cassis*
Var: *Noir de Bourgogne,
Royal Naples*
July, usually
Dep: Côte-d'Or,
Saône-et-Loire

• CHERRIES *cerises*
Var: *Bigarreau, Marmotte
de l'Yonne*
June to mid-July
Dep: Yonne

• RASPBERRY *framboise*
Var: *Rose-de-Côte-d'Or*
June-July (variable)
Dep: Cote-d'Or, Yonne
One of the few French
varieties of raspberry
grown commercially; has
a wonderful aroma.

Fils of Nuits-St-Georges make a sensational crème de fraise des bois (wild strawberry), remarkably true to flavor as the fruit is not cooked in any way; its alcoholic strength is high at 20 percent but crèmes can be 16 percent or less, which also makes them cheaper.

The Japanese artichoke (crosne), properly choro-gi, was introduced to Paris from Japan in the 1880s via Crosne in the Essonne (Seine-et-Oise). Fashionably taken up in those days of orientalia, it survives as a delicious curiosity only in pockets now. Sully-sur-Loire in the Loiret is one pocket. St-Seine-l'Abbaye in the Côte-d'Or is another. They are a slightly waxy, small root, sometimes confused with jerusalem artichokes (topinambours); the only other place I know that cultivates them regularly outside Japan is the market gardens around Wellington, New Zealand.

There are less exotic but equally delectable specialities - the asparagus of Auxonne, red and white haricot beans, the cherries of the Yonne, aniseed and hop shoots (jets d'houblon) - but there is also a huge, broad and general variety of more common vegetables and fruits. Most were once enjoyed primarily in the soups of one sort or another found in every region, but just as universally are now served lightly, elegantly and individually.

BOUILLIE FOR THEM

In Franche-Comté there was a long delight in barley broths, now declined. But it is there, rather than in

SOME LIKE IT HOT

Although Dijon is the spiritual and historical home of the mustard that bears its name, Dijon on most mustard jars now simply indicates a style of mustard and may be used by any mustard maker in France who meets the *appellation contrôllée* laws.

All mustard is made from black mustard seeds (*brassica nigra*) or brown mustard (*brassica juncea*) or some mixture, which are initially ground into mustard flour, coarse or fine. This has a negligible smell and no apparent taste when first put onto the tongue; but contact with water releases the oil and the bite. Exactly what is done to this mustard flour is what determines each style of mustard. To become *moutarde de Dijon* it is mixed with unripe grape juice but other styles will use wine, cider, beer, a mixture or just plain water. The strength depends on how much mustard flour is used in proportion to the liquid and whether or not any other solids such as sugar or other flours are included. The most difficult part of the operation, particularly if you want a hot mustard, is conserving the oil, which evaporates at temperatures of 40°C.

Most of the mustard eaten in France (90%) is Dijon-style, but the mustard seed is no longer exclusively grown in that region, although it grows very well there, discovered, they say, when Roman troops scattered seeds by the roadsides as they tramped backwards and forwards through the three parts of Gaul.

Mustard making was important in Dijon as long ago as the 13th century when the seeds were aged and ground with cloves, and cinnamon - but not allspice as some will tell you, for this had not yet come from the New World. The firm of Grey-Poupon, established in 1777, further enhanced the city's reputation by developing a recipe that used white wine.

Milder mustards are indicated by such labels as gentle (*douce*), yellow (*jaune*), brown (*brune*), green (*verte*) and violet (*violette*). Flavored mustards are *moutardes aromatisées* or a *moutarde aux aromates* if there is some complication of flavoring; if something simpler is used, the label is likely to tell you, as in *moutarde aux fines herbes* or *moutarde à l'estragon*.

Moutarde à l'ancienne is almost always relatively mild and made with coarsely ground seeds, a process that inhibits the release of some of the mustard oils. But in such a huge market, over 50,000 tons eaten in France alone each year, manufacturers will say and do almost anything to attract your attention.

Burgundy, that you might be offered a form of bouillie, the thickened porridge of grain meal which was the major sustenance of the region for aeons. The Francs-Comtois call it gaude, and make it of corn meal, cooked with water until very thick and served with milk or cream, perhaps wine. It may be sugared and served as a dessert, or left to cool, cut into squares and fried, like the polenta of Venice. The closest you are likely to get to anything remotely like the warm, thick goo of bouillie is fondue, made from mountain cheeses, and proper to the Franche-Comté via Switzerland, but certainly incorrectly described as fondue bourguignonne .

Once the reliable 19th-century strains of American wheat came to Burgundy, which had always had supplies but which now grows three times as much as it eats, the Burgundians slowly turned their backs on such food in favor of more plentiful and varied breads, and still pride themselves today on the range baked there.

Cheese

This is a cheese-lover's heaven. Champagne's cheeses naturally blend with those of Côte-d'Or giving more types of chaource and washed-rind cheeses. The rest of Burgundy makes a farmyard of cheeses, mainly chèvres, but some include cow's milk or a mixture, the mi-chèvres. In Franche-Comté, you find two famous styles of cheese, gruyère and cancoillotte, both of which require some explanation.

Gruyère is a word commonly misused, particularly in France, where it has become a generic name for all the great, cooked mountain cheeses which we are more likely to associate with Switzerland - emmental, gruyère, comté and beaufort. If it were not confusing enough to people who don't know which cheese has the holes, a French gruyère does have a considerable number of holes, which a Swiss one should not have. Perhaps you should avoid all known words and go for comté or beaufort as they are so rarely seen outside France. The Comtois use them for cheese fondues, of course!

And there is cancoillotte, a lesser version of fromage fort, fermented leftovers. To be exact, it is not really cheese at all, for the basic ingredient is mettons, which is made by heating whey, to solidify all the protein not already coagulated – that is, all the protein in milk that is not casein. Some sources say that farmwives make their mettons by heating curds, but I find this rather unlikely, for the point of both mettons and cancoillotte is the thrifty use of a whey that would otherwise be wasted or fed to animals.

Although long, this is not an exhaustive list, especially when it comes to chèvres, but these are the names you are most likely to see.

•Bleu de Gex/Haut-Jura: AOC Blue cheese from the highest pastureland of the Jura, where exceptionally varied flora give the milk of the montbéliarde cows a unique flavor. It is made by hand in traditional ways from raw milk; progressive salting gives both body and crust a special texture and an uneven marbling of blue-green which often clumps together. Recommended season is May to October, for then you know the cows have grazed on the best of fresh herbage of the Haut-Jura. This blue has such subtlety of flavor it is recommended that you eat it before other cheeses if you have a choice.

•Bressan: A soft, truncated cone of medium-flavored goat's cheese, which is best in summer and autumn, and which sometimes is a mi-chèvre.

•Bresse-bleu/Bleu de Bresse: Commercial blue cheese created in 1950 and based on saingorlon, itself created to copy the soft blue gorgonzola of Italy. An unaggressive flavor and nice creaminess from its 5 percent fat content.

•Bouton-de-culotte: See mâconnais.

•Cancoillotte: Very ripe mettons (qv) heated with brine then mixed with butter and eaten warm on bread or toast. Sometimes garlic, white wine or other flavorings are used. Beware of any grayish look, this cheese keeps for only a short time.

•Cendré d'Aisy: A soft cow's milk cheese in disk or truncated cone shape. Cured in marc for two months or so then stored in wood ash. Mild smell until cut; very strong flavor. Sometimes called Aisy cendré.

•Charollais: Goat or cow's milk, or a mixture. Hard, nutty cheese commonly used for fromage fort when aged.

•Chèvreton de Mâcon: Horrid small buttons of chèvre stored for use in winter, when they are grated into fromage fort. Dark brown and brittle with an appalling smell, and only likely to be found in real specialist shops or in small town markets. Who had the nerve to eat the first one?

•Cîteaux: A really delicious, rich but unaggressive washed-rind Trappist cheese still made by monks. Their abbey remains the only reliable source. A treat.

•Claquebitou: Fresh soft goat's milk cheese flavored with garlic and herbs. Mainly domestic but some enterprising goat keepers may sell to you direct - look for signs as you drive in the area.

•Comté/gruyère de comté: AOC cheese made for over 1,000 years. Deservillers is possibly where gruyère was created. The manufacture of comté is concentrated in the massif of Jura but spreads throughout Franche-Comté. Only milk from the montbéliarde and pie rouge de l'Est cows may be used. A cooked, pressed cheese, matured 3 months (minimum) to 10 months. It should be almost odorless but have a nutty, fresh taste whether young or matured and may be enjoyed all year round. NB: A local gruyère may almost be the same cheese, but uses different milk. See page 118.

•Dornecy: A fairly uncommercialized chèvre or mi-chèvre made in and around the town of the same name, weighing just over 200g/8oz; although very

goaty, the smell should be light.

•Ducs: A commercial brie/camembert type cheese in a cylindrical shape made from pasteurized cow's milk.

•Emmental français: Although mainly a product of Haute-Savoie, this French version of the Swiss cheese with the holes has been made here since the early 19th century, when German-Swiss cheesemakers immigrated. Aged cheeses are thought best November to May, but young ones are enjoyed all year round.

•Epoisses: A small round cow's milk cheese regularly washed with marc. Develops a penetrating smell and powerful flavor. Often kept in ashes over winter or used in fromage fort. Also available is L'ami du Chambertin, which is epoisses washed in Chambertin. Lucky thing!

•Fromage fort: Not often marketed; essentially old or overripe cheese mixed with butter, sometimes with leek water, sometimes with marc or with herbs, and then sealed in a pot, with occasional stirrings, for several months. It may explode; if I eat it, I do. Eaten on bread or toast with a little onion or garlic, it is the truest example of an acquired taste I know.

•Les Laumes: A brick of cheese washed with water, coffee or wine. Eaten freshish after three months, or aged, when it becomes extremely spicy and strong. Best in autumn and winter.

•Lormes: A chèvre or mi-chèvre of classic truncated cone shape with thin, blueish rind and strong flavor. Look for it in Lormes or around Clamecy.

•Mâconnais/Chevreton de Mâcon: Small, rather firm chèvre with only faintly goaty flavor but which may also be

eaten very fresh, when it is rather creamy. May also be a mi-chèvre or all cow's milk; these are available and good all year round. When stored over winter they become dark brown and rank. These are then called boutons de culottes and used for fromage fort.

•Mamirolle: A washed-rind loaf of pasteurized cow's milk that is rather richer in flavor than might be expected.

•Metton: Essentially a tasteless nugget of whey cheese, made by boiling whey, the method that creates Italian ricotta; almost exclusively aged and eaten as cancoillotte (qv).

•Montrachet: A rather delicious and creamy chèvre made in a cylinder about 10cm/4in high and matured only a week or so, wrapped in chestnut or vine leaves. A commercial operation. If only fresh goat's milk is used, it is best from the end of spring until autumn.

•Morbier: Also made in the plateaux of Champagne. A fruit of the mountains, a pressed cheese best tasted in spring if you can find one that is artisanale. A disk of 5-8kg/13-18lbs - the one with the streak of black soot (from the cauldron) through the middle.

•Pierre-qui-vire: Made at a monastery of the same name in St-Léger-Vauban, it is the expected washed-rind disk, only 10cm/4in diameter and on straw. It is stronger in smell and flavor than many such cheeses and is best in summer and autumn. Monsieur Androuet of Paris says it is also eaten fresh after draining.

•Pourly: Although aged a month, this cylinder of almost 300g/12oz of chèvre is not as pungent or goaty as some smaller or younger such

THE MOUNTAIN RANGE

Borders are political, while the mountains, the forests and rural traditions are far more constant. Nowhere is this more clearly expressed than in the Franche-Comté and neighboring areas of Switzerland. Why should things be different? At one time France, Switzerland and the majority of Germany were part of the Roman Empire. The Franche-Comté has been variously claimed by Burgundy, Germany, and Spain and only became permanently (well, you never know . . .) French during the reign of Louis XIV. Ask them, and I suspect you will find that to the remote mountain people, it makes little difference who is producing the correct *gruyère*. Modern marketing men however have encouraged the controversy.

Some believe that gruyère took its name from the Swiss Gruyère valley; however, closer inspection reveals that during the days of the Roman Empire, *gruyèries* were forests and officers *gruyèrs* were the officials who managed them. The cheesemakers of the time had to buy wood to fuel their twice-daily makings from the

officiers gruyèrs, who in turn would accept cheese as payment for the wood. It is only subsequently that the word became linked to Switzerland's great cheese-making area, as it did to several places in the Franche-Comté and Savoie.

As in Switzerland, the Franche-Comté cows, the esteemed *montbéliardes* and the *pie rouges de l'Est*, make the transition each summer from the lowlands to the rich mountain pastures. Here they enjoy as many as 50 grasses and herbs, which lend an irresistible aromatic quality to the milk and cheese. It takes around 530 liters, the yield of 30 cows, to make a typical mountain *gruyère de Comté*, but most farms only own around 15 cows and therefore work on a co-operative basis, delivering their milk to a jointly owned village dairy. Today this is typically done by truck, however the use of mules is still common in all mountain areas.

In both France and Switzerland the making of gruyère has been linked to that of *vacherin*. Where once the trees of the gruyèries supplied the fuel for

cheesemaking, they now generate the aromatic bark used to encircle vacherin, a cheese of the winter months. This cheese is - comparatively - a recent invention, apparently developed during the 18th century and a result of the trials of small-scale mountain farming. In the winter months, this region of France may be afflicted by temperatures as low as -30°C, making it difficult and unfruitful for small farmers to take their meager quantities of milk to the dairy. Rather than attempt to create a Comté gruyère from several days' milking, they chose to start making a smaller cheese and encircled its oozing paste with spruce bark from the forests.

French *vacherin du Mont d'Or* is now also known as *vacherin du Haut-Doubs*, a rather unsuccessful attempt to clarify confusion between it and Switzerland's *vacherin Mont d'Or*, which is made from pasteurized milk. In case you were wondering, the majority of Mont d'Or and its peak lies well inside France.

cheeses. Recommended for mutual enjoyment with fine white burgundy.

•Rouy: A commercial product, and as it is from the north of Burgundy (relatively), it is a washed-rind one, square and boxed; pretty positive flavor and taste. Cow's milk.

•St-Florentin: Mainly commercial production these days; cow's milk cheese washed with brine, best in summer, autumn and start of winter. Always a most assertive presence on all one's senses.

•Septmoncel: a variation of the name of Bleu de Gex.

•Soumaintrain: Becoming uncommon, it is essentially a farmhouse (original) version of

St-Florentin. It is considered even higher in flavor and smell; but there is or was a custom for eating them very fresh, so I should, rather, nose around for that version.

•Tomme de Belley: Something to jump at if you find it, not a large tomme but a small brick of chèvre or mi-chèvre weighing less than 200g/8oz. Medium, nutty flavor. Farmhouse made but less and less so.

•Vacherin du Mont-d'Or/du Haut-Doubs: One of the most important on the AOC list, for it is one of the few genuinely seasonal cheeses, made only in autumn and winter when the herds return from the plateaux of Haut-Doubs. Always circled with a band of

spruce and packed in a spruce box, it is recognized by its deeply wrinkled top surface, caused partly by the bottom sticking firmly to the container. Washed regularly with brine, it has a distinct odour of milk but a rich, sweet, creamy flavor with just a breath of resin from the spruce. As it is cured from 2-4 months, depending on size, expect it in good condition only from the end of autumn until winter's end. Only the milk of the montbéliarde and pie rouge de l'Est cows may be used.

•Vézelay: Farm-produced chèvre that is unlikely to stink you out; not dissimilar to Lormes (qv).

Pastries, Desserts & Confectionery

The abundance of grain of most types meant that, as baking became more sophisticated, Burgundy was always a leader in producing variety in breads and amusing goodies for the end of a meal. The oldest, as in most regions, are galettes, crêpes, and Burgundian beignets, which are not just any old doughnut. Even today the light, deep-fried paste may surround acacia flowers and the honey-muscat flavor of elderflowers (sureau); although not so popular these days, this once was considered irresistible; it still is in other countries. The most famous of these light, deep-fried balls of batter must be pets-de-nonne, which the Francs-Comtois reckon they invented, but so do the Burgundians and several others. The claim is disputed not so much over the undoubted superiority of the recipe but over the wish to bathe in the glory of having invented the name. In case you're not certain, it means nun's farts.

A huge variety of things sweet is offered in the big centers, with Mâcon, Auxerre, Sens, Beaune and Besançon all recommended. As there are eggs, there are meringues and macaroons everywhere and any number of cookies based on almonds with names that change from center to center. Nevers, and others, makes barley sugar (sucre d'orge), and as anise is grown here, it's worth looking both for the pain d'anis of Autun and other centers of the Morvan and the aniseed sweets of Flavigny (see below). Apples, pears, Auxerre cherries and other soft summer fruits are served hot and cold in tarts and crêpes of various kinds.

SWEET MEDICINE

Similar to dragées but with a heart of anise instead of almond, Anis de l'Abbaye de Flavigny have a romantic history incorporating medicine, monks, the Romans and the old spice trail.

The name of the village comes from the Roman Flavinius, who built a villa in the area after the 52 BC war between the Gauls and Romans. It is likely that it was around this time that the Romans introduced the aniseed of the Mediterranean to Burgundy.

Much later, in 718 AD, an abbey was founded in Flavigny, around which the village was built. It was the abbey's monks who developed the production of the candy, and although there is no written record of the occasion, it is said that around 873 AD a monk of Flavigny offered three pounds of aniseed candy to Pope Jean VIII when he came to consecrate the abbey. Anis de l'Abbaye de Flavigny seems to have been offered to personalities visiting the village ever since.

After the French Revolution, in 1789, the monks left the abbey and a few of the village's inhabitants began making their own brands of the candy. Around the 18th century, these family-run manufacturers began to unite and establish themselves in the ancient abbey.

Anise (Pimpinella anisum) originated in Egypt and India and was regarded by the Chinese as sacred. Herbalists and cooks have always used various parts of the plant in medicine and cooking but it is the seeds that are most prized. Chewed by themselves, they sweeten the breath and aid digestion, hence their development as comfits.

The dragée was first mentioned in 1220. At that time apothecaries were still being confused with confectioners and it is small wonder, as the apothecaries would coat medicinal spices such as aniseed, coriander and fennel with honey to form épices de chambre, a mouth sweetener and digéstif. When cane sugar was introduced to Europe, dragées such as sugar-coated almonds and Anis de l'Abbaye de Flavigny we know today developed.

It is possible to plant and cultivate aniseed in Flavigny but even ancient manufacturers of the sweet were most likely to do as they do now and import aniseed from the Mediterranean where it is better fed by the sun.

LA GOUGÈRE AND LES GOUGÈRES

Although a specialty of both the Aube in Champagne and the Côte-d'Or and using only the gruyères of Franche-Comté, gougère is particularly associated with, and found all over, Burgundy. It is simply a choux pastry studded with cubes of a gruyère of some type. Today it is often made very small as an elegant warm accompaniment to drinks, but in any case, shape or style, gougère is an excellent accompaniment to red or white wines, and may be served in place of cheese before dessert.

If you are driving into Burgundy from Champagne, Sens is one of the first important culinary centers and is recommended for its version, but it is the town of Tonnerre that claims its original invention.

It is important not to confuse gougère with the goyère of northern France, which is a tart made with maroilles cheese, or with gouerre, which is a potato and cheese cake.

Do it yourself using your favorite choux pastry recipe studded with roughly chopped gruyère; in a pinch Dutch gouda will do. Never use grated cheese. Drop the paste onto a lightly greased baking tray, either in large spoonfuls to make a ring (la Gougère) or in separate large and small spoonfuls to make individual gougères. Glaze with beaten egg yolk and bake in a moderate oven (180°C/ 350°F) for 20 to 35 minutes, according to size.

Once you have mastered the basic style - and it may be made heavier or lighter - you may like to experiment by adding herbs or spices. I use cumin seeds, which is not an uncommon flavoring in Franche-Comté.

WORTH FINDING

• *Cacau de Paray-le-Monial*: Cherry clafoutis.

• *Cassissines*: Small, black-currant-flavored sweeties from Dijon.

• *Flamussel*: Either a sweet omelette with fruit or a sweetened fresh-cheese tart.

• *Gouère*: Apple tart.

• *Mais*: A local name for fruit tarts.

• *Nonettes*: Associated particularly with Dijon, these are iced gingerbread cakes and thus associated with ...

• *Pain d'épices*: Common in many parts of France but very much a special association with Franche-Comté and Dijon, although Reims was once almost the sole center of manufacture. The idea of actually mixing flour with honey apparently came from the Arabs via knights returning from Crusades; the Arabs in turn are thought to have learned it through trading with the Chinese or Mongols. When the Romans made honey cakes, they poured it onto the baking after it was cooked. Spicy but rather dry to many, pain d'épices is nice with the touch of anise almost compulsory in Burgundy; it often includes nuts or dried fruits. Try it cut from a slab in the market, or bought packaged to take home from somewhere famous and grand like Mulot and Petitjean in Dijon, who also sell cassis and other liquers, plus ...

• *Rochers de Morvan*: Amazingly real-looking marzipan recreations of pebbles. Great to look at, boring to eat.

LIQUEURS

The relative newcomer cassis, which is available in several alcoholic strengths, has overshadowed the other fruit-based drinks of this area. There are liqueurs or crèmes made true to their flavors in many wine centers. Nuits-St-Georges is very good. Anything made with plums – mirabelle, prunelle or prunes sauvages (sloe) – will be terrific in my experience, but it is to the Franche-Comté for something more unusual. Once Pontalier was an important center for making banned absinthe; now gentian is a common flavoring for both apéritif and digestif, and liqueurs or white spirits may be found made from pine, cherries or plums. The wine makers of the Jura also make marc, which in turn is mixed with grape juice to make maquevin, a ratafia; hypocras is spiced sweet red wine, a cold sangria in fact. Sochaux makes well-reputed beer.

ARBOIS À BOIRE

Arbois is the capital of wine making in the Jura, and was where Louis Pasteur began his experiments by boiling.

The trade here is overbearingly dominated by one company, Henri Maire, and under many brand names you will find appellation arbois contrôllée - red, white and rosé wines plus a sparkler often called "mad" wine (vin fou).

Best bet is the Arbois rosé, here usually called gris rather

A DRINKER'S GUIDE

Value for money is a term that would usually be considered mutually exclusive with wines from Burgundy, given the price usually charged and the extreme variability of both wine makers and vintage. The main red grape of Burgundy, the pinot noir, is the neurotic of the grape variety world and is notoriously difficult to cultivate. That people persevere is testament to the fact that at some early, formative time in their lives, they had the opportunity to drink a quality Burgundy. The effect is unique; this wine commonly makes rough businessmen into poets.

For this section we split the red and white wines as vintages can differ markedly between the two main grape varieties, the pinot noir and the chardonnay, given the comparative dependability of the latter. The gamay used to make Beaujolais is hardier and less temperamental (see page 159).

RECENT VINTAGES
1994 Reds: A big difference between the best and the rest. Rain washed out the vintage. 1994 Whites: Rain also affected the whites, giving short-life drinking wines.

The chablis was successful but a small vintage.
1993 Reds: The best wines were good and may have a long future, but sadly rain spoiled the general vintage. 1993 Whites: Very satisfying, fruity wines that are a pleasure to drink. 1992 Reds: Big, average quality vintage. 1992 Whites: An excellent vintage, lots of elegant fruit. Comparable and probably superior to the 1989s. 1991 Reds: A little hail affected the vintage but some quality wines were made that will keep. 1991 Whites: A rather poor vintage, also weather affected. Wines to drink up and not worth spending big money on. 1990 Reds: The last in a great trio of vintages, possibly the finest of the three, with very high fruit. 1990 Whites: A good vintage with a lot of very attractive wines made, but not to keep. 1989 Reds: Number two excellent vintage, although few truly outstanding wines were made. Very concentrated wines, a broad vintage and one to keep. 1989 Whites: Initially thought to be really good but a lack of acidity in some of the wines is making some seem old

before their time. The best wines however are excellent and may be the best of the 1980s.
1988 Reds: A lusciously fruity year that took people by surprise with its quality. Wines to keep and to drink. 1988 Whites: Also clean fresh fruit but not so successful as the reds. 1987 Reds: The best are good but are being drunk now. 1987 Whites: Fairly bright fruit but not quality. 1986 Reds: Being drunk now but a highly perfumed vintage from the best producers and a good example of the reason people love Burgundy. 1986 Whites: A great year in Chablis but the white 1986s are perhaps not as good as the 1985s. 1985 Reds: A difficult vintage. Some, the best, are just getting better, while others are fading. So, an excellent year, in parts. 1985 Whites: Most of the white is already drunk but those that were not are tasting better than when they were.

PREVIOUS GREATS
The best red and white burgundies of 1983 are still going strong, after an excellent vintage for all wines of the region. 1978 was an excellent year for chablis.

than rosé. They are not your usual bunch of sweet and scented rosé, but fully fermented out to be dry, full flavoured, among the best of the type you'll enjoy anywhere, and perfectly suited to being drunk through most meals without feeling

you are compromising.
Two other Jura specialities are vin jaune, a strong, sherry-like dry white wine usually drunk as an apéritif, and vin de paille, a rarity these days. It used to be made by drying bunches of ripe grapes on straw (paille)

mats to concentrate their juices, making a deliciously rich sweet wine. Look out for it; it will last forever.

Bon Marché

Below is a selective list of markets plus some fairs (*foires*) of special interest. Check with the local Syndicat d'Initiative (SI) for precise locations and time changes.

YONNE

Aillant-sur-Tholon *Tue;* Ancy-le-Franc *Thur;* Arces Dilo *Thur;* Auxerre *Tue, Fri, Sun AM;* Avallon *Thur, Sat;* Bléneau *Tue PM;* Brienon-sur-Armançon *Tue, Fri;* Chablis *Sun AM;* Champignelles *Thur;* Charny *Tue PM;* Chéroy *Tue;* Courson-les-Carrières *Thur;* Flogny-la-Chapelle *Tue;* Joigny *Wed, Sat;* Migennes *Thur, rummage sale 1st Sun Aug;* Monéteau *Wed;* Pont-sur-Yonne *Wed, Sun;* Rogny *Wed;* Sens *Mon, Fri;* Serbonnes *23 & 24 Aug;* St-Florentin *Mon, Sat (veg), rummage sale 1st Sun Sept;* St-Julien-du-Sault *Sun;* St-Sauveur-en-Puisaye *Wed;* Tonnerre *Wed, Sat;* Toucy *Sat;* Vermenton *Tue, Fri;* Villeneuve-la-Guyard *Mon;* Villeneuve-l'Archevêque *Sat.*

NIÈVRE

Arleuf *Fair 17th of month (except Aug);* La Charité-sur-Lire *Sat, Prize Poultry Fair Dec;* Château-Chinon *2nd Mon each month, 29 Oct;* Corbigny *Fri, 2nd Fri Dec (poultry);* Decize *Fri;* Entrains-sur-Nohain *Wed;* Fours *Farm produce & poultry on Fair Days (see SI), Turkey Fair 2nd Sat Dec;* Lormes *Thur;* Lucenay-les-Aix *4th Thur of month, Poultry, Rabbit, Butter & Egg Fair 2nd Mon in month;* Luizy *Fri (poultry):* La Machine *Wed, Sat (veg);* Nevers *Daily;* Pouilly-sur-Loire *Fri;* Rouy *Thur (poultry);* St-Amand-en-Puisaye *Mon;* St-Bénin d'Azy *Fair 1st Mon of month;* St-Honoré-les-Bains *Mon, Tue, Thur, Fri during thermal season;* St-Pierre-le-Moutier

Thur, Fri; St-Révérien *Sat, 4th Tue of month;* St-Saulge *Fri (eggs, butter, poultry) 1st Aug Summer Fete, flower float, procession;* Tannay *4th Mon of month;* Varzy *Thur, Poultry market 2nd Thur Dec.*

CÔTE-D'OR

Arnay-le-Duc *Thur, 6th day each month exc. Mar & June (7) and Dec (5);* Auxonne, *Wed, Fri;* Beaune *Thur, Sat;* Châtillon-sur-Seine *Sat, Tue (occasional);* Chenove *Wed;* Dijon *Daily AM, Tue, Thur, Fri;* Les Laumes *Wed;* Marsannay-la-Côte *Thur;* Montbard *Tue, Fri;* Nolay *Mon;* Nuits-St-Georges *Mon, Fri;* Pontailler-sur-Saône *Sat (Fair 4th Sat of month);* Saulieu *Sat;* Semur-en-Auxois *Tue, Thur, Sat;* Seurre *Tue, Fri;* St-Jean-de-Losne *Sat;* Vitteaux *Fair 1st Thur of month.*

SÂONE-ET-LOIRE

Autun *Wed, Fri;* Beaurepaire-en-Bresse *Wed;* Bellevesvre *Fri;* Bourbon-Lancy *Sat, Fair Days;* Buffières *Thur;* Buxy *Thur, Chalon-sur-Saône *Wed, Fri & Sun (poultry);* Charolles *Wed, Bull Fair Wed before 4th Thur Oct;* Chauffailles *Mon;* La Clayette *Mon;* Cluny *Sat;* Le Creusot *Tue, Thur, Fri, Sat;* Cuiseaux *Fri, Chestnut Fair 29 Oct;* Digoin *Fri, Sun;* Epinac *Sat;* Etang-sur-Arroux *Turkey Fair 1st Mon Dec;* Joncy *10 Dec (poultry);* Louhans *Mon;* Lugny *Fri, Wine Fair 6 Dec;* Mâcon *Sat, National Wines of France Fair May 20 (8 days);* Marcigny *Mon;* Matour *Thur;* Mervans *Fri;* Montceau-les-Mines *Mon, Thur, Sat;* Montchanin *Wed AM, Sat PM;* Montpont-en-Bresse *Thur;* Montret *Tue;* Palinges *Fri;* Pierre-de-Bresse *Mon;* Romenay *Fri;* Sagy *Thur;* Sanvignes-les-Mines *Fri;* Sennecey-le-Grand *Fri;* Simandre *Wed;* St-Bonnet-de-Joux *Fri;* St-Gengoux-le-National *1st & 3rd Tue of month;* St-Germain-du-Plain *Thur;* St-Léger-sur-Dheune *Tue;* St-Martin-en-Bresse *Wed;* St-Pierre-le-Vieux *Thur;* St-

Vallier *Wed, Fri;* Tournus *Sat;* Verdun-sur-le-Doubs *Thur.*

HAUTE-SÂONE

Faucogney et la Mer *1st & Thur;* Fougerolles *Fri;* Héricourt *Wed AM, Sat PM;* Jussey *Tue;* Lure *Tue;* Melisey *Wed;* Plancher-les-Mines *Fri;* Ronchamp *Sat;* Servance *1st & 3rd Mon of month;* St-Loup-sur-Semouse *Mon;* St-Sauveur *Sun (Sept), 1st & 3rd Sun (Oct-May);* Vauvillers *2nd Thur of month;* Villersexel *1st & 3rd Wed of month.*

DOUBS

Arc-et-Senans *4th Wed of month;* Audincourt *Wed & Sat AM (Fairs) Spring Market (1 Apr), rummage sale (29 July);* Baume-les-Dames *3rd & 4th Thur of month;* Besançon *Daily ex Sun;* Colombier-Fontaine *2nd Wed of month;* Damprichard *Wed, Sat;* Fresches-le-Châtel *Fri;* Mandeure *Sat AM, rummage sale May;* Maiche *Wed, Sat;* Montbéliard *Fri, Sat;* Morteau *Tue, Sat, Fri;* Pontarlier *1st, 3rd, 5th Thur of month, (Fair 2nd & 4th);* Pont-de-Roide *Fri;* Rougemont *Fri (Fair 1st & 3rd Fri);* Seloncourt *Fri;* Sochaux *Thur;* St-Hippolyte *3rd Thur of month.*

JURA

Annoire *Wed PM;* Arinthod *1st Fri of month;* Beaufort *Fri;* Bletterans *Tue;* Champagnole *Sat;* Chaumergy *Thur;* Châtillon *2nd Thur of month;* Clairvaux-les-Lacs *Wed (June, July, Aug), 3rd Wed of month rest of year;* Dole *Tue, Thur, Sat;* Les Hays *Wed AM;* Lons-le-Saunier *Thur;* Moirans-en-Montagne *Wed, Fri;* Morez *Sat;* Petit-Noir *Wed AM;* Pleure *Tue;* Poligny *Mon, Fri;* Salins-les-Bains *Sat;* Sellières *Wed;* St-Amour *Tue, Sat.*

Shopping around in Besançon Where and when: *Covered market (daily ex Sun); Covered street market (daily ex Mon & Sun);* pl de la Révolution *Tue, Fri, Sat;* Palente *(Tue, Sat);* Chaprais *(Wed);* Clairs-Soleils *(Tue);* St-Claude *(Tue & Sat);* Planoise *(Fri AM).*

🐀 BORDEAUX & THE DORDOGNE

AN UPSTART SUCCESS

"In which we...
• Meet the pest that made a better butter but confused the kitchens...
• Sip a wine we've put out in the cold and collect an abandoned bounty...
• Recover the leek and eat flowers in a château...
• Buy a "green chicken," needle some mussels, and discover the truth about lawyers' tongues and the bar...
• Meet a rapturous oyster, yellow chickens and the best salty lamb in France...
• Learn how to judge a beast on the hoof and which bay to leave...
• Share the charm of sarment, slice the best of tomatoes and find a pastis that you eat...
• Go in search of an unapparent royal hare..."

T he Charentes' dairying pastures, fat with contented cattle grinding grass into cream for the famous butter of the Deux-Sèvres, are a direct result of the devastation caused by phylloxera. Virtually all of these pastures are the graveyards of vines killed by the pest that did more to change the French way of agriculture than both World Wars. Where Burgundy planted black currants and soft fruits, and the south planted fruit orchards, these western slopes were put to grass, and cattle were brought in from Normandy.

If you have discovered the butters of Normandy and chosen a favorite, you'll have to start again. For, unfair as it may be, there are many who feel the upstart new butter of the Deux-Sèvres to be better and waxier even than that of Normandy. Beurre d'Echiré is unquestionably the best and found everywhere in France; but it has confused the kitchens of the area, for this is traditionally a place of pork fat and walnut oil and goat's milk, from which the cream cannot be separated.

Further south, you can enjoy that butter in more familiar surroundings and more visited areas - Bordeaux and Aquitaine. They were British for centuries, and much of what sustains great parts of the regions remains closely associated with the British way of life - claret in Bordeaux, cognac in Cognac, and vacation homes in the Green, White or Black Périgord of the Dordogne.

Claret, which is what only the British call their Bordeaux red wines, is an echo of those older kingdoms, when the wine exported was light and clear and called *clairette*. It became the generic name for all Bordeaux red wines, but a true clairette may still be bought, and drinks delightfully when chilled. I enjoyed it first on a restaurant terrace in Bordeaux with a pretty plateful called Les Trésors de la Mer - pieces of the freshest fish from the Atlantic made brighter with tiny cultivated mussels (*moules de bouchot*) and succulent with fat oysters from Arcachon. It was a boiling hot day and chilled clairette was being drunk by almost everyone, seemingly regardless of what they ate.

But it is unfair to think of Bordeaux only in terms of the opportunities she offers for drinking wines you might not find at home. Like all big cities, she does the same for food lovers. In her famous markets and in the broad, traffic-free streets of the center you will easily espy fly-away sweet pastry tarts (*croustades*) from Gascony, foie gras from the Landes, a truly encyclopedic array of fresh, mature and rotten goat's milk cheeses and, if you look carefully enough, the sweet specialities of Bordeaux itself. You'll also find a fair range of cognacs. A few hours' drive inland is the Périgord, one of the best known culinary areas of France associated mainly, I suppose, with geese and foie gras. For me it is not so much the food of the Dordogne that is the attraction, undoubted though that may be, but the surroundings in which you can enjoy it. Périgueux, capital of the lush rolling White Périgord, has the most entrancing of old quarters, now marvelously restored to match the

scarcely touched 17th-century splendor of Sarlat, the Renaissance queen of the Black Périgord, an area thickly wooded with oak and chestnut, darker and more mysterious as you approach the Gouffre de Padirac and Rocamadour.

There is a certain sadness in the Périgord, but one that is to the advantage of the traveler who has time. For much of it has been deserted by its owners - châteaux, cottages and farmhouses rattle empty in the wind, so you can walk or ride for miles through their lands. The bonus is their orchards and hedgerows, crammed in their rightful seasons with unwanted baskets of the bounty that made the area famous. Blackberries and sloes, chestnuts and walnuts, greengages and sudden golden walls of *mirabelles* are yours. It makes a lovely afternoon to wander thus, and if you put the ripest fruits into jars with an *eau-de-vie* or some flavorless pure alcohol, sold just for this purpose, you will have souvenirs of the day to enjoy long into the future.

Market days in the connected little squares of Périgueux are Wednesday and Saturday, and here the progress of the seasons and prosperity of the land is chronicled by the produce brought for sale. Autumn and winter are the most fascinating times, for then pearlescent lobes of foie gras are displayed naked in the chill air, while strung above them are the red-black-clotted, curling necks and head and crop and lungs of the birds from which they have been cut. I've never seen truffles among the wild mushrooms there during the season, but I'm told you might. One summer I bought my first bottle of walnut oil in that market, stoppered with a cork wrapped in newspaper, so we had to use it before we flew home. Next day was another first: sun-warm slices of tomatoes from Marmande sprinkled with walnut oil. I ate this celestial combination (at least as good as foie gras and trumpets) on the terrace of the Bellevue

Hotel and Restaurant, which looks from a flustering height over the Padirac Gorge to the crankily sited town of Rocamadour.

Yes, I've eaten superbly, but never as when we called at the slip-tiled château of Max and Barbara Freeman. By now they may have restored much more of it, but then (in 1979) they had a long way to go and were living in the basement, which was as big, and as grand, as many an "ordinary" country house. "We'll have to eat like peasants," Barbara said, rattling us up truffled foie gras she had canned herself, an omelette of scorzonera flowers, and some chocolates. The bread was thick and chewy rye from a village far enough away to be an expedition, but everything was an expedition from here; any trouble was repaid because the bread lasted so very long. The wine was Pécharmant, a Bergerac from close-by. Max swears the name means "charming fart," and refers to a time when an aristocratic lady of the court of one or another of the kings called Louis, broke wind rather noticeably while touring the vines. Courtly etiquette demanded the gaffe be ignored, but circumstances denied this as a possibility. Diplomatically, the host announced he was charmed and flattered by the "ill wind" and turned it to good, by declaring that the domaine's name would henceforth enshrine the lady's "charming fart" ...

Charcuterie

Charcuterie here is far from exclusive or typical of the region. Certainly, the markets are all packed with pâtés and both salted and air-dried parts of pig. The best by far are the local hams, famed in Poitou, but sweeter to my mind in Charente, for there cognac is used in the pickling, as well as herbs and spices.

Rillettes and rillons are regularly found; they actually belong to the Loire regions, and to make some proprietorial claim, I suppose, the latter are more likely to be called grillons.

The Dordogne is much given to stuffing meats, and so they use their foie gras to make galantines (cold) and ballottines (hot); and as even these are more likely to be made with poultry, they cannot strictly be called charcuterie. Poitou and the Charentes also make the same things, using their own foie gras.

My best discovery, mentioned elsewhere, was the poulet vert found in Jarnac's Sunday morning market, a pâté-type mixture flavored with every fresh spring green, including sorrel and dandelion, and baked in cabbage leaves; it is called farci in Poitou. I took some back in the plane to eat at home with thick slices of charentais ham.

Fish & Shellfish

The Atlantic coast of France has a good line in special fish and fish dishes, especially those incorporating the small, sweet, cultivated moules de bouchot, and a reputation for a number of fishy things you won't actually find. Caviar is one no-show, although as you doubtless did not expect it, this may not be a shock. Yet the Gironde does welcome sturgeons (called créat here) from March to June, when they swim up as far as the headland at Ambès to spawn. For most of this century extremely passable caviar was made from their roe, so much so that Pruniers in Paris, who were responsible for organizing the initial project, were largely supplied from here. Small amounts are said to be made today, but the increasing pollution of the river makes this unlikely. Still, the places you might try are Chenac-Saint-Seurin-d'Uzet, Talmont-sur-Gironde, Meschers-sur-Gironde and Mortagne-sur-Gironde, in that order. The end of spring is probably the best time.

The shad (alose) and its superlative roe is best between mid-April and mid-June. The sorrel you so often find in shad, or on it, is said not just to dissolve away most of the bones, but to neutralize some poison. Either there is no poison, or all shad are quickly stuffed with sorrel, for I know of no one who has died from eating them. This is not true when it comes to lampreys (lamproie), they of the hideous face and poisonous thread. Their preparation is so complicated, including the skinning and saving of the blood, and takes so long - at least two days - that few restaurants serve them. Some housewives still make lamproie à la Bordelaise - indeed I was given some, thick with the mandatory red wine and local leeks cut to the same size as the steaks of lamprey; but many more do not, or make a slightly easier (and safer) version with eel.

You will find superlatively cooked fish, especially in La Rochelle, France's second fishing port after Boulogne, and in Bordeaux. For a delicious change, accompany it with a lightly chilled red clairette. Marvelous!

On the Charentais coast, the most important oyster center is Marennes, renowned for its vertes de Marennes, (natives or creuses) which have fattened in the claires (salt marshes) at the mouth of the Seudre River. The center is unique in France for both breeding and fattening oysters, for the others do just one or the other. La Tremblade

is another important center close by.

The Bay of Arcachon in the Gironde is one of the biggest oyster-growing areas in France, and here as elsewhere pests and disease have all but wiped out the native plates, locally called gravettes. The prevalence first of the replacement portugaises and now of creuses or gigas from Japan, more suited to cooking, explains why oysters are found so often in hot dishes, on brochettes, in stuffings and the like. In many places raw oysters will be accompanied by small hot sausages in caul fat (crépinettes), sometimes also truffled. The combination of oysters and hot sausages is excellent.

Real oysters, or creuses, are also offered with lemon wedges or with shallot vinegar. Anybody who actually likes oysters, and who is not simply spending money conspicuously, will add nothing but the merest threat of lemon juice to the raw flesh of an oyster. Anything hot or sharp or acidic obliterates any delicacy or complexity of flavor. You may as well save money and eat something else.

Arcachon and Marennes, which were once famous for making an especially white salt, also rear every other type of shellfish including delicious small clams (palourdes). The mussels you'll cook yourself in an éclade will also turn up as a mouclade, richer than simple steamed mussels (marinière) through the addition of cream, a bouquet garni, garlic with cognac and/or pineau de Charente.

WORTH FINDING

• *Chaudrée*: A cauldron or *chaudron* (originally) of fish, including conger eel (*congre*) according to some, almost every other fish according to others, from white fish to cuttlefish (*seiche*). It is one of the grand specialities of Poitou and the Charentes. One of the most extraordinary places to enjoy it is on the Île-de-Ré, 5 miles/8km west of La Rochelle. Its white wines have a taste of iodine and salt. Around Ars-en-Ré they make a particularly fine sea salt, slightly pinkish.
• *Bouilliture*: A stew of freshwater fish, like a *matelote*; most often of eels, sometimes with prunes and garlic or shallots - rarely the two together if it is authentic.
• *Friture*: Fry-up of mixed small freshwater fish.
• *Langue d'Avocat*: Lawyer's tongue, the name for a particularly small sole (*cétaux* or *solette*). From the north Landes and associated with the Bordelais. Superb filletted,

wrapped around an oyster, quickly steamed and served with the unctuous wine and cream sauce *montée au beurre*.
• *Loup de Mer*: Sea bass, also called *loubine vrai* or *bar* here and southwards, but exclusively *bar* northwards and in Paris. A high percentage of bass sold grilled with fennel (*fenouil*) on the south coast in summer has come from the fishing fleet of La Rochelle.
• *Pain de Brochet*: Hot, savory mousse of pike.
• *Rogne, rogue*: The name for other lightly salted fish eggs made in the same towns that used to make caviar. It is the roe of the gray mullet (*mulet*), that is the basis of a proper Greek taramasalata.
• *Soupe de poissons*: Fish soup often not puréed as you would expect in the south. In Arcachon they tend to use the green-boned garfish (*orphie*), cook it with leeks, potatoes, onion and garlic, and serve the fish and vegetables separately.

Verdun-sur-Mer is well thought of in the Bordelais for its lobsters and crayfish. Fresh cod (cabillaud) is served more often than the salted version and large sardines, often called Royans after the town that specializes in them, are eaten grilled, but more often raw, much to the effroi or horror of the visitor. There is excellent variety of freshwater fish here too, including carp from the étang de Cadeuil in Charente, and trout, farmed in most places but excellent from the Candrea at Bergerac. In the Dordogne the eel is well flavored, but this could be said of the whole region. They are best, though, at their most un-eel-like fry stage, thin threads sizzled in a friture.

Regardless of its provenance in the Atlantic or Mediterranean, fish and shellfish here are both likely to be drowned in cream or the rich butter of the Charentes.

SHELL SHOCKS

Whichever letter of the alphabet the month contains, or doesn't, you'll always be able to enjoy oysters (huîtres). The theory about not eating oysters in summer is not based on any danger to your health but on thoughtfulness for the well-being of the oyster. It can only breed in summer's soupy-hot water, so you are either eating an oyster that has not yet reproduced (described as "milky") and are depriving yourself of future enjoyment, or will be presented with a thin, flabby one that has, and deprive yourself of present pleasure.

Two types of oysters are found in France today, the true oyster (ostrea edulis) known as the flat oyster, the plate, native or belon, and the creuse, a Japanese variety crassostrea gigas. The portugaise, which wasn't even an oyster but a gryphea angulata, and which stepped in earlier this century, when the natives failed, has in its turn been virtually wiped out by disease.

The true oyster promiscuously changes from male to female as it matures, some returning to masculinity for refresher periods. It is as well oysters cannot pivot upon their firmly anchored feet, for how would they know which way to turn? I think, though, we should not begrudge them any pleasure; an oyster's life is a chancy business. Out of a million eggs only a dozen or so will become spats and grow up to equivocate.

You are much more likely to be served the creuse or gigas, first introduced into the Brittany oyster farms in 1974. They are easily recognizable, much longer than plates, and have a very crinkled, tough, thick shell, even more so than the portugaises you may have learned to identify. The creuse does not change sex, and has an even more depressing rate of reproduction. They have quickly become accepted as an excellent alternative to native oysters and develop the same range of flavors and appearance, according to where they have been grown to maturity. In Brittany and in Normandy this is done in the mouths of rivers, and these are generally sold as huîtres, creuses or gigas de parc, and they tend to look yellow to cream. But on the coast of Charente-Maritime and Aquitaine, they are matured in claires, old salt marshes, where they feed on an endemic blue algae and turn a variety of shades of green; perversely the algae that allows oysters to develop such a delicate flavor is that which gives a musty taste to tap water.

Oysters are sold according to size, but also according to how they have lived immediately before you bought them.

•Claires: Are oysters that have spent a rather crowded couple of years in a farm, as they all do, then just a month in a claire, which allows them merely a breath of special flavor or color.

•Fines de claires: The kings and queens of oysters. After the usual two years in a farm, they will spend another 18 or 24 months in a claire, at only 5 or 6 to the square meter. The effect transforms them almost into another being, with a texture and flavor that makes them the foie gras of the sea.

•Huitres raptures: Overgrown oysters, rather too daunting to confront when raw, unless you are prepared to chew more than once. Instead, roast them on a barbecue or in a fiery-hot oven, flat side up, until just opening. Quickly pry open fully and tip a little garlic or herb butter onto the just set, warm oyster. Eat with a fork and lots of bread. You can imagine why initiates call them huîtres raptures.

MUSSEL BEACH

Whatever else you do in France, make yourself an éclade. No restaurant will do it, and if it does it won't be half as much fun. An éclade is something for a group or family to prepare; a couple will get more reward for their effort. First, find a beach, then take a large plank of wood and lay it firmly on the sand. If you like, you can then coat the board with a thin layer of sticky clay but this is not important. Now you take mussels, which must have been well cleaned and bearded - if they are permanently open they must be discarded. Build a little mound of sand, clay or anything non-flammable in the center of the board and then start arranging the mussels pointed end up. Lay them as tightly as possible one next to the other so they do not open prematurely. Once that is completed, cover the mussels with a thick layer of pine needles and set fire to it. If there is a fig tree about, you might cover the mussels with fig leaves before you strew the needles - not to disguise any nakedness but to make it easier to remove the ashes when the flames have subsided; the leaves add a syrupy flavor too. I suppose that, as long as you have a cache of pine needles, you might enjoy an éclade wherever there is a plank and mussels: but it'll never be the same as on a beach. Or as safe.

Meat, Poultry & Game

Classically, Poitou and the Charentes are snail country and the two regions have long-standing agreements to disagree about how snails are best cooked. The lumas of Poitou are usually simmered in wine or made into a ragoût. In the Charentes, they do the same to their brown-shelled cagouilles with perhaps a dash of cognac, or, sometimes, of tomato, and serve them hot, as a salad or in an omelette. Ruffec is the best place to eat Charentais snails. The cagouille has so dominated life here that the Charentaise have long been called cagouillards, for they are considered to have emulated the gastropod's slowness and delight in privacy. The snails of Cauderan were traditionally eaten in Bordeaux during the first days of Lent, apparently not being considered meat. Of course, the herbicides used in the vineyards have had the same effect as elsewhere and there are fewer genuine local snails and more imported ones.

Poultry here is specially good. In Poitou, Sauzé-Vaussay and Chef-Boutonne rear the almost white poitevin goose and excellent ducks to make the confits and foie gras more associated with the Dordogne or Gascony. Civray in Vienne makes particularly good pâté de foie gras. In Charente, Barbezieux raises wonderful poultry, including turkeys and geese. Flesh from those reared with fattened livers is considered sweeter of flavor. Down in the Landes, St-Sever is the most important meat and poultry production center, with a market long known for pigs, beef and the famous Landais poulet jaune. Bred in Charente-Maritime, the chicks

come here at a day old to be raised in the open air for 12 weeks on a diet based on corn. Packaged and numbered individually, tens of thousands are sent to markets and restaurants all over France. St-Gours and St-Vincent-de-Tyrosse produce most. There are plenty of geese, too, but Dax is the biggest center for foie gras. Ducks are slowly taking over from the goose here too, to make a year-round industry, although virtually every market will have fattened goose livers displayed for sale between November and February. If you can buy one vacuum-packed, which is big time in France, it will safely last a lengthy period before you get it home.

Perhaps more important than foie gras to the average visitor, is the pré-salé lamb of Pauillac, an important wine center 48km/30 miles from Bordeaux. Twice each day the Atlantic tide floods the marshy banks of the Gironde, and spring lamb feeding on the salty grass develops a flavor considered unsurpassed. But as they are eaten very young it needs a good palate to appreciate the delicacy of flavor, and to protect this the meat is often roasted in a crust of breadcrumbs and parsley. Certainly there will be no garlic, onion or shallot used unless summer has truly come and the animal is starting to mature.

Pauillac lamb is often served with potatoes sautéed with strips of black truffle, but I think the fattiness coats the tastebuds and disguises the lamb's sweetness. Other claims along the long coastline to present pré-salé lamb are probably true, for there are

pockets of production everywhere. In the Landes, they compete with pré-salé by rearing milk-fed lambs to give extremely pale meat with even more delicacy. Spring in Poitou - the center for goat-raising - also brings the chance to dine on kid (pirot) with oseille and vert d'ail, sorrel and green garlic shoots.

Because so much pork is raised for the fine hams of Poitou, there is a wide range of pork dishes offered, some of considerable eccentricity and of little interest to anyone not brought up to be so persuaded; one such example is the poitevin gigourit/ tautouillet - pig's head cooked with wine and blood . . . I'll say no more, except that you are more likely to find the full range of pork products in autumn. Charente also raises fine pork, which for the most part is presented quite simply, if not being used for unusual dishes. Tripe, more familiar to the visitor, is much esteemed in all this region and can be met in many guises.

There seems no closed season for another speciality from the same area, oreilles de veau. But you would have the satisfaction of knowing the ears came from calves of the highest breeding, beasts of either the parthenay or bressuire varieties - both regarded with esteem. Yet your beef talk is more likely to be of the entrecôte bordelaise, grilled over sarments de cabernet or cabernet vine shoots (you'll be lucky) and finished with a coating of shallot or bone marrow or both. In Bordeaux itself this often becomes a sauce based on red wine, thought to be a 19th-century Parisian "improvement." This dish's real ancestor is said to be the rat du chai, rats fattened under the vines and in the wine warehouses, for

until recently this was never an area known for edible beef. But once tastes changed universally from rat to beef, it became generally accepted that only a highly unusual local breed was proper, the cattle of Bazas in the Gironde.

Bazadais beef is well worth tracking down. The breed is ancient, the animals gray-coated with flattened but tiptilted horns, and naturally firm and tender, dark-red meat, with rather a lot of highly flavored marbling and fat. Castrated before it is a year old, each steer spends three years grazing on grass and then is stabled and fattened on hay, rye, barley and maize. They are never slaughtered until they are five years old, and the most beautiful are paraded through Bazas each jeudi gras (Thursday before Shrove Tuesday). How do you tell a beautiful bazadais? It must have a cul panoramique, that is horizon-to-horizon hindquarters, for the qualities of the meat are directly proportional to the size. Just a few shops sell guaranteed bazadais beef, for the long raising period makes it expensive. Messrs Beziade and Lafon sell it in Bazas. If you aren't cooking yourself you'll have to rely on restaurateurs. Expensive.

Other than hare (lièvre) there is precious little game nowadays, for the netting and eating of ortolans and other migrating songbirds has been forbidden by the laws of the EC. Of course, there will always be someone who knows someone who has a brother-in-law . . . You may find woodcock (bécasses) or, more likely, pigeons (palombes) and if you do you should be well pleased.

The Périgord reputation for fine food is hardly based on

the products found by summer visitors, for it is a region of confits, and of every kind of poultry stuffed with enriching livers, sometimes with chestnuts, and sometimes with truffles. Suckling pig is popular and so are pâtés, now most likely made from game birds that have been farmed, but better than nothing. Yet heed what I have said elsewhere about the French tendency to use such birds unhung so that there is not enough flavor to perfume the rest of the mixture, thus negating the effort.

WORTH FINDING

- *Bifteck poitevin*: Beef chopped with sorrel and bone marrow.
- *Civet de lièvre*: Jugged hare. A rich stew of hare that should be thickened with its own blood. *Lièvre à la royale*, one of the world's best-known least-seen dishes is probably native to one or all of these regions, but Poitou and Périgord seem strongest claimants. It is boned, marinated and stuffed with everything expensive (foie gras, truffles) braised for an extraordinarily long time in wine and finished with cognac and its own blood.
- *Dindon désossé*: Boned turkey braised with vegetables and wine.
- *Foie gras chaud*: As well as being served in cold slices, fattened liver is freshly baked or fried and served hot, as often as not with grapes and cognac.
- *Poulet à la Niortaise*: Chicken with fried potatoes and the local *rouge de Niort* onions.
- *Salmis de palombe*: Pigeons in red wine sauce. To ensure flavor and tenderness there should be one old pigeon for each young one.
- *Tourtière*: A great speciality in Angoulême, chicken and salsify pie, but there is quite a liking for tourtes of other white meats and these will often be called *pâté en croûte*.

Fruits & Vegetables

It was while dining at Courvoisier's château on the Charente in Jarnac that the point of this book struck me most forcibly. On earlier visits to the region, I had dismissed as fashion, or as outside influence, the appearance of leeks in any recipe - particularly when in such a gastronomic temple as La Rochelle. Leeks are northern, aren't they, and isn't this the area of garlic and shallots? Well, no. Ginette, longtime cook at the château made me realize leeks are important to all the west and much of the south, but are vital foundations of tradition from the Charentes, and in Bordeaux and Cognac especially.

The increasingly rare poireaux des vignes, strong-tasting wild leeks from the vineyards, at risk, like snails, from insecticide sprays, were the asparagus of the sabotiers, the country people. Dishes ranging from the rugged richness of lampreys in red wine or blood, to the delicate seafood porée in La Rochelle, would not be possible without the leek. Poitou's leeks, les jaunes de Poitou, are highly regarded in Paris. It was from Ginette that I also learned there are three types of bay leaf (laurier - basically laurus nobilis) the soupe for savory foods, the cerisier for custards and sweet soufflés and the fleurier, just for show. Her locally produced cookbooks said so, but my horticultural French was not up to pursuing the subject closely. Perhaps by cerisier she meant the cherry laurel, prunus laurocerasus, the leaves of which have a sour, cherry-almond flavor.

Légumes du primeur, baby spring vegetables, are grown all through this region, from the Marais of Poitou to the Dordogne (especially green beans - haricots verts) to Lot-et-Garonne, whence comes one of the best tomatoes in the world, the knobbly giant marmande.

All around Marmande the fields positively throb with growth. One of the best ways to see the gardens, the extraordinary orchards of espaliered fruit trees, and the watercress beds rinsed by the Garonne, is to go by train. The line goes through the fields from Bordeaux to the plum orchards of Agen, incidentally traversing the backyards of a number of famous wine châteaux; the views are more fulsome and more interesting than from your car. Simpler domestic gardens have as much to offer in spring; new wild leaves of dandelion or sorrel, and the green shoots of young garlic (aille). Dandelion (pissenlit) is made into soup. Look hard for fars or farci, which I have also seen called poulet vert (see Charcuterie), great with locally cured ham, and asparagus from the Landes.

In autumn, the excitement of the fields focuses on wild mushrooms, cèpes particularly, which should appear between September and mid-October. Bordeaux is the place most associated with them, and one of the many bordelais garnishes is based on cèpes, here authentically cooked in oil rather than butter. The major vegetable of the area is the broad bean (fève), which you will not need to go out of your way to find.

Artichokes (artichauts) are also grown and those of Macau come to market in Bordeaux already stripped of their leaves.

A major key to assessing the extent of local influence on the cooking throughout the area is the inclusion or otherwise of the shallot, for it is the secret of notably superior savor.

Onions are used, notably in one of the oldest of bordelais dishes, le tourin, a soup of onions, cooked in fat but not browned, a breath of garlic, thickened with egg yolks and poured over bread. Once he has eaten the bread, a local will pour in a glass of vin de l'année creating the chabrot, which so unites the people of this region.

Bordeaux likes raw vegetables, too, carrottes râpées for instance, and young artichokes with butter and salt. In some families it is only children who eat them cooked. The American habit of eating salads as a first course was early assimilated here, and welcomed by the salad growers north and south. Ruffec, incidentally, has its own variety of curly endive, chicorée frisée, and you'll easily find lamb's lettuce (mâche), pinkish oak-leaf lettuce (feuilles de chêne) and other unusual salads.

Expect, too, the occasional pumpkin (potiron) dish, cardoons (cardons), delicious small spinach pies (look on stalls in markets) and mojettes, yet another type of bean, so named they say because they look like nuns praying. Potatoes vary from simply cooked primeurs to the indulgence of pommes de terre Sarladaise, cooked in goose fat, with or without truffles.

Modern transportation means that the region can share fully the gigantic amount of fruit produced in one part or another. I suppose the most famous of all has to be melons - the charentais from the Charentes, the netted

LOCAL PRODUCE

VEGETABLES

- **ARTICHOKE** *artichaut*
  Var: *Blanc Hyperois,
  Chrysanthème Gapean* (violet)
  The violet is the one eaten
  raw so often
  Two seasons, spring and
  autumn
  Dep: Charente-Maritime,
  Gironde, Lot-et-Garonne

- **ASPARAGUS** *asperge blanc*
  Mid-July until November
  Dep: Lot-et-Garonne

- **BEANS** *haricots verts*
  June to October
  Dep: Lot-et-Garonne,
  Dordogne
  Based around Marmande
  and Villeneuve-sur-Lot,
  two thirds are for
  commercial use. Second
  biggest French producers.

- **CUCUMBER** *concombre*
  March until November

- **EGGPLANT** *aubergine*
  Var: *Violette de Toulouse*
  (white flesh)
  violette de Barbentane
  (green flesh)
  Mid-July until November
  Dep: Lot-et-Garonne

- **MUSHROOMS** *champignons
  de couche*
  Year round
  Dep: Gironde, Charente

- **ONION** *oignon*
  May to September
  Dep: Lot-et-Garonne

- **PEPPERS** *poivrons*
  Var: *Lamuyo, Esterel*
  July to November
  Dep: Lot-et-Garonne

- **POTATOES** (new) *pommes
  de terre de primeur*
  Var: *Sirtema, Alcamaria*
  May and June
  Dep: Lot-et-Garonne

- **TOMATO** *tomate*
  Var: *Marmande*
  March to November,
  summer or open-air
  grown ones
  Dep: Lot-et-Garonne,
  Dordogne, Gironde
  Lot-et-Garonne is one of
  the four most important
  production zones of France,
  as well as being the home
  of one of the world's best
  knobby tomatoes.

- **ZUCCHINI** *courgette*
  Var: *Seneca* (under glass,
  spring and autumn),
  Diamant (open air, main
  season) Mid-April until end
  October
  Dep: Lot-et-Garonne

FRUITS

- **APPLE** *pomme*
  Var: *Reine des Reinettes*
  Picked August-October,
  sold until next April
  Dep: Dordogne, Gironde,
  Lot-et-Garonne

- **CHESTNUT** *marron/
  châtaigne*
  Harvested September-
  November
  Dep: Dordogne, Lot-et-
  Garonne
  Marrons have an
  unsegmented single kernel;
  châtaignes are segmented.

- **GRAPES** (table) *raisins*
  Black *Chasselas* is followed
  by white *Muscat*
  August until November,
  peak October
  Dep: Lot-et-Garonne
  mainly

- **GREENGAGE** *reine-claude*
  July and August
  Dep: Lot-et-Garonne

- **HAZELNUT** *noisette*
  Var: *Fertile de Coutard*
  Harvested September or so,
  but cobnuts sometimes
  available earlier.
  Dep: Dordogne, Lot-et-
  Garonne
  Together with the Loiret,
  the Dordogne is the
  principal producer.

- **KIWI FRUIT** *kiwi*
  Var: *Hayward* (NZ)
  November until March
  Dep: Gironde, Landes, Lot-
  et-Garonne

- **MELON** *melon*
  Var: *Charentais*
  End June until mid-October
  Dep: Lot-et-Garonne
  Most grown in small family
  plots, ensuring proper
  attention.

- **NECTARINE**
  nectarine/brugnon
  Var: yellow and white,
  mainly foreign strains
  June until September
  Dep: Lot-et-Garonne

- **PEACH** *pêche*
  Var: yellow and white
  mainly foreign
  June until September
  Dep: Lot-et-Garonne

- **PLUM** *prune*
  Var: *Prune d'Ente*
  July onwards for drying
  Dep: Lot-et-Garonne
  Although juicy and sweet,
  these red-skinned and
  -fleshed plums are almost
  all dried for prunes - see
  pruneaux d'Agen. Dessert
  plums are grown in Gironde
  and Dordogne.

- **STRAWBERRY** *fraise*
  Var: *Belrubi* and *Favette*
  dominate main season
  March (forced) until
  October, peak May and June
  Dep: Dordogne, Lot-et-
  Garonne
  These are the two biggest
  production zones in France.
  Sometimes the Dordogne
  has a second crop in
  September. Centers
  includes Périgueux,
  Marmande, Agen.

- **WALNUT** *noix*
  Var: *Grandjean*, native to
  the Dordogne
  Harvested first fortnight in
  October
  Dep: Dordogne, Charentes
  The Dordogne and Isère
  (Rhône Valley) are the
  premier production zones
  in France.

orange-fleshed melon also called a canteloupe. This is grown all over France, sometimes under different names, but it is never better than on its home ground, especially when drenched with pineau de Charente. Drenching fruit with wine or spirits is a natural thing to do here. You will find many combinations, and now that the Charentes are investing so heavily to produce wines too good to be distilled for cognac and brandy, there will be more to come.

Bordeaux is especially fond of showing off its fruit bathed in its wines: strawberries are served in real Bergerac and the elegant white peach is complemented with chilled white Bordeaux, a sweeter Sauternes, or the lighter, sharper red clairette.

The Dordogne and Périgord areas both produce a fantastic amount of fruit and nuts, and have consequently developed extraordinary ways to enjoy them. Perhaps the most unusual is to split hot miques (dumplings) and to spread them with honey, jam or redcurrant jelly (something the visitor is unlikely to be offered in modern restaurants I reckon). But peaches and pears, apricots and cherries are just as likely to be simply preserved in local cognac, brandy or pineau, and served on or with really super ice cream or sorbet. Poitou, incidentally, does a very nice Louise Bonne pear, among others. And should you ever tire of spooning up the sumptuous Charentais melon in its natural state, Périgueux offers a confiture de melon for you to slip into your suitcase. I shouldn't bother with the heart-arresting prices of whole candied melons, for the perfume of the lightly unripe fruit needed for the process rarely overcomes the

preservative soup of sugar.

Most of the walnuts and hazelnuts of the Dordogne are pressed into oils which, although meant mainly for salads, I use to flavor butter for spreading on ordinary bread, or actually put into dough with more of the same nuts. These nut and raisin breads, available universally hereabouts and often made with rye (seigle) are utterly addictive and have the special appeal to travelers of lasting a very long time, so are marvelous with cheese and fruit for a lunch when you are en route to or from somewhere. Both these nuts and chestnuts are used for stuffing chocolates or are stuffed themselves.

Those that escape either might be crushed into purées or spreads or used to flavor a variety of interesting drinks in which the nuts (or sometimes peach leaves and kernels) have been marinated. Both are excellent ways to take with you two of the best products of these lands.

Don't leave without buying some walnut oil, huile de noix, so much better for the experience of buying it in the sensitively restored medieval lanes of Périgueux.

PRUNEAUX D'AGEN

Even in English, the French would prefer us to use the term pruneaux for dried plums. This is in order to disassociate this delicacy of succulent fruit from those hard, dry bullets produced elsewhere and sometimes floating in a liquid all too similar to the Thames for comfort.

Dried plums have been appreciated for eons - plum stones have been found among the remains of many ancient European civilizations and even in the tomb of

Tutenkhamen. It is thought that the Crusaders brought the Damas plum tree back from Syria - the Damas plum tree had certainly reached French shores by the end of the 12th century - and it is this tree's descendants that are used in the production of pruneaux today.

Typically pruneaux d'Agen are made from the fruit of the prune d'Ente, with their pink, bloomy skin and oval shape. The moisture content of the finished pruneaux is 29-35 percent, so it is imperative to select a variety of plum that does not ferment at the pit. There are also, however, prunes Robe de Sergent, named after the color of the jackets worn by sergeants of the town before 1789, and prunes Imperial, a variety renowned for drying in the 17th and 18th centuries.

The pruniculteurs' preference to produce semi-dried (demi-secs) prunes has in the last five years thoroughly revitalized the popularity of pruneaux d'Agen in France and abroad. They are harvested in September, when around 40,000 tons of plums are picked mechanically and by hand.

Large producers dry the plums rapidly; in 24 hours fruit passes through a continuous series of drying tunnels and is sterilized and preserved. Smaller producers, such as Château de Born, which boasts a 12th-century castle originally built by the English, dry only for a morning, then pack and sterilize the prunes in bags. Pruneaux d'Agen may be rubbed with eau-de-vie or orange, or filled and made into fourrés, at which point they become a confectionery item more than a fruit. Look for shops in the town that will devote entire windows to pruneaux delicacies.

Cheese

Chèvres predominate in this region, particularly in Poitou and the Charentes. Produced both commercially and domestically, they are quite sharp to the tongue.

•Bougon: A factory-made goat's milk cheese of Poitou with predictable nutty flavor; best spring to autumn.

•Caillebotte Cailleé: Actually means curdled milk. This fresh unsalted cow's milk cheese is made in farms and homes in Poitou, Brittany, Anjou and Maine. It has a mild creamy flavor.

•Caillebotte d'Aunis: A farm-made sheep's milk cheese from Deux-Sèvres. It is fresh, unsalted and very mild; packed in a wicker or rush basket, often served with fruit. Also made in Charente-Maritime. When molded and drained it is called pigouille.

•Chabichou fermier: Produced only on the occasional farm around Poitiers, a small truncated cone of chèvre.

•Cabichou laitier: Dairy-produced in Poitou, the Charentes and Touraine, a small truncated cone of chèvre with a full flavor and strong smell. Also seen as cabrichou.

•Chèvre long: Widely available in Poitou, Charentes and Touraine; a soft chèvre.

•Couché-Verac: A soft goat's milk cheese, wrapped in sycamore or chestnut leaves. Weighs about 250g/8oz. Best from late spring to early autumn; has a robust flavor. Named after the nearest town to its farm-based production.

•Echourgnac: Made by Trappists at the monastery of Echourgnac in the Périgord, a small washed-rind cheese with tiny holes in the body. A

COGNAC, BRANDY — OR BOTH?

Cognac, like so many of the good things in life, is the result of tax avoidance. Cognac's wines are always thin and of low value and really too weak to travel. Yet travel they did, by barge down river, and they were taxed willy-nilly on quantity alone. Often the wines didn't survive the journey, or if they did, no one wanted them at the taxed price. The joint solution was to distill, reducing the volume and increasing the robustness; the rest is history.

The use of "champagne" in connection with cognac, is a variation of the word for countryside (campagne), and descriptive of the actual soils in which the essential wines are grown: Grande and Petite Champagne cognacs are considered the best, named because their rough chalk-strewn soil is the same as that of Champagne. Other areas of grape growing for cognac are the borderies and the bois.

Most of the big cognac houses sell a cognac made only from the Grande Champagne area towards the top of their range. You may also see fine champagne, which means a blend of Grande and Petite Champagne cognacs and should not be confused with the fine that Frenchmen ask for in bars, which gets them a glass of anonymous firewater.

Be certain you are buying what you think you are . . . for although all cognac is brandy, all brandies are not cognac. Only when the word cognac appears on a label can you be guaranteed, by law, that the contents have been distilled from grape juice and that the wording on the label actually means something.

The generally used degrees and styles of cognac are based on age, but the quality depends solely on the blend of distillates used. It is important to know that, in France, the legal minimum age requirements for the levels of quality are lower than they are, say, in Britain. In the UK, three-star brandy must be at least three years old, in France only one. At the higher levels (VSOP/VO/ Réserve and Extra/XO/ Napoléon/ Vieille Réserve), cognacs will be up to two years younger in France than in Britain.

More unusual, and more accessible pocket-wise, is pineau de Charente, one of the few remaining examples of the old ratafias. Pineau is made by adding cognac to the freshly pressed juice of grapes. It can be red, white or rosé and when perfect is delicious, with a clean raisin-like taste that a few people confuse with simple sweetness. In my opinion it is better than wine or spirit for cooking and well worth taking home.

The museum in Cognac has a display concerned with its eponymous spirit; there is also La Cognathèque, a shop dispensing knowledgeable advice, but no samples. Courvoisier has opened an excellent museum under its riverside premises in Jarnac; there is one at Cognac Delamin too, and Hennessey's tours include its barrel museum.

mild, fruity flavor.

•Jonchée Niortaise: Mild and creamy in taste, a very soft fresh goat's milk cheese from around Niort in Poitou; also in the Vendée and Charente. Sometimes called Parthenay.

•La-Mothe-St-Héray: There is a robust flavor to this small soft goat's milk cheese made at the dairy of La-Mothe-St-Héray whence it takes its name. Also known in Poitou as Mothais or chèvre à la feuille.

•Lusignan: A fresh goat's milk cheese farm-produced in and around Lusignan in Poitou. Weighs about 250g/8oz. The cheese used in tourteau fromagé, a cheesecake with a blackened upper crust.

•Pigouille: A fresh creamy charentais cheese from the milk of cows, goats or sheep. Packed on straw, and varying in quality and price.

•Poustagnacq: A fresh sheep's milk cheese from the Landes, best in winter, but sometimes fermented longer in crocks.

•Rocamadour: Known also as cabécou de Rocamadour, made from sheep's milk in the spring and goat's milk in summer, the latter giving a nutty flavor to this tiny disk of cheese. When aged with wine or spirit in crocks they are called picadou.

•Ruffec: A richly flavored goat's milk cheese made in Ruffec and the northern part of Charente. A thick disk; from farms from the end of spring to autumn.

Pastries, Desserts & Confectionery

Honey, fruit, wine, cognac and chocolate in one proportion or another, are the traditional basis of sweet eating from Poitou through the Charentes and into the Dordogne. Surprisingly, the unctuous cream and butter of the Deux-Sèvres has not given rise to new creations, but enhances those of other départements, so pastries, croissants, brioches and the like seem universally to excel. Equally unexpected is the retained taste for baking with corn flour, which long ago replaced the old sweetish standby, millet, (although millet is remembered in the names given to the new versions). The same thing happens in the Limousin and Auvergne.

Fruit of every description is grown locally, and much of it finds its life extended by marriage with cognac, but glitzy packaging makes the coupling too heavy to carry unless you have a car. Fruits in cognac are also very expensive - you are better off buying duty-free liquor and making such treats at home. While in the area, however, eat the fruit fresh with cream, or in tourtes, tourtières and tartes - the tarte verte d'Angoulême breaks fruity ranks by being made from a paste of green almonds.

Beignets - doughnuts or shapes of fried, flavored dough - are pretty common and the much-vaunted merveilles are just that. Pancakes are less ubiquitous

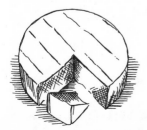

than elsewhere, although there are cruchades, made from a thick batter of corn flour. The macaroons are very good and are the basis of one of the best-ever confections made with chocolate, the Saint-Emilion.

The almonds that make macaroons also make marzipan (massepain), often shaped like sardines and fruits de mer, and the nougatine of

Poitiers. Whole almonds are baked into almost impossibly hard and chewy craquelins - I like those of Bordeaux. But if you need to keep children, friends or yourself amused in Bordeaux, search in its outstanding pastry shops for canalles. They look like tall little brioches and are made of corn flour, which gives a highly unusual, chewy but open texture. They are

recognizable by their coating of rich brown caramel and ridged sides (the canals). They seem unique to Bordeaux, and few other than natives of that city appear to know them. They travel well, though, so are excellent for picnics or munching en route.

A DRINKER'S GUIDE

Bordeaux is a region of two parts: the left bank, which contains all the famous names such as Latour and Margaux and which tend to be cabernet-sauvignon-based wines, and the right bank with areas such as St-Emilion and Pomerol, which are typically cabernet franc and merlot-based wines.

The drinking dates given here refer to classed growths and the top bourgeois châteaux only. The ordinary AOC bordeaux and similar wines, both red and white, are ready for drinking almost immed-iately. Most experts agree that a good Sauternes from a good vintage needs 10 years or more in the bottle, and a top white Graves at least 8.

RECENT VINTAGES
1994: Almost a great year. Looked good until the rains came and washed away the winemakers' hope. It is still an excellent year with great aging potential and not overpriced. A better year for merlot although some sweet wines are reasonable.
1993: A thoroughly washed-out year. Diluted wines that will probably

always disappoint.
1992: Even wetter. In fact, the wettest summer for 50 years in Bordeaux. These wines from wet years are to be drunk soon, if nothing better can be found.
1991: Rain did an incomplete job this year, with some of the early picking estates, usually the best, making acceptable wine.
1990: A great year and in contrast to the following wash-outs, one of the hottest years on record. Consequently the fruit flavors are much fuller than is usual in Bordeaux, but there are some great, extremely fruity wines, perhaps not for the longest aging. In Sauternes, this is said to be the best year since 1893! These will also be great, huge wines and one of the great unknowns is how these will develop - except that they will develop very, very well.
1989: A cabernet sauvignon year with some excellent wines made. The middle of what the Bordelaise call their trois glorieuses, along with 1988, when both the reds and the sweets were of top quality but of very

different character.
1988: The most classic of the '80s vintages, uniformly good or excellent. This is what claret should taste like. In Sauternes it was a mixed vintage, between the great and the very good.
1987: Definitely not a great year but some very drinkable soft wines, with merlots better and drinking now.
1986: Some very good wines made for long aging but the sweet wines seem to be the most successful of the vintage - some of them are wondrous.
1985: An exceptionally drinkable vintage and perhaps likely to remain so with some lovely jammy wines.
1984: The lesser wines are as they always have been - dismal. The better châteaux are drinkable, in a lean way.

PREVIOUS GREATS
1983 and 1982 produced great wines for long-term drinking, with the Sauternes very good indeed. Sweet wines from 1975 should be good, while the reds and whites from 1986 may still be interesting.

Bon Marché

DEUX-SÈVRES

Ardin *Sat;* Argenton Château
Thur; Le Beugnon *Every 2nd
Thur;* Bressuire *Tue;* Brious-sur-
Boutonne *Thur;* Champdeniers-
St-Denis *Sat;* Chef Boutonne *1st
& 3rd Sat;* Clessé *Sat;* Coulonges-
sur-l'Autize *Tue;* La Crèche *Tue;*
Lezay *Tue;* Mauléon *Fri;* Melle *Fri;*
Niort *Daily, esp Thur & Sat;*
Parthenay *Wed;* Sauzé-Vaussais
Thur; Secondigny *Mon;* St-
Maixent-l'Ecole *Wed;* Thénezay
Sun AM; Thouars *Tue & Fri;* St-
Varent *3rd Sun in month;*
Voultegon *Wed.*

VIENNE

Angles-sur-l'Anglin *Wed, Thur,
Sat, 1st Tue of month;* Availles
Limouzine *1st Wed of month;*
Bouresse *1st of month;*
Buxerolles *Thur AM;* Chatellerault
Tue, Thur, Sat; Chaunay *Mon;*
Chauvigny *Sat;* Civray *Tue;*
Coulonges *29th of month;* L'Isle-
Jourdain *1st Mon of month;*
Jaunay Clan *Fri;* Liglet *2nd of
month;* Luchapt *14th of month;*
Lusignan *Wed;* Mirebeau *Wed &
Sat AM;* Naintré *Sun AM;* Poitiers
Daily except Mon; Pouillé *1st &
3rd Wed of month;* La Roche-
Posay *Daily;* Rouillé *Fri;* St-Jean-
de-Sauves *1st Fri of month;*
St-Savin *Fri;* La Trimouille *8th of
month;* Les Trois Moutiers *Sat;*
Vendeuvre-du-Poitou *Tue;*
Vivonne *Tue, Sat.*

CHARENTE-MARITIME

Angoulins *Daily;* Aytre *Fri AM;* Le-
Bois-Plage-en-Ré *Daily (15 June
- 15 Sept), Thur (rest of year);*
Bourcefranc-le-Chapus *Wed, Fri;*
La Brée-les-Bains *Daily;* Château
d'Oléron *Daily ex Mon & Sat (Sat,
June 16 - Sept 15);* Couarde-sur-
Mer *Daily (summer);* Dolus
d'Oléron *Daily (summer);* La
Flotte *Daily;* Jonzac *Tue, Fri;*
Marennes *Tue, Fri, Sat;*
Mirambeau *Sat;* Montendre

Thur; Mortagne-sur-Gironde
Thur; Port-des-Barques *Daily;*
Pons *Wed, Sat,* Rochefort *Tue,
Thur, Sat;* La Rochelle *Daily;*
Royan *Daily (summer), daily ex
Mon rest of year;* Saintes *Daily ex
Mon;* Surgères *Tue, Thur, Sat;* St-
Denis-d'Oléron *Daily (summer);* St-
Genis-de-Saintonge *Every two
weeks;* St Georges-de-Didonne
*Daily (summer), daily ex Mon rest
of year;* Ste-Marie-de-Ré *Daily;*
St Martin-de-Ré *Daily;*
St Pierre-d'Oléron *Daily
(summer);* St Trojan-les-Bains
Wed, Sat; Tonnay-Charente *Wed,
Sat;* La Tremblade *Sat.*

CHARENTE

Aigre *Thur;* Angoulême *Daily;*
Barbezieux-St-Hilaire *Tue;*
Blanzac-Porcheresse *3rd Sat of
month;* Brossac *2nd & 4th Sat of
month;* Chalais *Mon;*
Chasseneuil-sur-Bonnieure *Sat;*
Chateauneuf-sur-Charente *Tue,
Thur, Sat;* Cognac *Daily;*
Confolens *Wed, Sat;* La Couronne
Sat; Jarnac *Daily ex Mon;* Mansle
2nd Mon of month; La
Rochefoucauld *Daily;* Rouillac
27th of month; Ruffec *Wed, Sat;*
St-Michel *Wed, Sat;* St-Séverin
2nd Tue of month; Villefagnan
Tue, Fri.

GIRONDE

Ambarès-et-Lagrave *Fri AM;*
Arcachon *Daily;* Audenge *Tue;*
Bassens *Sun AM;* Bazas *Sat (also
Cattle Fair);* Blaye *Wed, Sat;*
Bordeaux *Daily ex Sun;* Braud-
et-St-Louis *Mon, Wed, Fri (15
Mar - Oct) fruit, veg eggs,
poultry;* Cavignac *Thur;* Coutras
Wed & Sat AM; Créon *Wed;*
Frontenac *Fri AM;* Guitres *Onion
Fair 2nd Wed Sept;* Langon *Tue,
Fri;* Libourne *Tue, Fri, Sun AM;*
Monségur *Fri AM;* Pauillac *Tue,
Sat AM;* Pellegrue *Wed;* Podensac
Fri; Pugnac *Wed AM;* Reignac
Mon, Wed, Fri (prunes); La Réole
Wed, Sat; Sauveterre-de-
Guyenne *Tue;* Soulac-sur-Mer
*Daily (summer), Thur AM (rest of
year);* St-André-de-Cubzac *Thur
& Sat AM;* St Ciers-sur-Gironde
Sun AM; St-Emilion *Sun AM;* Ste-
Foy La-Grande *Sat AM;* St-Loubès
Mon AM;

St Médard-en-Jalles *Sat;* St-
Savin *Mon AM;* St-Seurin-sur-
l'Isle *Sat AM;* St-Symphorien *1st
& 3rd Sun of month;* St-Vivien-
de-Médoc *Wed;* La Teste *Daily;*
Oyster farming Fair/Exhibition
last week July.

DORDOGNE

Agonac *Sun;* Belvès *Sat;* Bergerac
Wed, Sat; Brantôme *Fri;* Le Bugue
Tue, Sat AM; Le Buisson-de-
Cadouin *Fri;* Champagnac-de-
Belair *Fair 1st Mon of month;*
Cogulot *Thur;* Excideuil *Thur;*
Eymet *2nd & 4th Thur of month;*
Les Eyzies-de-Tayac Sireuil *Mon;*
Lalinde *Thur;* Monpazier *Thur
(Chestnut Market Thur & Sun AM
Oct-Dec);* Montignac *Wed, Sat
AM;* Montpon Ménestérol *Wed;*
Neuvic *Tue, Sat,* Nontron *Sat;*
Périgueux *Wed, Sat;* Razac-sur-
l'Isle *Sat AM;* Rouffignac-St-
Cernin-de-Reilhac *Sun;* Serges
1st & 3rd Thur of month; St-
Astier *Thur;* St-Aulaye *Sat;*
Terrasson-la-Villedieu *Daily;*
Thenon *Tue;* Thiviers *Sat;*
Tocane-St-Apre *Mon;* Vergt *Fri;*
Villefranche-du-Périgord *Sat,
(Chestnut Market Sats Oct-Dec).*

LOT-ET-GARONNE

Agen *Wed, Sat & Sun AM, Fat
Geese Fair 2nd Mon Dec, Ham
Fair Mon before Easter;* Aiguillon
Tue; Astaffort *Mon* Cancon *1st &
3rd Mon of month;* Castejaloux
Tue, Sat; Castillonnès *Tue;*
Cocumont *Mon;* Fargues-sur-
Ourbise *Mon, Wed, Fri eve;* Fumel
Sun, Tue, Fri; Houeillès *Wed AM;*
Labretonie *Mon;* Lauzun *Sat;*
Lavardac *Sun AM;* Marmande
Mon, Thur, Sat; Le Mas d'Agenais
2nd Thur of month; Miramont-
de-Guyenne *Mon;* Monbahus
*Sun AM, 1st Sat in month (calves,
poultry);* Monflanquin *Thur;*
Nèrac *Sat;* Penne de'Agenais *Sun
AM;* Port-Ste-Marie *Sat AM;*
Prayssas *Sun, Tue, Thur (June-Aug
15) (fruit & veg), Daily (Sept-Nov),
(Chasselas Grapes);* Sauvetat-de-
Savères *Sun (poultry & eggs);*
Seyches *Fri;* Tonneins *Wed, Sat
AM;* Villeneuve-sur-Lot *Tue, Sat;*
Villeréal *Sat, 1st & 3rd Mon.*

⟨❀⟩ LIMOUSIN &
THE AUVERGNE

VALLEYS OF EDEN

"In which we...
•Identify rude food, and
find how Pompadour
spared servants from
blushing...
•Discover a thousand-
year-old corporation and
the meaning of
Millevaches...
•Cook famous carrots...
•Taste what Adam sat
on and the moldy beards
bartered for a bride...
•Fish in the Jordanne,
see sizzling springs and a
meatloaf crossed with
soufflé, taste
nutty oils...
•See the old hams that
became an auvergnat
sensation...
•Marvel at the kamikaze
chestnut that cracks its
own shell...
•Ride to find raspberries,
poke about blue chesses
and taste a 2,000-year-
old variety...
•Avoid herbs in innocent
guise but look for a cake
that commanded the
Black Prince's troops...
•Discover the water table
of the table waters..."

Contrast is an insidious word to a food writer, invidious even, for the frightful ease there is in using it, because it too often accurately describes the experience of a place. Yet, try as I might, I can't think of a better word to describe the singular appeal of Limousin and the Auvergne. In mitigation, there are, at least, lots of different contrasts.

If you know anything about either region, it is probably that they get pretty cold and pretty hot, and can drop from midsummer to midwinter in a few hours, and that they are high and fairly inaccessible and rather plain in parts, with sheep. That's all true enough and you'll get what you bargained for.

The foods thought most "typical" of these related areas are based on cabbage, on potatoes, chestnuts and pork. They are the thick soup/stews, the *potée auvergnat* and the *bréjaude* or *bréjauda* of Limousin. There are the usual arguments about which should have what, whether leeks and beet root, or a whole head of pig, or just this or that salted piece should be there, but these are modern scholarly arguments of little relevance, for such dishes are the basis of the cuisine of every region of France, the sons and daughters of necessity. What you saw was what you used.

But there were definite problems with what you ate with those hearty dishes. The solution here was often that of the Bretons, pancakes of buckwheat (*sarrasin/blé noir*). It is basic, rude, simple food, packed with calories needed to get you through days of hard work or harsh winter temperatures; thus the surprise of finding, also, associations with some of France's most sophisticated names and products.

It had never occurred to me that one of my heroines, Madame de Pompadour, was actually a *marquise* and a *duchesse* of a real place, but Pompadour is in Limousin and her château, much too unfashionably sited for her to have spent much time in it, became a stud farm after her death, and remains so. She would have known well the tapestries made in Aubusson, about 60 km/37 miles away from her château as the crow flies; they would have been used to cut out the draughts and the whispers of the palace, and to make discreet back-grounds for her intriguing *petits soupers.*

Her private dining room in Versailles was no place for servants to overhear gossip and inuendo either. To save their blushes and those of her guests, La Pompadour's table disappeared through the floor after each course, returning when summoned, suitably relaid. But she missed by one year the discovery that made Limoges famous: that in 1765 of kaolin at St-Yrieix-la-Perche and the subsequent founding of the porcelain industry, fashioning tureens and bowls and gold-rimmed services. They would have looked good on that table.

It was surprising (to me, at least) to find meat, beef in particular, has been important long enough for there to have been a corporation of butchers ever since 930. Since the 17th century *les bouchers* have had also the honor and duty of guarding the safety of all visitors. Incidentally, I'm not sure if the words are related but the verb *limoger* means to dismiss or retire someone. Perhaps being sent to Limoges was once considered a banishment.

They seem to have had plenty to do, these butchers, preparing the flesh of the Limousin cattle of the plateau de Millevaches, which disappointingly doesn't mean thousands of cows but lots of rivers. Indeed there are many, and water in every other form possible, except for thermal spas, which is the perogative of the Auvergne. The abundance of water makes the Limousin such a green luscious place in summer and the great stretches of thick, green vegetation and trees magnify its reputation for being so sparsely peopled. Of course, the water also nourishes the fruits and nuts of those trees, notably *reines-claudes* in the Corrèze, and makes fat the cherries (*cerises*) which in turn moisten *clafoutis.*

The Auvergne, which is the greater part of the Massif Central, is much wilder to see than the Limousin, and full of tall stories. Its *puys* are extinct volcanic cones reaching even higher, but loved quite as much as they are cursed for their inconvenience by Auvergnats. When the days are too hot to bear, you can always climb a mountain, and it will be cooler. Where there are mountains there are valleys and plains; thus, although it is true that grazing is sparse on the heights, so that only sheep and goats can be expected to live and lactate, down below are thriving gardens, pastures for dairy cattle, orchards, and farms to rival any. Vichy is a good example of an unappreciated agricultural center, and is encircled by market gardens (*cultures maraichères*), a renowned crop of which is carrots. I can't find anyone who actually knows what has so indelibly linked Vichy and carrots, but I'm quite certain that cooking carrots in bottled Vichy spa water is not the reason. This confusion has arisen because local cooks add a pinch of bicarbonate of soda and of sugar to the saucepan. The slight taste the soda leaves was thought to be from the local mineral water. My opinion is that the fame was originally based on the local technique, either cooking carrots in butter only or in so little water it evaporated to make a thick sauce by the time the carrots were cooked - add butter and chopped parsley, and *voilà*, Vichy carrots. Of course, any water used may have been from a local spring . . .

The contrast between what the uninitiated expect and what the locals feel about their country and their food is nowhere better illustrated than in Aigueperse, Puy-de-Dôme. The local view is that this was the very epicenter of the Garden of Eden. Of all the wicked fruits which hung from the trees of Paradise, *pralines* were the favorites of Adam and Eve. One day, God came visiting, and caught them having a right old feast. They apparently heard him coming - thunderbolts I presume - and attempted to dissemble with nonchalant lounging. But God knew better and made Adam stand up, revealing that he had been sitting on a couple. God was so cross he chased them both out of the garden. Much later the confectioners still make a speciality of the forbidden sweets that Adam - not Eve mind you - could not resist. More research required I think . . .

None is needed into the reputation the locals have for being as canny about money as the Scots. That's a fact. And like the Scots they've gone to make it somewhere else if times have been tough, usually opening small restaurants or shops specializing in the hams and charcuterie and excellent cheeses of the Auvergne. Auvergnat shops all over France, particularly in Paris, are always worth a visit.

Tomme incidentally is not a type of cheese, but the local name for cheese, and this is why tommes from the same area may be totally different types of cheese. What each will have in common is a fantastic story woven about it, some curious enough to be true. *Gaperon*, for instance, is a gray half sphere wrapped in ribbon, made from skimmed milk and flavored with garlic and black peppercorns. How pale and uninteresting is its modern life in cheese shops around the world compared to its once and proper place in society. Gaperons were the conspicious part of a young girl's dowry, hung outside her parents' house promiscuously to be counted, and allowed to grow beards of mold that dangled a foot or more. If you see lumps of garlicy mold hanging outside the house, and you are a single male, apply within.

There is plenty of confusion about what rightfully belongs to the culinary repertoire of the Limousin and the Auvergne. It's partly a matter of knowing quite where older boundaries, like those of the Aveyron and the Rouergue, belong. Because they are central surely it is expected that both regions have invaded and been invaded. Thus *bleu d'Auvergne* is meant to be like the roquefort of Aveyron, and cantal cheese is mixed into a potato purée (*aligot*) as carefully as in the Rouergue, and salads are seasoned with nut oils as in the Périgord. But just because you can't find the wines of Chanturgue, don't think chicken cooked in those wines was not the original *coq au vin*; it's simply that the vineyards are no longer with us. In any case, I shouldn't bother too much about the stories you hear, but concentrate instead on what you find. You may be surprised at the contrast . . .

Charcuterie

As pork features among the many riches of the Auvergne - marginally more than in Limousin - and as the climate is just right, air-dried charcuterie is extremely good. All through France you are likely to find stalls of traveling Auvergnats selling their andouilles, their air-dried sausages and, even better, the famed hams of the Auvergne; recommended centers of production are Ussel, St-Mathieu, Lezoux and Clermont-Ferrand. As well as the raw, the cooked ones are worth seeking out; in Lezoux, for instance, they are baked in pastry with madeira.

In Rochechouart on mardi gras you should find small pies of pork, spices and egg in pastry - a French pork pie. It is slowly being learnt, I believe, that they are good enough to be worth making at other times of the year. Pâtés are universally made, but are generally too strongly flavored for foreign palates when the local taste for pork liver predominates. Yet all of them are interesting for the variety of herbs and spices of the plateau that might be employed, including juniper. More to the general taste are the large tourtes, pastry-covered pies of pork and veal nicely spiced with pepper and cloves. Smaller are friands sanflorains, little sausages baked in pastry.

The presence of pigs means blood pudding (boudin). Chestnuts are often included and on a cold day or chilly evening the combination of hot boudin and the common Limousin garnish of red cabbage, with or without more chestnuts, is quite wonderfully warming ... even in summer you may need it.

WORTH FINDING

• *Fricandeau*: A *crépine* of pork; chopped, flavored pork wrapped in caul fat (*coiffe*).
• *Farcidure*: The name means "hard stuffing" and these are small dumplings based on buckwheat, a *hachis* of green leaves (like sorrel), and herbs. Sometimes wrapped in cabbage leaves as well.
• *Tripoux*: Small cushions of tripe stuffed with boned trotter flesh; they might well be made with mutton rather than pork, but are always flavored with cloves. Further south they will be called *trénels*, and the exact composition of the stuffing is, naturally, subject to many variations, argument and opinion.

Fish & Shellfish

The abundant freshwater fish found in the Limousin and Auvergne is most likely to be served to you in a friture almost certainly prepared in butter. Experimenters might dribble in a little nut oil, which is local, or olive oil, which is not. Auvergnat frogs were fattened and taken to 18th-century Paris, so renowned was their succulence, but they are fewer since the swamps of Limagne have been drained for pastureland. What remains - or what are imported - are served as simply as the fish, fried in butter. The mixed freshwater matelote based on carp and eels, pike, tench and so on is also made.

The treat to really go for - if you can find them these days - is the local crayfish (écrevisses). A simple and effective ploy in the Haute Auvergne is to cook them with fresh mint; delicious. Guéret serves them à la sauce sans nom - in a nameless sauce.

Pike (brochet) is stuffed and roasted and sometimes made into a pâté, a lazy but tastier version of a quenelle. You can be fairly certain that trout is wild and local and it will be served classically (au bleu if you are lucky), experimentally, or in local tradition, which might include cheese, vermouth or spinach. For the greatest of traveling fishy tales, order local trout in Aurillac - it will have come from the River Jordanne. Brits may welcome the regular appearance of jellied eels (anguilles en gelée).

Meat, Poultry & Game

Beef, lamb, mutton, veal, pork, turkeys, geese and chickens are all produced in one part or another of the valleys and high pastures of central France. Since the 19th century, Limousin has become the virtual meat factory of France. Its small cattle were primarily kept as workers but have subsequently been bred into the huge modern limousins with first-class meat – which has changed local cuisine. You'll find many products traditionally made from pork now sweetened and made more sophisticated with veal, or with parts of veal. Tourtes are an example.

Lamb and mutton equally thrive on the well-watered heights of the Auvergne, especially in Cantal. In Chaudes-Aigues they have been important far longer than has the pig, but are just one of the claims to fame of this place. It doesn't just have hot springs: the water positively sizzles at over 80°C.

Cantal is also an important center for raising turkey and geese, and in the north of the region, the Bourbonnais, you'll find a highly reputed race of chickens, the poulets bourbonnais. The name usually also indicates the bird will be served in typical sauce of cream and cheese.

Game is here limited and not as important as elsewhere. There is some fame for a method of preparing hare (lièvre en cabessal), differing from the exalted but complicted lièvre à la royale in the stuffing. You are unlikely to meet either but may find the wild rabbit (lapin de garenne). In the Auvergne it is more likely you will find boar (sanglier), sometimes in a daube which makes a change from roasts. Partridge (perdrix, and perdreau for young birds) is prepared with two of the local favorites – cabbage and lentils.

Some of the most famous dishes of the region were based on such songbirds as the thrush, which were stuffed with foie gras; but these may no longer be taken, being protected by the Common Market. The most surprising food fact is that coq au vin was first cooked here and was actually called coq au Chanturgue; it is deceptive of local restaurateurs to dub it au Chanturgue, for this is one of the wines that has all but disappeared since the vineyards have been replaced by pastures.

Chicken will also be found stuffed with chestnuts à la limousin or made into a tourte or chicken pie. Cherries, too, are combined with poultry. Anne Willan, in her book French Regional Cooking, has an excellent recipe for duck with the tart cherries that can be gathered wild in the hedgerows of this area .

• *Gigot brayaude*: Also called *cassette*. A most famous dish, almost a pot roast really, of leg of lamb cooked in a little wine on a bed of vegetables, potatoes usually included. Gault Millau publish the unresolved question of whether the gigot should be stuck with cloves of garlic or larded, but the former was all I found. It should be served with the usual mixture of vegetables in these parts – cabbage, red beans and onions.

• *Mortier*: A casserole from the Auvergne associated with Easter, which combines beef or veal with ham and chicken.

• *Pounti*: Described almost everywhere as a cross between a meat loaf and a vegetable soufflé, which is about as close as you could hope to get to encapsulating something mixing chopped pork or bacon with eggs, cream, ham and almost any green leaf or herb, plus, sometimes, raisins and prunes. When it includes sorrel or dandelion leaves in spring time, it is a somewhat lighter version of Cognac's *poulet vert* (see Bordeaux).

• *Pountari*: Not the same as pounti but a sort of sausage wrapped in cabbage leaves.

Fruits & Vegetables

If you are among the uninitiated and think of central France, as I once did, as an area of high, dry and scrubby fields nibbled at by scrawny sheep, you will thoroughly enjoy exploring the surprising range of its produce. For in between those plains, and much lower down, rich valleys grow an extraordinary choice of fruit, vegetables and grains.

Auvergne and Le Puy grow everything from petits pois to chestnuts, although cabbage and exquisite lentils (lentilles) are the best-known crops, turning up, with beans, green, white or red, whatever the season. The blue-green lentilles de Puy are protected by an AOC. Limagne and its plain is the most perfect example of the Auvergne's spread of produce. Its wheat fields are bordered by orchards producing sun-ripened apricots and other fruits for the excellent local confitures. Look out specially for the strawberries from Courpière, fresh or preserved.

The autumnal debris under chestnut trees is the place to find succulent cèpes in autumn. Spring offers the more sophisticated flavors of morels (morilles) and mousserons. Both garlic and shallots are important commercial crops in Puy-de-Dôme, but you should particularly plan to stock up on nut oils - either walnut (huile de noix) or exquisite hazelnut oil (huile de noisette). Both are used to finish the flavor of dishes cooked in pork fats and as the dressing for salads of all kinds. Corrèze (Limousin) grows the most and best nuts, and so may offer marginally better choice.

LOCAL PRODUCE

VEGETABLES
- **CABBAGE** chou pommé
  Var: none French
  Autumn and winter
  Dep: Creuse

- **SHALLOT** échalote
  Var: Longue, Demi-Longue
  Fresh June/July; available
  12 months
  Dep: Puy-de-Dôme

FRUIT
- **APPLES** pommes
  Var: Reinette Blanche
  and Grise
  Mainly September to October
  Dep: Corrèze

- **CHESTNUT** marron/
  châtaigne
  Var: Précoce Migoule
  (châtaigne), Laguepie
  eaten fresh; Dorée de Lyon
  Late autumn early winter
  Dep: Corrèze

- **HAZELNUT** noisette
  Var: None French
  July to September, fresh,
  then dried
  Dep: Corrèze

- **PLUM** prune
  Var: Reines-Claudes, Prune
  de Vars (July)
  Mid-July to early October
  Dep: Corrèze

- **RASPBERRY** framboise
  Var: none French
  June and July high season
  Dep: Corrèze

- **STRAWBERRY** fraises
  Var: Favette, Belrubi
  Forced start end April. May
  and June main season
  Dep: Corrèze

- **WALNUT** noix
  Var: Corne, Marbot
  Harvested September to
  January
  Dep: Corrèze

Limousin was one of the very first areas in France to enjoy the potato, long before Parmentier and the Revolution. Both here and in the Auvergne you'll find some of the most unusual and delicious potato ideas, often mixed with dairy products of one kind or another. Potatoes are creamed to go with salt cod, in pies, in farcidure. The gratin auvergnat is potatoes mixed with an equal amount of chestnuts.

Chestnuts with red cabbage is a classic Limousin mixture but they are just as often served separately; boiled chestnuts are boursadas, when grilled they are chauvets. They are usually the châtaigne rather than the marron and turn up almost everywhere in simple home cooking; perhaps that is why the debou circadour was developed - it neatly cracks open its own shell.

Limousin is one of the few French regions to grow Jerusalem artichokes (topinambours) and of all central France its southern département, Corrèze, has the greatest number of commercial crops - of apple, table plums and greengages, strawberries and raspberries, the biggest of all. Less common fruit includes the sumptuous mulberry (mûre), which may turn up with saddle of hare (râble de lièvre). And should you be walking or, blissfully, riding through August woodland or forest, you stand well to discover bilberries (myrtilles) or exquisite wild raspberries. With the wine you would, naturally, be carrying, a shady bough and a thou, who'd mind the lack of bread?

WORTH FINDING

• *Criquettes*: Potato pancakes, usually flavored with garlic in the Auvergne.

• *Farinettes*: Savory pancakes usually filled with vegetable mixtures.

• *Aligot*: One of the most famous dishes - a purée of mashed potato and fresh cheese (aligot is actually the fresh curd of cantal cheeses). Also associated with the Rouergue, which corresponds to the *département* of Aveyron, just across the border from Cantal.

• *Pastourelle*: The best of the many delicious auvergnat salads, dressed with a nut oil, cream, blue cheese, tarragon and chervil.

• *Gâteau de potiron et maïs*: A bread/cake of pumpkin and corn meal like that made in the Basque country.

• *Pommes de terre à la guerilla*: Potatoes sautéed then grated into milk.

• *Truffado/truffade*: Potatoes cooked with cheese, properly cantal, and then shaped into cakes and fried.

Cheese

The rich pastureland of this region - which includes Cantal, the Aubrac mountains and the massif of Auvergne - gives an excellent flavor to the milk of the cows and goats grazing there, in turn producing many excellent cheeses. There is a wide selection of blue cheeses made on mountain farms, including the bleu d'Auvergne, the celebrated fourmes and many other pressed-uncooked cow's milk cheeses and some fine chèvres and mi-chèvres.

• *Aligot*: Originating in the mountains of Aubrac, aligot is a fresh pressed cheese that has to be eaten within 48 hours of manufacture. Produced by small mountain dairies called burons, it is slightly sour with a somewhat nutty flavor; used in cooking.

• *Bleu d'Auvergne*: Only created in 1845 by a peasant of the Auvergne who added some of the blue mold he saw on his rye bread to his cheeses and poked them with a needle to ensure the air passages in which the mold might grow. Others in the area followed his example and so was born one of the newest cheeses to be honored with an AOC. Neither pressed nor cooked, the body should be very evenly molded with veins, firm to the touch and have a strong smell and full, savory flavor. It is always wrapped in foil, weighs 2-3 kg/4-6 lb (smaller ones 1kg/2 ¼lb) and can be enjoyed all year round. In effect a cow's milk version of roquefort.

• *Bleu de Laqueille*: Related to bleu d'Auvergne, this soft cow's milk cheese, now produced commercially, was developed about 1850. Foil wrapped, weighing 2kg/4 lb it has a keen smell, definite savoury flavor and is at its best in summer and autumn after its three month's curing.

• *Bleu de Loudes*: Sometimes called bleu du Valay although there is another cheese of this name with a higher fat content. This is a low-fat (25-35%) cow's milk cheese with a savory flavor and is similar to many other blue cheeses from small mountain farms in the region.

• *Bleu de Thiézac*: Made exclusively by mountain farms in the upper valley of Cère and the Jordanne, a soft cow's milk cheese not unlike bleu d'Auvergne although a little less smooth. A savory flavor, at its best in summer and autumn.

• *Bleu du Velay*: A 30-40% fat blue very similar to bleu de Loudes.

• *Brique du Forez*: Known also as chèvron d'Ambert or cabrion du Forez. A soft chèvre or mi-chèvre from the Auvergne, brick-shaped, 300-350g/ 12-14oz, which is cured dry on rye hay for two or three months and eaten summer to autumn. Chèvres have a bluish mold exterior; mi-chèvre are gray.

• *Cantal*: An AOC cheese also known as fourme de Cantal, this is one of the most ancient cheeses known, dating back at least 2,000 years. It comes from an area in the volcanic massif of the Auvergne where vegetation is luscious and excellent for grazing. A very large cow's milk cheese - it can weigh 30-45 kg/ 77-99 lb (although the cantalet weighs a mere 10 kg/22 lb) - it is pressed but not cooked and can be eaten young (le cantal jeune) or matured (vieux - about 4-6 months). With a light gray crust and ivory-colored body, it has a mild flavor, comparable to that of a good nutty farm-made cheddar. Made commercially throughout the year, it is also produced on mountain farms in the summer. It is used in cooking, in any way a cheddar would be.

•Cantalon: Produced in most of Auvergne, it is a cow's milk cheese very similar to cantal but smaller, weighing 4-10 kg/9-22 lb.

•Chevrotin du bourbonnais: A small truncated cone of goat's milk cheese that receives very little curing - no more than a week or two - and can be eaten fresh and creamy (with sugar if you want) or semi-dry, when it has a nutty flavor.

•Conne: Known also as chevrotin de bourbonnais, a cone of soft goat's milk cheese with a mild nutty flavor; made close to Moulins, center of the Bourbonnais in Allier.

•Coulandon/chaucetier: Eaten fresh, this soft cheese from the Allier is rather like fresh coulommiers but made from partly skimmed cow's milk.

•Fourme d'Ambert/Fourme de Montbrison: The AOC cheese we know probably emerged in the 8th or 9th century, although it has a history that predates the arrival of the Caesars. Fourme refers to molds in which the cheese is made. It is a typical blue pressed uncooked cow's milk cheese but has a rougher, more mold-covered crust than most; it is taller and thinner, too. Produced extensively in the farms and dairies of the Puy-de-Dôme plus some in the neighboring Loire (Rhône Valley) and five cantons around St-Flour. Although a little salty, it has a smooth fruity flavor.

•Fourme de Pierre-sur-Haute: Closely resembling the fourme d'Ambert, this blue cheese is made high up in the mountains of Livradois.

•Fourme de rochefort: Linked with the history of Cantal, this is a big cow's milk cheese with a lactic smell and,

BOTTLING IT UP

Nowhere else in the world are mineral waters consumed in such quantity and treated with such reverence as in France. The French drink some 300 billion liters of eau minérale naturelle each year, believing it to be an important aid to health, beauty and above all le foie. Over the last decade, sales of mineral water have been gaining at the expense of wine although they have recently plateaued, with volume consumption at a level around 94 liters per person per year. Still water is preferred in French homes - 75 percent of households purchase it as opposed to the 53 percent that purchase sparkling water.

All bottled waters are highly regulated by the French government, which has put them into three distinct classes. Bottom of the league is eau de table (table water), which can come from either a public or a private supply, but it must be drinkable and contain a certain number of mineral salts. Eau de source (spring water) must be of a specified origin and be drinkable in its natural state. A spring water gains the accolade of eau minérale naturelle if it is found by the National Academy of Medicine to be positively good for you, and can therefore be used therapeutically. Such is the French attitude to mineral waters, doctors study their different properties during training and can forbid or recommend different brands according to their minerals. According to law, mineral water must be bottled as it emerges from the ground, without any sterilization - in other words it reaches the public in its natural pure state. All aspects of collection, bottling and protection from pollution are subject to stringent checks and standards. Some mineral waters carry a d'intérêt public seal of approval, meaning the spring and surrounding land are even further safeguarded. Differing

tastes come from mineral salts naturally present in the water and usually waters such as Evian and Perrier are lower in minerals than brands such as Vichy, which has a more distinctive taste. Sparkling waters get their sparkle from carbon dioxide, found under carbonate rocks, which may be collected separately at the spring and re-injected at bottling - in fact, only Badoit has not been re-injected, amongst sparkling waters.

These are the most famous waters from France's 1,200 mineral springs and 100 spas.

•Badoit: Medium-strength flavor with a natural, light sparkle. Licenced in 1838, it was the first mineral water to be bottled and sold commercially for mass consumption. The source is St-Galmier in the Loire Valley, the spring emerging on the edge of Monts du Lyonnais. Recommended for nervous disorders. Much the most fashionable in France - because the bubbles are smaller and more elegant?

•Contrex: A still water with an earthy taste. The source was discovered in 1760, 383m/1,148 ft above sea level in the Faucille mountain range, near the French-German border. Contrex has a high calcium sulphate content and is popular with dieters because of its diuretic properties.

•Evian: A light, still water and the biggest selling bottled water in the world. The source is the water and the snow falling on the French Alps, which eventually collect in a deep bed formed in sands of glacial origin, naturally protected by two thick layers of clay. The average time it takes to filter through the sands is thought to be 15 years. Low in sodium and nitrate, it has diuretic properties, and being particularly pure, it is recommended by French doctors for kidney diseases, arthritis and gout.

• *Perrier*: Highly carbonated and one of the most popular imported mineral waters in Britain and America. The source was a resting place for Hannibal and the site of Roman baths in the 1st century AD. Its name comes from Dr. Perrier, who sold the spring at the turn of the century to AW St John Harmsworth, brother of the Fleet Street tycoon Lord Northcliffe. Harmsworth gave to Perrier its distinctive Indian-club-shaped bottle and coined the slogan "*Perrier - le champagne des eaux de table.*" Its effervescence comes from gases trapped by volcanic eruptions deep beneath the earth's surface, which travel up through porous limestone to mix with the water. The carbonated water collects in a basin of white sand topped with sand and gravel, which acts as a natural filter. Over several hundred million bottles of Perrier are sold each year.

• *Pierval*: Still spring water (*eau de source*), so not a mineral water. Pierval is low in mineral salts and sodium and has a pH very close to neutral, making it suitable for most people, in particular the very young. The source, the Pierval spring, is in the middle of the *parc* of the château of Pont-St-Pierre, in a small village near Rouen in Normandy.

• *St-Yorré*: Sparkling water with a strong taste of salt and bicarbonate. In the mid-19th century Monsieur Larbaud, a chemist and landowner, obtained authorization to develop the springs at St-Yorré, a small town in the Vichy basin. St-Yorré has subsequently expanded dramatically, particularly since the Second World War. Rich in potassium, calcium and sodium, this water produces a rapid revitalizing effect, making it particularly appropriate after exercise. It is also recommended to drink with meals, however for this I find its strong salty taste too intrusive. The waters of several springs with identical characteristics in the St-Yorré area are blended to produce the "Royale" blend.

• *Thonon*: A still water for all-day drinking, the source of Thonon is the Versoie spring at Thonon-les-Baines in the Haute-Savoie, near Lake Geneva. The thermal baths of Thonon are visited by many people seeking recuperation and of course, the cure involves taking the waters. Thonon, which has a very low mineral content, was authorized in 1963, making it one of the newer French mineral waters. It is almost sodium free and therefore recommended for families with young children and people on salt-free diets.

• *Vernière*: A lightly sparkling water with a slightly astringent taste due to its high level of magnesium salts. Vernière also contains bicarbonate of soda, sodium and calcium. It is naturally gassy, sourced in the heart of the Espinouse mountains in the Cevennes. Napoléon III granted Vernière mineral water status in 1861. An excellent digestif, and its good calcium level recommends it to growing children.

• *Vichy Celestins*: Still water with a slightly salty taste, high mineral content and naturally mildly carbonated. Its source is one of four springs bubbling out of Vichy, including Puits Carré, the hottest spring which emerges at 42.5°C and is used for baths. The Vichy resort was originally built by Julius Caesar and rebuilt several times, lastly by Napoléon III.

• *Vittel*: A still water with moderate mineral content, collected from springs discovered by the Romans. The spa specializes in kidney troubles and blood pressure.

• *Volvic*: Still water, low in minerals. The source is a valley in the Auvergne, filled over thousands of years with layers of volcanic rock, which filter the water. Volvic has a perfectly balanced pH (7.0), making it a popular water for skin care.

usually, a tangy flavor. Best summer or autumn.

•Galette de La Chaise-Dieu: A charming name - galette means flat cake and La Chaise-Dieu is the place of origin; thin, farmhouse disk of chèvre or mi-chèvre with a strongly nutty flavor; sometimes brick-shaped; blue or gray surface molds.

•Gaperon/gapron: The name is derived from a dialect word gap or gape meaning buttermilk and it is that, or cow's skimmed milk, that is used to produce this very low fat cheese. Pressed into a rounded cone shape and uncooked, it is flavored with garlic and black peppercorns. Light delicious flavor when fresh; used to be aged until a beard grew all over. Once part of a bride's dowry (see chapter introduction).

•Guéret: A small, low-fat (10%) cheese from the Creuse made from almost totally skimmed milk. May be aged in crocks up to 6 months and even through into winter. Possibly found in markets only. Known also as geusois or coupi.

•Laguiole: Pronounced laiole, this is a large AOC cheese related to the cantal but with an even herbier flavour, the cows grazing on pastures rich in thyme, fennel, gentian and broom in the Aubrac mountains. It is made only from raw full-fat milk; pressed but not cooked, made in mountain burons or creameries. Also known as Laguiole-Aubrac or fourme de Laguiole, it is best eaten after it has been cured at least 5 months.

•Murol: Produced in small factories in and around Murol; a milk-flavored cow's milk washed-rind disk.

•Pouligny-St-Pierre: This full-cream AOC goat's milk cheese gets its special savor from the wide-range of grasses and plants available to the short-haired goats in the pastures around Pouligny-St-Pierre. The cheese is at its best from April to October. Has a definite earthy taste; traditionally eaten only with dry white wines, usually a sauvignon from Touraine or Berry, or a white chenin.

•Rigotte de Pelussin: A small soft chèvre or mi-chèvre made in farms or small traditional dairies. A slightly nutty taste, best enjoyed between late spring and autumn.

•St-Nectaire: An outstanding AOC cheese of great antiquity - Louis XIV was fond of it. It's a pressed cow's milk cheese, made in farms and dairies in a large area of southwest Puy-de-Dôme and the north of Cantal. The crust is brine-washed during curing to encourage molds varying in color from white to red and violet. Best eaten in summer and autumn; often used in cooking, this semi-soft cheese should have a light mushroom smell and sweet but rounded flavor.

•Salers/Fourme de Salers: An AOC cheese that obtains its characteristic savor from the fragrant grasses, bushes and berries (including bilberries) that the cows feed upon in Cantal and its surroundings. Made from raw, full-cream cow's milk, it has an earthy flavor that strengthens with age. Matured for 3-12 months.

•Tomme de Brach: Related to fresh-drained roquefort cheeses, this tomme from the Corrèze is made from sheep's milk but has no internal veining. Best in spring and summer, it has a distinct sheep smell and strong taste; mainly farm-produced.

•Vachard: Made only in farms in the Dore mountains, this is a 20 cm/8 in disk of pressed uncooked cow's milk cheese.

Pastries, Desserts & Confectionery

Best known of the edible sweet delights of central France is the clafoutis, usually associated etymologically only with Limousin, but commonly made throughout the Auvergne too, particularly in Allier. Often called other names - millat, milla, mias millard and tuillard (Vichy) - but essentially a good old-fashioned baked batter pudding, classically containing fresh unpitted black cherries, but just as often you'll find grapes, plums or red currants. Today's freedom of culinary interpretation means one might come to you thicker, thinner or in some other way different from what you expect - if it includes black rum, so much the better. Clermont-Ferrand has had a sugar refinery of sorts since the 18th century and as this began processing only cane from the Caribbean, rum was bound to turn up. Cognac or kirsch are just as likely to be used.

Clermont has actually been famous for sweetness more than 400 years, preserving with honey local apricots and angelica (angélique) and making superior fruit pastes and jams, or confitures which are noticeably thinner and runnier than a British jam or American preserve. Many other centers do the same admirably, notably Riom. But for locals with aspirations, sugar was used to sweeten the same batter as a clafoutis, a ritzy alternative to the natural sweetness of fruit; this sweet, baked pancake is the flognarde or flaugnard, and really only worth ordering if it is to be doused in the region's fruity alcohols, or covered with fresh fruit and cream.

The cold nights of the central plateau are perfect for producing crisp apples and voluptuous pears. Everyone makes tarts and flans (with cherries or chestnuts too) and you may also find covered pies of apple paste or sucre de pommes, something the Americans make and call apple butter or apple cheese. In puff pastry, like turnovers, these are often called chaussons. Even better are cakes made with unusual local varieties of pear; gargouillau is the best known of these. Piquenchagne or picanchagne and le poirat are also pear pies or cakes, sometimes in combination with walnut.

With chestnuts and hazelnuts growing here and almonds from the south easily available, you'll find nougatines, marzipan, macaroons and the like. The barley grown here but used for maltings in northern breweries makes a famous barley sugar (sucre d'orge) in Vichy. The noisettes of Aubusson are little cakes flavored with hazelnuts. A reminder of the occasional harshness of the climate is seen in the use of the reliable buckwheat crop, here often called sarrasin rather than blé noir, and used in pancakes (galettes), called galetons in Haute Vienne and tourtons in Corrèze. Rye flour (farine de seigle) is used for bourioles, a yeasted pancake.

In a sublime confluence of indulgences, Royat makes what many feel are among the best chocolates in the world using the fruits and liqueurs of the surrounding countryside. Make sure you go there, and make sure you have plenty of money. Good barley sugar, glacé fruits and fruit pastes, too.

There is but one caveat for the sweet of tooth. The herbs grown here extensively for medical use flavor many innocent-looking pastilles. Some are distinctly unusual! Stick to names you recognize, or to other chocolates, like the palets d'or of Moulins, or move on to fouaces. These are also called pompe and, like the fougasse and pompe of Provence, are sweetened dough spiked with glacé fruits.

BETTER BATTER PUDDINGS

The *clafoutis* of Limousin is typical of many ancient puddings throughout Europe based on pouring a sweet batter onto fruit then baking the mixture. Ripe cherries feature in the best-known version, but any fruit can be used; the mixture may be enlivened by rum, cognac or other spirits and you can use your favorite pancake batter.

For a more spectacular effect, pour oil or butter into the baking dish and heat to piping hot. Add fruit, heat well in the oven, then pour batter over it and pop it immediately into a very hot oven. It will rise to the occasion like a Yorkshire pudding and can be taken directly to the table.

From the Bourbonnais in northwest Auvergne comes the related *gargouillau*, based on an unusual pear and blackcurrant combination and a rich batter mix with single cream.

Mix together a couple of eggs, 75g (⅓ c) sugar, 25g (scant ¼ c) flour and 300ml (1 c) cream into a liquid paste. Peel and chop half a dozen pears and mix into the paste with a few ounces of black currants. Pour into a buttered pie dish and bake until set (about half an hour). Serve warm, with more cream, of course. You might find it easier to manage in individual ramequins.

Bon Marché

Below is a selective list of markets plus some fairs (*foires*) of special interest. Check with the local Syndicat d'Initiative (SI) for precise locations and time changes.

HAUTE-VIENNE

Aixe-sur-Vienne *Sat, Sun;* Ambazac *Thur;* Bellac *Wed, Fri,* Châteauneuf-la-Forêt *Last Sat in month;* Châteauponsac *Sun;* Coussac Bonneval *3rd Thur in month;* Eymoutiers *Sun, 1st & 3rd Thur (except May, Sep & Oct);* Limoges *Daily;* Magnac-Laval *8th Jan, April, Dec, 22nd other months;* Nantiat *Fri;* Rochechouart *Tue, Thur, Sat;* St-Junien *Daily;* St-Léonard de Noblat *Sat;* St-Paul *Tue before Mardi Gras;* St-Yrieix-la-Perche *Sat.*

CREUSE

Aubusson *Sat;* Auzances *Tue;* Bonnat *Wed;* Bourganeuf *Wed;* Chenérailles *5th & 20th each month, 2nd Sun May & Oct (poultry);* Gouzon *Tue;* Le Grand Bourg *2nd & 17th of month;* Guéret *Sat;* Jouillat *Thur;* Moutier-Malcard *Sat;* Nouziers *Sat;* Peyrat-la-Nonière *Sat;* La Souterraine *Thur, Sat;* St-Etienne de Fursac *5th & 19th of month;* St-Marc-à-Loubaud *Sheep Fair 25 Aug;* St-Pierre Bellevue *Lamb Fair 4th Sept;* Vallière *Thur.*

CORRÈZE

Allassac *Daily;* Arnac Pompadour *Tue, Thur, Sat;* Beaulieu-sur-Dordogne *Sat;* Brive-la-Gaillard *Tue, Thur, Sat;* Chamboulive *Sat;* Donzenac *Thur, Sun;* Lubersac *Summer Fete (flower procession) Sun after Aug 15;* Marcillac-la-Croisille *14th & 26th each month;* Neuvic *Wed;* Objat

A DRINKER'S GUIDE

The Auvergne uses its many wild herbs to make liqueurs and apéritif drinks. *Verveine, gentiane,* and sloe (*prunelle*) are found beside more familiar flavors, such as raspberry (*framboise*) and strawberry (*fraise*). Le Puy's *Verveine de Velay,* green or yellow, is well known and there is a juniper-flavored *genièvre* and an unexpected *mandarine.* You may see lots of barley growing but once it is malted it is shipped off to the brewers of the north. Don't miss the underrated wines of St-Pourçain-sur-Soule from the Allier - for several years the producers have been trying to upgrade from VDQS to AOC but unfortunately without success. And in between meals you might like to try the beer of Clermont.

Daily (summer), Wed, Fri, Sun rest of year, Lamb Fair 4th Mon Jan; Treignac 6th & 22nd of each month; Ussel Wed, Sat; Uzerche 20th of each month.

ALLIER

Bourbon-Larchambault Wed; Cerilly Thur AM; Cosne d'Allier Tue (2nd Tue poultry); Coulanges Thur; Lurcy-Levis Mon, Poultry Fair 4th Mon Oct; Marillat-en-Combraille Thur (poultry); Mayet-de-Montagne Mon; Montluçon Tue, Wed, Thur, Fri, Sat; Moulins Fri; Néris-les-Banis Thur; Neuilly-le-Réal Thur; St-Pourçain-sur-Sioule Sat; Varennes-sur-Allier Mon; Vichy Wed.

PUY-DE DÔME

Aigueperse Tue; Ambert 1st & 3rd Thur of month; Les Ancizes Comps Wed; Ardes 2nd & 4th Mon; Arlanc 2nd & 4th Mon; La Bourboule Sat, daily in summer; Brassac-les-Mines Sun AM; Chatel-Guyon Fri; Clermont-Ferrand Mon; Combronde Every 2nd Mon; Cournon d'Auvergne Thur; Courpière Every 2nd Tue; Cunlhat Wed; Issoire Sat; Maringues Thur (farm produce); Menat Wed; Messeix Thur; Olliergues Sat; Picherande Cheese Market every fortnight from 10 Jan; Puy-Guillaume Wed; Randan Fri; Riom Sat; Sauxillanges Tues; St-Alyre-d'Arlanc 2nd & 4th Sun of month; St-Dier-d'Auvergne Thur; St-Donat Every other Sat (pigs, cheese); St-Genès Champespe Thur (cheese); St-Gervais d'Auvergne 2nd Mon of month; Thiers Sun; Vernet-la-Varenne 1st & 3rd Mon of month; Vic-le-Comte Thur.

CANTAL

Allanche Tue; Aurillac Wed, Sat, Fair days; Chaudes-Aigues Mon; Condat Tue; Lacapelle-Barrès 1st Mon of month; Laroquebrou 2nd Fri of month (and 4th Fri in summer); Marcenat Thur; Massiac Every 2nd Tue; Mauriac Tue, Fri;

Maurs Thur; Marat Fri; Neussargues-Moissac Fri every two weeks; Neuvéglise every 2nd month; Pierrefort Wed; Riom-lès-Montagnes Sat; St-Flour Mon every two weeks, Wool market last Sat June; Trizac Tue (summer), every 2nd Tue (rest of year).

HAUTE-LOIRE

Allègre Wed; Alleyras Mon, Wed; Bas-en-Basset Wed; Blesle Thur; Brioude Sat (Pig market 1st & 3rd Sat) of month; Champagnac-le-Vieux Fri; Costaros Mon; Craponne-sur-Arzon Sat; Fay-sur-Lignon Wed; Landos Tue; Langeac Tue; Lavoute-Chilhac Sun; Lempdes Tue; Loudes 1st & 3rd Tue of month; Mazet St-Voy Thur; Le Monastier-sur-Gazeille Tue; Monistrol-sur-Loire Mon; Paulhaguet Mon; Pradelles Sun; Le-Puy Wed, Fri; Retournac Wed; Sauges Mon (calves), Fri; Solignac-sur-Loire Tue; St-Didier-en-Velay Wed; St-Front Fri; St-Julien Chapteuil Mon; St-Just Malmont 1st & 3rd Thur of month; St Paulien 2nd & 4th Tue of month; Ste-Sigolène Tue; Vorey Sun; Yssingeaux Thur.

RHÔNE, SAVOIE & THE DAUPHINE

A CHRISTIAN IN THE LYONS DEN

"In which we...
- *Shop for our lessons and find gratification in gratins...*
- *Follow a liqueur to Spain and back and worship a new monarchy...*
- *Look for a faded reputation but revel in charcuterie...*
- *Enjoy undiluted pork liver, meet the unusual fish of Annecy and learn which frogs have fat legs...*
- *Trace the source of the essential crayfish...*
- *Go nuts in Grenoble, even though they do not, and visit the potato's first French home...*
- *Discuss an unfair cushion, sip a protected vermouth and buy the cherriest kirsch of all...*
- *Discover that mountain hare can be good for you...*
- *Pine for honey bonbons and find which cheese is the perkiest..."*

Many offer to teach you to cook in France, but few do it as well as American Aileen Martin and her French husband, Chef Jean Berrard, at Moule Martin, just above Annecy. Madame Berrard believes food must be relevant, used to enhance experience rather than to fuel you for it. Her classes often start by driving down to the markets of Annecy and handing each student a different shopping list. One must buy flowers and ground almonds, another is sent to find *lavaret* or *lotte du lac*, another for local peaches and a chicken from Bresse, another for oil from Nyons and olives from Nice, walnuts from Grenoble or cheese from Franche-Comté. It's a marvelous way to bring any place into focus, for once you are looking for something specific, you see everything else as well, instead of it all passing you by in an agreeable but incoherent haze.

This is also the best way to use the information in this book; decide on something that specially interests you - seasonal, basic or frivolous - before you wander in a market or village center and you'll see more than you imagined possible.

It is a strange grouping, these three *départements*, each highly distinctive and ranging from the highest heights to the most fertile valleys. If there is a link to be found other than that of geography, it must be the individuality each has retained, and that's why I so much like driving east towards the mountains once I've touched base in a few centers along the Rhône.

The Dauphiné makes no culinary bones about taking exactly what it wants from neighboring styles of food, particularly claiming as its own the gratins of Provence and the Languedoc; but in return it usually makes them more interesting. The most famous, and often shamefully abused, is *gratin dauphinoise*, a dish of sliced potatoes baked in a thin layer with rich milk; eggs and a little *gruyère* are sometimes added but not authentically, and onion has no place at all.

If the sheer simplicity of that surprises you, so will the tremendous variety of other gratins. Most are of vegetables, and late in the year there will be a gratin of cardoons (*cardons*) and of wild mushrooms, of tripe or of pumpkin (*potiron*) and, during summer, of soft fruits and of pears. Some of these will be topped with a little sauce, some with breadcrumbs, and there will be cream, eggs and perhaps almonds on the fruit versions but hardly ever a sight of that bane of good taste, a thick blanket of bubbling grated cheese thrown over the top.

On the border of Isère and the Rhône is Vienne, once the seat of a local lord, the Dauphin of the Viennois, the childless last of whom agreed to cede his lands to the then king of France, Charles V, if his title remained as that of the heir to the throne. It was centuries before Vienne had another hereditary monarchy, but after World War I, the family Point came and took over La Pyramide restaurant. First they, then their son Fernand, turned this into one of the most influential restaurants France has ever known, brilliantly executing or reinterpreting classics of the kitchen and creating new ones, inspiring the careers of dozens of

modern luminaries - and there is the rub. La Pyramide, the pride and joy of the Points, unwittingly also opened a Pandora's box, which led to the modern school of sensation, where everything goes with everything, particularly if it hasn't been done before - a school in fact that misses the Point.

The Dauphiné actually makes more wine than the Rhône Valley but is more famous for one of the world's best-known liqueurs, Chartreuse. It is a drink that encourages mental images of monks macerating herbs and flowers and barks in cellars, guarding ancient secret formulae and methods unchanged for centuries - but the monasteries of France have been remarkably less secure than in Protestant countries. They were stripped of their possessions during the Revolution but allowed to return in 1816, about which time many of the liqueur-making houses went into serious production of what had previously been medicinal brews. In 1903 many were expelled again, including all of the Carthusians who began making Chartreuse at Tarragona in Spain, thus explaining the version still made there. In 1940 all was forgiven again and, with new premises, Chartreuse of green and yellow has been making you feel better, or worse, ever since.

In a perverse settlement of the debt to other *départements* for borrowing their styles, the Dauphiné makes a great deal of walnut oil, but sends most of it away, for there they consider it much too strong a flavor, although upwardly mobile restaurants will have followed the fashion for it.

Immediately north and somewhat higher is Savoie. Long independent, then part of the Italian conglomeration, it became French only after a referendum in 1860. Gratins have crept this far north, but the difference in geography also means more dairying and more cheese; here the common *gratin savoyard* actually mixes potato with cheese and moistens both with stock, usually of veal or beef. In autumn wild mushrooms are layered between the cheesy potatoes, great for the potatoes, dreadful for the mushrooms, and marvelous without the cheese.

Among the cultivated and wild fruit and vegetables that flourish so wonderfully in the valleys of Savoie you find many wheat fields, the grains of which are usually used for making pastas. An older crop is red peppers which, cooked, peeled and served in oil, have been associated with the region for centuries, as has a special liking for nutmeg as a seasoning, particularly suited to the milk, cream and butter made and used so lavishly. But for me the greatest seasoning found here is not imported from some far-off hot country but dug from its own damp earth - the white truffle.

The white truffle season is shorter and earlier than that of the black one - from October to the first snows of December - but it repays by many times any trouble or expense you may incur. For a start, even a rank amateur can know in a second if it is a real *tuber magnatum* or one of the lesser white truffles. Real ones have a scent that knocks you out, reeking sweetly of vice and irresistibly savory for its insinuating promise of new sensation.

There is excitement to be garnered even if you are not interested in that sort of thing, for you never risk wasting money on a white truffle that has had its flavor cooked out of it - it is always eaten raw. And best of all, although it is arrestingly expensive, it is sliced so tissue-thin over dishes, and in such small quantity, that your pocket would be silly to complain. No better cushion for shavings of white truffle has been found than egg dishes or a real, runny risotto. The south of the Rhône merges so easily into Provence that there is confusion about what belongs to which, for both olive and almond grow there, and glacé fruits and *marrons glacés* are prepared on either side of the border. Of course these are modern borders, but this goes only a

short way to explaining the old arguments over which town from which province invented, say, *cailettes*.

My interest though lies in the north, in Lyon, which is translated into English by adding a letter to make it Lyons. For me, this is the center of a more modern argument, that of deciding if it really deserves its reputation as one of the great culinary centers of France, indeed of the world.

The Rhône and the Saône, which converge here, and its central geographical location, certainly have given Lyon access to the best of the produce of surrounding regions. It once was capital of the Burgundians and has such historical links with Beaujolais that its wines are said to be the third river of Lyon. But access to good produce is no guarantee of universal excellence, as many a Briton will testify. I think the trap fallen into has been to judge all of Lyon by the few, a lesser example of the world judging French food by the standard and style of haute cuisine.

Certainly there are now some sensational places to eat in Lyon and its environs, glittering with names internationally famous, and Lyon has served some famous banquets in its time. And there does seem to have been a Golden Age, the age of the *mères*, which began in the second half of the 19th century. Coinciding with more interest in leisure time and competition for its trade, a number of wine traders and bars started to offer a continuous choice of snacks and simple bourgeois food in the same way the brasseries of the north had always done. It naturally fell to the wives, the mères to do the cooking, which gradually took over in importance from the wine. These small places are, or were, the *bouchots* of which so much has been written.

But the mères who did so well are now dead, and the bouchots have been translated into hamburger and fast food joints, no more startling an advance than the bouchots first were. Lyon is resting on a reputation for accessible, honest food that only existed for some 50 years or so. Before then she had little praise from travelers, and since then somewhat less if you read reviews of unstarred restaurants.

If you go to Lyon confident of its expertise and excitement you may be denied pleasure. It is a big city, with all the modern big-city hunger for change and novelty. Once you have eaten in one of the famous or recommended restaurants you are on your own. Personally I have eaten badly more often, and more reliably so, in Lyon than anywhere else in France, and had service so grossly rude on the Place Bellecour

that I endured the wait of one hour for my order to be taken in a half-empty restaurant simply for the thrill of a good story. Be suspicious, do your homework and appear knowledgeable and confident.

One of the most French things you can do is to go to Lyon for lunch from Paris on the wonderful TGV trains, and at least you will arrive. If you drive into Lyon you may not eat at all, for the traffic system is such that I once drove around the center for an hour without discovering the way in. Perhaps it was one more warning that Christians should have nothing to do with Lyons . . .

Charcuterie

Lyon is the center of a gigantic commercial charcuterie-making operation, with a range of products exported nationally and internationally. Modern techniques, refrigeration and humidity control mean any product of the pig, whether native to valley or mountain-top, can be made. Thus in Lyon, and in most contiguous places, the charcuterie enthusiast will have a choice unmatched elsewhere. You

WORTH FINDING

• *Andouilles/andouillettes*: These are not unexpected - but the comments of long-reigning mayor Edouard Heriot are. He's supposed to have said that only two things leave a bad taste in the mouth, politics and *andouillettes*. In Lyon they are often made with veal intestines rather than pork.

• *Caillettes*: Liver-based baked dish with spinach or chard. It's common in Provence but also found in the Dauphiné, Drôme and Ardèche. Indeed, Aubenas claims to have invented it. The only way I know to enjoy pork liver relatively undiluted.

• *Cervelas*: The same fine-fleshed, fat sausage found elsewhere in France, once made with brains. Today, very likely to be studded with truffles and pistachios; certainly so in Grenoble. Unlike the German *cervelat*, which is a slicing

sausage, this is to be served hot. If you are buying them to cook yourself, older ones will be better value, for what truffle content there is will have had time to perfume the pork somewhat.

• *Farçon*: A large cervelas made in Montélimar.

• *Jésus de Lyon*: an air-dried salami, one of many of this name. Fat and tapering and tied with strings. The coarsely chopped flesh and fat indicate a sweet flavor.

• *Rose/Rosette de Lyon*: One of the biggest of air-dried salami-type sausages, made of pure pork, chopped and stuffed into the final length of a pig's large intestine. Some say it is so called because this length is always a rosy pink color, others more vociferous declare it simply describes the appear-ance of the puckered and tied

sphincter (if it is left attached).

• *Saucisses de Lyon*: There are two sausages of this name, and confusion is not uncommon. One is a long air-dried sausage, the other a boiling (fresh) sausage. This latter is more common and used for the region's famous sausage dishes - with hot potato salad, in brioche, etc. It is little different from, and may be called, garlic sausage (*saucisse à l'ail*).

• *Roulade de tête de porc*: Salted pig's head cooked whole, boned and rolled. If it is *pistachée*, it may be studded with pistachio nuts, or with whole cloves of cooked garlic, which would indicate some influence of the Languedoc.

• *Sabodet*: A boiling sausage for eating hot, made from pig's head and rind and shaped like a *sabot* (clog).

Fish & Shellfish

will also see both in-town and country signs exhorting business, sincere signs earnestly protesting that a local shop's jambonneau, saucissons and cervelas are veritably of their own manufacture. If the claim seems possible, look also for the genuine things from nearby regions, judru from the Jura, Jésus de Morteau smoked over pine and juniper, hams from Burgundy's Morvan, or, more unusual, smoked hams from Celliers or Taninges in Savoie. The herb- and pepper-wrapped air-dried sausages associated with Provence are made here too, and will be none the worse for that. Some villages make whole boned hams with a dried herb coating - delicious and now being commercialized in Feillens (Bresse). The herb-flavored sausages of Annecy are called pormoniers.

Commercialism, mainly of the best kind, is such that in Lyon I tend to forget any quest for local foods. As in Paris, I take advantage of tasting and learning about whatever looks good or sounds familiar and profit from the rare chance to compare, surely the greatest reward of traveling.

Freshwater fish - and what is done with it - is fairly predictable in the Lyonnais and the Rhône Valley.

Carp, perch, tench, etc. are served in many a guise, but down the Rhône Valley you might find rather more of the friture, an incursion from the south or west but done in butter rather than olive oil. Pauchouse - a fish stew - invades the north from Burgundy, then reverts to the more usual name of matelote.

In Lyon, fish are kept alive and healthy in great freshwater tanks through which the Rhône and Saône flow ceaselessly. You will undoubtedly be offered quenelles de brochet, which translate somewhat boringly as pike dumplings, or poached fish cakes. They are a purée of pike, eggs and something farinaceous, and should be light, sweet and delicate. Too often the farinacea dominate, through heavy hand or light mind. When they are good, quenelles count mainly for praise upon the technique that has made them light; when they are bad they are even more boring. If it is the flavor of pike you are after, I suggest pike roasted, or with some cream-based sauce. Of course, it might be that quenelle lovers are more enamored of the sauce Nantua which regally accompanies them.

Sauce Nantua is based on the essence of écrevisses, the freshwater crayfish that abound in the rivers of Savoie and the Dauphiné quite as much as they do in Franche-Comté. Écrevisses come gratinéed; stock made from their shells is used to flavor mousses of chicken livers in the Bugey; beurre d'écrevisses accompanies poultry from Bresse; and enriches sauce Nantua. Various manufacturers in the puddles of industry that surround Lyon pack quenelles and sauce Nantua into cans, sometimes under the banner of one of the region's master chefs. These are quite good enough to serve at home.

Deep in the lakes of Léman and Annecy, there are types of salmon rarely found elsewhere. The finest fleshed is the omble chevalier (char), not unfamiliar to determined fish enthusiasts (I have eaten one in Sweden). More unusual are the white-fleshed lavaret, the fera, and, in December only, the gravenche; any of these may be stuffed or, if your visit coincides with the seasons, served in sauces of cream perfumed with morilles or cèpes. The lotte des lacs is a burbot, but tastes rather different from those of the river; as well as firm white flesh, which is often filleted and fried like perch, it has a specially succulent liver served as a separate specialty. On the shores of Lake Léman, where trout weighing 15kg/34lb have been landed, there is a soupe aux poissons.

In the parts of the Bresse that fall into this region, frogs are excellent and are gratinéed or poached in cream and wine; and eels, although becoming less common, should be offered in stews or in pâtés. Incidentally, if your frog's legs seem par-ticularly plump and rounded, they are most probably imported.

Meat, Poultry & Game

The chickens and turkeys of Bresse belong as much to this region as to Burgundy geographically. Anyway, Lyon has always exploited its crossroads position and called many things from neighboring regions its own; charollais beef is one, which is grilled as often as it is cooked in wine; along the banks of the Rhône and in the Dauphiné, local beef is cooked slowly in a daube.

Pork rules as a fresh meat. Like beef, it's usually found served fairly plainly cooked, and onions and potatoes are usually on the plate too. This can be assured with cochonnailles - the boiled head, trotters and odd other pieces of pig served with onion sauce and the ubiquitous hot potato salad. In Savoie you might be offered pork cutlets with cooked pears, which is a far better idea.

Savoie is also where you're more likely to meet local lamb, its sweetbreads, brains or liver. Veal, a speciality of the Dauphiné is sometimes served with ham and cheese, or with vegetables and fresh chestnuts - à l'aixoise - but always delicious with cream and wild mushrooms. These are the best ways to enjoy local poultry too. In the Dauphiné look for the turkeys of Cremieu. Lyon and its mères are jointly credited with a number of chicken dishes of world renown. The one always mentioned is en demi-deuil (half mourning), with slices of truffle stuck under half its skin; frankly you can't expect to find it easily, it will be very expensive, and unless fresh truffles are used and have been allowed to sit under the skin for 24 hours, the exercise is one of inconspicuous consumption. When you are in the region, look to chicken with cream, with vinegar (au vinaigre) or anything with mushrooms, cultivated or wild. Sometimes it will be as well to go for a simple roast of poulet de Bresse, a casserole or some version of coq au vin. At least you will be spending your money on the quality of the chicken rather than risking it on a soi-disant truffle.

What game there is comes from Burgundy or the Alps, where it is mainly feathered - partridge, quail, pheasant, woodcock (perdreau, caille, faisan, bécasse). Even if killed on the wing they may well have been bred on farms, and so the likelihood of their flesh having been affected by a few weeks' freedom and a wild diet of mountain herbs and berries is largely fanciful. Much of the game-bird crop goes into making pâtés, which suffer from the French habit of not hanging game for enough time to allow any development of the flavor, and of expecting the roasted flesh of a bird to retain any of its native savor when layered and baked in a rich farce of pork and veal. If you like pâté, I suggest you slice into the rougher, more robust pâtés campagnards.

Wild rabbit (lapin or lapereaux de la garenne) is recommended if it is from Monteynard, but the hare (lièvre) is what excites those with a yen for really fulsome flavor. Some would say that civet de lièvre, hare cooked in wine and finished with cream and its own blood, was born in the mountains of Savoie.

Fruits & Vegetables

The sweet natural rewards for those who wander from summer's beaten tracks and into Savoie are myriad. For hence come some of France's best strawberries and most of her raspberries. Pears are fabulous, and the apples aren't bad. Cherries and plums are harvested and if you literally leave even these untouristy roads there are wild berries - cherries (merises) and strawberries (fraises des bois) to gather yourself. Closer to the beaten track, Vienne has long been renowned for its cherries.

The Dauphiné matches this abundance with its walnuts (noix de Grenoble), honored with an AOC and savored throughout the world. They are candied, made into cakes, put into brioche mixtures called fanciful things by every village pâtissier. Nuts that don't make the grade are pressed to make walnut oil (huile de noix), but this is little used by the Dauphinoises, who consider it indigestible. Silly them. Just over the département's border, Briançon (Hautes-Alpes) makes an even rarer culinary almond oil. In the south both the Ardèche and Drôme produce excellent chestnuts, and make marrons glacés and sugar-preserved fruits of all kinds, an artisanale tradition that became commercialized when the silk industry was crippled in the 1880s.

The Ardèche can claim, but doesn't do it loudly, to be the first place in France to grow the potato. In 1540 a Franciscan monk from Toledo planted some in St-Alban-d'Aÿ. In 1585 the truffole (one of many names celebrating it as a truffle for everyday use) was already a commercial

LOCAL PRODUCE

VEGETABLES
- GARLIC ail
  Var: White: Thermidrôme, Messidrôme, Blanc de Lomagne. Pink: Rosé d'Italie, Rosé dur Var, Fructidor. Violet: Rosé de Lautrec, Germidor
  Harvested June and July but younger and earlier often too.
  Dep: Rhône

- ZUCCHINI courgettes
  Var: Seneca (under glass spring and autumn), Diamant (open air, main season)
  Mid-April to end November
  Dep: Drôme, Rhône, Ain

FRUITS
- APPLE pomme
  Var: Reinettes, Reine des reinettes
  Harvested July to September
  Dep: Drôme, Ardèche, Rhône, Isère, Savoie

- APRICOT abricot
  Var: Bergeron, Polonais (Orange de Provence)
  Mid-June until August 18th
  Dep: Drôme, Ardèche, Rhône

- CHERRIES cerises
  Var: Bigarreau, Moreau, Reverchon
  June until mid-July
  Dep: Drôme, Ardèche, Rhône

- CHESTNUTS marrons/châtaigne
  (marrons have only one kernel in each shell)
  September until end November
  Dep: Ardèche

- BLACK CURRANTS cassis
  RED CURRANTS groseilles
  July 8th to 20th

- GRAPES raisins
  Var: among many, Chasselas and Muscat
  September and October
  Dep: Drôme, Ardèche

- GREENGAGE reine-claude
  Early August for 6 weeks

- KIWIFRUIT kiwi
  Var: Hayward
  November through to March
  Dep: SE corner of Drôme

- MELON melon
  July until mid-September

- NECTARINE nectarine/brugnon
  Var: White: fuzalode
  Yellow: mainly American strains
  June-ish until start September
  Dep: Rhône, Ardèche, Isère

- PEACH pêche
  Var: mainly yellow American strains, white Amsden
  Early July to October
  Dep: Rhône, Drôme, Ardèche, Isère

- PEAR poire
  Var: Guyot, Williams, Louise-Bonne d'Avranches
  Early July to end October
  Dep: Rhône, Drôme, Ardèche, Isère

- RASPBERRIES framboise
  June to end October
  Dep: Rhône, Ardèche, Haute-Savoie, Drôme, Isère, in that order. The most important area; most varieties grown are British and most of the crop is used for syrup, confitures and so on.

- WALNUTS noix
  September to November
  Dep: Isère, Drôme

crop, and by the early years of the 17th century, the Dauphiné and the Auvergne had adopted it.

Drôme and the Dauphiné both sport the white oaks associated with the presence of black truffles, but Savoie is the place for the lesser-known but infinitely more aromatic white truffle. If you buy a whole one fresh, store it air-tight and cushioned with rice grains to protect it all round. Back home, keep it in a covered bowl with eggs for a couple of days, then make scrambled eggs with unsalted butter and cream.

Wild mushrooms are specially good in the mountains, too, both the morilles and delicate mousserons of spring and the hunkier cèpes of autumn. Enjoy them simply - in omelettes, with artichokes or in cream by themselves or with the exceptional poultry or fish. Local stories of poaching across borders, of the skullduggery of this or that mushroom collector, make excellent digestifs.

In general, the range of vegetables used is a bit more adventurous than many areas. The cardoon (cardon) is a feature of late summer, served with bone marrow (moelle). Squash (courge) is made into soups with cream or served au gratin.

The great plains that lie among the mountains and gorges of eastern France grow a great variety of cereals, and much of the wheat is used to make pasta (pâtes alimentaires).

It is not fair to think of Lyon and its region as living permanently on a cushion of frying onions (the white ones from Roanne are said to be best). The Île-Barbe has supplied wonderful salads for countless centuries. Ampuis would easily satiate you with

her apricots alone. Nonetheless, few would disagree that to eat a galette lyonnaise, a fritter of potato and onion, is about as accurate a picture of the foundations of the region's food as you could hope to get.

GLACÉ FRUITS AND MARRONS GLACÉS

Ardèche (Rhône) and Vaucluse (Provence), are the most important French centers for preserving fruit and chestnuts in sugar syrup. Privas and Aubenas are particularly famous for their marrons glacés, which used to be very much artisanale with many small, private manufacturers, but after the silk industry's crisis in the 1880s, Privas in particular began larger scale manufacture in central factories.

Glacé chestnuts can be made only from marrons, the chestnuts that have a single kernel in the shell; those with more kernels are châtaignes and these are broken up for use in confectionery and canned purées of chestnut, plain or vanilla flavor. Marrons glacés are especially expensive because of the twin difficulty of peeling the skin and the extreme delicacy of the nut once it has been lightly cooked, a process they do not need. Look for marrons brisés, the broken ones, at a cheaper rate. Good for putting into desserts.

Fruits for this sort of

processing are usually picked before they are fully ripe (one reason they often have so little flavor), then waxed and stored in brine until needed. After washing, stalking or pitting, they are soaked in increasingly stronger sugar solutions, vanilla-flavored in the case of the poached chestnuts. Once saturated, fruit is given an outer coating of sugar which is quickly baked on to form a shiny, preservative coating.

Apt (Vaucluse) is an important center for crystallizing fruits and from Collobrières (Var) come marrons glacés, but many small family confectioners (confiseurs) will make their own. The most famous, and hardly small, is Aubers in Nice which has an extraordinary range. But think before you splurge; many glacé fruits are dreadfully disappointing, retaining little recognizable flavor. Tiny poires Williams, abricots (apricots) and mandarines (mandarins) are best, I reckon, and the preserved figs (figues) of Grasse are worth the investment - for real ostentation you can even buy whole melons or pineapples complete with their leaves. Watermelon (pastèque) is an example of a fruit that offers more than it delivers - you are better off looking for jams (confitures) and other sweet spreads of individuality, such as that of eggplant.

Cheese

There is a marvelous assortment of cheeses available in this area, many of them domestically produced. In the mountains of Savoie there are countless varieties of gray tomme and many chèvres and mi-chèvres to be found. And this region is the home of the so-called prince of gruyères - Beaufort.

•Abondance/Tomme d'Abondance: Made from partly skimmed milk up in the mountain chalets of the Abondance valley and the surrounding valleys of the Drasnes. Weighing from 5-15kg/11-33lb. With the usual grayish rind of these tommes, it has a creamy taste that varies from subtle to rich. They are best eaten in summer and autumn.

•Arômes au Gêne de Marc: Rigottes, St-Marcellins, pélardons or picodons cured in fermenting marc. The bigger ones are even more strongly flavored.

•Arômes de Lyon: Like arômes au gêne de marc but cured in crocks of white wine.

•Beaufort: Called the prince of gruyères by Brillat-Savarin, this AOC member of the gruyère family is produced in the high Alpine regions of Savoie in small dairies and alpine chalets. Made from raw cow's milk, notably from the tarines breed, these large disks can weigh anything from 20-70kg/50-157lb. Usually matured for 6 months, it is best eaten at any time except autumn. The surface should be smooth and brown with reddish tints. Fruity to the nose, the flavor has the nuttiness associated with this type of cheese.

•Beaumont: Related to all the Saint-Paulin cheeses, this commercially made cow's milk cheese is disk-shaped with a light-yellow rind, possesses a mild creamy flavor and is best eaten in summer and autumn.

•Bleu de Ste-Foy: A lightly pressed blue cheese mostly made in the farms and mountain chalets in and around Ste-Foy. It is flat and cylindrical in shape, weighs 2-3kg/4 1/2-6 1/2lb and has a savory flavor.

•Bleu de Sassenage: Mentioned more than 300 years ago by Olivier de Serres, this cow's milk bleu is still made in traditional dairies in Le-Villard-de-Lans (the Dauphiné) and the neighboring plateaux of Vercors. Weighing 5-6kg/11-13lb it is matured for 2 or 3 months. Best eaten in summer and autumn. Light colored with little smell and a savory taste.

•Bleu de Tignes: Best in summer and autumn, a lightly pressed blue of cow's milk made in a flat cylinder and tasting, well, like a blue cheese. Also known as tignard.

•Bressan: A domestically produced chèvre or mi-chèvre, a small truncated cone in shape. Soft with a light goat smell and flavor ranging between savory and extremely fruity. Good summer and autumn.

•Cervelle de Canut: A mixture of beaten fresh curds, garlic, herbs, vinegar, wine and oil, aged a little then served as an hors d'oeuvre or dessert; also called claqueret Lyonnais.

•Chambarand: Made the traditional way by monks (it is also known as trappiste de Chambarand) this is a small washed-rind disk made with cow's milk. Mild, creamy flavor.

•Chevrotin d'Aravis: A mild-flavored chèvre or mi-chèvre made in chalets in the massif of Aravis. Matured for 2 months and best eaten in summer and autumn.

•Chèvrine de Lenta: Only available in Bonneval (Savoie), this chalet-produced pressed cheese with a sharp flavor is made from the milk of goats grazing on summer pastures over 2,000m/6,000ft around Bonneval-sur-Arc or Lenta. Best eaten in summer.

•Claqueret Lyonnaise: See Cervelle de Canut.

•Colombière: A washed-rind cow's milk cheese related to reblochon, colombière is produced exclusively by farms in the massif of the same name. A 600g/1 1/2lb disk with pink-white rind, it has a mild flavor.

•Fondu au Marc: Also known as fondu au raisin, a factory-produced cheese with a rind of toasted grape seeds.

•Grataron d'Arèches: A 200g/8oz chèvre made in the mountain chalets of the Doron valley in Beaufort. It has a strong tangy flavor. Hauteluce is similar.

•Persillé d'Aravis: Very unusual for a chèvre in that it is a pressed blue cheese. Made in farms and chalets of the massif of Aravis (Savoie) with a savory flavor best enjoyed in summer and autumn. Known also as grand-bornand and persillé de Thones. Weighs about 2lb/1kg.

•Persillé du Mont-Cenis: Summer pasturing, which gives the highest-quality milk from cows and goats, makes the best of these large blue-veined cheeses. Matured for 3 months. Very strong flavor.

•Picadon de l'Ardèche/Picadon de la Drôme: Its name is a provençal word meaning to prick or sting. This AOC goat cheese from the mountains of the Ardèche and Drôme (but also the Dauphiné) has a history that stretches back for centuries. In this region, goat's milk was the only type available but because goats do not give milk during winter, this full-cream cheese was also matured for use as a staple food. Shaped to a small flat disk, the cheese has a white mold or a reddish washed-rind appearance. If it is labeled affiné méthode Dieulefit, it means that it has been matured at least a month to give a more pronounced flavor. Really at their best from late summer to autumn.

•Reblochon: A fascinating AOC cheese from Haute-Savoie known since at least the 14th century. Dairy farmers would not milk the cows dry when the steward came to check the yield, but once he had gone, the high-fat second milking was used to make this special cheese which was the perk or rebloche of the job. Made from full-cream raw milk, the cheese is gently pressed but not cooked, and has a washed rind and pinkish-white skin. It generally weighs just over 500g/1lb and is always sold in a wooden box. At its best in summer and autumn, it should have a slightly dank smell but a creamy delicate flavor that leaves a pleasant hazelnut aftertaste.

•St-Marcellin: Once produced on farms from pure goat's milk, this small (75mm/3in) disk of soft mild cheese is now made commercially only from cow's milk; a few goat farms still produce the original chèvre (known also as Tomme de St-Marcellin). Although it has a 50% fat content, a clear bite of acidity balances this. The

rind is thin and blue-gray in appearance.

•Tamié: A rather "farmy" washed-rind cow's milk cheese made by monks in Tamié (Savoie).

•Tarare: A high-fat (75%) triple-cream cow's milk cheese from the Lyonnais.

•Tommes des Allues: Domestically produced on the pastures of Miribel (Savoie); a pressed goat's milk cheese, fairly large, 3-4kg/7-9lb, really eaten only in autumn after the 2-month curing period of milk from summer's pastures.

•Tomme de Savoie: Produced by farms, fruitières and factories, this is the best-known tomme. A low-fat (20-40%) cow's milk cheese with gray rind and mild nutty taste. Usually weighing between 2-3kg/4-7lb, it can be enjoyed from the end of spring through to autumn. Variations are enormous, from use of skim or low-fat milk to simple changes of name –

tomme de Belleville, boudane, etc. Often marinated in marc.

•Vacherin d'Abondance: Related to the Swiss vacherins of the Joux Valley, this soft, mild-flavored cheese with washed rind is shaped like a thick pancake; usually best in late autumn and winter, from the controlled richness of stall-fed cattle's milk.

•Vacherin des Aillons: A soft cow's milk cheese similar to vacherin des Bauges.

•Vacherin des Bauges: An ancient cheese dating back to the Middle Ages before fruitières and cooperatives existed, when mountain dwellers made only small cheeses and did not yet know how to prepare cooked ones. Farm produced, it is a thick pancake of washed-rind cheese made from cow's milk. Best eaten at the end of autumn and in winter, it is packaged with a strip of bark. It savors of resin and has a creamy taste.

LIQUEURS

Chambéry makes the only vermouth in France to have an appellation. It is wonderfully dry and herby. Dolin is the best-known shipper in Britain and the U.S., but there are others. It also makes the less well known Chambéryzette, a vermouth flavored with wild strawberries (fraises des bois), which is said not to last very long in the bottle. Génépy, made throughout the area, is not unrelated to vermouth, being a maceration of mountain herbs in alcohol; you should also find cherry liqueur – liqueur de cerises or de merises if the cherries are wild. These

fruits may also be found as cerise sauvage, and the kirsch made from them in Allevard is probably the best you'll ever taste. Le Grand-Lemps makes a liqueur of originality but far less so than Voiron, where you find the modern distillery and caves of Grande-Chartreuse; or you can see the old ones at Fourvoirie. You can visit every day except Sundays and holy days.

Less exciting perhaps, but more generally useful, might be the knowledge that Savoie also makes rather good hard cider from its apples.

Pastries, Desserts & Confectionery

The abundance of fruit and nuts means you can expect even more of the tartes so associated with France. In high summer the pâtisseries who make their own ice creams and sorbets really go to town. Many of them will also make small quantities of confitures too - runnier than our jams but very true to flavor.

As the almonds of Drôme and the south are so near, macaroons and marzipan-based cakes and confectionery predominate; the pain de Châtillon alone is different, for this is a macaroon brightened with saffron.

Chocolate is as good in the scintillating air of Savoie and the Dauphiné as in the sparkle of Lyon's boutiques. Chambéry makes particularly marvelous liqueur-flavored chocolate truffles. Chartreuse flavors bonbons; so do local raspberries, and aromatic honeys. Mégève honey was famed well before her winter slopes became popular, and most Dauphiné varieties are very fine. The dark honey of pine (sapin) is the most aromatic, the wild flower ones vary from strong to delicate. Chamonix makes terrific bonbons from its honey.

NORTHERN EXILE

The Gamay grape was effectively exiled from Burgundy in 1366, but found a new, welcoming home in the granite hills south of Macon where it has flourished. Other areas of France, such as the Loire and the Aude, grow Gamay as well, but the wine they make from it is lackluster compared to Beaujolais. If you have only ever experienced poor Beaujolais Nouveau and judged it to be a pile of over-marketed twaddle, read on and let me convince you to try again.

Some years ago, Beaujolais was taken in barrels from the farms on the hills north of Lyon to the city's bars and restaurants where it was enjoyed for its young, vigorous, fresh and fruity flavor - a touch of summer to take the edge off the autumn chill. So good was it, that soon the Parisians wanted Beaujolais Nouveau as well, so the barrels were taken to the capital. In order to avoid any compromise, the wine was regulated by law but because of the demand, it had to be bottled.

Beaujolais can drink well at this young age because of the special way in which it is made: instead of being destalked, lightly pressed and placed in a barrel for the juice to take the color from the skins on which it is rested,

MONTELIMAR NOUGAT

Montélimar's *nougat* is considered some of the finest in the world. Fortunately, it is not as sickly as the 200-year-old story of its origination. A young kitchen boy is said to have been in love with the daughter of Lord Adhémar. One evening as he was dreaming of her, full of despair, he put some fine provençal honey in a bowl and believed, for a moment, that he could see the gold of her hair. Then he put some almonds in the bowl, for they were the color of her eyes. He thought, when seeing the *pralines* he scattered in the mixture, that they were like her crimson lips. He placed the bowl on a stove and, as this fragrant blend was cooking, he saw the eyes, mouth and golden hair of the girl he adored. He then decided to whip some egg whites, which reminded him of her delicate skin, and fold them into the mixture. Montélimar nougat was born.

In order to qualify as Montélimar nougat, the almond mixture may only be aerated with hen's eggs and/or hen's egg whites, the sweetening agents used must contain at least 25 percent pure honey and sweet peeled and grilled almonds and pistachios must represent at least 30 percent of the weight of the finished product.

Provence nougat is different. It is not aerated and should be blond in color. Sweet almonds and/or pistachios and/or hazelnuts must represent at least 30 percent of the finished product and additional flavoring may come in the form of aniseed or coriander. Again, the sweetening agents must contain at least 25 percent pure honey, and the syrup in which this is included will be cooked until highly caramelized.

RICH, DARK & HANDSOME

Driving over the vine-clad hills and down into the town of Tain l'Hermitage, one can immediately sense why the wines of the area are said to taste of chocolate. In the 42°C heat we experienced in particular, the whole region breathes it, for in the center of Tain l'Hermitage is the pretty factory of Valrhona, one of the world's finest quality chocolate makers.

French chocolate differs from the Swiss in that it tends to be dark rather than milk. Valrhona specializes in *grand cru couvertures*, single-bean varietals with a particularly high cocoa-solids content. All the cocoa beans are roasted by origin as well as type, because one variety of cocoa bean, such as the trinitario grown in South America, will taste very different from the same variety grown in the Caribbean. And these will be quite different again from the criollos grown near the Indian Ocean, or the forasteros from Brazil or the Ivory Coast.

Sugar and minor ingredients such as natural vanilla seeds and lecithin are added to the beans after roasting, then the lot is ground. A fine chocolatier will grind to a level around 13 microns; the tongue can detect the particles of anything above 20 microns so you know that chocolate with a powdery, grainy texture has not been finely ground.

Conching is another process that contributes to a fine chocolate's smooth, velvety texture. Still not fully understood even by manufacturers, conching is a mysterious but very important method that affects chocolate not unlike the maturing of cheese or wine; it gives chocolate its character, balance and final texture. A hollow drum, something like a cement mixer, swirls the ingredients; the friction thus generated causes the chocolate to mix and transform. Most good-quality chocolates are conched for six to 12 hours; Valrhona's is conched for more than 100.

When the conching is finished, the chocolate is in liquid form, ready to be tempered. This process ensures that the chocolate crystallizes properly, and produces fine chocolate's snap and shine. It is warmed to 55-60°C, at which point it is completely melted, and then cooled to 29°C, when the chocolate begins to build its crystalline structure. If chocolate were not tempered, it would stick to the mold and appear dull, gray and moldy.

You can recognize fine chocolate by its appearance. The cocoa solids content, listed on the packet, is a clue, but it is a misconception that the greater the cocoa bean content the better the quality of the chocolate per se. This is far too simple a formula. Cocoa bean content is very important, but once manufacturers begin to flirt with high numbers (60 percent and above) the cocoa bean is actually more inclined to exhibit its flaws. It's like saying that if you brew a cup of coffee you'll have a better flavor if you put ten spoonfuls in the pot instead of two. So when you open a packet of good chocolate, the aroma should waft out enticingly. Look also for shine and test that the chocolate snaps when you break it.

Visit Valrhona's factory shop in the center of Tain l'Hermitage and you can taste the company's *bonbons*, which unlike their chocolate bars, are not widely available outside France as they are made with fresh cream. These are interesting because in Tain L'Hermitage they find it a tad sacrilegious to add flavorings to fine chocolate – among the dark chocolate bars you will find only one milk variety and one flavored with hazelnuts, certainly none filled with strawberry cream and the like. At this high standard, they don't need it.

Beaujolais' grapes go stalks-and-all into huge vats in which they just sit. The grapes at the bottom crack to give the wine color, but the rest remain intact, allowing the fermentation to take place within the grape itself. This first fermentation of Nouveau lasts around five or six days, while for a cru Beaujolais, it will be ten days or more. That is why the wine completes its secondary fermentation early enough to be drunk in November.

Unfortunately, by the late 1970s, worldwide demand for Beaujolais Nouveau had doubled, more land was planted to fulfil the orders coming in, even from supermarket chains. The expanded vineyards took in the Bas Beaujolais, which runs from Villefranche to the Tourdine River by Lyon. Here, the soil is chalk, not granite, acceptable for the production of ordinary Beaujolais or the Nouveau. This left the northern area of Beaujolais free to concentrate on the great cru or village wines - everyone was relatively happy until they hit a poor summer, as they did in 1980, then 1984 and 1993. In 1993, for example, thunderstorms and hailstones fell in the southern area, it rained during the harvest, filling the grapes with excess water, and there was no sun. The yields were down, quality was poor.

In the north, however, the vineyards are protected by the granite hills, the weather patterns are completely different and therefore so is the wine. As much of the Beaujolais Nouveau harvest comes from the south, the secret is to purchase Beaujolais Villages Nouveau from the north. The ordinary Beaujolais will fade rather quickly but a good Beaujolais Villages will drink well from November to Christmas - don't touch it again until Easter, when it will awaken from its winter slumbers to herald the spring.

WORTH FINDING

- *Bugnes.* Specially big doughnuts or *beignets* seen mainly on festivals and holidays.
- *Gâteau Savoie.* Associated specially with St-Genix-sur-Guiers, a large brioche-type cake incorporating *praliné*, as far as I can determine.
- *Matefaims.* Spelled many ways, but meaning "appetite killers"; very big pancakes to fill up with at the end of a sparing meal, or if made savory, at the start of, or instead of one. Found mainly in the Savoie in this region, but elsewhere in France too.
- *Pognes.* In most places a large crown of sweetened brioche baked with a fruit topping which, once autumn comes, may be exchanged for squash, of all things. In the Dauphiné, a pogne is more likely to be an open tart, albeit with the same variation of topping.

A DRINKER'S GUIDE

The wines of Savoie are not built for long life and should be drunk as young as possible. The drinking dates shown here refer to the good wines of the northern Rhône. Ordinary Rhône wines are for drinking within 2 or 3 years of the vintage.

RECENT VINTAGES
1994: Seemed washed out and was the earliest vintage in recent history, but starting to look very successful and may be great.
1993: Light wines that are fruity and pleasant.
1992: Not a good year.
1991: The northern Rhône was better and the fourth good vintage in a row.
1990: Another northern Rhône year, with a large drought.

1989: A southern Rhône year. Small crop but good wines.
1988: Some wines are very tannic but others are more balanced. There were quality wines made throughout the region.
1987: Some good wines.
1986: Only the best names made good wine.
1985: A great year. Some luscious wines with great aging potential and tempting drinkability now.

PREVIOUS GREATS
The year 2000 and later will be the best time for drinking the wonderful Hermitage and Côte Rotie wines of 1983 and 1982. 1979 was another good year for Hermitage and is worth drinking now. Wines of 1978 can be drunk now or even later.

Bon Marché

Below is a selective list of markets plus some fairs (*foires*) of special interest. Check with the local Syndicat d'Initiative (SI) for precise locations and time changes.

AIN
Bellegarde-sur-Valserine *Mon, Tue;* Belley *Sat;* Bourg-en-Bresse *Wed, Sat, Poultry Fair 3rd Sat Dec;* Brenod *Tue;* Champagne-en-Valronmey *Thur;* Châtillon-sur-Chalaronne *Sat;* Collonges *Tue;* Culoz *Wed;* Gex *Mon, Thur;* Lagnieu *Mon;* Montrevel-en-Bresse *Tue;* Nantua *Sat;* Oyonnax *Mon, Thur, Sat;* Pont-de-Vaux *Wed;* St-Denis-en-Bugey *Sat;* St-Etienne-du-Bois *Mon;* St-Laurent-sur-Saône *Sat;* Vonnas *Thur.*

RHÔNE

Belleville *Tue;* Bessenay *Thur,* daily fruit market (early AM) May-July; Bron *Daily (Sun AM),* rummage sale 13 May; Caluire-et-Cuire *Thur, Sat AM;* Chambest-Longessaigne *Wed, Sat AM;* Condrieu *Daily fruit market (May-Oct);* Cours-la-Ville *Mon, Wed, Sat;* Fontaines-sur-Saône *Wed & Thur AM;* Grivors *Tue AM, Wed, Fri & Sun AM;* Grigny *Thur, Tue;* Haute-Rivoire *Thur PM;* Irigny *Thur AM, Wed & Sat PM;* Lyon *Daily;* Meyzieu *Wed, Sat;* La Mulatière *Tue, Fri;* Neuville-sur-Saône *Fri;* Oullins *Tue, Sun AM;* Rillieux-la-Pape-Crepieux *Sat AM, Sun, Wed, Fri AM;* Sérézin du Rhône *Tue PM;* Ste-Foy-les-Lyon *Tue, Wed, Thur, Sat (all AM);* St-Laurent-de-Chamousset *Mon;* St-Martin-en-Haut *Mon;* St-Priest *Tue, Wed AM, Thur, Fri, Sun AM,* Thurins *Thur;* Valsonne *Wed;* Vénissieux *Tue, Wed, Thur, Fri, Sat, Sun;* Villeurbanne *Daily except Mon.*

LOIRE

Ambierle *Thur;* Balbigny *Mon;* Belmont-de-la-Loire *Tue;* Boen *Thur;* Bourg Argental *Thur, Sun;* Chambon-Feugerolles *Mon, Wed, Fri, Sun;* Charlieu *Sat, Silk Market 2nd Sun Sept;* Chazelles-sur-Lyon *Tue, Fri, Sat;* Feurs *Tue, Fri;* Firminy *Tue, Thur, Sat, Sun;* Maclas *Thur;* Montbrison *Sat, Tue (June-Oct);* Montrond-les-Bains *Thur;* Neulise *Tue;* Noiretable *Wed, Sat;* La Pacaudière *Wed, Sat;* Pelussin *Sat, Sun;* Rive-de-Gier *Tue, Fri;* Roanne *Tue, Fri, Sun;* Roche-la-Molière *Wed, Sat;* Sorbiers *Fri;* Sury-le-Comtal *Wed;* St-Bonnet-le- Château *Fri;* St-Chamond *Tue, Thur, Sat, Sun;* St Etienne *Mon, Fri, Sat (summer),* St-Galmier *Mon;* St-Georges-en-Couzan *Wed;* St-Germain-Lespinasse *Thur, 1st, 2nd, 3rd Wed of month;* St-Jean-Soleymieux

Tue; St-Just-en-Chevalet *Thur;* St-Just-St-Rambert *Thur, Sun;* St-Martin-d'Estréaux *Thur;* St-Priest-la-Prugne *Mon;* St Romain-le-Puy *Fri;* St-Symphorien-de-Lay *Thur;* La Talaudière *Tue;* Veauche *Wed, Fri, Sat;* Villars *Thur.*

ARDÈCHE

Annonay *Wed, Sat;* Aubenas *Sat, Wed in chestnut season;* Bourg St-Andéol *Wed;* Burzet *Wed, Sun;* Cheylard *Wed;* Chomerac *Thur;* Coucouron *Wed;* Joyeuse *Mon, Wed, Fri, Chestnut Market Sat from 1st Oct, Grape Market daily;* Lamastre *Tue;* Largentière *Tue;* Montpezat-sous-Bauzon *Thur;* Le Pouzin *Tue;* Privas *Wed, Sat;* Satillieu *Tue;* Serrières *Fri;* Ste-Eulalie *Violet Fair Sun after 12 July;* St-Felicien *Fri;* St-Martial *Thur;* St-Péray *Wed, daily fruit market May-Sept;* St-Pierreville *Thur during chestnut season;* Tournon *Sat;* Vals-les-Bains *Sun, Thur in summer;* Vernoux-en-Vivarais *Thur, chestnut market during season (no fixed days);* Villeneuve-de-Berg *Wed.*

DRÔME

Anneyron *Tue;* Bourge-de-Péage *Mon, Fri, Sat, Sun AM;* Buis-les-Baronnies *Daily (during cherry and apricot season), Wed & Sun (during olive season);* Châteauneuf-de-Galaure *Wed;* Claveyson *Asparagus Market Mon, Wed (15th April-15th July), Leeks Oct to 15th April;* Crest *Wed, Sat;* Die *Sat;* Dieulefit *Fri;* Donzère *Sat;* Le Grand Serre *Tue;* Hauterives *Tue, Livron-sur-Drôme *Tue, Sat;* Montélimar *Wed, Thur, Fri, Sat;* La-Motte-Chalancon *Wed;* Nyons *Daily;* Pierrelatte *Fri;* Portes-les-Valence *Mon, Thur AM;* Romans-sur-Isère *Tue, Wed, Fri, Sat, Sun;* Saillans *Sun;* St-Paul Trois

Châteaux *Tue;* St-Rambert d'Albon *Fri;* St-Sorlin-en-Valloire *Mon;* Tain-l'Hermitage *Sat, Daily 31 May-Aug (fruit & veg);* Valence *Daily ex Sun.*

HAUTE-SAVOIE

Annecy *Tue, Wed, Sat, Sun AM;* Boege *Tue AM;* Bonneville *Tue, Fri;* Chamonix-Mont-Blanc *Sat AM;* Evian-les-Bains *Tue, Fri;* Faverges *Wed;* Le Grand Bornand *Tue;* Les Houches *Mon;* La Roche-sur-Foron *Thur AM;* Rumilly *Thur AM;* Sallanches *Sat;* Samdens *Wed AM;* St-Gervais-les-Bains *Thur AM;* St Jeoire *Fri;* Taninges *Thur AM;* Thones *Sat;* Thorens Glières *Wed;* Viuz-en-Sallaz *Mon AM.*

SAVOIE

Aiguebelle *Tue;* Albens *Fri;* Albertville *Thur;* Bourg-St-Maurice *Sat;* Bozel *Sat;* Chambéry *Daily;* La Chambre *Thur;* Le Chatelard *Mon;* Les Echelles *Tue;* Lescheraines *Fri;* Modane *Thur;* Montmélian *Mon;* Moutiers *Tue;* Novalaise *Thur;* Le-Pont-de-Beauvoisin *Mon;* La Rochette *Wed;* St-Béron *Wed;* St-Genix-sur-Guiers *Wed;* St-Jean-de-Maurienne *Sat;* St-Pierre-d'Albigny *Wed;* Ugine *Wed AM, Sat;* Yenne *Tue.*

ISÈRE

Beaurepaire *Wed;* Bourg d'Oisans *Sat;* Bourgoin Jallieu *Thur;* Brignoud *Tue, Sat;* Chasse-sur-Rhône *Thur;* Cote-St-André *Thur;* Cremieu *Wed;* Domène *Thur;* Le Grand Lemps *Tue, Fri;* Grenoble *Tue, Fri;* Moirans *Sat;* La-Motte-d'Aveillans *Wed;* La-Mure-d'Isère *Mon;* Pontcharra *Thur;* Pont-de-Beauvoisin *Mon;* St-Jean de Bournay *Mon;* St Marcellin *Tue, Fri, Sat;* La-Tour-du-Pin *Tue, Sat;* Vienne *Sat;* Virieu *Fri;* Viriville *Tue, Sat;* Vizille *Tue;* Voiron *Wed.*

GASCONY & THE SOUTH

SOUTHERN COMFORTS

"In which we...
* Shop for garlic tops
and a soldier's line up...
* Discuss the future
under canvas and find
food fairs with
musketeers and Spanish
music...
* Smell violets and find
what should be a
sausage in Toulouse...
* Put trout under a
blanquette and enjoy the
influence of Basques
and Catalans from over
the border...
* Discover what is
suprême about fattened
ducks, and where
musketeers make
policeman's eyes pop...
* Brew up some snails
and find God in velvet
trousers...
* Count the cloves not
the kernels...
* Taste a chartered
cheese and a cake with
wings, that sounds like
stew...
* Discover where fruit
and nut lovers really feel
chez soi..."*

This is an enormous region, sprawling eastwards from the very bottom of the French Atlantic coast to just short of Marseilles, bounded to the south by the Pyrénées and to the north by the towns of Agen, Cahors, Rodez. It was to Gascony that I wanted to go, but to find Gascony these days needs determination and the very oldest map you can lay hands on.

Officially it doesn't exist; and neither do the Quercy, the Rouergue, and Comté de Foix, and other places which people think they live in, and talk about, and travel to and from. They've all become part of modern *départements*. Thus once you determine where Gascony might be, you find it spilling into all kinds of administratively untidy areas, into Aquitaine in the west and the Languedoc in the east - and isn't there also something called the Midi down here? Indeed there is, and to add confusion it is in the middle, even though that's not what it means; Midi actually means "towards the South" or "south facing." Notwithstanding, Gascony was where I wanted to go, so I headed for Auch, home of d'Artagnan the musketeer and vaunted as the capital of Gascony.

It was spring and I first took a train from Bordeaux, speeding comfortably through the backyards of vineyards where activity was just starting, through the market gardens of Marmande where tomatoes were growing plump under plastic cloches, and alighting in Agen where the plums were plump enough to burst on the boughs. I was on my way to Hôtel de France in Auch to visit André Daguin and his wife and to see what the market had to offer.

André Daguin had fascinating stories to tell of the Gascony of only a few decades ago - of how he saw neither milk nor cheese as a child and cannot take either now. Cattle were used solely for ploughing. Even goat's milk and its cheeses were something developed over the last 20 years. The food of the Gascon was simple and by today's standards dangerously high in protein, fat and salt. Goose, duck and pork were the basis - hot in *confits* in winter, cold confit in summer, fresh sometimes, or a mixture of salt and fresh in *garbure* or, sometimes, in certain versions of *cassoulet*. The greatest portion of

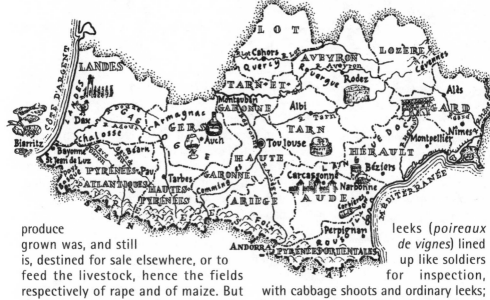

produce grown was, and still is, destined for sale elsewhere, or to feed the livestock, hence the fields respectively of rape and of maize. But then, as now, spring always brought goodies to relieve a monotonous diet. Mme Daguin took me to inspect the market.

When we walked across the Place de la République to the cathedral about which the market is set, I was expecting great stacked stalls. There were some, selling early strawberries which hit you at a hundred paces with their syrup-sweet perfume, even so early in the morning. But this was not an organized commercial market, this was a meeting place for people young and old who had come to town for the day with a bundle of what they thought might make a franc or two; it was a chance to escape the thrall of the land and gossip a little. It was the posies of flowers I noticed first, small knots of blue and gold, yellow, white and violet, laid in bright buttons under a few garlands of lilac or branches of other blossom, gathered, you imagined, while hurrying for the bus. Most of the vegetables and salad greens I was looking at had not been bundled. They were so few they were simply spread flat on scraps of newspaper or on brown paper bags that had been split and opened. Garlic tops (*aillet*) and wild leeks (*poireaux de vignes*) lined up like soldiers for inspection, with cabbage shoots and ordinary leeks; later in the year cabbage flowers would be offered, to boil and eat with vinegar and oil. The variety of salad stuffs, and the eating of it, is only a few decades old, again the results of wars and immigration. This time it is the Italians, who are indeed everywhere but who have generally added little to what they found, with one small exception: you find marvelous pizzas, but they are now becoming a national dish of France.

A further reason for being in Gascony in spring or early summer (and even pretty landscapes need brightening with activity and noise sometimes) is the *foires*, fairs agricultural and cultural that combine modern technology with fun-fairs, fireworks and serious panel discussions under canvas, such as "Whither foie gras?" - it's true, I went to one in Castelsarrasin. There's generally a gastronomic stand or tent, to taste the wines or to eat local prunes and cakes, or even to talk to small producers of foie gras and charcuterie, which is the most interesting experience of all. (The wine, incidentally, is more worth tasting than ever before, now the growers are turning towards controlled, low-temperature fermentation and producing delightfully clean and elegant wines). *Foires aux Bandas* include roving bands of brass and percussion, *Bandas et Panas,* clearly with musical roots in Spain.

The *Foire d'Auch* lasts from the first week in April to the first week of May; in smaller places it may be just for a day, but there will be one somewhere almost every weekend, until it's too hot.

Having found some of Gascony, it was by train again, to Toulouse, middle of the Midi. Here you may eat violets, and are reminded of it in every shop selling sweetness of one kind or another. It is strange to be famous for both chunky sausages and violets, but Toulouse is, and violet essence is available in chocolates, bonbons, even in liqueur for the rugged individualist.

The Midi has only one highway of note, few railway lines and produce that lends itself to the attentions of such creators as the 14 chefs of La Ronde des Mousquetaires. You'll certainly come back with something to think about - I'm still thinking about foie gras steamed with scallops . . . and what you do with violet liqueur after you have sniffed it once . . .

Charcuterie

The pigs, the food they eat and the climate combine throughout Gascony and the south to make excellent charcuterie of all kinds, although pâtés are less common than salted, preserved products. Between the Cévennes and the Cerdagne ranges of Languedoc particularly, air-dried sausages are marvelous. So, too, are the jambons crus, notably from the Black Mountain area close to Toulouse and from Ariège. Buy sausages from the mountains; the labels will say fabrication montagnarde, séchage nacturel à 850 m d'altitude, for instance.

As well as the raw hams enjoyed at the start of meals (often with the local figs or, in the spring, with radishes or young, raw broad beans), equivalents to our bacon are common. Oeufs à la causalade (Ariège) are simply eggs and bacon. Breakfast by any other name . . .

Blood puddings (boudins)

are common and in Béziers they contain pine nuts, whereas the boutifarces of Roussillon include bacon and herbs. Galabart indicates a particularly large blood pudding and melsat a white sausage based on pork rather than poultry. In Aspet, the end of the pig's intestine is used to make a giant air-dried sausage, the marinoun, holding 2-3kg/4-6lb pork when first made; it is the same idea as the rose de Lyon (see page 152).

The most famous product, and one you are more likely to find and afford than the foie gras variation, is the saucisse de Toulouse. To be worthy of the name, such sausages must first be made only with back fat, neither too firm nor too soft. The flesh and fat must be cut into large pieces by knife; small pieces or machine-cutting might lead to a texture that will break or split. The pepper must be a mixture of two-thirds finely ground and one-

third whole grains, and the mixture must sit 48 hours before being put into skins. If they are served à la languedocienne they are rolled into a spiral, sautéed in good fat with garlic and herbs and served with tomato, parsley and capers.

JAMBON DE BAYONNE

Amber of color, firm of fat and fragrant, *jambon de Bayonne* is France's most important ham, with a 40 percent share of the country's dried ham and charcuterie market and an international reputation. There are around a hundred individual artisan producers of Bayonne ham selling exclusively at a local level. You may find it intriguing to purchase some at the markets and compare with the jambon of the larger producers, such as Chevallier, which has several factories in the area and sells under the label Grand Adour, or the

THE CASSOULET WAR

Only the very wise or the very foolish should dare any attempt conspicuously to be knowledgeable in France about *cassoulet*; even worse is to voice a preference for one version over another, or to declare which is the original. For these are questions that divide towns and villages, even - it is said - families. There are three main protagonists; Castlenaudary (Aude), Carc-assonne (Aude) and Toulouse (Hte-Garonne). All three present the same base as Castelnaudary, which seems to have the best claim as originator: white haricot beans with pork rind, garlic, a little onion with clove, a little carrot, a little bay, thyme and parsley. Other parts of the pig, salted or otherwise, are added from time to time, place to place. Carcassonne adds lamb or mutton, sometimes even partridge (but you'd be lucky); Toulouse, the most complicated version, adds mutton or lamb too, plus its famed chunky sausage and preserved goose (*confit d'oie*) or preserved duck (*confit de canard*). These are but guidelines, and the basis of the conflicts. None of the additions is as important as the basic treatment of the beans. They must be well soaked, which starts germination and sweetens each bean. And the cooking must be long and slow enough to blend the flavors, reducing the cooking liquid (water) to voluptuousness but retaining the shape and texture of the beans. It is common to sprinkle the top of the cooked cassoulet with breadcrumbs and, once these have crispened, to stir them in and let another crust form. This can be done less dramatically and without adding the crumbs, simply by removing the top of the container. Needless to say, there are strong arguments for allowing anything from seven crusts to form to none at all. When Gault Millau interviewed chefs for a modern view only a third felt it at all necessary, and

then only once; yet they also said it should be done twice for holidays and three times for weddings . . .

It's considered that only an earthenware container allows a cassoulet to cook at the low temperature and slow speed that guarantees results. And thus Castelnaudary's claim to be originator of the dish, for close by is the town of Issel and since time unknown its potters have made the *cassole d'Issel* for baking slow stews.

Those villages and establishments that want to avoid the battle about which or who is right, there are variations of the basic idea under other names, notably *estouffat*, and other words like that, indicating a dish of local origin cooked very slowly. Some of these, as in Montauban, may contain that upstart new arrival, the tomato (horror!). But tomato's acid sharpness balances the richness for the uneducated palate of those from outside the area or who are foreigners. When I make dishes of this sort I also use more herbs and take advantage of the extraordinary effect red wine has on beans (improving even baked beans from a can). Whatever your version, the inclusion of goose fat (*gras d'oie*) adds marvelous velvety flavour and texture; you can buy it in cans. The real problem with cassoulet is that it is murderously unsuited to summer eating, and you are ill-advised if recommended to do so unless there is an un-seasonal plunge of temperature. Yet in the Hte-Garonne, you might go for *mongetado*, local beans cooked with onions and pork rinds, considerably lighter than a cassoulet.

A cassolette incidentally, is not a lesser, lighter or smaller version, but an indication that you are to get a small helping of something savory or sweet in a small dish of the same name.

20 small companies that produce 5,000-15,000 hams a year.

Despite, or maybe because of, its popularity, there have been no formal regulations governing the manufacture of jambon de Bayonne. One producer has been lobbying for proper controls since 1952 and, over 40 years later, it looks as though he may finally get a result with the proposed AOC status and the introduction of a logo to guarantee authenticity.

A dry-cured, lightly smoked ham, most is not made in Bayonne but 40 miles away at Orthez in the warm, humid Ardour valley. Authentic jambon de Bayonne will come from pigs bred within a prescribed area around the town and fattened on corn. Also lending a characteristic flavor to the meat is the coarse gray salt from the springs at Salies-de-Béarn. The salt is rubbed into the ham each day for three days before the meat is left to pickle in a brine of red wine and herbs for three weeks. After mild smoking, the ham is rubbed with coarse red Basque pepper (*piment d'Espelette*) and hung to mature for 7-12 months.

Slice jambon de Bayonne thinly to eat raw with melon, figs or baguette (no butter, because nothing should interfere with the flavor of the fat). Dry-cured hams are largely wasted in cooking, except when their particular flavor is used to point a dish. If this appeals, try jambon de Bayonne with omelettes and *piperade*, chicken dishes and Basque stews.

Fish & Shellfish

is one of the best areas in the world for these two fish and for other "blue" fish including mackerel; this is often presented under a nom de guerre such as grillade du golfe. You'll look in vain here for the cassoulet - fish and

There is a certain amount of freshwater fish in Gascony (pike, perch, tench, some écrevisses and truites des gaves in the Pyrénéean streams) but they are not really important. The rivers Garonne, Ariège, Tarn and Aude contain much the same population. In Limoux trout is served like veal in a blanquette - in this case not just a white wine sauce but a sauce made with blanquette de Limoux, the local sparkling white wine. In Uzès (Gard) trout and other such fish are braised in sorrel (oseille) for a summer dish. In the northern Pays Basque the River Adour still attracts salmon, one of the few in France with a run big enough to justify the expectations of being served a local salmon.

For sea fish the west of Gascony - Gers, Hautes-Pyrénées and the Midi - rely on ports such as St-Jean-de-Luz for deliveries. The haul includes delicious fresh tuna (thon), gurnard (grondin) and hake (merluche/merluz). This last is a great local favorite cooked à la koskena with peas, potatoes and asparagus, sometimes given the Spanish name salsa verde.

It's a different story down east, where warmwater fish, shellfish and crustacea come directly from the Mediterranean coast of Languedoc-Roussillon to the ports of markets. As the Languedocians were always more interested in the land than the sea, much of the business of catching and eating fish has a Spanish or Catalan flavor, as it was the men from over the border who did most of the fishing.

Sète is by far the most important port with Port-Vendres, almost on the Spanish border, the center for sardines and anchovies. This fishy things from the sea are the greatest attraction. And the biggest is oysters.

The parcs conchylicoles (oyster beds) of the Étang de Thau (Hérault) were farmed by the Romans but then ignored until the 1930s. The oysters of Bouzigues are considered the best and have the special advantage of being in season year round. Among the oysters, you may note the occasional presence of a pied de cheval, horse's foot, named for its size and shape. I'd love to hear of someone who has actually tried one.

Clams (palourdes) are also grown and mussels are cultivated on loosely woven nets, then eaten raw with a thread of vinegar and chopped shallots. But they'll also be eaten à la brochette, à la marinière or stuffed à la Sétoise with sausage meat then braised with tomatoes, shallot, garlic and olive oil. The mussel season is June to September, so summer visitors can spend no better balmy evening than in the company of a raw seafood platter raised high in the middle of their table, glittering dully with ice cubes, sporting a strand or two of seaweed, and smelling of the sea.

In Sète, keep an eye out for the cigale de mer (literally sea cicada). This extraordinary creature, a flat lobster, looks

like a huge woodlouse before cooking turns it red, and is said to make a chirruping like a cricket; it is exquisitely sweet. All along the coast the sardines, anchovies, mackerel and tuna are superb and sèche, spelled seiche everywhere else, and which is cuttlefish, is served with a rouille (garlic mayonnaise with hot red pepper). You might find saffron included in fish dishes, especially soupy ones, and plainly cooked fish is likely to be basted with one of the many local vermouths; in Agde they use it in their bouillabaisse.

Early in summer, enjoy some of the best anchovies in the world; later they'll be sold rock-salted, and the friend who told of his purchase in Couilloure said: "Every last fish in the bag tasted of fresh anchovy instead of the smear-on pizza taste."

Anchoïade, the garlic, oil and anchovy paste, is used a lot in amuse-gueules (appetizers).

The bouillabaisse, bourride and soupe de poissons found along the provençal coast prevail here too with variations, but the amazing southern preoccupation with salted fish from the north is now mercifully on the wane. Locally caught tuna (thon rouge or thounina, dialect) is only a fifth of the size of the deepwater type and makes an interesting change from the red mullet (rouget), bream (daurade), sea bass (bar), crabs, eels (anguilles), whiting (merlan) and the rest. A tip for the self-catering: fish sellers wrap your purchases in paper printed with good recipes.

Meat, Poultry & Game

Things have changed on the plates of Gascony and Languedoc-Roussillon quite as much as they have on the land, where vineyards are turning into apple orchards. For although still a food to be reckoned with, the goose is no longer sole queen of cuisine; her consort regnant is the duck. But it's her own fault. As explained in the section on foie gras, the duck is far more biddable than the goose, reproduces more often and is thus more profitable. Its fattened livers (foie gras de canard) are generally considered superior in flavor and appearance. There is plenty of it, hence the emergence, in the last 25 years or so, of the magret or maigret de canard (the former is dialect), essentially a boneless suprême of duck breast. The magret should properly only be the breast of a duck fattened for its liver, for eccentrically, such ducks present a thinner breast than usual with less fat, too. But this is generally misunder-stood and now any old duck breast might be called a magret. More duck means more preserved duck (confit de canard) too, and thus once-goosed dishes are now ducked. Everywhere, chefs are exercising themselves to make more of this bounty, particularly in combination with summer's superb vegetables and salads.

Chickens and turkeys, too, are part of the edible birdlife of the area, with Gascon turkeys well prized throughout

FOIE GRAS & FOIE GRAS DE CANARD

Because geese are so relentlessly independent, and refuse to breed more than once a year, the season for fresh fattened goose livers only starts in early winter, with a peak coinciding with demand at Christmas time. But demand is now so great throughout the year that most foie gras served in France, especially in summer's tourist season, must be imported from Eastern Europe and Israel.

Today, though, it is *foie gras de canard* you are more likely to meet, and this fattened duck liver is also more likely to be made in France. The emergence and current domination of ducks' livers is largely due to the passion of one man, André Daguin of Hôtel de France in Auch, once capital of Gascony. Over 20 years ago he realized it was only the hot Gascon summers that prevented *foie gras de canard* being available all year. Ducks are bred year-round for the table, but no one ever fattened them in summer's months, for the birds could not be kept in good enough condition. By constructing cool pens protected from the sun, and by using refrigeration, a virtually new industry has been born. Those who have been privileged enough to compare geese and duck livers invariably prefer that of duck, for it is richer and more complex. From the cook's point of view, ducks' livers are less likely to explode in cooking or to break down into an expensive pool of liquid fat.

Foie gras is specially important to two main areas, the contiguous zones of Gascony, Landes and the Dordogne, and in Alsace, with Strasbourg as the center. The major difference between the products of the two areas is that in the north, the livers are mixed with spices and gently massaged and molded to encourage voluptuousness; in the south they are not man-handled, and if there is any flavoring it is likely to be that of armagnac.

Although it will never be cheap, you are best advised to start your experience of eating foie gras in a restaurant. Nowadays it will be served cold as a first course, or be included freshly cooked on a warm salad (*salade tiède*) as the first course. At the Château de Montreuil I've eaten it on a bed of *mâche* (lamb's lettuce), in Alsace stuffed into a pheasant breast. In the Languedoc it might be baked in pastry or lightly fried with grapes in a traditional kitchen, but Daguin serves it with scallops or salts it and serves it raw.

You will argue for days about the correct accompaniment for foie gras; it is an argument complicated by the fact that until early this century, foie gras was always served at the end of the meal, when there were dessert wines about. Thus even when ordering it as a first course, a luscious, chilled sauterne is often chosen, but it must be one that is balanced by a little acidity (don't say I said so but Austrian dessert wines are cheaper and more balanced than many French styles). White burgundy, an Alsatian *vendange tardive*, red wine, amontillados, madeira, Madiran and champagne all have their advocates.

If you want to bring foie gras home, resist canned livers of any type, for the best flavor comes only from cooking at low temperatures; those required properly to sterilize canned goods are far too high. In any case, if you look at the label, you are invariably not buying goose liver but some mixture with pork and/or other fats. Those with a ludicrous 1% or so of truffles are even less value for money. As a Christmas or other treat, buy only *demi* or *semiconserves*, sometimes called *mi-cuit*, which are always in glass and have a life of several months under refrigeration. They are as good as anything you will prepare yourself and, as cooked foie gras improves with age, you can pack some into your suitcase or carry-on bag with confidence.

These days you can more readily buy raw foie gras or foie gras de canard in vacuum-sealed packs - I have done so in the Marché aux Grand'Hommes in Bordeaux. This is by far the cheapest source, and is safe to transport without refrigeration. Incidentally, you cannot judge the quality of a fattened liver by its color. The introduction of the yellow hybrid corn to replace the old white type means yellow flesh and fat, which can disguise defects.

In Gascony, the Landes and the Périgord, keep your eyes open for farms that will welcome you to see how foie gras is made. In Gascony there will be more chances than anywhere else because foie gras de canard is made all year round. Look for signs saying *gavage*, the term for force feeding, if that is what you want to see, or *dégustation* if you would rather concentrate on tasting the finished product.

France. One of the most interesting poultry dishes is alicot/ailcuit, chicken giblets cooked with potato, carrot and garlic, but the best version is made with turkey (giblets are gesiers and really authentic recipes should include the wings, ailerons, explaining the name). When you are in the Rouergue/Aveyron, beware of confusing this with aligot, which is a purée of potatoes and cheese. All poultry goes with almost anything and so almost every part of a bird may be stuffed with or served with any combination of olives, raisins, nuts, chestnuts, prunes and bitter oranges. They may be spit-roasted with a garlic croûton in the gullet, or roasted or boiled as poulet farcie au pot.

In the area abutting the Agenais (Lot-et-Garonne) there is much acclaim given to oie farcie aux pruneaux (goose stuffed with prunes). As it takes four days to make properly, you'd be better off looking for stuffed goose neck (cou d'oie farci), a sort of sausage.

Many ancient and honorable dishes are disappearing, in many cases in pursuit of a less fatty diet, but just as often because they take too long to cook. Cassoulets will flourish for some time I expect and so will the main beanless, long-cooked stew of mixed meats, the famous garbure of Gascony. Three or four different parts of different animals cooked slowly with vegetables (gerbe means a bunch or bundle of them), with cabbage added at an earlier or later stage according to your sophistication, is fast becoming a special occasion dish rather than a family staple. The new musketeers of Gascony, La Ronde des Mousquetaires, an association of the best chefs, made garbure for several hundreds of journalists and dignitaries in Auch's magnificent Corn Market. The chefs' modern lighter touch made it

thoroughly delicious and there was an enjoyable frisson waiting in line as you spied a choice piece of chicken, for instance, and hoped it would still be there when you were. Even in the spring evening, balmy rather than summer sultry, eyes were popping and foreheads sopping. A policeman said the temptation to eat too much of it, resisted by few, was why he ate garbure only rarely. We were served it all in one plate, but properly the broth and the meat and vegetables should be separate, with the last of the broth mixed with wine, the waste-not want-not custom called faire chabrot practiced here.

Sheep are better equipped than cattle or pigs to graze on such stubby plains as the Causses. Uzès and Quercy are also important centers. Mouton might actually be mutton rather than lamb, and thus able to survive being cooked in rich daubes or civets, roasted with juniper (genièvre) or served with the extraordinary concoction of Toulouse, cité rose or aux briques, a mixture of blood pudding, sausage, preserved duck, tomato and garlic. They do things with mutton tripes, too, like tripoux (see Limousin & the Auvergne) and manouls, and with lambs' head (cabassol).

Daubes of beef are associated with Albi and Carcassonne, but veal is more common these days, perhaps with a lemon sauce or with green olives. Those of advanced culinary theory will appreciate the knowledge that even in France some things cannot be called anything French; bulls' testicles become a distinctly Spanish criadillas when served in Nîmes.

There is little game to

speak of, although there once was, especially around Narbonne, but it was senselessly double-decimated between the two wars by literal overkill and insensitive husbanding. There was even a type of mountain goat, the isard in the Comté de Foix (Ariège); the small game birds, ortolans, thrush, warblers (becfigues) and so on are now protected by EC regulations. Some hare, wild rabbit (lapin de la garenne), pigeons and partridge (perdreau) are all that are left now. It is really worth ordering one if it is from the Foix, for the flesh tends to be perfumed by its heady diet of lavender, juniper and thyme. À la catalane should mean it is accompanied by a sharp sauce of bitter oranges.

A cargolade is more easily found, a sort of brew-up of snails in white wine or snails grilled en masse. In the Languedoc more than anywhere else in France, snails are served in ways more interesting than with butter and too much garlic; the best are those which include nut oil or nuts, which underpin the nuttiness of a good snail: à la gayouparde, Sommiéroise or Lodévoise; à la Narbonnaise mixes mayonnaise with almond milk.

Pork is most likely to be used for charcuterie, or included in the many mixed meat dishes; but suckling pig is often enjoyed at special occasions.

HOME CONFITS

A confit is any fatty meat pickled with salt then preserved in fat, usually more of its own, traditionally prepared in autumn to store protein for winter. Confits of goose, or of duck, used to be the most common, usually

only the legs and thigh, but now the greater number of ducks being bred for making foie gras in Gascony mean both that duck predominates there, and that breasts are preserved too.

The process is simple and easy to do at home. The meat is covered with salt and left to pickle lightly for a day or so according to taste. Some flavoring is usually included, too – bay, peppercorns, that sort of thing. Once the unabsorbed salt has been brushed away, the meat is cooked gently to render most of its own fat, then covered completely with fat and cooked until falling from the bone. Ideally goose is cooked in goose fat, duck in duck fat and so on. Pork pieces are also preserved, and in some cases, chicken (poulet en confit). Once packed in the cooking fat, it must mature at least a week before being eaten, but is usually kept much longer when, like anything salted, it will slowly harden and the fat may develop a taint: this is more likely if the preserving fat is being used for a second or third time. When served, confits are heated in the fat so any pieces of skin crisp up again. They are usually served with potatoes sliced thinly and browned in the same fat, although this is being changed by thoughtful French chefs who may serve them shaved thinly onto salads as a first course.

Fruits & Vegetables

Garlic haters, go home. This is the heart of garlic growing and eating, with Tarn probably the place where more is used than any other part of France. Known also as aulz rather than ail, it's used in more interesting ways, too. When I poked around the market in Auch on Saturday morning, I discovered aillet (sometimes aillé) the green shoots of young garlic, used as we would chives or scallions. It was also the only place I found genuine wild leeks (poireaux des vignes) offered, too - I would have given anything for a kitchen to play in that day.

Generally Gascony and its near neighbors prefer to use cloves of garlic whole rather than chopped or crushed. This is flagged by the use of pistache in descriptions of dishes, sometimes meaning the cloves have been stuck into, say, a leg of lamb, or used in daube or ragoût, as the ragoût de mouton of the Haute Garonne, also called cassoulet Luchonnais. If the cloves are just lightly crushed in their skins, the eventual flavor is relatively subtle, and if the cloves have cooked long enough their flesh will have melted into a buttery sweetness that is beguiling, addictive, unlike garlic, and hell the next day.

The extraordinary range of vegetables grown from the Atlantic to the Mediterranean find themselves in an even bigger range of soups and stews, generally heartier than you would imagine such a climate would indicate. These are mainly winter dishes but in summer at midday the locals rely on the equally numberless variations of salad as a mainstay, albeit with a little confit de canard. Salade de Cévennes is nicer than the Waldorf, with which it has affinities; it is diced potato, celery and walnuts. In Languedoc or Roussillon you will be more likely to be offered the green olives of Lucques or the longer, more savory black picholines. And the bread is guaranteed to be good and honest, and interesting, for cereals have been a major crop for centuries. Early in the 19th century, Tarn and Haute-Garonne made quite a lot of wine, but now vineyards are being converted to orchards. Many look to the Golden Delicious for their future prosperity, but no apple can thrive without cold nights to develop texture and skin color. Some growers who have seen, and tasted, the better crisper apples being developed elsewhere in the world are now turning to the vines of the kiwifruit, the monkey peach from the Yangtze Valley, perfected by New Zealand.

Millet used to be a staple used for the porridge-like bouillie or millas, but it has been replaced, even though the name has not, by corn from America. The use of corn for human food is considered eccentric in most of France. Most of the corn is not sweet, but grown for the sustenance of the huge population of animals and poultry. The great mesh-sided stores of dried corn-cobs seen everywhere are as nourishing a sight for the culinary traveler as the reality of cornfed chickens or turkey on the plate. There is some little local complaint, for the yellow hybrid variety most commonly sown is not considered to produce such

LOCAL PRODUCE

VEGETABLES

- **ARTICHOKE** artichaut
  Var: Violet de Gapeau
  March to June and October to December
  Dep: Pyrénées-Orientales, Vallée de la Garonne

- **ASPARAGUS** asperge
  Var: White and green*
  Early March to mid-June
  Dep: Garde, Hérault, Aude, Pyrénées-Orientales
  One of the most important areas in France; some primeurs are forced for mid-February. *In France, green asparagus is still two-thirds white.

- **CAULIFLOWER** choufleur
  Var: Boule de Neige, Erfut, Rex Aramon, Brio, Claudia
  October until January 15th
  Dep: Gard

- **CELERY** céleri branche
  Peak in October
  Dep: Pyrénnées-Orientales, Hte-Garonne
  Second biggest producer after the Loire.

- **EGGPLANT** aubergine
  Var: West: Violette de Toulouse (white flesh); East: Violette de Varbentanne (green flesh)
  End May to mid-November
  Dep: Gard, Tarn-et-Garonne

- **GARLIC** ail
  Var: white: Messidrôme, Thermidrôme, Blanc de Lomange; pink: Fructidor, Rosé d'Italie, du Var, de Lautrec; violet: Germidour, Cadours
  July and first two weeks of August
  Dep: Tarn-et-Garonne, Gers, Tarn, Hte-Garonne
  The principal French production zones; the relatively uncommercialized garlic of Quercy, which includes some of Tarn-et-Garonne and some of the Lot is considered the sweetest and the least likely to be bitter in cooking. In addition to the amount grown in domestic gardens, each French person buys an extra 800g/2lb a year. France imports more garlic from South America than it exports to European markets.

- **LEEK** poireau
  Mainly autumn/winter
  Dep: Hte-Garonne, Tarn-et-Garonne

- **LETTUCE** laitue
  Var: white and green cabbage varieties plus icebergs, batavia, curly endive, etc.
  Open-air: November until March
  Covered: December until March
  Dep: Pyrénées-Orientales, Gard, Hte-Garonne
  The Pyrénées-Orientales produce 40% of winter lettuce and 65% of scarole, (frisée, etc.).

- **ONION** oignon
  End March until September
  Dep: Hérault, Gard

- **SHORT-DAY ONIONS** oignons de jours courts
  Ready from end of May to end of July

- **PARSLEY** persil
  Var: Le Commun (most perfumed); Frisé (crinklier)
  Year round
  Dep: Pyrénées-Orientales
  Over 25% of French production.

- **PEPPER** poivrons
  Var: Lamuyo, Esterel
  June to early November, but later in southwest
  Dep: Gard, Tarn-et-Garonne, Pyrénées-Atlantiques

- **POTATOES** (new) pommes de terre de primeur
  End May to end July
  Dep: Gard, Pyrénées-Orientales, Hérault, Pyrénées-Atlantiques

- **TOMATO** tomate
  Var: Beefsteak

LOCAL PRODUCE

East: End April until start December
West: Gard, Hérault, Pyrénées-Orientales, Tarn-et-Garonne
Gard is a most imprtant center, but Pyrénées-Orientales are first on the market with quantity, in May. As well as growing an average of 2kg per person, the French buy 8.5kg/20lb of tomatoes per person per year.

- TURNIP *navet*
Var: long: *Nantais, Croissy, Milan;* flat: *de Nancy, de Saint-Benoît, Jaune boule d'or*
September until April
Dep: Gard, Hérault, Lozère, Hte-Garonne

FRUITS
- ALMONDS *amandes*
Var: mainly introduced
Green: June/July; Main harvest: August to October
Dep: Hérault, Aude, Hte-Garonne, Pyrénées-Orientales

- APPLE *pomme*
Var: *Reine des Reinettes*
East: July/August; West: September/October
Dep: Hérault, Gard, Hte-Garonne, Tarn, Tarn-et-Garonne, Lot, Gers, Ariège

- APRICOT *abricot*
Var: *Rouge du Roussillon, Rouge de Rivesaltes, Précoce de Boulbon*
Early June until early August
Dep: Pyrénées-Orientales, Gard
The Pyrénées-Orientales is as important as the Drôme as a premier production zone, but crops 10-20 days earlier, peaking about the end of June.

- CHERRIES *cerises*
Var: *Bigarreau,* red and white, *Berlat*
Mid-May to end June
Dep: Gard, Hérault, Pyrénées-Orientales, Tarn-et-Garonne, Aveyron. Céret (Pyrénées-Orientales)

is usually the earliest place to harvest followed by the Gard. Remoulins and St-Quentin are important centers.

- CHESTNUTS *châtaignes*
Harvest begins September
Dep: Lot, Hte-Garonne

- GRAPES *raisins*
Var: *Lavallée, Cardinal, Chasselas, Muscat; Chasselas de Moissac* are AOC
East: August until November; West: September until December
Dep: Gard, Hérault, Tarn-et-Garonne

- GREENGAGES *reines-claudes*
Various varieties over season
July until October
Dep: Tarn-et-Garonne, Gers, Lot

- HAZELNUTS *noisettes*
Var: *Fertile de Coutard*
Harvest starts September
Dep: Hte-Garonne
Green hazelnuts, cob nuts, are often available earlier for snacking.

- KIWIFRUIT *kiwi*
Var: *Hayward*
December until April
Dep: Tarn-et-Garonne, Hte-Garonne, Tarn, Pyrénées-Atlantiques

- MELON *melon*
Var: types of *Charentais*
June until mid-October
Dep: Tarn-et-Garonne, Gers, Lot
Accounts for 30% of the French crop, often sold under name of production area but all are charentais; much of the production is on a small scale to protect quality.

- NECTARINES *nectarine/ brugnon*
Var: *Fuzalode* (white, mid-July)
Yellow ones are American strains

End May until end August
Dep: Pyrénées-Orientales, Gard, Tarn-et-Garonne, Hte-Garonne
More than half of the French crop comes from the Pyrénées-Orientales; vallées de la Salanque, de la Têt, du Tech: Perpignan is an important market for them. Moissac, Montauban and Toulouse are important centers, too. Nectarines have a free stone; brugnons do not.

- PEACH *pêche*
Var: *Genadix* 4 & 7 old white; rest of white and yellow fleshed are American
June until early September
Dep: Pyrénées-Orientales, Gard, Hérault, Tarn-et-Garonne, Hte-Garonne.
Pyrénées-Orientales and Gard produce about 50% of the nation's crop, with a continuously extended season as new strains are included.

- PEAR *poire*
Var: *Williams, Guyot, Beurré hardy, Passe-Crassane* (winter)
Mid-July to mid-September
Dep: Tarn-et-Garonne, Gard, Hte-Garonne

- PLUMS *prune*
Var: *Prune d'Ente*
June to September
Dep: Tarn-et-Garonne, Gers, Lot, Gard
Huge production almost exclusively for processing of one sort or another; but delicious fresh if you have the chance.

- STRAWBERRIES *fraises*
April/June and mid-August/October
Dep: Tarn-et-Garonne, Gers, Hte-Garonne, Lot

- WALNUTS *noix*
Var: *Grandjean Marbot*
Harvest starts in September
Dep: Lot

delicately flavored flesh as the old but less prolific white corn, which gave also a less startling color to flesh and fat.

Pumpkin is another delicious vegetable often given only to animals but here commonly used to advantage; in the Pays Basque there is a delicious pumpkin bread, easily spotted for its warmth of color and recommended for its amicability of flavor. Its combination of pumpkin, corn meal and dark rum owes nothing to local tradition, however, for all three are from the New World, and are more likely to have crossed the border from Spain.

The vegetables associated in the northern European mind with the Midi – eggplants, tomatoes, zucchini, beans, artichokes and the like – are all here, of course, and constantly being used in more ways than with oil and garlic. The zucchini blossom will be stuffed, the eggplant combined with wild mushrooms in Nîmes. The cèpe might be found solo in a daube of distinction, but there is more to wild mushrooms than that. The Béarn, for instance, has a wide range of wild mushrooms in the valleys of Ape and Ossau. As well as cèpes there will be the slightly earlier oronges, an edible amanite of which the oronges des Césars is the best, and the psalliotes des prés, related to and almost the same as the cultivated variety, and also including champignon rosé, with a pinky-brown, scaled skin which I bought in August in Toulon's Cours Lafayette market; they have a richer, stronger flavor and keep their shape and texture remarkably well in cooking. If you are in the south in spring, you might be rewarded instead with mousserons or the crinkly-

capped morilles. Like cèpes, they are equally wonderful dried.

Lentils are a favorite in the Lozère through the proximity of the Auvergne, but the most unusual vegetable must be the salsify (salsifis) which is fried and sweetened before serving.

Béarn, and the valleys behind the coasts of the Pays Basque, grow a remarkable range of vegetables; the latter being the center for the cultivation of several varieties of red pepper, sweetish or hottish, which dominate the cooking and condiments of the area. Esplette is the center of the business of sun-drying and selling them. A naive belief that the rest of France was as fortunate in the bounty of their horticultural harvests as his home in the Vicomté de Béarn is what I think led Henri IV to promote the belief that each family might aspire to a weekly poule au pot.

Potatoes, yet another import from the Americas, are combined there with peppers and, as throughout the region, both with the traditional cooking media of pork fat and oil and in combined olive oil and butter, too. In north Languedoc, criquettes are potato and garlic pancakes. In Ciboure, potatoes are puréed with beans, garlic, olives and shallots to make the distinctive purée Ciboure. Marjoram (marjolaine) is used in the southwest, for stuffing peppers or with masses of parsley in soups. Parsley is the most common garnish, persillade. The proximity of the Spanish border explains the regular but not common use of saffron.

Cheese

Although the range of cheese made locally is not enormous it covers a wide spectrum. The greatest opportunity offered is to compare roquefort cheeses, for some will have more veins, some less, some will be fresher, some more aged. A gentle stroll through a market or along a village street will offer a choice you will never find back home. Look too for the plain soft sheep's milk cheese in cartons; if you can keep it chilled, it is a delicious but somewhat startling spread for picnics.

Take the plunge and try other local blue cheeses, too, made with cow's milk. Lovers of

---

THE GOAT WOMAN OF CORBIÈRES

Englishwoman Penny Lyman-Dixon has finally found her niche, and it's 200 hectares of French mountain shared with 40 goats, 40 sheep and her partner Peter. On the farm, La Gigude, the 16-hour day begins at 4:30 AM with the first of the two milkings. Each of the alpine goats produces around 3 liters of milk a day, enough for six unpasteurized *pélardon*. The cheese is sold fresh after three days, a little older and it is demi-sec, and after six weeks *sec*, which for you and me can be roughly translated as bullets. In the winter, when there is more milk, Penny produces *tommes*.

The cheese can be found at markets at Perpignan and on the Roussillon coast. Enjoy as sold, or try marinating the fresh cheeses in oil flavored with wine, garlic, thyme, rosemary and the like for two days. In cooking, the pélardon can be added to salads, wrapped in puff pastry, or rolled into balls and coated in herbs and nuts to make savory goat's cheese truffles.

goat's milk cheese will find cabécous, but my favorite is bethmale.

•*Amou:* A west-Gascon farm-made sheeps' milk cheese (45% fat) in the shape of a thick disk, cured for 2-6 months, thus mild to sharp. May be used in cooking. Fragile golden rind, lightly oiled.

•*Ardi Gasna:* Basque for "local cheese." This is a nutty-flavored sheeps' milk cheese made in the mountain farms of the Pays Basque. Used in cooking and sometimes eaten when a little moldy. Best end of spring to autumn.

•*Bleu des Causses:* AOC cheese clearly related to bleu d'Auvergne geographically and in culinary terms. Made for centuries; now produced commercially (although cured in natural caves), it is a non-cooked non-pressed blue cheese with moderate veining. Eaten all year, although a winter cheese (whiter and drier than a summer one) has a more vigorous flavor. Adds savor to pasta and potatoes and, oddly enough, to grilled meats or the juices of roast beef and other meats. Production in Lot, Aveyron, Lozère, Gard and Hérault, an area which includes, but is bigger than, Les Causses.

•*Bethmale:* A large disk of cows' milk cheese made in the Comté de Foix. At its best in spring and summer, it has a haunting flavor becoming sharp. Really wonderful.

•*Bleu du Quercy:* Commercially produced blue closely related to bleu d'Auvergne (45% fat); a soft blue with strong smell and positive savory flavor. From Figeac area particularly: best in autumn and winter.

•*Bossons macérés:* Look for this home-produced cheese only in small markets. Produced by macerating dry tommes de chèvre in a mixture

MIRACLE OF THE MOUNTAIN

The mysterious, deep caves formed by the collapse of the Combalou mountain are the natural cellars for the maturation of *roquefort,* one of the world's most ancient and respected cheeses – and unique among these in that it is made from sheep's and not cow's milk.

The mass of fallen rocks stretches for around 2km and is 300 meters wide. The oldest and largest caves are owned by the *Société Anonyme des Caves et des Producteurs Réunis de Roquefort* and situated at the top end of the rock mass where the first inhabitants of the area built their small huts along a fissure in the mountain.

It is believed that each cave has its own personality, which is passed on to the cheeses as they mature. Roquefort's flavor is attributed to the cheese ripener's skill, the spores of the *penicillium roquefortii* that exist naturally within the caves (although these days the mold is cultivated in a laboratory and sprinkled into the milk at the dairy), and the caves' *fleurines,* the cracks in the rocks through which air flows affecting the temperature and humidity of the caves. The master cheesemaker controls the flow of air through the fleurines by adjusting a series of ancient wooden doors.

Roquefort is made exclusively from the milk of Lacaune sheep, farmed in the area for thousands of years. Each cheese is turned 5 times a day while it drains, after which it is placed for at least 3 months in the caves.

Roquefort has a sticky surface, a white, unevenly veined body (it crumbles easily) and an incomparably rich flavor, both savory and salty. It must be left to reach room temperature – wrapped – before eating, and can be enjoyed year round.

of white wine, olive oil and marc: a local fromage fort, in fact.

•*Cabécou d'Entraygues:* Made on farms around Entraygues-sur-Truyère and the immediate area in the Aveyron, these are very small disks of chèvre or mi-chèvre with a mild to nutty flavor. Cabécou is a generic name for a group of small chévres of this type derived from the word for goat in Languedoc patois - cabre.

•*Cierp de Luchon:* Also known as bethmale.

•*Esbareich:* A large flattened loaf of sheep's milk cheese made in the mountain cottages of the Pays Basque, it has a mild flavor becoming stronger as the cheese matures (2-6 months). Grate like parmesan when mature.

•*Iraty:* Another Basque cheese, this time from the Basse Navar. Made in mountain homes from a mix of sheep's and cow's milk. A large flattened loaf with washed rind and strong flavor variable according to the exact mixture of milks used.

•*Livernon:* A soft goat's milk cheese, also called cabécou de Livernon.

•*Montségur:* Relatively new, very bland washed-rind cheese made commercially of pasteurized cow's milk down in the Pyrénées of the Ariège.

•*Les Orrys:* Named after a mountain village in the Comté

de Foix, a large flat cylinder of cow's milk cheese, pressed and uncooked with a fairly strong flavor. Often used grated on food.

•Ossau-Iraty-Brébis-Pyrénées: Remarkable AOC cheese that is made from the milk of two types of sheep: manech and basco-béarnaises. Lightly pressed with a dry brushed crust that can vary from a yellow-orange to gray, a creamy white body and rich earthy flavor. Best from late spring to the end of autumn. The hot curd is broken up by whisking, then the cheeses are hand-shaped, treated with gros sel, and matured about 3 months in a humid atmosphere at less than 12°C.

•Pélardon des Cévennes: Péladon is the generic name for several cheeses of this type - small soft chévre with a nutty flavor.

•Passe l'An: A large very hard cheese with a low fat content (28-32%) cured for at least 2 years; it not surprisingly has a distinct flavor; a commercial attempt to imitate Italian grana cheeses; mainly used as such.

•Picodon de St-Agrève: St-Agrève is the place to buy this rich, nutty small disk of chèvre although it is also found in the Cévennes. Best in summer and autumn.

•Picadou: A very powerful small cheese, wrapped in leaves; made from sheep's or goat's milk; called cabècou when cured in crocks.

•Rogeret des Cévennes: Small goat's milk cheese; red-blue rind and a keen nutty flavor. Made around Lamastre.

•Roquefort: In 1411 Charles VI signed a charter giving the inhabitants of Roquefort-sur-Soulzon the monopoly on making this, the best-known of all blue cheeses. Made only with full cream, raw sheep's milk, roquefort naturally has an AOC.

Pastries, Desserts & Confectionery

In Castelsarrasin, there was a man selling gâteau à la broche, like the German baumkuchen. Batter is dribbled onto a slowly turning skewer over a fire until the layers build up into a cake; a bit dry. There was also a gâteau de noix with chocolate icing and a rich stuffing of nuts and honey, packed on wooden slats. It lasted some days in my suitcase. Back home the rich, rather short crust and filling were excellent. The manufacturer, La Coupiagasse, based in Coupiac, makes a wide range of broadly authentic baked goods.

The word pastis is complicated in Gascony. It is used both for its constantly refreshed stew, and for a dessert creation found in the Landes and most places south of Bordeaux, yet made with a paper-thin pastry related only to the strudel leaves of Austria and to the phyllo pastry of Greece and the lands of Islam. Leaves of the lightly vanilla-flavored pastry are torn raggedly, perfumed with armagnac and orange-flower water then folded twice, piled

with lumps of butter into a baking dish and baked into un gâteau qui a des ailes, a cake with wings. La croustade is the same wondrous pastry, which should look as fine as a bridal veil before it is baked, but adds layers of apple or plum and sugar. Anyone you see walking on tip-toe while balancing a cakebox on Sundays, is almost certainly carrying a pastis or croustade from the pastry shop to grace a family lunch.

Castelnaudary and other places follow the example of the Ardèche by making crystallized fruits, but Toulouse, capital of the Midi, does it to violets. Indeed her violets flavor bonbons and fill chocolates - even perfume a liqueur. A more universal flavor perhaps is licorice (réglisse) and Uzès is the French licorice capital, producing more than half of all that's consumed. There is a fine range of licorice confectionery (bou d'Zan particularly) but the major part of the crop goes into pastis aperitif drinks such as Ricard.

If ever there was a home for fruit and nut lovers, this is it. In the southeast corner, the Pyrénées-Orientales produce France's best apricots plus excelling peaches and raspberries. The Agenais grows its famed plums for the world's best prunes, often still dried in old-fashioned prune ovens by the orchards. Pruneaux fourré, prunes stuffed with a paste of almonds and themselves, taste too wonderful to imagine. From old and new orchards in the west and east

---

WORTH FINDING

• **Coques**: A brioche studded with angelica (angelique).
• **Flônes**: Associated with the marvelously named town of Ste-Affrique, these are made from the whey of sheep's milk, thickened with egg yolks and flavored with orange-flower water.
• **Nênes**: Again something to find in Ste-Affrique, this is an aniseed cake.
• **Pinus**: Small anise cakes from Lunel.

tumble barrels full of greengages, apples (although frankly the area is too hot to expect much quality) and pears, often found happily relaxed in armagnac.

Preserved fruits in sugar, alcohol or both, are common throughout the region. In Gascony, fruits are poached with spices in red wine; on the Côte Vermeuil - Perpignan and thereabouts - fruit is more likely to be served fresh, mixed in a salad and all the more welcome on your plate for its customary slurp of Banyuls wine.

Preserved or fresh fruit, and the syrupy jams (confitures) made from them, adorn thick pancakes (pannequets), or are dipped in batter and deep-fried, beignets. I specially liked the sudden appearance here of the blood-juiced pomegranate (grenadier) and the sensuously perfumed quince (coing), normally more associated with the preserves of Spain and Portugal. Thin lacy-edged pancakes (crêpes en l'air) are mixed with eggs and water and fried only in lard, then basted with a fruit eau-de-vie.

Walnuts, hazelnuts, almonds and pine nuts from the tall parasol pines of the coast (noix, noisettes, amandes and pignons) add snap, crunch and richness to a huge variety of nibbles and cakes. A great speciality of the Pays Basque, turrones or tourons, of Spanish birth, are almond-nougat loaves stuffed with these local nuts and other fillings. Nuts go also into the nougat of Limoux and the richer, darker nougat noir you'll specially find in Perpignan. Rosquillas is an almond cake from Roussillon: and gimblettes and petitsjeans are almond biscuits, ideal for nibbling with a glass of wine.

Less publicized than its peppers is the excellent Basque summer crop of figs, plums, table grapes and, best of all, cherries. If you miss the season do not fret, for the sensational chocolate-makers have combined them with their product for centuries.

THE PIES OF PÉZANAS

When Clive of India escaped from the heat of battle and business for the winter of 1766 to stay in the Château de Larzac, near Pézanas, he brought with him both Indian servants and a taste for sweet mincemeat pies. It was thought these pies of chopped mutton, sugar and lemon peel were invented by, or an ethnic speciality of, the Indians, but they are simply a rare survival of the original pies brought back to Europe from Araby by the Crusaders.

Pézanas still bakes them according to what is said to be the original recipe: four parts of brown sugar, two of minced mutton, one of mutton fat, one of beef suet, ideally from veal kidneys, and some grated lemon peel - all baked in an elegant French version of a hot-water crust. Béziers has its own version, but it is considered impolite, i.e. dangerous, to be heard comparing the two. They may be sold as *pâtés de viande sucrée* or *de Pézanas/Béziers*. In Béziers, other, simpler fillings may be used including fish. In Nîmes, there are *pâtés de mouton*.

SPIRIT OF THE SOIL

Some think armagnac inferior to cognac. Its bouquet is earthier, more obvious, less subtle, they say. But it's important to realize that the two brandies aim at completely different styles: the best cognacs seem to capture the soul of the grapes from which they were made; armagnac's rich flavor reflects the soil on which its grapes were grown.

Many of the largest armagnac producers are partly (or wholly) owned by cognac houses and the differences are sometimes blurred. This is a pity because armagnac has a strong character of its own. The traditional still, the *alambic armagnacais*, is mainly responsible. Distilled only once, armagnac thus retains many of the volatile flavoring components that are lost in the second distillation that cognacs endure.

Armagnac is essentially a region of small producers, many of whom sell direct to the public. At most road-side shops, farms and market stalls you may taste first.

Within the region, the best confusingly comes from Lower Armagnac (*Bas-Armagnac*), while most of the lesser stuff that finishes up inside expensive bottles of fruit in armagnac comes from Upper Armagnac, (*Haut-Armagnac*). In between comes Ténarèze, which produces a lighter style of spirit.

When you find single vintage armagancs on sale, remember the oldest lose much of their character as they age, as well as being horrifyingly expensive.

There are two mixed drinks you will find regularly: *floc* is grape juice and armagnac; a *pousse-rapière* is armagnac with orange and a sparkling white wine.

Bon Marché

Below is a selective list of markets plus some fairs (*foires*) of special interest. Check with the local Syndicat d'Initiative (SI) for precise locations and time changes.

LANDES

Aire sur l'Adour *Tue;* Capbreton *Wed;* Dax *Fri, Sat;* Gabarret *Wed;* Geaune *Thur;* Hagetmau *Wed;* Labouheyre *Thur;* Mont-de-Marsan *Tue;* Montfort-en-Chalosse *Wed;* Peyrehorade *Wed;* Pouillon *Thur;* Roquefort *Sat;* Sabres *Sun;* Soustons *Mon.*

PYRÉNÉES-ATLANTIQUES

Artix *Wed;* Bayonne *Tue, Thur, Sat, Charcuterie and Ham Fair Wed, Thur, Fri of Holy Week;* Bedous *Thur;* Biarritz *Daily;* Hendaye *Wed, Sat;* Laruns *Sat;* Mauléon Soule *Tue;* Monein *Mon, Thur May-Oct (Fruit & Veg); Cattle Fair 7 Oct;* Navarrenx *Tue;* Nay-Bourdettes *Tue;* Oloron-Ste-Marie *Tue, Sun AM;* Ossès *Thur AM (Mar-April), every 2nd Thur rest of year;* Pau *Daily, Mon (poultry, cattle, foie gras & chestnuts Oct-Feb);* Salies-de-Béarn *Daily;* St-Jean-de-Luz *Tue, Fri.*

HAUTES-PYRÉNÉES

Argelès Gazost *Tue;* Arreau *Thur;* Bagnères-de-Bigorre *Sat;* Maubourguet *Tue (veg, poultry, rabbits);* Pierrefitte-Nestalas *Sat;* Sarrancolin *Tue;* St-Lary-Soulan *Sat;* St-Pé-de-Bigorre *Wed;* Trie-sur-Baise *Tue;* Tarbes *Thur;* Vieille-Aure *Tue.*

GERS

Aignan *Mon;* Auch *Wed, Thur, Sat;* Beaumarchés *Mon AM;* Cazaubon *Fri PM, Sat AM;* Condom *Wed;* Eauze *Thur;* Gimont *Wed;* L'Isle-Jourdain *Sat;* Lectoure *Fri;* Marciac *Wed;* Miélan *Thur;* Mirande *Mon;* Plaisance *Thur;* Riscle *Fri.*

TARN-ET-GARONNE

Beaumont-de-Lomagne *Garlic Market Tue, Turkey & Capon Fair Sat,* Castelsarrasin *Thur, Poultry Show Thur before Christmas;* Grisolles *Wed;* Lafrançaise *Wed;* Molières *Tue;* Montauban *Sat;* Montech *Tue;* St-Antonin-Noble-Val *Sun AM;* St-Nicholas-de-la-Grave *Mon.*

LOT

Bretenoux *Sat;* Cahors *Wed, Sat;* Castelnau-Montratier *Tue & Thur, Sun (20 June onwards);* Figeac *Sat;* Lalbenque *Truffle Market Mon (Dec-Mar 20);* Mayrinhac-Lentour *Mon, Wed, Fri (plums);* Souillac *Mon, Wed, Fri;* St-Céré *Sat.*

AVEYRON

Decazeville *Fri, Sat;* Entraygues-sur-Truyère *Fri;* Laguiole *Sat (May & June);* Macrillac-Vallon *Sun;* Millau *Mon, Wed, Fri;* Najac *Fri, Ham Fair 4 Mar, 20 April;* Rignac *Wed;* Rodez *Wed, Fri, Sat;* St-Affrique *Tue, Thur, Sat.*

TARN

Albi *Sat, 2nd & 4th Tue of month;* Castres *Mon, Thur, Sat, (Cattle);* Gaillac *Fri;* Graulhet *Thur;* Labastide Rouairoux *Thur, Sun;* Lautrec *Fri;* Lavaur *Sat;* Lisle-sur-Tarn *Sun;* Mazamet *Tue, Sat, Sun.*

HAUTE-GARONNE

Auterive *Fri;* Bessières *Mon;* Cintegabelle *Tue;* Cugnaux *Sat;* Grenade *Sat;* L'Isle-en-Dodon *Tue (Poultry), Sat;* Lanta *Sat;* Lévignac *Tue;* Montastruc-la-Conseillère *Sat (eggs & poultry);* Montesquieu-Volvestre *Tue;* Montréjeau *Mon;* Muret *Tue, Sat;* Ramonville-St-Agne *Wed;* Toulouse *Daily ex Mon, Garlic Fair 24 Aug, 15 Oct.*

ARIÈGE

Ax-les-Thermes *Tue, Thur, Sat;* Daumazan-sur-Arize *1st Fri of month (poultry market retail 11:30-12);* Foix *Wed, Fri;* Laroque-d'Olmes *Thur, Sat;* Lavelanet *Wed, Fri;* Mazères *Thur;* Mirepoix *Thur, Sat (veg);* Pamiers *Tue, Thur, Sat;* St-Girons *Sat AM;* Seix *Thur.*

PYRÉNÉES-ORIENTALES

Banyuls-sur-Mer *Tue, Thur, Sun AM;* Le Boulou *Thur;* Cerbère *Daily AM Wed;* Collioure *Wed, Sun AM;* Estagel *Daily ex Sun;* Ille-sur-Têt *Daily ex Sun;* Maury *Daily ex Sun;* Millas *Tue, Thur;* Port Vendres *Sat;* Perpignan *Daily;* Prades *Tue.*

AUDE

Carcassonne *Daily;* Castelnaudary *Mon;* Chalabre *Sat;* Labastide-d'Anjou *Thur, Sat;* Lézignan-Corbières *Wed;* Limoux *Tue, Fri;* Narbonne *Thur, Languedoc Exhibition May.*

HÉRAULT

Agde *Thur;* Balaruc-les-Bains *Tue, Fri;* Bédarieux *Mon;* Bessan *Tue, Sun;* Béziers *Fri;* Cazouls-les-Beziers *Tue;* Florensac *Tue;* Ganges *Tue, Fri;* Lamalou-les-Bains *Tue;* Marseillan *Tue;* Montagnac

Fri; Montpellier *Tue (wine);*
Palavaz-les-Flots *Sun;*
Pézenas *Sat;* Pomérols *Mon.*

GARD

Beaucaire *Olive Market Thur
& Sun (Oct-Dec);* Beauvoisin
Daily; Bessèges *Thur;*
Calvisson *Grape Market Aug
Truffle Market Tue Nov-
March;* Clarenzac *Olive
Market Wed & Sat Oct 5-end
of harvest, Grape Market
daily in season;* Congénies
*Olive Market Tue & Fri (Sept-
Jan);* Connaux *Daily (April-
June)* Jonquières-et-
St-Vincent *Fri (fish), Tue, Fri,
cherries May-15 June, grapes
Aug-15 Sept;* Les Mages *Fri;*
Marguerittes *Mon, Tue, Thur,
Fri (olives);* Meynes *Daily
(asparagus, fruit April - June);*
Montfrin *Tue, daily (fruit &
veg May-Jan);* Nîmes *Daily;*
Redessan *April-June
(cherries), July-Sept (grapes);*
Rochefort-du-Gard *Late
Tomato Market 2/3 times a
week 20 Sept-1 Dec;* St-
Gervasy *Asparagus Market
April-June;* St-Jean-du-Gard
Tue, Sat (summer); Uzès *Sat;*
Vers-Pont-du-Gard *Mon,
Wed, Fri, Cherry Market daily
in season.*

LOZÈRE

Aumont Aubrac *Fri (May);*
Barre des-Cévennes *Sat;* Berc
Thur; La Bastide-Puylaurent
Wed; Le Bleymard *Sat;* La
Candurgue *Tue;* Chanac *Thur;*
Florac *Mon & Fri;* Ispagnac
Tue & Sun; Malzieu-Ville *Sat;*
Marvejols *Sat;* Meyrueis *Thur,
Sat;* Nasbinals *Tue.*

PROVENCE

SERVANTS OF THE SUN

"In which we...
•Find more water than we thought and little places in the country - with bread for dinner...
•Return to the village baker with leftovers...
•Discover the mistake of modern chefs - and how not to recognize onions...
•Consider who sells the most authentic food...
•Give some pâtés the bird, find a saltwater caviar, the best hay in France and the laws that inhibit restaurants...
•Eat a provençal truffle under the moon and meet a kissing cousin...
•Find capers being cut in bottles, get an earful of puddings, and cook for a village lunch...
•Visit the three wise virgins who look after their oil, and enumerate a Christmas pudding..."

The French say the Mediterranean ends where the olive trees stop growing. But when I drive south, I reverse that. For me the Mediterranean starts where I see my first grove of olive trees. They are a sure sign that wines have changed to pink, olive oil is replacing butter and pork fat, and a more masterful southern sun commands a veritable cornucopia of fruits, flowers and vegetables to swell and to sweeten.

Between those first ancient signposts and the first sight of the Mediterranean, the wild scrubland of the *garrigue* partners voluptuous manicured fields to become both herb garden and perfumery. Almond trees succor pastry chefs and confectioners. Bees buzz honey from lavender and mountain flowers, from jasmine and orange blossom, honey that once preserved the luscious glacé fruits of Apt but now drenches cakes and pastries or makes the black nougat (*nougat noir*) of St-Tropez. In summer there will be wild raspberries, in spring wild asparagus and mushrooms to join *limaçons*, snails to be cooked and sucked directly from their shells, and in winter black truffles, if you know where to look. And then, affirmation that I've arrived, the fish, noticeably better in the cooler weather, but always welcome for its color and freshness and unfamiliar flavors.

Bruised by the sun and battered on her leading edge by tourism, the south of France is pictured by many an enthusiastic eater as an Elizabeth David or Peter Mayle chapter come to life, redolent of garlic and tomatoes, of dishes robust with olive oil and summer's herbs. The reality is often startling in its subtlety, restrained and simple.

In culinary terms there were three areas of Provence until rail and irrigation canals began to give some sense of unity. Down by the Mediterranean, which was clean enough to swim in only when fashion dictated you did not, they ate well, of fish.

Because there were fishing boats and a tradition of trade with other coasts of the Mediterranean, olive oil was imported for repacking: in such ports as Nice or Aigues-Mortes (when it was on the sea), taste was developed for the basil and pine nuts of Genoa, oranges from Majorca, the pastas of the Maghreb and Southern Italy, and for the cloves and cinnamon that came west through Venice.

Behind the coast the swallows swoop over the orange-pantiled villages of valleys and small plains where garlic, chard, chickpeas, peaches and cherries grew. This was the best place to drink, too, for vines are jollied by the sun into producing lakes of wine with high alcohol levels. "Here, m'sieu," I was often told, "we are servants of the sun. It is too hot to grow elegant white wines, too hot to drink heavier red wines. We had to choose grapes that would yield us a rosé wine, to be drunk cool with whatever we were eating."

Further inland, past the *sere garrigue* of scrub and pebble, where the hills begin to swell into the mountains which will eventually become Alps, olive trees rule, deep-rooted on fragile terraces constructed to conserve what little topsoil has accumulated over the centuries. Olive trees also serve to protect smaller crops and shade the goats, sheep and few chickens needed for protein. Cattle were virtually unknown in Provence until after World War I - there was little pasture for them to graze on and even less for them to drink.

Surprisingly, there is plenty of water throughout the area, for it is one great drain for the snows of the Alps. But it is not widespread, or flowing in a tracery of rivers and rivulets. It is not close to the surface, and worse, it is rarely where you would choose both to live and garden. . . . In Provence it was almost unknown, historically, to live where your food grew, and it is thus that there are only rare examples of great country houses or estates here. Any travelers' tales of luscious profusion are based on the gardens fed directly by the Rhône, the Durance or few other rivers.

The laboring men and women who were the backbone of Provence built a society that relied on "little places in the country" - *cabanons*. Groups of families would first settle in a place with freshwater springs that was also easy to protect with fortifications, hence the great number of hilltop villages, each with central wells fed by the even higher Alps. From this fortified family retreat you had regularly to journey to your parcel of agricultural land, often far enough away to require you to shelter in your cabanon several nights, and to carry with you what you expected to eat or drink. The simplicity of bread scraped with garlic and dribbled with his own oil was all a tired man could bring himself to prepare. The luckier might add a salted anchovy or two to make *anchoïade*, but all would have wine.

Once back in the village, you enjoyed the convenience of a central baker, whose large bread ovens would cook the dishes impossible to handle

CUISINE PROVENÇALE

Over in the Var, there's a school with no lecturer that happens in a karate club's hall in La Roquebrussane, the hometown of Reboul, author of one of the bibles of provençal food (*La Cuisinière Provençale*, 1895). Here local housewives cook with your assistance and you learn at their apron stings, as they did from their mothers. Many of the recipes aren't provençal, some aren't authentic - but it's a terrifically entertaining way to spend a morning, and you'll learn buckets if your French is good enough. The small cost includes lunch (three-course menu), prepared during the morning and upon which most of the villagers descend like vultures. With the long tables, local wine and some home-made *vin cuit* or *vin d'oranges* as an apéritif, it's the closest you'll ever be to village life without living there.

This remarkable experience is yours for a whole week once a month from February to November, but only on Wednesdays during August. For details, contact the energetic Madame Caulet (whose husband is the local doctor), Chemin de la Palu, 83136 La Roquebrussane, Tel: (94) 86 93 36.

degree of culinary unity in the area.

It is a fascinating exercise to ask old people what they consider the real tastes of the south to be. Universally, they will first indicate spit-roasted game and birds, for the south was once crammed with game and songbirds. But just as frosts regularly murder the olives, forests have burned and suffocated their inhabitants, and as food the fat songbirds are now forbidden by EC law. *Brouillard*, scrambled eggs thick with black truffles, is another nomination, and so, less surprisingly, are the sharp tangs of thyme and of summer savory (*sarriette*); most older housewives maintain that today's chefs and cooks use too many herbs and that, properly, none should be recognizable in a finished dish, not even onion.

When you discover the living food of the south it is unlikely to be where you thought it might be. If, as seems fair to me, it is food based solely on the wide range of fresh local produce then the galaxy of innovative starred chefs - such as Roger Vergé at Mougins - may well be more provençal than the auberges you seek so diligently in the countryside; almost 70 percent of French frozen vegetables are used in such small places, and their eggplant and garlic, cucumbers and tomatoes - even their oils and olives - have come from North Africa because they are cheaper. The food is not necessarily less good, it simply isn't provençal.

The real food of the south is warmer and more subtle than the dry land or the million-dollar excess of hamburgers, pizza and chips of the coast, and the wine will be smoother and more sophisticated. Today there will be butter and cream and oils other than olive. Be prepared to be seduced, but beware, for the sun-ripe nectarine on a roadside stall is probably from an American tree, and the luscious tomatoes from Spain . . .

over the open fires of a provençal kitchen, common still in many a tall village house. The baker would, for instance, cook and brown the stuffed, olive-oil bathed vegetables - the *gratins* and *farcis* which were the canny country way to use up leftover pieces of treasured meat from the spit.

Essentially, the people of the south traditionally relied on the same three products that had sustained and encouraged the growth of the great civilizations of the Mediterranean - the olives, wheat and wine the Romans had perfected for them. For those with no fish, there was a little cheese and milk from sheep and goats, but not until the tomato arrived from the New World - only in the 19th century - was there any

Charcuterie

Although many a southern family was once sustained by a pig or two in the yard, I cannot think pigs have ever been as important here as in other regions, and thus you will find true local charcuterie difficult to identify. Most pork seems to have been converted into salted products and then used in cooking, so any *saucisson sec* you find is likely to have come in from the southwest, from the Lyonnais, or, if you are lucky, from the chestnut-fed porkers of Corsica.

Generally, what charcuterie Provence made had two distinguishing features: it was stored in oil and more commonly contained blanched greens, chard or spinach - and, naturally, herbs. Such a mixture of pork and greens is cailettes, which is likely to be served to you often. The air-dried saucisson which has endured is from Arles. Both the Camargue and the uplands of Provence are spoken of as producing excellent air-dried hams. Worth looking for, but be wary in any place that does not look as though it caters only for locals.

WORTH FINDING

- **Cailettes/gayettes**: Meatballs of chopped pork liver or slices of liver plus blanched chard or spinach, flavored with herbs, baked in a terrine and eaten cold.
- **Saucisson d'Arles**: Air-dried sausage made traditionally from 75% pork and 25% beef from the nearby Camargue. Distinctive flavor comes from the *lardons* included, from the quality of the natural gut used and its spicing with whole black peppercorns, paprika and garlic. Much is still made authentically, and hung to ripen in *séchoir*.
- **Pâté de merles**: blackbirds or *de grives* (thrushes). Their manufacture is now forbidden, though you will still be able to taste these pâtés from cans. Worth doing once, but even the whole birds preserved in a farce taste only of the pork which surrounds them. I suspect the only way to enjoy such flesh is spit-roasted.

Fish & Shellfish

The arc of Mediterranean from Spain's Costa Brava to the Côte d'Azur is one of the most important areas in the world for anchovies; they're just as good as sardines when young, but by the time July comes, housewives along the coast know they are good for salting and pissaladière, a type of local pizza, or anchoïade.

In today's world, there's no longer need to come south to eat these and other well-known specialities - red and gray mullet, bream, mussels, conger, sea bass or langoustines. Instead you should look for different ways of enjoying them or, better, discover something you can't get back home. Try the mussels of Marseilles with saffron and rice from the Camargue, the raw, iodine-perfumed pulp inside potato-shaped violets in Toulon, the telline, a sort of clam of the Camargue, or the famed, rich stew catigau of Martigue's freshwater eel. Look, too, for grilled gurnard (grondin), or fresh tuna, or rascasse, a basic ingredient of bouillabaisse, served with capers, an important local flavoring. Best for firm, sweet flesh, in my view, is the chapon.

There is one essential rule for enjoying Mediterranean fish - they should live in water but die in oil, olive oil. Fennel, bay and lemon are the most authentic flavorings with chopped, mixed parsley and garlic, and perhaps onion, commonly for color except in the Camargue.

FISHY TREATS

Self-catering in villas is one of the best ways to give yourself fishy treats. Once you've exhausted the familiar, here are some of the un-familiar you might like to bring home from the market. Sometimes you'll see them in restaurants, and you'll encourage the others by ordering them.

Clams (clovisses or palourdes) and limpets (patelles) may be found raw on platters of seafood. Sea urchins (oursins) provide a rich roe, but favouilles are small crabs and some people eat them all. Seiche, supion, muscardins and poulpe are all local names for types of cephalod or squid-octopus related things. The spinard and the esquinade (especially associated with Nice) are spider-crabs, the former being rather giant-sized and more difficult to eat than the latter, and thus usually cheaper; both might be served with a vinaigrette rather than mayonnaise.

More daring are sea anemones (orties) which should be stripped of their tentacles, marinated in vinegar, cooked in oil and served with lemon or in omelettes and fritters.

Poutine is the fry or alevins of sardines (although some local fishermen disagree with this) and used like whitebait. But before they become poutine, the eggs can be found attached to the shaded side of rocks close to the shore between April and July. Easily collected now you know where to look, they are skinned gently then fried in olive oil, a provençal saltwater caviar.

Best of all is the saupe, a pale yellowish fish with brilliant golden stripes, sometimes sold as fausse (false) daurade (sea bream). It is generally despised, for dining exclusively on seaweed it is thought to develop a pronounced flavor. The trick is to scrape away the black lining of the gut cavity. Then, baked with a splash of white wine, saupe rewards you by being le seul poisson avec un vrai goût de la mer - the only fish with a true taste of the sea. I've tried it - it's true.

BOUILLABAISSE

This is a saffron- and oil-rich fish stew, originating in Marseilles. The name supposedly comes from the French words for "to boil" and "to lower": for once the cauldron had boiled it was taken from the heat.

There is no common consensus about the recipe except that it must not be served with "eyes" of oil on the surface, indicating the mixture had not been boiled to emulsify the oil with the other liquids, and that fennel and saffron are

---

WORTH FINDING

• **Aïoli**: Mayonnaise stiff with garlic. Commonly served with salt cod (morue) or raw vegetables (crudités), when it is aïoli garni.

• **Anchoïade**: The basic staple of yesteryear. Many variations exist on a combination of mashed salted anchovies, olive oil and garlic on bread. In Corsica they would, and may still, add figs.

• **Boumiane**: Anchovy-flavored tomato and eggplant stew.

• **Bourride**: Important fish stew based only on firm, white-fleshed fish (congre, lotte, chapon). Served over toasted bread with rouille, a garlic-flavored mayonnaise into which some of the cooking stock is mixed, together with chili or other hot red pepper.

• **Boutargue/Poutargue/Caviar de Martigues**: Great and now expensive delicacy, this is the salted, dried and pressed roe of the gray mullet (mulet) served sliced. A very ancient thing; made in summer, it lasts only until November.

• **Brandade de morue**: Paste of soaked and poached salt cod whisked with warm oilve oil, milk (recently) and garlic. Truffles sometimes used to be added. If the cod has not been properly prepared by a very long soaking, this will be the filthiest taste experience of your life.

• **Catigau d'Anguilles/Catigot**: Eel stew with tomatoes, garlic and red wine, indicating it is from the Camargue. Also includes onions, celery, bay, orange peel and cloves.

• **Daube de muscardins**: Cuttle-fish in their own ink with tomatoes, red wine, etc. Considered one of the Camargue's greatest treats.

• **Homard**: Lobster. In high season, the best ones retreat from the sun. If you insist, look for small ones with dark purple shell (when uncooked) from Corsica; their color indicates they have not descended to the depths, and the fierce sun will have darkened their shells and sweetened their flesh.

• **Loup de mer (bar) au fenouil**: Sea bass cooked with fennel; an expensive cliché but worth it once or twice.

• **Pissalat**: Condiment of salted anchovies perfumed with cloves, and olive oil.

• **Soupe de poissons**: Fish soup. Basic ingredients are poissons du rocher, a tumble of tiny bright fish from the rock bottom. Generally these are stewed then puréed. Usually served with grilled bread and a rouille. Order it only in a reputable restaurant, or if you have enough French, ensure it is rich with flavor rather than red-hot with pepper, when it is a waste of time.

essential. You may find grudging agreement that the dish should include at least some *rascasse, chapon, galinette,* a little *congre,* perhaps some *rouget* and some *St-Pierre.* But opinions divide furiously on whether there should be shellfish or crustaceans.

Remembering this was originally a hearty meal created to reward fishermen at the end of their toil, it is difficult to emulate its manufacture properly on shore. The sailors threw "one for the pot" into the cauldron as they fished; and as the fish sat with some olive oil, and some fennel, some herbs and onion, there was an exchange of flavors as they marinated in juices of their own creation. This marinating of the ingredients seems authentically to be more important than precisely which fish are included and in what proportion. Cooking over a wood fire, so that a flavor of smoke is absorbed, is largely a thing of the past, but wondrous it must have been, from reports.

Once marinated, the *bouillabaisse* is boiled, and in today's more sophisticated times, finer-fleshed fish are added last: the broth and fish are served separately. To be honest, the fish is almost always overcooked (paying for a bouillabaisse that includes lobster is lunacy) and few people who have a palate order it twice.

The Toulonnais version always includes mussels and potatoes, the ingredients about which locals argue most. Although now common, it is not correct to accompany the dish with *rouille* as this properly belongs to *bourride.*

Meat, Poultry & Game

The south of France has never been a place for large grazing animals, neither cattle nor horses. Even though there were and are domestic pigs, most of the flesh eaten regularly was game, game birds or songbirds.

Real treats came from domestic animals, the most important being sheep. From the highlands down to the plains, you'll find herds of sheep everywhere. The sheep of Provence have been famed for the succulence of their flesh for centuries, and historically, many of the most envied daubes or stews of the area are properly based on lamb or mutton. It could never be claimed that these specialities were staples, except perhaps for the pieds et paquets of Marseilles; most ewes were kept exclusively for milk, to make into such fresh cheeses as brousses. When they were past that, the flesh

WORTH FINDING

• *Alouettes sans têtes*: What we call beef or veal rolls or roulades - thin slices of meat wrapped around a stuffing and braised. Also known as *paupiettes.*

• *Boeuf en daube*: See *Daube.*

• *Broufade*: A piquant local type of stew marinated like a daube but using rather more vinegar, plus those local standbys, anchovies and capers.

• *Canard aux olives*: Duck with olives. The olives are usually blanched and added towards the end of the cooking and so do not add much to the basis of the dish, but delicious nonetheless. Lamb with olives is better.

• *Civet*: A stew or *daube,* ideally of game, in which the blood is used as a thickener; but this is rare these days.

• *Daube*: A stew, usually of beef nowadays, cooked very slowly in a locally made earthenware pot called a *daubière.* A daube would traditionally be cooked overnight in the kitchen fire's ashes, thus an authentic daube must be cooked long and slow. The cooking method explains why they were often only eaten cold, in their own jelly, the next day. The meat must always marinate awhile in vinegar and oil. Fresh herbs, salt pork, a little onion and some garlic are the basic flavorings and red,

white or rosé wine is added to the cooking later. Root vegetables or leeks have no place in a proper daube, but some orange peel is a common provençal addition. Some old recipes also include a few cloves and a piece of cinnamon. Wild mushrooms might be added, fresh or dried, if available. Beef being fairly recent down here, the daube you find in Avignon made with mutton or lamb is more likely to be authentic.

• *Escargots à la sucarelle/ Limaces/Limaçons*: A small white provençal snail (not a *petit-gris*). Part of the shell is cut off so when served with a spicy stew of tomatoes and sausage, you can pick them up one by one and suck them; also known as *à l'arlésienne.*

• *Estouffade*: A type of pot roast of a piece of meat with herbs and other aromatics; the container is, properly, hermetically sealed; also called *étuvée.*

• *Lapin à la sarriette*: Rabbit is popular in many ways but the most typical is rabbit braised in wine with savory.

• *Pieds et paquets/Piedpaquet*: Sheep's feet cooked with tied packets of tripe. Don't leave Marseilles without eating them at least once.

• *Râble de lièvre*: Saddle of hare, most often flavored with juniper berries.

was of little use even to themselves. Male lambs invariably found themselves welcomed directly onto the spit, for the gigot of Easter, which is universal still.

There are two distinct types of lamb or mutton to look for. The sheep from Sisteron, fed on the mountain herbs and grasses of the uplands, and those from the commune of Arles, largest in France, especially from Nîmes and the plains of the Camargue to the west and of Alpilles and the Cau to the east. Arlésien grass and hay (foin) is so fragrant that such culinary luminaries as Gault Millau have long suggested it should be granted a protective AOC rating! It gives flesh such flavor that the pré-salé animals of the north are rendered effete and bland by comparison - or so any red-blooded Arlésien will argue!

Goats are kept for milk, cheese and meat, but they are much less important than sheep. Uncontrolled shooting for sport and ill-advised culling to protect crops means you'll be lucky to be served local game anywhere but private homes, yet if you are well inland in late summer, autumn or winter, who knows? Shooting parties are back as the forests refill with animals after the decimation of recent

THE TREE THAT WILL NOT DIE

If you cut me, you make me more beautiful. If you pull me out, you hurt me. Only if you destroy me completely do I die.

Provençal Proverb

The gnarled olive tree - its leaves symbolic of peace and love, its fruits of resurrection and renewal, its oil used for baptisms - thrives only on a narrow border of sea-lapped land. It can't grow at heights and won't grow far inland. It is the touchstone of provençal life, and the oil mill, unchanged in its function, remains essential to every-day life.

The olive tree's reputation is based on its reliability, for nothing short of dynamite can guarantee the death of one. Even the disastrous snows of 1985 killed the trees only above the ground.

Both green and black olives come from the same tree, for green olives are simply unripe ones. Some varieties are good both green and ripe, others better as one or the other.

Green olives are usually gathered about the end of August for by autumn the fruit will be turning violet. The finest black olives are only truly ripe in the coldest months of winter and their harvest can be a raw, chill task. The less common wrinkled olives are the raisins of the olive world, left on the trees until the new season's sun begins to desiccate them and concentrate their flavor.

The *Lucques* and *Nyons* are considered the *grandes dames* of olives, but there is also the *manzanille*, the *sevillane*, the *turquoise*, *sigoise*, *pansue* and *royale*, *tanche*, *aglandau*, *cayon* . . . the list is as long as for any other fruit. The markets of Nîmes are an important center for stuffed green olives; Nyons and Carpentras for black ones in brine. Menton olives grow especially big and make a luscious oil.

GREEN OLIVES
• *La Picholine*: Small, elongated and pointed. Fine, savory flesh proportionately generous for size of stone. It keeps a long time in brine and is harvested in October in the Gard, Hérault, Bouches-du-Rhône and Pyrénées-Orientales.
• *La Lacques*: Elongated, rather curved, pointed tip; sometimes dented in the curve. The fine flesh parts easily from the small stone. Gathered in October in Hérault and Aude.
• *La Salonenque*: Pear-shaped, but usually broken for use in cooking, where the slight bitterness it retains is welcome. Harvested in September and October in Bouches-du-Rhône.

BLACK OLIVES
• *Nyons/Tanches*: Round, heart-shaped with large stone and superb flesh. It ripens first to a violet color and then deepens to a rich plum-black. Fully ripe in December and January in Drôme and Vaucluse.
• *Le Cailletier/Olives de Nice*: A little olive with shining black skin, rarely seen outside Provence. Very perfumed flavor and the proper one to use in Niçoise cooking. Ripe in February or March and grown only in the Alpes-Maritimes.

Fruits & Vegetables

forest fires. There are certainly enough wild boar (sangliers) about Draguignan and Brignoles to be a threat to the young shoots of the vines, a favorite snack. One nameless restaurant did serve me a pâté de sanglier, but it was apparently illegal to do so. Extraordinarily, laws of hygiene prohibit restaurateurs dealing directly with small producers of specialty products and then selling them. But wild rabbit (lapin de la garenne) or, closer to the coast, farigoulette if it has dined upon wild thyme, and hare (lièvre) flavored with local juniper berries are commonly offered on menus; hare from Ventoux is recommended. Poultry does not thrive here, but some ducks do, and get served with green olives. Quails (caille), to be spit roast or barbecued in vine leaves, and guinea fowl (pintadeau) are farmed here and there; some turkey too.

Travelers in the Camargue, are the only ones likely to try local beef, usually charcoal grilled. The flesh of the bulls of the Camargue is well reputed, but as the ritual bullring fights do not end in the animal's death, this is harder to test.

The real glory of the meat here is less what it is than how it is prepared, cooked very long and very slowly, with a piece of orange peel to blend the herbs and wine, and to add a haunting tang. These are the daubes, estouffades, civets and broufades which never seem quite right in summer, but which make being here in autumn or winter so very rewarding.

In Aix-en-Provence there were golden zucchini blossoms to stuff and steam or fry; in Cannes Old Town armfuls of fresh herbs to take as gifts; in Nice in mid-summer early champignons rosés, a rich wild mushroom from the woods, marvelous to find for it keeps its texture and shape when cooked; outside the walls of Aigues-Mortes in the Camargue there were barrels and buckets and tins and jars of green and black and violet olives each differently flavored and marinated, first to sample and then to copy in the jars in the boot of my car; in Les Arcs tiny new broad beans (fèves) were to eat raw, dipped into grated parmesan as the Romans did; and in the square of Méounes, fragile stems of wild asparagus - this is how many of my memories of Provence start, with the specialities I bought from its markets. The most vivid are of a Sunday morning spent in the gigantic ribbon of stalls along the Cours Lafayette in Toulon, where I discovered stall after stall of white peaches and nectarines (called brugnons blancs if there is a clingstone), fruit I thought came only in cans at Christmas time. Two days earlier I had been honored, given a lustrous black provençal truffle by the woman who had first found it. I wanted to eat it in Provence and to prepare a meal of local produce to enhance and surround it.

That night, with the moon hung full above the vineyards, we ate under a bay tree. The peaches and nectarines were sliced, dribbled with raspberry vinegar (an old thing here, where raspberries still grow wild), topped with mint and served on slices of the sweetest air-dried ham there is, from Corsica. Then I cooked fresh noodles, made with local wheat, and bought in Toulon's covered market. The night before we had eaten quail barbecued in vine leaves, one of the few culinary uses for the leaves here; the birds' bones had been making a rich, dramatically reduced stock while I shopped. Half the truffle perspired its fragrance into this sauce for hours, and now I sliced the rest into the sauce too and, as its perfume ballooned, poured it warm, but not hot onto the pasta. Then a salad, with raw plum tomatoes for the first time, and a little brousse, a little more wine from our friends from Domaine de Chaberts ... it had been a perfect provençal meal, and day. And the only time I have enjoyed (or detected?) the flavor of black truffle ...

But only in the last 35 years, with the coming of irrigation canals, has the south become a garden of orchards sweet with the perfume of apricots in Vaucluse, with cherries in Olargues and Remoulins. There had been some - and perfumed violet figs and melons in Cavaillon - but now everything can grow, and flourish. The paradox is that this fertility cannot fully be exploited, either to service the local tourism or France itself, for what is not flourishing is agriculture. Most of the land remains divided into small jealously held family plots, so the benefits of modern bulk harvesting and handling procedures cannot be used to

LOCAL PRODUCE

VEGETABLES

- **ARTICHOKE** *artichaut*
  Var: *Blanc Hyperois, Violet du Chrysanthème*
  March to June (most important)
  Dep: Var, Bouches-du-Rhône, Vaucluse.
  Hyères is the most famous center, followed by Marseille and Cavallion.

- **CABBAGE** *chou*
  Var: pointed varieties, *Tête de Pierre, Châteaurenard*
  All year, peak March/April
  Dep: Bouches-du-Rhône, Vaucluse
  Surprisingly, Bouches-du-Rhône is the country's biggest producer.

- **CARROT** *carotte*
  Var: *Touchon, Nantaise*
  New carrots August to September, matured until February
  Dep: Vaucluse, Bouches-du-Rhône

- **CAULIFLOWER** *choufleur*
  Var: spring varieties grown for harvesting in autumn: *Boule-de-Neige, Aramon, Rex*
  September to December

- **EGGPLANT** *aubergine*
  Var: *Violette du Barbanne* (green flesh), *de Toulouse* (white flesh)
  June to September (height)
  Dep: Bouches-du-Rhône, Vaucluse, Var, Alpes-Maritimes
  The Bouches-du-Rhône produces over 40% of all French eggplants; Carpentras and Cavaillon are major market centers.

- **GARLIC** *ail*
  Var: *Rose du Var, d'Italie, Fructidor, Rosé de Lautrec*
  Harvested mid-July to mid-August
  Dep: Vaucluse, Bouches-du-Rhône
  Vaucluse is one of the top three production zones. Provençal garlic is generally smaller-bulbed than that of Drôme and the Rhône valley. Cavaillon specializes in fresh garlic, Aix-en-Provence in dried. Vaucluse specializes in white garlic, Bouches-du-Rhône in white and pink varieties.

- **LETTUCE** *laitue/chicorée*
  Var: every conceivable type
  All year, except summer
  Dep: Bouches-du-Rhône, Alpes-Maritimes, Vaucluse.
  Bouches-du-Rhône is the second biggest producer after the Pyrénées-Orientales; the Alpes-Maritimes are on the second rung.

- **ONION** *oignon*
  Var: various
  Mid-May to mid-September
  Dep: Bouches-du-Rhône, Vaucluse
  The region around Aubagne (Bouches-du-Rhône) is the most important for white onions. Fresh ones will appear as early as spring. Cavaillon and Avignon are major market centers.

- **PEPPER** *poivron/piment doux*
  Var: *Gros Carré de Cavaillon*
  June to mid-November
  Dep: Vaucluse, Bouches-du-Rhône, Alpes-Maritimes, Var
  The Var and Bouches-du-Rhône produce 70% of the national crop. Cavaillon, Carpentras, Châteaurenard, Marseille and Salon de Provence are major markets, Berre et Crau and Aubagne are major growing areas.

- **SHALLOT** *échalote*
  Var: various
  Fresh June to August or so
  Dep: Vaucluse, Bouches-du-Rhône
  Not a major crop locally but the long, wine-streaked shallots found here are considered the sweetest and most succulent of any.

- **TURNIP** *navets*
  October through to April
  Dep: Bouches-du-Rhône, Vaucluse
  Two of the four most important zones in France.

- **TOMATO** *tomate*
  Var: different every year

make prices competitive. Although the area exports internally most of the apples, pears, zucchini, spinach, cherries, apricots, parsley, peaches and figs grown in France, it does not dominate the market; the local tourist industry largely feeds it fodder with fruit and vegetables imported more cheaply from North Africa and Spain and Italy.

A complication for the visitor wishing to luxuriate in the produce of the south is that many varieties - sometimes the best - aren't French in origin. Most yellow peaches and nectarines, most cherries and many soft fruits are American or Canadian strains. But a judicious peek at the boxes or the price labels will usually tell you the variety, so you can pick French varieties and that's why these are listed in this book.

The dearth of meat in the south meant historically that once you had nibbled on almonds and olives, vegetable dishes absolutely dominated first and main courses, in soups and in stews like ratatouille, in gratins and in farcis of zucchini, eggplant and, latterly, tomatoes. The equal paucity of ovens in most houses meant that fruit, fresh or dried, was and is the most common way to end a meal.

LOCAL PRODUCE

April to November: open-air from end June only
Dep: Vaucluse, Bouches-du-Rhône
Almost 40% of all French tomatoes are grown here.

- ZUCCHINI *courgette*
Mid-May to September.
Dep: Bouches-du-Rhône, Vaucluse, Var, Alpes-Maritimes
Bouches-du-Rhône produces almost 25% of the national crop.

FRUITS
- APPLES *pommes*
Var: *Reine de reinettes* (best in August)
Mid-July to November
Dep: Vaucluse, Bouches-du-Rhône.
Much of the product is the dratted Golden Delicious, but some Granny Smith is grown in Bouches-du-Rhône and Vaucluse which together produce about 20% of French apples.

- APRICOT *abricot*
Var: *Hatif Colomer, Orange de Provence, Luizet, Rouget de Sernhac, Bergeron*
End July to mid-August
Dep: Vaucluse, Bouche-du-Rhône

- CHERRIES *cerises*
Var: *Bigarreau, Coeur de Pigeon, Napoléon*
Mid-May to early July

Dep: Vaucluse, Bouches-du-Rhône, Var
Vaucluse produces almost 25% of the national crop. Most varieties are not native. Biggest centers include Carpentras, Cavaillon, Châteaurenard, St-Didier and Vallegregues.

- GRAPES *raisins*
Var: Black: *Livan, Alphonse Lavalle, Muscat de Hambourg, Ribou*; White: *Gros Vert, Dattier de Beyrouth, Chasselas*
August to October, with later and earlier crops
Dep: Vaucluse, Bouches-du-Rhône, Var

- MELON *melon*
Var: *Charentais, Galia, Ogen,* Honeydew and new types
May until October with peak July to mid-September
Dep: Vaucluse, Bouches-du-Rhône

- NECTARINES *nectarine/ brugnon*
Var: *Fuzalode* (white); yellow are all American varieties
Mid-July to mid-August
Dep: Bouches-du-Rhône, Vaucluse, Corsica.
Crau et Contat, Châteaurenard, Senas and Salon are the centers in Bouches-du-Rhône, Cavaillon and Carpentras in Vaucluse. Basically similar,

nectarines differ from *brugnons* by having a free stone.

- PEACH *pêche*
Var: White: *Genadix*; Yellow: all imported varieties
June to early September
Dep: Bouches-du-Rhône, Vaucluse, Var
Avignon is one of the biggest centers.

- PEAR *poire*
Var: *Guyots, Williams, Alexandrine Douillard,* plus some winter pears - *Passe-Crassane*
Peaks July to September but continues until end November
Dep: Bouches-du-Rhône, Vaucluse, Alpes-Maritime.
Bouches-du-Rhone grows almost 20% of French pears.

- PLUMS *prune*
Var: all yellow or green types generally French.
Red-fleshed Italian variety starts with July;
Japanese varieties ripen about June 15th and other types continue until early August
Vaucluse and the two other départements produce almost half the national crop.

- STRAWBERRIES *fraises*
Var: *Fayette, Belrubi*
Approx: March to May
Dep: Vaucluse, Bouches-du-Rhône

A summer vegetable I recommend you try is Swiss chard (blette), like a tastier spinach but with a broad white stalk that is often cooked and eaten separately in a sauce or gratin, but is sweet enough to slice thinly when raw into a salad; especially look for sweet tarts of blette leaves (tarte aux blettes). This is the kissing cousin of an old British dish made with spinach and sometimes called Florentine Tart that was popular from the time of the Crusaders right up to until late 19th century. Later in the year, cardoons (cardons), a member of the thistle family, become so important to some families that Christmas is not complete without a gratin of them.

Not unexpectedly, the EC is having its effect in Provence and there is the common battle about which varieties of which may be grown. But the most startling sight in the new provençal agriculture was self-generated, in the Camargue. It had been simply swampy and unproductive, but wildly beautiful with its white horses and wild bulls and sensational birdlife. Now areas are being semi-drained and used to grow rice. It's not the best rice in the world, although the red strain is quite interesting (see below), but it is perfectly usable, and after a few year's production, each paddy field is further drained and turned into orchard, garden or pasture. It's a bit hard on the succulent eels that liked the Camargue the way it was, but once they have been simmered to the local taste, the flavor of the Camargue's rice is the perfect though poignant partner.

The Camargue also boasts a vast area of shallow lagoons producing salt of high quality. The harvest takes place in September, before autumn's heavy rains. The salt is stacked into magnificent white mountains, then graded and packed.

RED RICE

The farmers of the Camargue had never had success growing the red wild rice indigenous to their region; the stalk sheds its grains when they ripen, making it virtually impossible to harvest. However, in 1980 René Griotto discovered that, while he wasn't looking, some of this wild rice had struck up a relationship with the short grain variety he had been growing and they decided to become one. From this single stalk, he harvested what grains he could and planted them. In 1992 René began selling the result commercially and remains the only source of what has become known as Camargue red rice. An interesting addition to the larder, and a great base for pilafs and stuffing mixtures, Camargue red rice has a sweet, earthy flavor and a chewy texture. In fact, it tastes remarkably similar to what it is: a cross between wild and short-grained brown rice. If you don't like them, you probably won't like them. If you do, you will.

WORTH FINDING

• *Aïgo boulido*: Garlic-flavored stock (often just water boiled with garlic in it) served over oil-soaked bread, either as a light supper or, often, as a quasi-medicine.

• *Artichauts à la barigoule*: Can be one of two dishes, both based on very young spring artichokes. They are either stuffed with, among other things, a special local mushroom called barigoule or simply braised in wine and oil with a garlic and parsley stuffing.

• *Caviar Niçois*: A purée of anchovy fillets, black olives, garlic, thyme, mustard and oil - clearly a relation of *tapénade* (qv).

• *Farcis*: Stuffed vegetables cooked in oil. The fillings were always based on restes (leftovers) and may still be, so only buy from what seems to be a reputable and busy shop.

• *Pan bagna/bagnat*: Speciality of Nice originally but now universal; indispensible for picnics. Split a long or short bread roll, sprinkle with olive oil, fill with mixed salad, and leave to marinate.

• *Pissaladière*: Although tempting to call it the pizza of Provence, it isn't quite right. The topping should consist of onion purée cooked in olive oil, flavored with anchovies and a few olives. Any other addition, especially tomato, makes it a pizza.

• *Pistou*: Provençal pesto made with a paste of basil, garlic, sharp cheese and olive oil and used in a bean soup.

• *Ratatouille/ratatouia*: Essentially a stew of summer vegetables in olive oil (with no other liquid), made with whatever vegetables are most abundant. Eggplants, tomatoes, zucchini, red and green peppers, lots of good oil and garlic are the basics, plus some onion. Herbs are not traditional or necessary if you have been generous with the oil. If you make some and it really needs a lift, basil works. And if you want to keep it for a while, you must boil it up 24 hours after you make it or it will ferment.

• *Salade Niçoise*: Apparently not mentioned by any of the old food writers, which probably explains the many variations. Gault Millau nevertheless think it is established enough to say the real one is made from the following: segments (never slices) of tomato, radish, peppers, broad beans, onion, black olives, garlic, anchovies and a dressing made of olive oil and pounded anchovies. Modern versions seem to substitute green beans for the broad variety and tuna fish is a common addition, which is welcome if it is of a worthwhile quality.

• *Sauce poivrade*: Sharp pepper and shallot sauce with an effective amount of vinegar; for brochettes, game etc. Once thickened with blood.

• *Tapénade*: Something else called "poor man's caviar," but actually made more like Gentlemen's Relish. Although some sources say it is timelessly ancient, the much respected J-B Reboul says (on page 71 of *La Cuisinière Provençale*) that it was invented by "our friend Meynier at the Maison Doré in Marseille" . . . *Tapéno* is the Provençal dialect word for capers, for tapénade turns out to be not so much a purée of black olives but one of capers and olives. Olives, capers, anchovies and olive oil are the basics, but marinated tuna, lemon juice, and even English mustard are included in seemingly authentic recipes. It is used as a dip or a spread and is good with hard-boiled eggs.

• *Tarte aux blettes*: An important relic of the past, a sweetened but still rather savory open tart based on *blettes* (chard) or spinach. Here it is flavored with sugar, currants, pine-nuts and spices, sometimes set in an egg custard to bind it. Very Middle Eastern but traditionally here for aeons. Savory French versions include anchovies and olives.

TRUFFLING MATTERS

Yes, I was surprised to find truffles in Provence too, so thought if this section appeared here, instead of in the Dordogne, it might fire your imagination rather more, and be more likely to help you stop wasting money.

The essential information about black truffles (*tuber melanosporum*) is this - those in cans and glass jars are less than a pale shadow of them-selves; like canned foie gras, the fabled elegance of flavor is destroyed by the preserving process. They are just not worth the expense. Some that are semi-preserved in small glass jars, often privately, are marginally better for having been exposed to lesser heats. Don't expect culinary fireworks if you've bought, or used, the equivalent of damp squibs. In addition, the flavoring action of black truffles is a mysterious process, acting more as an enzymic catalyst. It must both be raw and sit in the food for some time if you are to get any result, or be gently poached or baked at a lowish temperature to be enjoyed by itself in generous amounts. It is mere posturing to slice canned truffle over something and to serve it straight away. You may as well slice a black olive or some dyed gelatin - some places do. And if all that weren't enough to put you off, there are black truffles and lesser black truffles and only the expert can really tell whether the warty black thing offered you is worth the money - there's no way your nose alone can do the job.

The truffle's widespread home ground is around the roots of certain white oak trees, truffle oaks (*chênes blancs truffés*), in an area around the edge of the Massif Central, roughly southwards from the Dordogne, then swinging in a curve through upper Languedoc

and Provence and up the Rhône Valley and into parts of Alsace. Opinions clash over whether there are varieties of black truffles or whether like other natural products, some are good and some are better; hence the arguments over the merits of truffles from this or that area. Yet often the reason for disappointment is the method of preservation.

Down the ages, the truffle harvest has swung slowly through a pattern of paucity or plenty; right now it is paucity. Only 50 years ago it was common to harvest 50kg/112lb a day (!) in Provence, and to buy a fistful for a few francs. Thus there are many folk memories of grating them thickly into omelettes or eggs scrambled in olive oil (*brouillard*), but only after the truffle had sat with the eggs for 24 hours to perfume them. Poached or baked truffles were sliced thickly into potato salads, and on Christmas Day into salads of wild leaves (*salade sauvage*). They were lavished raw into pâté mixtures, left uncooked overnight, chopped into the stuffings of game birds or sliced into matchsticks and poked under the skin of a gigot of lamb instead of garlic. You could even eat them whole, roasted in ashes.

The biggest stupidity of the truffle business is that they are in greatest demand for Christmas, when they are actually at their least interesting and barely ripe. The season begins in mid-November or so and continues until the middle of February, when they are ripest, most flavorsome, and cheapest. In most places, trained pigs or dogs are used to find the truffles, which may be as much as a foot underground; but most country folk out walking in likely spots will be seen tapping the ground with a

stick as they walk towards the sun. Once the light glitters on a disturbed swarm of tiny transparent flies, they've found a truffle.

Throughout the season, truffles straight from the ground might turn up at any market; but there are recognized truffle centers. If you go, expect little of the exuberance of the usual market. Nothing happens until an agreed time, often as late as 10:30. Until then most vendors will sit silently with pathetic ragged bundles, feigning disinterest. At a given sign, often a bell, their black diamonds will be revealed. If you have advice or nerve, you'll certainly save money on one hand, and by using fresh truffle will get far better value on the other. Carry them sealed in a jar full of rice, which prevents any damage, and keep them cool and dark and they'll last a few days easily. But if you are in a truffle area for some time, you may like to take the astonishing advice of some of the older inhabitants of the hill towns of the Var. They, traditionalists to a man, are now brushing and cleaning their truffles, wrapping them in foil - and deep freezing them. They are as good as fresh if defrosted rather quickly in warm olive oil. The far more fragrant, reliable and more expensive white truffle (*tuber magnatum*) is, strangely, more accessible in its short season, from October until the first snows of December. This is because it is always eaten raw, shaved thinly over eggs or rice or hot brioche, for instance, and thus you pay only for what you eat. White truffles are found in Savoie, especially around Chambéry.

Happy truffling. But if in doubt, go for the chocolate ones.

OLIVE OIL

Olive oil is one of the world's marvels. The best requires no processing other than cold pressing and will last for years in a cool, dark place. The great stone storage tanks of the old oil mills needed only to be drained annually, to remove any debris that may have settled, for the oil to last another year . . .

French olive oil has a lower acid content than that of other countries, but within each grade there will be enormous variations of flavor depending on the exact mixture of olives used, how ripe they were, even the temperature on the day they were picked. When you visit an oil mill on a quiet day, ask if you can sample the oil from several of the storage tanks. Each will be a different day's pressing and each one will taste a little different.

The word virgin or *vierge* indicates the oil has been obtained only by mechanical pressing, and that it has not been subsequently treated in any way. The insignia *"Huile de Provence"* is a guarantee of quality. In terms of quality it is generally considered that

the lower the acid content the better.

There are three types:
• *Vierge extra*: Irreproachable quality and flavor, and guaranteed not to have an acidity of more than 1%.
• *Vierge fine*: Equally irreproachable, but with an acidity of 1.5%.
• *Vierge, vierge courante* or *semi-fine*: Excellent quality, but with an acidity of up to 3%.

Huiles d'olives raffinées is oil made by refining virgin oil that originally had an unattractive taste or was too high in acidity. *Huile d'olives* pures is made by mixing virgin oil and refined oil, sometimes called Riviera oil.

Whenever you are in the south you won't be too far a drive from an oil mill, although they are by no means as common as winemakers. You'll easily be able to find their locations from tourist offices, but real enthusiasts should know that the oil of La Lacques, around the corner in Languedoc, is considered to be among the best.
Ets. Roger Michel is at Opio, straight up the D4 from

Antibes, passing through Biot (where you can see and buy the famous handblown glassware). There, at the 15th-century mill, you'll also find other regional products.

Much further west there are five mills north of Marseilles on either side of the A7. Closest is at La Fare-les-Oliviers, where local olives, *aglandaus* and *saurines*, combine to make a very individual oil. You might also go to Maussane-les-Alpilles, Mouriès, Beaumes-de-Venise and, perhaps best of all, Les Barronnies at Nyons.

But before you go, visit the *Musée de l'Olivier* in the château of Cagnes-sur-Mer. Or if you are in Provence during late July or August, head for Ampus to visit the fascinating private, free museum of Mon and Mme Martin, on the place de la Mairie. Open every afternoon during that time, it explains everything - history, culture, cultivation, olive pickling, oil pressing - even soap making.

THE HERBS & FLOWERS OF PROVENCE

The most successful indigenous plants of the south of France are those that meet the challenge of the sun with glossy reflective leaves, deep roots and a protective vapor of aromatic oils: sweet herbs. Once you reach the

south, herbs are likely to be uppermost in your mind, but don't expect them to be uppermost in flavoring your food, for the authentic way to use herbs here is with great restraint, so that they add savor without an independent obtrusive presence.

The mixture of herbs sold as *herbes de Provence* is nice,

and it is useful, but do not be misled by the inclusion of lavender or lavender flowers. Lavender is used, exceptionally, to flavor some sweets and a liqueur, but its inclusion in this herb mixture is to disguise the low quality of the other ingredients.

Basil is very popular but apart from its role in *pistou*, a version of the Genoese *pesto* that you particularly find in Nice, it had no part in provençal food until the past few decades. Like saffron in Marseilles, it is not native and came back with sailing and fishing fleets – and remained in port. Chervil, coriander, tarragon, fennel, marjoram, oregano, parsley and sage are mainly commercial crops. Chives are grown too, but rarely used as they are considered "northern"; the exceptions are the nouvelle restaurants which put them on course after course thus swamping what delicate flavor there might have once been there.

But just as drinkers can follow wine routes, any eater can ramble to find the true herbes of Provence, particularly by following the ancient walking paths to and from the hill towns, or, my favorite, from Peillon to Peille; you'll find beds of thyme and field thyme (*serpolet/farigoule* – some restaurants now perfume sauces just with the blossoms), rosemary (*romarin*), bay and juniper. Most specially provençal is summer savory (*sarriette*), also known as donkey's pepper (*poivre d'âne/pèbre d'ai*). It grows only in the foothills and mountains and thus does not belong to coastal recipes; it is particularly liked by, and good with, rabbit and hare.

Bottles of herb-flavored oils and vinegars are hardly authentic, but are interesting additives to a cook's repertoire; much better to make your own by taking herbs you have picked and macerating them in oil you have bought direct from the press.

Cheese

With one rare exception, all provençal cheeses are variations of the one style, a small, round, white, sometimes crumbly, fresh cheese called a brousse. *It is mainly made with sheep's milk but it might be made with goat's milk. The creamy freshness should outweigh any "sheep" taste. It is sometimes mixed with fresh or stewed fruit or perfumed with orange–flower water to be used as a dessert cheese. These dessert cheeses go perfectly well with a chilled, dry provençal rosé wine; in fact, I don't think red or white wines match them at all. Brousses are best in autumn and winter;* banon *(see below) all year depending on which animal is lactating.*

*•*Banon: *The best-known version of* brousse *is this commercially produced cheese. Small, clear-flavored and wrapped in chestnut leaves, it is mainly made in the* départements *of* Isère, Drôme *and* Vaucluse. *I like it slightly chilled, which complements the clean, lactic flavor. When mixed or coated with summer savory it will be called a* poivre d'ai *or* pèbre d'ane, *which are local names, meaning "donkey's pepper" (these versions are not*

wrapped in leaves). Look carefully when you buy a banon, for the time-honored tradition of making cheese with whatever milk was closest persists. Thus you will find them made with cow's milk, sheep's or goat's milk, or any combination.

*•*Brousse du Roue: *Made on the Roue peninsula;* Brousse de la Vésubie *in the* Comté de Nice.

*•*Sarriette: *A very creamy, commercially manufactured cheese, flavored with savory. Other equally large cheeses for cutting on deli counters are made with a provençal tag or flavor, and most are a double-cream or triple-cream type, so they go bad quickly. Great for picnics, of course.*

*•*Tomme de Camargue/ Tomme Arlésienne/Tomme Gardien: *Lightly pressed sheep's milk cheese flavored with ground thyme. Some cheesophiles like the sheepier taste it develops when it is more aged.*

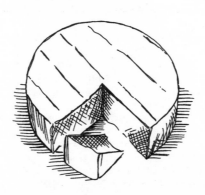

Pastries, Desserts & Confectionery

To call desserts in the south of France a bit of a pig's ear is no insult. As there were few ovens in private houses, any cooked sweetness had to be deep-fried. Almost the only kind were pieces of flat dough shaped like an ear, oreillettes; they were often flavored with an orange-flower water.

In any traditional house fresh and dried fruits and nuts are still the most common way to end meals, although on Sundays you will find bought ice creams or sorbet and the ubiquitous crème caramel or îles flottantes, clouds of poached meringue afloat in a sea of custard crème anglaise and topped with caramelized sugar. Expensive or "modern" restaurants will probably offer a gratin of seasonal fruits in a

light sauce of eggs and ground almonds.

Where apples and pears and quinces (coings) grow, medieval tastes often prevail; quinces especially might be rolled in honey or sugar and baked in dough.

The cooking school I found in La Roquebrussane teaches a number of sweet dishes based on the almond: baked pears stuffed with a macaroon mixture, orange-flavored barquettes from Nîmes, cookies flavored with aniseed, a lemon flan, and green figs baked with rum and served with cream. They are certainly more appealing than the peeled and baked broad beans that once joined your sweet store of raisins and almonds.

LES TREIZE DESSERTS

On Christmas Eve in Provence *les treize desserts* are arranged on a table with *le pain Calendal*, a big round wheat-flour loaf, surrounded by 12 smaller ones representing the apostles and decorated with berries and bay leaves. The casual visitor is unlikely to be invited to share this family tradition, but it makes fascinating reading, for it is a summary of the most common ways to end provençal meals throughout the year.
• *La Pompe*: A fairly dry orange- or lemon-flavored bread; dipped into *vin cuit* (see next page), it swells or pompes. Its provençal name is *lou Gibassie*.
• *Nougats*: All varieties including pistachio (*pistache*)

and pine nut (*pignon*).
• *Les Quatre Mendiants*: raisins (*raisins secs*), peeled almonds, dried figs and walnuts, indicating the mendicant orders of the Dominicans, Carmelites, Fransiscans and Augustines respectively.
• Dates (*dattes*)
• Mandarin oranges (*mandarines*)
• Oranges (*oranges*)
• Grapes (*raisins*)
• Melon (*melon*)
• Chestnuts (*marrons/châtaignes*), often roasted
• Apples (*pommes*)
• Pears (*poires*)
• Prunes (*pruneaux*)
• Quince jelly (*gelée* or *pâte de coings*), usually home-made but also from pâtisseries.

A DRINKER'S GUIDE

Over the past ten years, Provence has been a mecca for winemakers who want to do something a little different from the norm. The consistent climate, abundant sunshine and cheap land have allowed some of the most interesting wines made anywhere in the world to be created.

Mas de Daumas Gassac, popularly known as the Latour of Languedoc, is one of the most expensive new wines made in the south but offers exceptional value for its quality. Domaine de Trevallon is another stunning wine and, like many of these newer wines, is organic. Another is Domaine de Richeaume, made on the side of Mont St Victoire opposite to that so often painted by Cézanne.

Other wines to look out for in particular are Domaine Tempier, Château de Bellet, Mas de la Dame, Mas Gourgonnier and anything made by Olivier Julien.

In general, the wines of Provence are at their best at two or three years old and wines older than five years are unlikely to please.

Only the traditionally made, old-style Châteauneuf-du-Papes and the best Gigondas need aging.

A number of Provence's other alcoholic drinks are first rate. The suburb of Ste-Martine in Marseilles is the home of Ricard *pastis*, which differs from the Parisian anise drinks such as Pernod in that it is based on licorice. If you want to drink it *à la marseillaise* you should add five times as much water.

Marseilles is also the home of France's second most important vermouth, Noilly Prat. Unusually, it is matured by exposing it to the sun and sea breezes in barrels, which contributes to its aroma and salty tang. It is the finest vermouth for cooking.

Wine-based apéritifs abound and they may be flavored with fruit, nuts or herbs. In Forcalquier, *Rinquinquin* is made with peaches and peach leaves, others are made with nuts, *Colignac* with quince. In many of the houses I visited, liqueurs had been made by macerating herbs in alcohol; in Ampus I was offered a pungent verbena version. There is also *vin cuit*, not wine at all but boiled down grape juice and *vin d'oranges*, oranges macerated in red wine with added spirit.

CHATEAUNEUF-DU-PAPE

Châteauneuf-du-Pape was an important wine-growing region of around 1,000 hectares well before it became the favorite of the Catholic church. In 1309 Bertrand the Goth, Archbishop of Bordeaux, was elected Pope Clement V. As relations between the king of France and the papacy in Rome were strained at this time, and as Italy was additionally at war, Clement stayed in France and established his court at Avignon.

His successor, John XXII, enlarged the Avignon estates and built a summer palace on the foundations of the old castle in Vaucluse. This new castle - Châteauneuf-du-Pape - took 15 years to build and the surrounding vineyards became the pope's property. With the pope's return to Rome in 1410 however, the area and its wines sunk into obscurity. The palace was subsequently destroyed in religious wars, (then restored and destroyed again by the Germans in 1944).

The 18th century saw the area revitalized, and individual estates established a reputation.

Thirteen grape varieties are permitted in the making of Châteauneuf-du-Pape wines, eight red and five white. The reds are well rounded and full flavored with a characteristic flavor of red fruits. The bouquet appreciated by connoisseurs is typically of old leather, mushrooms and licorice.

The village sprawls down the gentle hillside which is dominated by the ruins of the château. It is a pretty area in which to spend a day cycling through the vineyards - English-speaking guides are available. The largest producer in the area is the family-owned Château Mont-Redon, which boasts 95 hectares of good stony soil and makes around 350 thousand bottles of red and 70 thousand bottles of white each year. For a taste of regional specialities, dine at the Restaurants Le Pistou or Le Verger des Papes in the village.

thought to come from the Black Périgord, with those from Sarlat perhaps the very best.

MAJOR TRUFFLE MARKETS
In the Ardèche: Bourg-Saint-Andéol; *in the Drôme:* Pierrelatte, Buis-les-Baronnies *and* St-Paul-Trois-Châteaux; *in Vaucluse:* Valréas, Carpentras *and* Orange; *in the Gard:* Uzès. *There is a Truffle Museum at*

Sorges, *which is between the truffling centers of Thiviers and Périgueux, and an experimental truffle farm near Coly.*

Bon Marché

Below is a selective list of markets plus some fairs (*foires*) of special interest. Check with the local Syndicat d'Initiative (SI) for precise locations and time changes.

VAUCLUSE

Apt *Sat;* Avignon *Daily ex Mon;* Bédarrides *Mon;* Bollene *Mon, daily (March-Oct);* Cadenet *Mon;* Carpentras *Daily (April-Nov), Fri (Winter), (Vine plants, truffle, game);* Cavaillon *Daily;* Courthézon *Fri, Sun AM;* Entraigues-sur-Sorgues *Wed;* Grillon *Truffle Market Mon Nov-Mar, Melon Market daily 10th Aug-Sept;* Lauris *Mon AM, daily 15 Sep-15 Nov;* Malaucène *Wed, daily May-June (asparagus & cherries, etc.);* Mondragon *Tue;* Monteux *Daily;* Orange *Daily (15 May-15 Oct), Mon, Wed, Fri (fruit & veg), Thur (poultry) 15 Oct-15 April);* Pernes-les-Fontaines *Sat AM;* Pertuis *Fri, daily 10 June - 31 Aug;* Piolenc *Mon AM;* Le Pontet *Thur AM;* Sault *Wed;* Sorgues *Daily (eve), (May & June cherries and veg), Sun;* Ste-Cécile-les-Vignes *Sat AM;* St-Didier *Daily 10 May-30 June (cherries), 25 Aug-30 Oct (grapes);* St-Saturnin-les-Avignon *Mon;* Le-Thor *Grape Market daily Aug-Oct;* La-Tour-d'Aigues *Tue;* Vaison-la-Romaine *Tue;* Valréas *Wed AM, Mon, Wed, Fri & Sat PM (April-June);* Védène *Tue;* Visan *Fri.*

BOUCHES-DU-RHÔNE

Aix-en-Provence *Tue, Thur, Sat;* Arles *Tue, Wed, Thur, Sat;* Aubagne *Daily;* Châteauneuf-les-Martigues *Weekly;* Châteaurenard *Daily;* Fos-sur-Mer-Pal *Wed, Sat;* Istres *Daily in harvest time, Tue, Thur, Sat other months;* Mallemort *Fri;* Marseille *Daily;* Martigues *Thur, Sat, Sun;* Peyrolles-en-Provence *Wed, daily April-June;* Port-de-Bouc *Daily;* Port-St-Louis-du-Rhône *Daily;* Rognonas *Daily;* La Roque d'Anthéron *Daily June, Mon, Wed, Fri rest of year;* Salon-de-Provence *Wed;* St-Rémy-de-Provence *Wed, Sat;* Tarascon *Daily;* Trets *Daily ex Mon.*

VAR

Aups *Wed & Sat AM;* Barjols *Tue, Thur, Sat;* Brignoles *Sat;* Callas *Thur, Sat;* Collobrières *Thur, Sun;* Cuers *Fri AM;* Draguignan *Wed, Sat AM, Junk Fair 4 days in 2nd half Feb;* Flayosc *Mon;* Fréjus *Daily;* Gonfaron *Thur AM;* Hyères *Daily AM,* Le Lavandou *Thur AM;* Lorgues *Tue AM;* Le Luc *Fri AM;* Méounes-les-Montrieux *Thur AM;* Ollioules *Mon, Wed, Fri;* Pignans *Thur AM;* Le Pradet *Fri AM;* Rians *Fri AM;* Salernes *Wed & Sun AM;* Le Seyne-sur-Mer *Daily;* Signes *Thur AM;* Six-Fours-les-Plages *Tue, Thur AM, Sat;* Solliès Pont *Wed AM;* St-Maximin-la-Ste-Baume *Wed;* St-Raphaël *Daily;* St-Tropez *Tue, Sat;* Toulon *Daily (ex Mon 15 Sept-15 Mar);* La-Valette-du-Var *Daily AM;* Vidauban *Wed, Sun AM.*

ALPES-MARITIMES

Antibes *Daily;* Breil-sur-Roya *Olive Fair mid July & 19 Oct;* Cagnes-sur-Mer *Daily;* Le Cannet *Daily;* Cannes *Daily;* Le Colle-sur-Loup *Wed, Fri;* Grasse *Daily;* Guillaumes *Sun, daily in summer;* Menton *Daily, Lemon Fair end Feb;* Nice *Daily;* Puget-Théniers *Sun;* Roquesteron *Wed, Sun;* St-Etienne de Tinée *Sun AM, Mon (18 Nov-25 Dec);* St-Sauveur-sur-Tinée *Tue;* Valbonne *Grape Fair 4 Feb;* Vence *Daily;* Villars-sur-Var *Sun.*

ALPES-DE-HAUTE-PROVENCE

Barcelonnette *Wed, Sat;* Castellane *Wed, Sat;* Château-Arnoux *Tue, Wed, Fri, Sun;* Digne *Wed, Sat, Lavender Fair 26 Aug-3 Sept;* Entrevaux *Fri, Sun;* Forcalguier *Mon;* Manosque *Sat;* Moustiers-Ste-Marie *Fri;* Riez *2nd Sat of month, Truffle Fair Wed & Sat AM Nov-Feb;* Seyne-les-Alpes *Tue, Fri;* Sisteron *Wed, Sat;* Valensole *2nd Wed of month.*

HAUTES-ALPES

Abriès *Wed;* Briançon *Wed, Thur;* Chorges *Thur;* Embrun *Sat;* Gap *Wed, Thur, Sat;* Guillestre *Mon;* Laragne-Montéglin *Thur;* Rosans *Wed (15 June-15 Sept);* Serres *Sat;* St-Bonnet-en-Champsaur *Mon;* Veynes *Thur.*

ALL THE FUN OF THE FOIRE

The French hold *foires* on saint's days, holy days, public holidays, at the change of season and at the drop of a hat. Virtually no animal or edible plant glides foire-less through life - look out for the Charolles Bull Fair, a chance to see *charollais* beef on the hoof. Most towns and large villages have an annual foire to celebrate their own continued existence. The Syndicat d'Initiative will give you information on these. Easter and Pentecost (*Pâcques* and *Pentecôte*) are especially good for fairs: look out for them on *Jeudi Gras,* the Thursday before Shrove Tuesday (*Mardi Gras*), Jeudi Saint (Maundy Thursday), and *Dimache des Rameaux* (Palm Sunday).

poiré 24
poireau(x) 20,34,56,59,69,172
  des vignes 130,164,171
pois 34
poissonnerie 8
Poitou 67,129,132-33
poitrine farcie 43
poivrons 131,172,188
pomme(s) 45,69,131,142,155,
  173,189
  tarte Normande 21
pomme(s) de terre 20,59,130,
  131,172
  à la guerilla 143
  en robe de chambre 46
pommeau 24
Pommery, Madame La veuve 32
Pompadour, Madame de 138
pompe 147,194
pont-l'Evêque 22-25
porché 57
pormoniers 153
pot-au-feu 32,45
potée 33,40,45,58,112,137
potiron 58,130,150
potje flesch/vleesch 30
Pouilly Blanc Fumé 73
poularde en vessie 154
poulet(s) 113
  bourbonnais 141
  de Bresse 57,113,154
  aux chipolatas 68
  farci au pot 170
  gris 67
  jaune 128
  Lochoise 68
  au Meursault 112
  à la Nazairienne 58
  à la Niortaise 129
  vert 125,130
poulpe 55,184
pountari 141
pounti 141
pourly 117
pousse-rapière 177
poustagnacq 134
poutargue 184
poutine 184
praires 18
pré-salé 15,19,57,67,128,
  129,186
prepons 70
pretzel 41,49
prune (s) 44,45,70,131,142,
  173,189
  sauvages 120
pruneaux 71,132
  fourré 134,176
prunelle 120,147
psalliotes des prés 174
puits d'amour 60
pyramides 70
pyrénées 39,163

quart maroilles 36
  see maroilles
quatre-quarts 60
quenelles de brochet 9,55,65,
  140,153
quetsch 45
queue de boeuf 112
quiche 47
Quimper 60
quinquins 36

râble de lièvre 143,185
rabot(te)s 21
radis 20,69,114
ragoût de mouton 171
ragoût d'oie/gansvoresse 44
raie 55
raifort 45
raisiné picard 36

raisins 131,155, 189
rascasse 31,183
rat du chai 129
ratafia 28,51,120
  de noyau 51
ratatouille/ratatouia 188,190
Ré, île-de- 126
Reblochon 157-58
Redon 58
réglisse 176
reines-claudes 9,44,68,131,
  138,155
relais routiers 11
repas du cochon 113
restaurant(s) 11
restoroute 11
Rhône 149
Ridel, M. 22
Riesling 44
rigolettes 72
rigotte(s) 157
  de Pelussin 146
rille d'oie 65
rillettes 63-5,125
rillons 65,125
Rinquinquin 195
rochers de Morvan 120
rogeret des Cévennes 176
rogne (rouge) 126
rollot 36
Romorantin 71
Roquefort 146,174-76
rose/rossette de Lyon 152,165
rosette du Morvan 110
rosquillas 177
rôtisserie 8,11
roucou 22
rouget 31,168,185
rouille 9,56,168,184,185
roulade de téte de porc
  152
roux 18
rouy 118

sablés 21,72
sabodet 152
safran 70
saindoux 54
St-Benoî(s)t 71
Saint-Emilion 135
St-Florentin 118
St-Gildas-des-Bois 59
St-Léger-Vauban 117
St-Malo 54,55,68
St-Marcellins 157-58
St-Nazaire 58
St-Nectaire 146
Saint-Paulin 22-3,59,157
Ste-Ménéhould 29
salade de Cévennes 172
salade Niçoise 190
salaisons 8
salami de palombe 129
salers 146
salon de thé 11
salsa verde 167
salsifis 174
Sancerre 62,71,73
sandre 43
sanglier 44,113,141,187
sanguette 17
Santranges-Sancerre 71
sardines 55
sarments 112
sarrasin 53,60,138,147
sarriette 182,193
sauces(s)
  beurre blanc 55-6,62,65-6
  bretonne 58
  Nantua 153
  poivrade 190
  poulette 55
  rouille 9

Vallée d'Auge 18
velouté 18
saucisse(s) 30,110
  de Lyon 152
  au muscadet 65
  de Strasbourg 42
  de Toulouse 165
saucisson 12,110,153,183
  d'Arles 183
salmon 43,56,63
saupe 184
saupiquet 110,112
Sauternes 132,135,169
schankelas 49
schifela 42
schmalz 43
schnitz 44
seiche (sèche) 126,167,168,184
Seine-Maritime 24
sel gris 57
selles-sur-Cher 71
septmoncel 118
shops 8
  see hypermarkets
  see under Paris
socca 194
sole 17,18
solognotes 68
songbirds 4,32,129,141,182,185
sorbets 8,63
Sorel, Agnès 62,64
sottises 36
souche 66
soumaintrain 118
soupe aux/de poissons 126,
  153,168,184
spaetzli 41
spinard 184
Stanislas of Poland, King 44,
  48,50
Stosswihr 45
sucre
  de cerises 21
  d'orge 36,119,147
  de pommes 21,36,146
suppefleisch 43
suprême 23

table d'hôte 10
tabliers de sapeur 154
taliburs 36
tamié 158
tanche 43,65,111
tapénade/tapéno 190
tarare 18
tarte 49,159
  almond 21
  aux blettes 189,190
  flambée 47
  à la Linz 49
  normande 21
  oignon 45
  renversées 68
  au sucre 36
  Tatin 71,74
  verte d'Angoulême 134
tautouillet 129
taverne 11
telline 183
tergoule 21
terrine 8,17,54,57
  flamande 30
terrinée normande 21
thionville 48
thon 55,167
  rouge (thounina) 168
thoro 167
tielle Sétoise 167
tomate(s) 59,69,131,172,189
tomme 138,157,174
  des Allues 158
  de Belley 118
  de Brach 146

de Carmargue
  /Arlésienne
  /Gardien 193
de Savoie 158
topinambours 115,142
toupie 45
tourin, le 130
tournon-St-Pierre 71
tourons 177
tourte(s) 113,129,135,140-41
  (au) fromage 134
tourteau 55
tourtière 129,134
tourtons 147
traiteur 8,42
Tranche-sur-Mer, La 66
trappiste de Chambarand 157
trénels 140,170
tripe(s) à la mode 19
tripe(s) de thon 167
tripée 32
triperie 8
tripière 19
tripoux 140,170
Troo 71
trou normand 24
trouville 23
Troyan cendré 34
truffado/truffade 143
truffés 151,156,191
truffole 155
truite
  blanquette 167
  au bleu 43
  à l'estragon 18
  au poivre bouilli 31
ttoro 167
tuillard 146
turrones 177

vachard 146
Vacherin
  d'Abondance 158
  des Aillons 158
  des Bauges 158
  Mont-d'Or 118
Valençay fermier 71
Valençay laitier 71
veau flammande 32
veau de lait 12
venaison 65
Vendée 67,68,134
vergeoise 33
vermouth 70,140,195
verneuil 71
vert d'ail 129
verveine de Velay 147
Vichy 138,144
vieux Lille 36
vieux puant/gris 35
Villandry 64
villebarou 71
vin   see also individual
  wines
  cuit 182,195
  gris 43,120
  d'oranges 182,195
vinegar 10
  cider 24
  Orléans 70
violets de Toulon 31
vive 18
vol-au-vents 47
volaile 12
volailler 8,42
Vosges 40,41,43,47,49
Vouvray 73
VSOP 133

waterzooi 31
wine tasting 35
winstubs 41

*Primarily an index of French terms relating to food